SAVING TATUM

SAVING
TATUM

SAVING TATUM

MICALEA SMELTZER

© Copyright 2014, 2016, 2017 Micalea Smeltzer

All rights reserved. This book or any portion thereof may not be reproduced or used in any manner whatsoever without the express written permission of the publisher.

This is a work of fiction. Names, characters, businesses, places, events and incidents are either the products of the author's imagination or used in a fictitious manner. Any resemblance to actual persons, living or dead, or actual events is purely coincidental.

Cover Design: Emily Wittig

Photography by Regina Wamba at Mae I Design

Editing by Wendi Temporado of Ready, Set, Edit

Formatting: Micalea Smeltzer

To anyone who has had to break before they could mend.

YOU ONLY LIVE ONCE,
BUT IF YOU DO IT RIGHT,
ONCE IS ENOUGH.

–MAE WEST

PROLOGUE

I JOLTED AWAKE AT THE SOUND OF SOMEONE TRYING TO beat down our front door. I sat straight up, the blankets pooling at my waist. My head twisted to look at the blinking orange numbers flashing on the clock beside my bed. Three in the morning.

Fear slithered down my spine like a serpent.

Nothing good came from someone at your door that early in the morning.

I heaved my tired body out of bed. My muscles were stiff and overworked from a rigorous cheerleading practice the night before.

I opened my bedroom door and poked my head out. I saw

my mom and dad coming out of their bedroom. A baseball bat was clutched in my dad's hand. What did he think he was going to do to an intruder with that? Knock them out? Besides, if someone was trying to break in, why would they be knocking on the door?

"Stay up here, Tatie," my dad warned in a stern voice, quietly tiptoeing down the steps. My mom followed him even though he warned her to stay put as well.

I kept watch on the door.

My dad looked through the peephole and muttered, "What the hell?"

Swinging it open, I saw red and blue flashing lights and an officer stood at our door.

I rolled my eyes. The neighbor's kids were probably vandalizing again.

I was about to close my door and get back in bed when I heard the officer speak.

"Mr. and Mrs. O'Connor?" he asked. He was young and nervous, obviously new to the police force.

"That's us," my dad answered, "is there a problem?"

The officer shifted nervously, clearly not wanting to talk.

Finally, he found the courage to speak—to deliver the most devastating news I could imagine. "It's about your son, there's been an accident. I'm so sorry to tell you this, but he didn't make it." His face was somber, eyes downcast.

My mom let out a piercing, soul-crushing wail, and started to fall. My dad's arm held her upright.

But there was no one there to hold me up.

I crumbled to the floor, clutching at my chest.

I couldn't breathe.

I was suffocating under the pressure.

He didn't make it.

He was dead. My big brother—my best friend—was gone.

"I'm sorry," I heard the officer say one more time before my dad closed the door. His cries soon joined the sound of my mother's.

Tears streamed down my face, but my sobs were silent.

Graham was gone. In a matter of hours, he'd been ripped from my life forever. I'd just seen him at dinner and we'd been talking about school and how I'd be cheering at the football game on Friday. He was telling me how proud he was of me.

Everything had been perfect. The way it was supposed to be.

Something like this wasn't supposed to happen.

I felt like my whole world had been tilted on its axis. I felt lost and afraid. I didn't know which way was up or down.

This was Graham's last year of high school. He was supposed to leave for college and study to be a lawyer like our dad.

He. Wasn't. Supposed. To. Die.

None of this was supposed to happen.

My perfect life wasn't supposed to explode like this.

But it did.

Overnight, I went from having it all to having nothing.

I watched my mom close herself off from everybody.

I watched my dad spend his every waking hour slaving over his job so he didn't have to think about Graham, or mom, or even me.

I watched myself slowly spiral from a carefree happy girl, into a complete and utter cynic.

And I knew exactly who was to blame for everything.

Jude Brooks.

CHAPTER ONE

I smiled giddily as the Professor explained our final assignment. As he talked, an idea formed in my mind. I knew exactly what I wanted to write about. As a journalism major, we were always writing papers and doing interviews, but this one was to count for fifty percent of our final grade. I wanted to make sure mine stuck out.

"The next time I see you, I'd like for you all to have an idea for your paper. Come to me for final approval before you leave class Wednesday."

When the professor dismissed us, I calmly made my way down the steps to his desk.

"Professor Taylor?" I asked, my voice soft and hesitant.

He looked up, pushing his glasses up his nose. "Yes, Miss O'Connor?"

I rocked back on my heels, clasping my books tightly in my hands. "I already know what I want to write about." My fingers nervously tapped against the books in my hands.

"All right." He steepled his fingers. "What is it?"

I swallowed thickly, praying to the journalism gods that he approved of what I wanted to do. I was already getting exciting about it. "I have a friend here who's studying to be a nurse, I thought maybe I could shadow her and learn more about the process of going into the medical field. I want it to be more than a question and answer session. I want to delve into all the hard work these students go through to become our health care providers." With a sigh, I waited patiently for him to think it over.

He nodded slowly, mulling it over. "It sounds interesting. Go for it."

My eyes widened in surprise. I couldn't believe he'd agreed so readily. I'd been preparing a speech in my head to argue my case.

"Thank you!" I exclaimed. Sobering, I said in a calmer tone, "Thank you so much. I'm really excited about this."

He chuckled. "Miss O'Connor, I think you're always my most excited journalism major. It's refreshing. It reminds me why I wanted to do this job in the first place."

"Thank you again," I told him, resisting the urge to hug him, because that would be majorly awkward. Before he could change his mind, I jogged up the steps and out the door.

I headed across campus to the cafeteria. It was a crisp March afternoon. Some days were downright freezing, while some held the promise of spring. I let the small amount of sun filtering between the tree branches warm my face. I smiled, my blonde hair swaying around my shoulders. I couldn't believe that in a few short months I'd be graduating. It didn't seem real. Once college was over, it was time for real life. While I was mostly excited, there was a small part of me that was terrified. I'd never liked the unknown.

Once in the cafeteria I got my food and sat down at the usual table I shared with my best friend Rowan ... and sometimes Jude. God, I hated that guy with every fiber of my being. Unfortunately, he was also friends with Rowan, which meant I was kind of stuck with him.

Rowan took the seat across from me, dropping her bag on the floor. With a heavy sigh, she poured dressing on her salad and used a fork to swirl the leafy pieces around the bowl. "I'm so tired." She propped her head on one hand and took a bite of her salad. "Between classes, and wedding planning, on top of the kids, I'm beat."

I frowned. "I'm sorry."

"It's my own fault," she huffed, pulling her long light brown hair into a ponytail. "I should've told Trent that I wanted to wait longer to get married. But he was adamant on not waiting more than a year." She scrubbed a hand over her eyes. "At least he's been helpful, but there's only so much a guy can do when it comes to wedding planning." She rolled her eyes.

With a clatter, Jude dropped his backpack on the table. I glared up at him. "Can you not put your stuff down gently like a normal person?" I asked him.

"No." He grinned, backing away to go get his food. Everything Jude did got on my nerves. It was like he had a special talent for irritating me.

Rowan and I fell into silence. I itched to ask her if she'd help me with my project, but I wasn't sure if I should in her current mood.

Jude finally joined us again and I couldn't stand it anymore.

"Row?" I cleared my throat.

"Yeah?" She looked up, wiping a piece of lettuce from

her lip.

I explained my paper and what I wanted to do. Her face fell.

"Oh, Tate, I wish I could help you but I'm far too busy." She frowned, looking at me sadly.

I groaned. "But I already got my paper approved! Come on! I won't be in your way!" I begged, desperation overtaking my tone.

"I can't, Tate. Not with all I have on my plate. I'm really sorry." I knew she was, but it didn't make me feel any better.

I buried my head in my hands. Great, now I had to start from scratch.

"You can shadow me."

"What?" My head snapped up and I glared at Jude. "No way."

He sighed heavily. "Don't be stubborn, Tate—"

"Once again, *you* are not allowed to call me Tate," I interrupted him.

Grinning, he said, "*Tatum*, I can help you with your project. Now be a good girl, nod your head, and accept my help."

Why? Why did Jude have to be studying to be a nurse too? Life was cruel and unfair.

Nibbling on my bottom lip, I did what I had to do. "Okay." I couldn't believe I was agreeing to this. I was willingly going to be spending time with Jude Brooks—the guy who singlehandedly ruined my life.

Mondays sucked.

So did desperation.

"That was easier than I thought." Jude smirked, crossing his hands behind his head. "This is going to be fun."

"No, it's not *fun*," I spat the word. "It's my final paper. I need a good grade for this, so don't screw with me." I pointed a finger at him.

"You need to chill. You're too stressed. You know what's an excellent stress reliever?"

"What?" I asked, even though I knew I shouldn't.

"Sex."

My eyes widened. "Oh, really. Are you suggesting I have sex with you?"

His grin became even bigger. "I mean, if you're interested I could always show you a good time. I promise to make it worth your while." He winked.

"Keep dreaming," I muttered, returning my attention to my lunch.

"I don't have to dream. I'm not giving up on you, Tate."

I looked up then, choosing to ignore him calling me Tate again. "There will never be an 'us.' Besides," I said, leaning closer and lowering my voice like I was letting him in on a secret, "it's not like you're hurting for a little fun between the sheets." I nodded toward all the girls that had their eyes on Jude. I might hate the guy, but he was hot—in that All-American sort of way. With his brown hair and eyes and that grin, he drew women to him like a magnet. Everyone on campus knew he was a player, but most girls didn't care. They were more than happy to be a notch on his bedpost. Not me, though, and I knew that was the real reason Jude wouldn't leave me alone. I was the only female on campus that posed a challenge. I wished he'd leave it alone. It was annoying. If he wasn't friends with Rowan I'd kick him for all his schoolyard antics—like right then, he was trying to play footsie with me. What were we? Five?

He gasped dramatically and put a hand over his heart, like he was offended by my words. "I deserve to have some fun while I wait for you to wake up and realize that we're perfect for each other."

I rolled my eyes and turned my attention back to my food. I wasn't wasting any more of my time on Jude. I couldn't believe I was going to be stuck shadowing him ... hours of just the two of us. It was like my own personal hell.

"Well, ladies, this has been nice and all, but I need to go," Jude mumbled, standing up and grabbing his backpack. He shoved his phone in his pocket and grabbed an apple off his tray, sticking it in his mouth. He gave us a salute and headed out the double doors.

Rowan looked across the table at me and sighed. She did that a lot. "I really am sorry I couldn't help you, but at least there's Jude. I mean, it won't be that bad, right?"

I glared at her. "That bad? I hate him."

"But *why*?" she asked. "He's not a bad guy at all, Tate. He's really nice once you get to know him. I wouldn't be friend's with him otherwise."

"You don't understand." I squirmed in my seat. "You don't know him like I do."

"You're right." She grinned like the cat that ate the canary. "I know him better."

I was over this conversation. I knew even if I told her the truth, I'd never be able to make her see.

We finished our lunch in silence and went our separate ways.

When classes were over, I met Rowan for our almost daily study session in the library. A lot of the time Jude joined us, but today wasn't one of those days. When my homework was done, I knew I couldn't put off the inevitable any longer. I had to go home, back to the place I dreaded the most.

"I'll see you tomorrow," I told Row, shrugging my backpack

on. She barely nodded at me as I left. Even though she had her fiancé, Trenton, to take care of her now, she still wanted to get her degree and have a job. I couldn't blame her. I craved my independence too. There was something satisfying about knowing you could stand on your own two feet without anyone else's help.

I made the drive home blasting the radio and singing along. I enjoyed the noise because once I got home there would be nothing but silence.

Once upon a time we'd been a happy family. We'd laughed and talked and sometimes even fought. But that was before Graham died. Now we were broken, merely a fragment of the family we'd once been. We lost the glue that held us together.

My dad buried himself in work, and when he was home he was always angry, yelling at me and telling me to do better.

Mom retreated into herself. Her eyes now held a vacant, lost look. She stared listlessly for hours out the window, and it was like she was always watching for Graham to return.

I worked hard to be the perfect daughter, to be *noticed* by them, but it did no good.

I didn't know why I kept trying.

I parked in the driveway and headed inside.

The house was dark. Not a single light on. Unfortunately, that was normal.

"Mom," I called out. No answer. "Mom?"

I found her standing in the kitchen by the sink, looking out the window. She didn't move as I approached.

"Come on, Mom," I whispered, taking her hand in mine and pulling her away.

I led her to the living room and forced her to sit on the couch. I turned the TV on, but it wasn't necessary. She wouldn't watch it.

"I'll make dinner." I kissed her forehead.

She did nothing to acknowledge my words. It was like I didn't exist ... or maybe she was the one that didn't exist. Watching someone you loved wither away to nothing was hard. She'd lost a lot of weight since Graham died seven years ago. I swear, she couldn't weigh more than a hundred pounds. She was skin and bones.

I really hated the look that was always in her eyes now. Like she was lost and didn't know where she was. It hurt that she couldn't be strong enough to be there for me. At the same time, I understood. Graham was the golden boy. He was the perfect son and brother. I loved and admired him. He was my best friend growing up and unlike other siblings we never drifted apart. I missed him every day, but I refused to shut down like my parents. Graham might be gone, but I still deserved to live my life.

I made dinner, took a plate to my mom, and then sat by myself at the kitchen table.

It didn't matter if my mom or even my dad was here, I was always alone when I was home.

The moment Graham was buried we stopped being a family.

I knew in the amount of years that had passed I should be over it, but I wasn't. I missed my mom and dad, but there was nothing I could do to fix the mess we'd become.

I was torn about leaving. Most people had already moved out of their parents' place, but I was scared of what would happen to my mom if I left. I was starting to crave my independence, though. I felt trapped by the memories. I wanted a fresh start, but I wasn't sure I was going to get one.

I guessed only time would tell.

CHAPTER TWO

"Tatum!"

I jumped and fell out of my chair.

"Dammit Jude!" I exclaimed, glaring up at his laughing form.

"Shhhh!" hushed a girl at the table beside me in the library.

"Sorry, I couldn't resist," he chortled, reaching a hand down to help me up. I refused his hand, getting up on my own. I would never need Jude's help—you know, except for with my paper, but that didn't really count, right?

"Don't you ever do that again." I glared at him, wiping my jeans free of lint and Lord knows what else that coated the library floor.

"No promises." He grinned, taking the seat beside me.

"What do you want?" I asked, returning to my computer.

"I thought I was helping you with your paper, or have you changed your mind?" He scooted the chair back and propped his legs up on the table, crossing his hands behind his head. He was the picture of ease.

"I wasn't planning on working on it today." I tapped my fingers against the wood table with irritation. I felt his eyes staring a hole into me. I wanted him to go away.

"Come on, don't be a party pooper. I'm on my way to the nursing home now." He bumped my shoulder lightly with his hand and I flinched. "I don't bite, Tate ..." He lowered his feet and leaned toward me, his grin wicked. "Unless you want me to."

"No, no, no, no way." I stood, gathering my belongings. "I knew this was a bad idea. Forget I ever agreed to this. I don't need your help. Not now, not ever."

I knew I wouldn't be able to put up with Jude for an entire month. I'd have to come up with a new idea for my paper.

Before he could reply, I hauled ass out of there.

I heard his footsteps pounding behind me, but I refused to turn around and look at him.

It didn't take him long to catch up to me.

His hand wrapped around my arm and he pulled me against his chest.

"Let me go!" I cried, trying to wiggle free.

His whole body pressed against mine and I didn't like how good it felt. Jude was the last person on the planet who should turn me on.

He released me and I whipped around to glare at him. "Why won't you leave me alone?"

"What can I say? I'm very determined." Crossing his arms over his chest, we ended up in a stare down. "I said I'd help you with your paper, and I intend to keep that promise." Lowering his voice, he said, "I've never been able to figure out why you hate me so much."

I rolled my eyes. "The fact that you don't know says a lot."

I started to walk away again, but he grabbed my arm to halt me.

"Jude," I warned, only he didn't release me this time. He stepped up behind me, his long lean body adhering to my shadow.

"Come on, Tatum." His free hand skimmed over my shoulder. "You know you don't want to change your project, just let me help you. Hell, you might even find that you actually like me." His voice was low and coaxing.

"Not likely." I wrenched my arm from his hold. Taking several deep breaths, I tried to calm myself down. Realistically, I needed Jude's help with this, and being stubborn would get me nowhere. Squaring my shoulders, I did the responsible thing. "Thank you for offering to help me with this. I know you didn't have to." Tucking a stray piece of blonde hair behind my ear, I mumbled reluctantly, "I'd be happy to accompany you to the nursing home."

"Good." He grinned, his eyes sparkling with victory. "By the way, I appreciate the fact that you're trying to be nice and all, but drop the formalities. It's weird."

He reached for my hand and started pulling me along.

"Whoa, buddy." I dug my heels into the sidewalk. "Where do you think you're dragging me off to?"

"My truck." He looked at me like I was stupid.

"I can follow you," I declared.

"I veto that idea." He stared me down. Jude could be intimidating when he wanted to, but I was not one to cower. Life had been cruel to me the last few years and I'd become tough because of it. "I think you need to get to know me. The *real* me, since you insist upon hating me, you should at least know exactly what it is you're hating."

What the hell?

"Who are you? Yoda?" I looked at him incredulously.

"I want to make a bet with you." He grinned impishly.

"A bet? What kind of bet?" Now I did start to squirm. This had "bad news" written all over it.

"How long do you need to shadow me for your paper?" he asked.

I wasn't sure where he was going with this, but I answered anyway. "A month."

His smile widened. "I bet that at the end of four weeks you'll find that I'm really a nice guy."

"Oookay. What do you get if you win?" I was scared to ask, but I had to know what he could want so bad that he'd be willing to make a bet.

"A date." He waggled his eyebrows and licked his lips suggestively. If I were a meaner person I'd push him off the sidewalk into oncoming traffic. It was the least he deserved for being such a perverted jerk.

"If I win and still hate you in a month, what do I get?" I tilted my head slightly, waiting for his response.

His eyes widened in surprise, like he couldn't believe I might actually agree to this. I wasn't as much of an uptight bitch as he believed.

"If you win, I will gladly kiss the stick up your ass." He chuckled, scratching his jaw. He held out his hand to me. "Deal?"

"Deal."

We shook on it and my fate was sealed.

I started to head toward my car, but he stopped me once more. Since I wasn't in the mood to argue anymore, I let him lead me to his truck. It was an old beat-up blue Ford. It was nothing special, but I knew Jude loved that truck more than he loved pretty much anything. Even though it was old, it shined like it was brand new.

He opened the passenger door for me. I rolled my eyes at his pathetic effort to be a gentleman. I wasn't fooled.

He slid into the driver's seat and I noticed for that first time that he was no longer wearing the jeans and t-shirt he'd worn earlier. Instead he'd changed into a pair of blue scrubs. He looked professional and capable in them—two things I never thought I'd associate with Jude Brooks. I wondered what had made him decide to get into nursing, but figured that was a question better left for later.

"Let's play a game," he suggested, starting up the truck. The engine roared and I resisted the urge to cover my ears with my hands.

"What kind of game?" I was hesitant to play any game Jude would come up with.

"How about each day I help you with your paper I get to ask you a personal question and you *have* to answer it honestly. If it makes you feel better you can ask me one question too."

I sighed, figuring this was all a part of his ploy to get me on his side. He didn't know it, but there was nothing he could do to ever make me like him. So, I agreed. After all, what could it hurt?

"Fine. Ask me whatever you want." I shrugged, looking out the window.

He grinned widely, reminding me of a little kid when you gave them a toy. Maybe I shouldn't have agreed to this. He'd probably either ask me something sexual, or why I hated him so much. Neither of which I would answer.

"What's your favorite candy?"

I swiveled toward him, my mouth parting in shock. "What?"

"What's your favorite candy?" he repeated, smiling like he knew exactly what I had expected him to ask. "It's a simple enough question."

Flabbergasted, I was unable to answer him for a moment. Finally, I opened my mouth and replied, "Twizzlers. The cherry kind. That's my favorite."

"Twizzlers." He mulled that over. "I would've never guessed that."

"What's *your* favorite candy?" I asked, since I really didn't care to ask him any personal questions. I did not want to get to know Jude.

"Hmm." He tapped his fingers against the steering wheel as he thought. "Probably gummy bears."

"Gummy bears?" I laughed.

His face fell. "What's wrong with gummy bears? They're delicious!"

"Nothing," I said, fighting a smile, "I just didn't expect that to be your favorite."

"What did you expect then?" he questioned, eyes on the road.

I thought for a moment and answered, "Airheads or Sour Patch Kids."

"Bleh." He made a face, gagging for extra effect. "I don't do sour. Only sweet. That's why I like you."

I shook my head and looked out the window once more, my bad mood instantly returning. I didn't like it when Jude said stuff like that. I didn't want him to pursue me, or even actually *like* me as a person. I hated him, so I didn't deserve his attention.

I started to laugh to myself, because up until a moment

ago, Jude and I were having a civil conversation. I hadn't been thinking about what he'd done to me—how he ruined my life—and he'd just been any other guy. I wished he could stay that way. I didn't like all this hate bottled up inside me. Anger was like a poison, slithering through your veins and tainting the things you did and said. He deserved my hate for what he did, for what he *caused*, but the hate was only hurting me and not him. I'd lived with it for so many years I didn't know if I'd ever be able to let it go.

We arrived at the nursing home and I followed him inside. He pulled an ID badge out of his pocket and fixed it to his shirt. The doors slid open and the smell that accompanied every medical building assaulted me. It was one of my least favorite smells—sterile and lifeless.

"Hi, Trudy," Jude greeted the older woman behind the desk. "You're looking more beautiful than usual today. Did you do something to your hair?" She immediately turned into a swooning and blushing teenager. My God, was I the only female that was immune to his charms? Get it together, people. He wasn't *that* good-looking and he was downright annoying.

"I did." She batted her eyelashes. "I curled it."

"It looks good." He grinned. "Who am I seeing today?"

She handed him a chart and then looked at me. "Who are you?"

"Oh, uh, I'm here with him. He's helping me with a, uh, paper," I stammered. It wasn't like me to act that way but I didn't want this woman to get the impression that I was his girlfriend and we'd be sneaking off to the nearest broom closet.

She looked to Jude. "Is this true?"

Jude grinned and leaned against her desk so he could talk to her and watch me at the same time. "Look at her face,

Trudy. Does that look like the face of someone that would lie to you?"

"Um ..."

"Don't worry," he continued, "sadly, she is telling the truth. I wish I could tell you that she's here because she loves me so much she can't bear to live a moment without me in her sight. But Trudy." He frowned, putting a hand to his heart and fake tears pooling in his eyes. "Sweet Tatum here does not feel that way about me. No matter how hard I try, she does not want to be my lover. It has left me broken hearted and I'm only left with the hope that helping her with this paper will somehow make her see that she's the girl I'm going to marry."

"Oh, you poor thing." Trudy reached out, patting his hand. Her gaze swiveled to me and she glared like I was an evil wench for breaking Jude's heart. I had news for her; he didn't have a heart to break. If he did, he wouldn't have destroyed my life. To me she said, "Don't get in any trouble."

Me? Trouble? That was laughable.

"See you later, Trudy." Jude leaned over and kissed the older woman's cheek before scampering away. Her blush from earlier deepened and she reached up to touch her cheek. "Come on, Tate."

"Don't call me that," I grumbled, trailing after him as I dug a pen and paper from my backpack.

"If I can't call you that, can I at least call you Tater Tot? Or maybe just Tater?"

I kicked the back of his knee and he stumbled.

"I assume that's a no then." He chuckled, straightening his scrubs.

"You bet your ass that's a no," I muttered. I scribbled the date in my notebook and then pointed to the clipboard he held as we walked down the hall. "So, I'm guessing you visit different patients when you're here?"

He nodded, suddenly becoming all business. "It's a rotation and they mix it up. They want us to get a feel for different issues patients face, since there's such a wide variety."

He glanced down at his chart and stopped in front of a door. Looking over his shoulder at me, he waggled his brows. "Showtime."

BY THE TIME Jude dropped me back off at school to get my car, I had a new respect for nurses and all medical personnel. They had to deal with some crappy stuff, all with a smile on their face. Remembering the Jude I'd known in high school—yes, I'd been subjected to attending the same high school as the douchebag—I couldn't believe he was willingly taking care of people. It didn't seem like him. If someone had asked me back then what I thought Jude would be when he grew up, I probably would've replied with gigolo. I hated to admit it, but Jude was surprising me. It didn't mean I was starting to like him, though. It would take far more than his career choice to change my opinion of him.

CHAPTER THREE

I HATED WEEKENDS.

Weekends, for most college seniors, probably meant studying with a little fun time thrown in.

There was no fun time for me—hadn't been in a long time.

I was stuck in this hellhole and the most exciting thing that ever happened to me was the rare late-night study session at the local coffee shop/restaurant Griffin's with Rowan.

I used to be okay with that, but not anymore. I wanted a *life*, not … whatever this was.

I lay across my bed with my head propped against my hand. I'd finished my homework hours ago and had nothing else to do. I wondered how different my life would have been if Graham had lived—if he hadn't wrapped his car around a tree.

I'd never know.

My phone chirped with a text and I rolled over to retrieve it from the table beside my bed.

I opened the text from Rowan.

Get your ass out of bed. We're going to a party.

No way. I typed back.

Yes u r. Don't be stubborn. I need u 2 go so I'm not alone.

I sighed. Parties weren't my thing and I knew they weren't Rowan's, either. I needed to get out, though, and this looked like the only way.

With a huff, I typed, **Ok.**

I'm sure Rowan was surprised I caved so easily. I wasn't the most agreeable person in the world.

We'll be there in 5. Was her reply.

Since I was chilling in my pajamas, I scurried around to change. I didn't have the wardrobe for a party, so I had to make do. I shimmied into my favorite pair of jeans and put on a plain, black, long-sleeved t-shirt. It was nothing fancy, that was for sure, but I didn't care. At least I'd be comfortable. I dabbed on a bit of makeup, not much, but enough to not look like I'd rolled out of bed, and braided my hair.

My dad wasn't home, and since my mom was practically comatose it wasn't like I had to worry about sneaking out. Besides, I was twenty-two so technically I was free to do what I wanted, so why did I feel so caged?

A familiar black Dodge Challenger was parked by the mailbox. It was Trent's—Rowan's fiancé—car.

As I approached the parked car, Rowan hopped out and moved the seat so I could slip in the back.

"Evening, lovebirds," I commented.

I might joke about Rowan and Trent's deep love for each other, but those two had been through *a lot* and I truly was happy they'd been able to work it out. Rowan used to be so anti-love but after she almost lost Trent she turned into such a sap. If they weren't so perfect for each other I would miss the old Rowan.

"Nice to see you too, Tate." Trent chuckled, pulling away.

Like I always did, I looked back at my house. I didn't know why, but I felt like one day it might not be there to return to. It shouldn't have even mattered to me, since it hardly felt like a home.

"So," I started and swiveled forward, "where's this party?"

Rowan looked back at me, sweeping her long sandy hair over her shoulder. "Well, it's at Jude's."

"Are you fucking kidding me?"

Rowan flinched at my words and tone. I rarely ever cussed, and when I did it usually involved Jude in some form.

"I wouldn't have come if I knew it was at his place," I grumbled, crossing my arms over my chest. My lower lip threatened to jut out like a pouting child. "I already spent all afternoon with the guy, and now you expect me to spend the night with him too?"

"Not the whole night ... unless you want to." Trent winked as he looked back at me from the rearview mirror. Rowan smacked his arm.

"It's a party, Tatum." She sighed, exasperated with my behavior. "You might not even see him."

"Why are you guys going?" I asked. "Don't you have something better to do? Like sit around and stare into each other's eyes? Or plan a wedding?"

"Jude invited me and I wanted to get out for a bit." Rowan shrugged. "This is my last chance to do something like this."

I guessed she was right, what with taking care of two kids. Rowan and Trent had a son together, a son Trent didn't even know he had until a little over a year ago. In fact, I hadn't even known Rowan had a son. She'd claimed he was her brother, and no one had a reason to doubt her. After her mother died, she also got custody of her little sister, Ivy.

I didn't say any more, because I didn't want to ruin tonight for Trent and Row. They didn't get out enough as it was. At least they were happy unlike most people.

I didn't know where Jude lived, but when we turned down a street lined with cars, I knew this must be where the party was. The townhouse was close to campus and I figured other college kids had to occupy the neighborhood to put up with all the people hanging around and the loud music. Trent parked the car along the street and we all hopped out. I suddenly felt very nervous. I hadn't been to a party since high school and it hadn't ended well.

I followed behind Trent and Rowan. I kept my head low—afraid of being recognized. To this day, some people still only saw me as Graham's little sister—he'd always been popular and people older and younger than us knew who he was—and I couldn't handle the looks of pity. He'd been gone for seven years now. I would always miss him, but I was no longer grieving. But when people looked at me with such sadness it always brought back memories better left buried.

I stepped into the townhouse and was shocked by the amount of people inside. I really regretted agreeing to this now. I hated mingling and I refused to be Trent and Row's third wheel all night.

"I'm the designated driver," Trent turned around to tell me, "so feel free to drink whatever you want."

"I don't drink," was my response. I had never taken one sip of alcohol, not since Graham got drunk and crashed his car.

Trenton's brows drew together. Before he could say anything more, I separated myself from them. I heard Rowan call my name but I didn't turn back.

The three-level townhouse was packed with fellow college students. I didn't recognize most of them. Probably because I'd never made the effort to get to know anyone besides Rowan.

I pushed through the crowd of bodies, heading to the second level. I hoped it would be less crowded. *Wrong.*

There were buckets of ice, overflowing with bottles of beer. That wasn't what I wanted. I sauntered over to the refrigerator, pushing people out of my way when I needed to, and searched for a bottle of water.

Mountain Dew.

Coca Cola.

Dr. Pepper.

And beer. Lots of beer.

Was this all college guys drank? They were going to have liver failure before their thirtieth birthday.

I grabbed a bottle of Dr. Pepper—it might not have been water but at least it wasn't alcohol.

Some heavy rock song played from an iPod dock sitting on the counter. I was tempted to replace it with mine—which was filled with country, but I wasn't in the mood to get in a fight with Jude or anyone else, for that matter. I didn't even want to be here. I wanted to go home. Was it acceptable to stay five minutes and leave? I totally would if I had my car.

You know, it was just my luck that the one time I wanted to get out and agreed to go to a party it would have to be at Jude's. I couldn't escape him no matter how hard I tried.

I spotted a couple making out on the couch. A part of me was disgusted by their display, but a small piece was jealous. I'd never had a relationship like that. I wasn't saying that I was the Virgin Mary, but I'd never been in love. There had never been a guy I pined for from afar. I hadn't kissed someone in the rain. Or fought and made up. I hadn't found someone worth sharing the darkest parts of myself with, or even the good parts.

I turned away from the couple before I got overly emotional for no reason.

I moved through the people gathered in the middle of the living room, looking for a place I could hide out until Rowan and Trent wanted to leave.

I spotted a door leading out onto the deck. No one was out there, since it was such a chilly night, so I decided to make my escape there.

I was almost to the door when I spotted a bowl of gummy bears on the coffee table. I couldn't stop myself from smiling as I recalled Jude telling me he loved them.

Feeling devilish, I reached out for a handful, then decided to take the whole bowl. They were my gummy bears now.

Nobody paid me any attention as I slid open the deck door. I'd long ago realized that even though Graham was the one that died, I sort of became a ghost too. I'd allowed that to happen by avoiding people, and refusing to get to know new ones, so it was my own fault.

The deck was small with two chairs. I picked one of the plastic Adirondack chairs and looked up at the shining full moon and twinkling stars. It was such a pretty night. I thought people didn't appreciate the beauty of the night sky enough. There was something breathtaking about its simplicity.

I propped my legs up on the railing and popped a gummy bear in my mouth. It tasted so good that I ended up eating another, and another, until half the bowl was gone and my stomach was starting to feel upset.

I laid my head back, my eyes feeling heavy. I *would* be the person to fall asleep at a party.

To keep myself awake, I chewed on some more gummy

bears—probably not my most brilliant idea since I was already feeling sick. At least it would give me an excuse to leave.

I shivered from the cold, but I wasn't desperate enough to go back inside and deal with that mess. I pulled my phone out of the pocket of my jeans, checking for a text from Rowan. Nothing. *Grrreat.* We had to have been here for at least an hour already. Surely that was enough time and we could leave. My bed was calling my name.

I sent her a text, asking her when they'd be ready to leave.

When I didn't receive a response in five minutes, I was tempted to chuck my phone off the deck out into the dark void.

I didn't.

The deck door slid open and I jumped at the grating sound. Relief flooded my system. Rowan hadn't text because she was coming to find me.

Only it wasn't Rowan walking toward me. I didn't have good enough luck for that to be the case. Instead, it was Jude.

He wore a pair of jeans and a plain white tee. His feet were bare and he was the picture of ease. He sat down in the chair beside me, smiling crookedly. "I was looking for you," he said simply.

"Me?" I questioned with a raised brow. "Why?"

He shrugged. "When Rowan said you came, I was surprised. This doesn't seem like your type of thing." He nodded toward the door that kept us barred from the craziness inside.

"It's not," I agreed, looking away from Jude. "That's why I'm out here. By myself," I added, hoping he'd get the message and leave. He didn't. Jude never did what you wanted him to. He always had to go against the grain. If there was ever anyone that I'd saddle with the label of REBEL it was Jude. Some of the things he'd done in high school were borderline illegal. He was always looking for something stupid to do and a girl's pants to get into. He was charming and never had a problem with accomplishing either of those things. Except with me.

"You know you prefer my company to being alone," he joked, his eyes twinkling with laughter.

"I've had my fill of you for the day," I grumbled, propping my head up. I was really starting to get nauseous. I knew I shouldn't have continued to eat those dang gummy bears. Jude's presence was also adding to my upset stomach. I could only handle so much of the crazy things that came out of his mouth.

"I'd like to fill you up."

My eyes bugged out. "You did not just say what I think you said."

His smirk widened, and he scratched at his jaw—almost as if he hoped the gesture would help mask his smile. "I did, and I meant it."

Leaning toward him with my eyes locked on his I spat, "Never gonna happen. Get that through your thick skull, Brooks." That's when I got a whiff of his cologne and my gag reflex kicked in. "Oh, God." I slapped a hand over my mouth. I stood quickly, forgetting about the gummy bears in my lap. The bowl fell to the ground and the gummy bears littered the surface.

Jude's eyes flicked from the gummy bears to me and back again. "Shit. How many of those did you eat?"

"A lot," I replied when I had control of myself.

"Shit," he repeated, thrusting his fingers through his hair so that it stood up wildly. "Those were soaked in vodka."

"*What?*" I shrieked, my voice so high that Jude flinched from the sound. "Who the hell does that?" I cried.

His laugh echoed around us—the kind of laugh that shakes your whole body and leaves tracks of tears down your cheeks.

"It's a party, what did you expect?" he asked when he had control of himself.

"Not this." I pointed to the mess on the deck. "You forgot to mention the vodka part when you told me you liked gummy bears."

Still laughing, he said, "I only soak them in vodka for parties."

"I can't believe this," I muttered, burying my face in my hands.

He stepped toward me and his cologne hit my nostrils once more. I gagged and dove for the door.

I ran through the house, looking for a bathroom. A line had formed outside a door of what I assumed was my destination. I was so screwed. I did not want to get sick all over the floor of Jude's townhouse. That would be enough ammunition for him to make fun of me for the rest of my life—or at least until college was over and I never had to see him again.

A hand reached out for mine, before I could wrench it away I saw that the hand belonged to Jude. "This way," he said, guiding me through the hallway and up a third set of steps.

His pace was quick, trying to get me to a bathroom before I got sick. I had news for him, he'd better have me there in seconds if he wanted to avoid that.

He stopped at a door, pulled a key out to unlock it, and shoved me inside.

It was obviously a bedroom, but bless his heart there was a bathroom. I ran for it, collapsing to my knees. My stomach heaved, trying to rid itself of those dang bears.

I startled when Jude's fingers gently coasted against my

neck, but then he was pulling my hair back and I was sick again, so there was nothing I could do to stop him.

Jude was the last person I would ever want to see me like this, so of course I was stuck in a bathroom with him. That's just how my life worked.

And the most ironic part of it all was the fact that I was drunk on gummy bears. I didn't even drink! How did stuff like this happen to me?

Once I was done emptying my stomach, Jude let go of my hair. I hoped he was going to leave me alone, but my luck wasn't that good.

He grabbed a washcloth from under the sink, dampened it, and knelt in front of me. I blinked heavy, shock-filled eyes at him as he gently cleaned my face.

I knew he saw the surprise in my eyes. Jude Brooks was taking care of me. The only words to describe this situation were: What the fuck? Clearly, I was drunker than I thought and I'd stepped into some parallel universe. This was not good. I did not want to start liking him. He was the reason my brother was dead, and that was enough ammunition to hate him for the rest of my life.

"Gummy bears are the devil," I muttered, causing him to belt out a deep, throaty laugh. Taking a deep breath, I told him, "I'm fine." I stood shakily, using the bathroom wall for support.

"You're not fine, Tatum," he growled, using his body to close me in so I couldn't edge toward the door. "You're clearly not used to drinking and those gummy bears will really get to you."

"I don't need you to look out for me." I groaned. "I'm fine on my own. I don't need you or anybody else to try and save me."

I put a quivering hand against my forehead, feeling dizzy from my outburst.

"Tate." He grabbed my shoulders to keep me from wobbling.

I collapsed against him, unable to hold myself up anymore. His strong arms wrapped around me. I was never going near a gummy bear ever again. Those things were dangerous.

Jude swept my legs out from under me. Before I could protest, he laid me down on the softest surface imaginable. Maybe I wouldn't argue with him.

I curled my body around the pillow and smiled. "This feels nice."

He chuckled in response. He laughed at me a lot. I didn't know why. I wasn't very funny.

"Is this your room?" I asked, crooking my elbow over my eyes to block out the glow of the light. It hurt my eyes. "Why'd you lock the door?"

"So no one can get in." His tone of voice told me exactly what he thought of that question. "No one is allowed to have sex in my bed that isn't me."

"Does this mean you want to have sex with me?"

I don't know what made me ask the question. I guessed I'd blame it on loose lips courtesy of gummy bears.

I felt the bed dip down beside me. For a moment, my heart stopped, as I feared he'd taken my words as invitation. I rolled my head to the side to look at him but found that he was staring at the ceiling. I looked up too, and noticed the ceiling was decorated with those peel and stick stars and moons lots of kids have on their bedroom ceiling. I wondered why he had them here. He wasn't a kid anymore and I wouldn't think Jude, being a twenty-two-year-old male, would want something like that in his bedroom. I hated to admit it, but maybe I was wrong about him. I really didn't know that much about *him* as a person. Everything I knew was based on assumptions from what I saw and heard. I did know one thing, and that was that he was responsible for my brother's death. I wondered if that fact weighed heavily on his shoulders. Probably not. Based on what he'd said about not being able to figure out why I hated him so much, I'd bet he wasn't even aware of the damage he'd caused.

I wished I could be more like him—not caring what other's thought of me and doing whatever the hell I wanted.

I'd stopped being carefree a long time ago.

"I want to have sex with you." I startled at his voice. He'd taken so long to answer that with my foggy brain I'd completely forgotten that I'd asked him anything. "But I know you don't want that." He turned his head slowly to look at me. His warm brown eyes caused something to stir in my stomach that I didn't even recognize. Despite my hatred of Jude there had always been *something* between us, and I'd always tried my hardest to squash it. The last year, having to share my best friend with him, had somehow managed to soften my heart toward him—and I hadn't even realized it was happening. It didn't mean I actually liked him, though. That would never happen. "When I touch you like *that*," he started as he reached out with his index finger to graze my lips, "you're going to *beg* for it. You're going to want it, and you're going to scream my name because it's the only word you can remember."

My breath faltered. "You're crazy."

"No, I'm not."

He rolled onto his back once more, crossing his arms behind his head, looking up once more at the glow-in-the-dark stickers on the ceiling.

I was too tired to move and my heavy eyes soon closed. I was asleep within minutes.

I really hoped I still hated Jude when I woke up.

SUNLIGHT WARMED MY SKIN. I blinked open my eyes wondering why I'd fallen asleep with the blinds open.

Only they weren't open and the heat wasn't from the sun.

A very heavy, manly arm was draped over my chest and I was pulled against a body where I was cradled like a teddy bear.

What the hell happened last night?

I tried to lift the arm off me, but it was futile.

I really hoped I hadn't done something stupid, but since my clothes were still on chances were good that I was safe.

Since I couldn't move, I looked around at the room.

That's when the memories flooded me.

With a strength that I didn't know I had, I scrambled from the bed and fell on the floor. The noise caused Jude to stir. I hopped up in time to see him stretching his arms above his head and yawning loudly. I kept backing up until I ran into the wall.

This had to be a really bad dream or a cruel joke.

There was no way I slept all night in a bed *cuddled* against Jude.

"Morning, darlin'," he chortled, running his fingers through his already mussed dark hair.

"Why am I in your bed?" My voice was shriller than I intended. I was in shock, to be honest. I grasped at my shirt, trying to pull it down from where it had ridden up to expose my stomach.

"You fell asleep." He rolled over and stood, cracking his back. "You were too cute to wake. Don't worry, I didn't fondle you in your sleep." He waggled his fingers innocently. "I'm not *that* desperate."

"You're not desperate at all," I stated, knowing just how many girls he had probably 'fondled' in this room. "I can't believe Rowan abandoned me," I muttered, anger filling my body. Some friend she was.

"She didn't." He shrugged easily, opening a dresser drawer. He pulled out a fresh shirt and removed the one he wore. I forced my eyes to the ground so that I didn't stare at his chest. I couldn't help wondering how he was so muscular. Between school and his volunteer hours I doubted he had very much time to work out.

"What do you mean she didn't?" I asked once he'd put on the clean shirt.

"I let her know what happened. She checked on you, and since *she* trusts me, she left you alone." Shrugging, he added, "To be honest, I think she would've had Trent carry you out of here but she said something about not knowing how to get you into your house. Are your parents strict or something?" he asked. "You still live with them, right?"

I wanted to laugh. My parents strict? They didn't care what I did. Not anymore.

"It's complicated," I answered, tucking a piece of blonde hair behind my ear. I felt extremely uncomfortable and I wanted nothing more than to get out of here, but I didn't have a car, which meant I was dependent on Jude. Something told me this situation had played out exactly as he wanted.

"Since you're here ..." He crossed his arms over his chest and his shirt rode up a bit, exposing his smooth stomach and the small patch of hair that disappeared beneath the waistband of his jeans. "Maybe we should go somewhere."

I cocked my hip to the side and stared him down. I was not going to play games with Jude. I wasn't in the mood.

"If you're taking me anywhere, it's home."

"All right." He grabbed his keys off the top of the dresser and spun the ring around on his finger. "Let's go then."

I was surprised he agreed so easily. Maybe he knew the chances of me spending the day with him were slim to none.

As we walked through the townhouse I noticed more than one person passed out in the hallway. One guy raised his head and gave Jude a thumb's up. My mouth fell open in shock as I realized what the guy believed had transpired between Jude and me. There was no need to correct him; he'd only think I was lying. I was stuck looking like I was doing the walk of shame. This sucked.

Once in Jude's truck I gave him the directions to my parents' house.

As soon as he parked in the driveway, I hopped out with no intentions to look back.

"See you later, Tater Tot."

I whipped around, that nickname grating on my nerves. He started to back out of the driveway and when he looked back at me I waved my middle finger at him.

He simply laughed at the gesture, so something told me I hadn't proven anything.

CHAPTER FOUR

I SLID INTO THE TRUCK, GLARING AT THE DRIVER.

"I don't understand why you need to drive me. I'm perfectly capable of driving my car and following you. There's no need for this." I waved my arms around wildly to encompass the truck.

Jude chuckled, shifting the truck into gear. "Yes, there is Tater Tot." He smirked like his ridiculous nickname for me was so clever and cute. I wondered what he'd think of it when I stabbed him with a pencil—or whatever other sharp object I could get my hands on. "If you didn't ride with me, we wouldn't get to have such enlightening conversations. And remember our bet?" I nodded reluctantly at his question. "This is the perfect time for each of us to ask our one question."

Buckling the seatbelt, I stifled the urge to roll my eyes. "I deserve a giant bowl of ice cream for dealing with you."

"With gummy bears on top?"

I gagged at the mention of those devilish little creatures. "Never. Again," I assured him.

He chuckled. "I really am sorry about that, just so you know."

"I'm sure you're very apologetic," I muttered, my voice laced with sarcasm as I looked out the window.

"Let me put it this way, I'm sorry you got sick, but I'm not sorry I got to spend the night with you."

I looked over to find him watching the road, his expression serious. There was no crinkling of his eyes or smirk on his lips. He was serious.

I chose not to comment on that. I'd probably only end up getting in an argument with him if I did and, frankly, he wasn't worth it.

As silence stretched between us, he asked, "What's your favorite color?"

Once again, I was surprised by the simplicity of his question.

I didn't look at him as I answered. "It always changes, depending on my mood and where I'm at, but right now it's orange."

"Why?"

I decided to answer instead of telling him he'd already asked me one question. Sometimes, I just needed to talk to someone—about anything—it just really sucked that I was stuck with Jude.

"Because of that—" I nodded out the truck window at the setting sun. "It's beautiful, warm, vibrant ..." It was everything I wasn't. "It comes every evening, but it's always slightly different—the colors brighter and more vivid, or dulled depending on the weather. It's always pretty, though."

He cleared his throat. "I wasn't expecting that detailed of a response."

I shrugged. The answer was more for myself than him, anyway. Even if he did ask.

"What's your question for me?"

I ignored him for a moment, so I could gather my thoughts. I rolled the window down and let it whip my hair around. It was really still too cold outside for this—winter was only beginning to melt away—but I didn't care. The cold air helped to calm me.

"Why did you help me?" I don't know why that was the question that popped into my head. It wasn't even really the one I wanted to ask, but apparently my mouth had different ideas.

"What do you mean?" His gaze flicked briefly my way—long enough for me to see his thick brows furrowed together across his forehead like a caterpillar.

"Why did you help me the other night, when I was sick? You didn't have to do that. I'm sure you had more important things to do than hold my hair back as I puked confetti," I said the words quickly, desperate to get them out. I'd felt antsy since Friday night. I'd spent most of my weekend pacing my house, and when I couldn't take that any longer I hung out at Griffin's and got buzzed on coffee.

He chuckled at my confetti comment but quickly sobered. "I don't know why you hate me," his voice softened and when his eyes briefly connected with mine I was shocked to see *hurt* shining so clearly in them. "I'm actually a nice guy. Yeah, yeah, I know I've been with a lot of girls, and never in a relationship, but ... it's easier not to get attached." His voice had quieted so much with the last bit that I wasn't even sure I heard him. I really wondered what he meant by that comment, but I'd already asked my one question and I didn't want to push my luck.

We fell into silence for the rest of the drive to the nursing home.

I was cursing myself for not getting something from the vending machine at the library before we left. It was already five o'clock and I was used to eating dinner at this time. I didn't dare tell Jude I was hungry. Not even when we passed a McDonald's and my stomach rumbled like a jumbo jet.

"Was that—?"

"No," I quickly cut him off. "I don't know what that was. Maybe a plane." I proceeded to look out the window, totally playing up the plane thing.

He laughed, banging his fist against the steering wheel. I was surprised tears weren't streaking his cheeks at this point, since he was laughing so hard. Like the kind of laughter that shakes your whole body. "I will never understand why so many girls won't admit they're hungry."

I hated being compared to anyone else, especially lumped into a category as ambiguous as *girls*. Honestly, what did that even *mean*?

"Fine, turn around and take me to McDonald's so you can watch me devour a Big Mac."

He looked at the clock on the dashboard and shrugged lightly, immediately executing a very dangerous U-turn that had illegal written all over it. "We've got time," he said when he saw my open-mouthed expression.

"You could have killed us!" I cried in shock at the Duke's of Hazzard move he'd pulled.

"And before you got your Big Mac?" he joked. "That would've been a shame. But you're okay, so it's all good."

"You infuriate me," I seethed, glaring out the window.

After Graham's wreck, I was always scared to be in a car. For a long time, I wouldn't even drive. The stunt Jude had pulled startled me. I didn't like not being in control.

I didn't stay mad for long once I saw the McDonald's. I was too hungry to care.

Jude pulled his truck around in the drive-thru and placed our order. I slid over beside him and yelled into the speaker that I wanted a Hi-C and an Oreo McFlurry. When I returned to my previous position he shook his head, a small almost boyish smile lifting his lips.

"What?" I prompted, pushing stray pieces of hair out of my eyes. It was honestly too long now, but I refused to cut it.

"You're going to have a severe sugar rush in an old folks' home. I'm really looking forward to watching this play out." His smile grew wider and I was sure he was probably imagining something silly—like me singing, dancing, and spinning around in wheelchairs.

"I'm hungry," I responded, "and no meal is complete without dessert."

"That doesn't explain the Hi-C," he countered, sitting up a bit to grab his wallet out of his back pocket. "That drink is for five year olds, and doesn't it turn your tongue blue or something?"

"Red," I answered, "and you're not paying for my food." My protests went unheard as I dug through my backpack for the money I kept stashed there.

He handed the lady working at the window his credit card and tilted his head to look at me. "Last time I checked, it was the gentlemanly thing to do."

"Last time *I* checked," I countered, smiling despite the fact that I shouldn't be enjoying this at all, "there was nothing gentlemanly about you."

"Touché," he chuckled heartily, scratching his chin as he waited for her to hand him his card and the receipt.

Once he had it he pulled up to the next window where they handed us our food.

He busted out in laughter at the sound I made upon smelling the food. I was starved and the smell of a greasy cheeseburger was calling my name. I didn't think I had ever wanted anything more than I wanted that burger.

I set my food in my lap and handed Jude his so he could eat as he drove. He promptly shoved a handful of fries in his mouth, chewing loudly. The fries stuck out of his mouth like the tentacles of an octopus. I couldn't help laughing. "What?" he asked around the mouthful. He took a large sip of his soda and said, "Isn't this how everyone eats their fries?"

"No." I shook my head, eating one single fry to make a point.

He shrugged. "I'm a man and that's how we eat fries."

"Maybe if you were a caveman," I mumbled under my breath, but he heard me even over the music blasting from the radio.

"Cavemen didn't have the convenience of drive-thrus or the salty deliciousness of French fries."

At his words, I realized I would never win in an argument with Jude. Well, more like neither one of us would win. We were both far too argumentative and neither of us would back down.

I took a bite of my burger, unable to hold back a moan. I really needed to stop forgetting to eat. It wasn't healthy.

As I chewed, I watched Jude out of the corner of my eye and noticed him squirming in his seat. "What are you doing?" I asked, and then when he explained I really wished I hadn't.

"I'm a guy, and when you make noises like that I can't stop

my reaction."

My eyes flicked down and then away. "Oh," was all I could say. I could have come back with something rude, but then I would've looked like an idiot and I didn't want to argue with him anymore. Especially since I still had to spend the majority of my evening with him.

Jude parked in the back lot of the nursing home and we finished our meal in silence. He looked longingly at my Oreo McFlurry, and I told him, "You should've gotten one."

"And maybe you should share," he suggested with a coy smile, like if he flirted with me it would make me willingly give up the most delicious substance on Earth. I was pretty sure ice cream could solve all the world's problems. I always had the freezer stocked with it.

"Come anywhere near my ice cream, Brooks, and I will not hesitate to bite you."

"Biting makes things interesting."

"Not if I bite your hand off," I replied easily. "Whatever will you do then?" I eyed the noticeable bulge straining against his jeans.

"Guess you'll have to help me with *that*, Tater Tot."

"I'll gladly help you to an early grave." My words shut me up, and Jude too. I wasn't sure if it was for the same reason, though. I thought of Graham. Of that twisted sheet of metal wrapped around a tree. How we had to bury him in a closed casket because there wasn't much left. I shouldn't have had to bury my brother at that age. He was far too young with his whole life ahead of him. My parents shouldn't have been around to watch their oldest child lowered into the ground. From the moment Graham died, my life was filled with *shouldn't*. I hated that word now. I hated a lot of things. Mostly myself.

"I'm sorry," Jude whispered. I'm sure he'd guessed where my mind went.

"Don't fucking apologize when you don't mean it," I snapped. My tone was icy calm, but my words were more heated than normal. I didn't normally get upset over much, but Jude and anything involving Graham always got my temper stirring.

"I do mean it." His words were almost a plea, trying to get me to *believe* that he was a good guy. But he wasn't. He killed my brother and he didn't even know it.

My anger got the best of me and I threw the half-melted McFlurry at him. Ice cream splattered everywhere. All over him, his clean scrubs, the cab of the truck, and even me.

I got out of the truck, slamming the door behind me. I started walking in the opposite direction. I wasn't sure where I was going. It didn't matter. I had to get away.

But Jude had other plans.

"Tatum!"

He was right behind me and there was no escape. I whipped around so fast that he stopped in his tracks. I was crying, I felt the tears now, but I hadn't even known they were there a moment ago. All my anger, all my frustration bubbled out of me. I couldn't hold it in anymore. That's what I'd been doing for seven years. I had to crack eventually and now was that moment.

"I hate you!" I screamed at the man in front of me with vanilla ice cream and Oreo's caked into his hair and scrubs. "I hate you so fucking much that it eats me up inside! I can't stand to look at you, knowing what you did! That it's *your* fault! It's not fair that you get to parade around like you own the place, fuck every girl you see, and my brother is dead because you couldn't keep your fucking dick in your pants!"

Jude's mouth formed a perfect O of shock as I yelled at him. "You destroyed my life! You stomped all over it and you didn't even care!" I couldn't breathe I was so worked up. I clutched at my chest. Now that I was yelling I couldn't seem to stop. I needed to get it all out in the open. I was sick of holding everything in and pretending I was okay when I wasn't. I was always the person plastering on a brave face when inside I was breaking apart. I didn't care what Jude thought of me, and since he was the source of every ounce of hatred I felt, I guessed it was appropriate that I lost my cool with him. "I lost not only my brother, but my best friend! One day he was there and the next he wasn't! My mom won't even *look* at me anymore! Did you know that? It's like I'm a ghost in my own house! My dad's barely even there! When you killed Graham, you killed them too! And you might as well have killed me, because I've never been the same!"

"Tate, I don't know what you're talking about." His voice was deceptively calm. I could see the storm brewing in his eyes. He was pissed, but he was trying not to show it. If I wasn't mistaken there was some fear too. He should be afraid.

"Don't play dumb. You know exactly what you did," I spat.

"I really don't."

I wanted to punch him in the face. Maybe it would knock some sense into him, but probably not.

The fight was leaving my body and I turned to leave once more.

I wanted to forget about Jude, this stupid project, and definitely how nice it had been to be snuggled in his arms.

At sixteen years old, I had vowed to hate Jude Brooks for the rest of my life for the damage he'd caused. I was not about to break that promise.

CHAPTER FIVE

After I walked away from Jude, Rowan was kind enough to pick me up and drive me back to school to get my car. Then she insisted on following me home and she hadn't left yet. She sat beside me at the bar that extended from the island in the kitchen. I had a bowl of vanilla ice cream with three Twizzlers in it. After all, I hadn't really gotten to eat my McFlurry. I propped my head up with one hand and slowly ate the ice cream with the other. Normally, ice cream always made me feel better. Not now, though.

"You have to tell me what happened," Rowan pleaded, looking at me with wide hazel eyes.

"No."

"It's in the code of Best Friends," she continued. "So, you have to tell me."

"Then don't be my best friend, I really don't care."

"Tatum." The way she said my name was the tone of a mother scolding her child.

"Rowan."

Her lips pursed and we ended up in a staring contest. She caved first and I ate a Twizzler to celebrate my small victory.

"I just want to understand why you hate him so much. I think I deserve an explanation. I've been dealing with you two for over a year now. And I don't care what you say, but there's definitely chemistry between you guys. Oh, my God," she gasped, "is that why you hate him? Did he screw you over in high school or something?"

"Absolutely not." I was appalled that she'd suggest such a thing. "I have never, and will never, be one of his play things."

"Then explain it to me." She eyed me, waiting for me to cave.

She reached for the spoon that lay in my bowl of ice cream but I swatted her hand away. "Get your own."

"Fine, I will."

Rowan made her own bowl of ice cream and sat beside me once more. I was lucky that when we got there my mom was nowhere to be seen. Usually, when I got home and she wasn't downstairs it meant she was in Graham's room. I always knew not to bother her when she was in there.

In all the time that I'd been friends with Rowan this was the first time she'd ever set foot in my house. I'd never wanted to explain my family to her and she didn't know about Graham. She was the only normal thing I had in my life.

"I'm not leaving here until you give me some answers, Tate." She eyed me and her look was determined. Rowan was a woman of her word, so I knew I better spit it out or she'd be sleeping on the floor of my bedroom.

I started from the beginning, telling her about Graham and his girlfriend and how Jude slept with her. I told her about Graham's supposed accident, and how I found a suicide note in his bedroom and knew it was no accident at all.

"Jude mentioned that to me a long time ago," she whispered, "he said you kicked him in the balls for sleeping with your brother's girlfriend."

"I did," I confirmed. "I wanted to do a lot more than that, actually," I muttered, looking away. "Graham wasn't even dead yet then. That happened a week later."

"I still don't see how Graham killing himself has anything to do with Jude."

"It has *everything* to do with Jude." I glared at her. "Wait here."

When I was sure she wasn't going to follow me, I jogged upstairs and opened the drawer in the table beside my bed. I pulled out the folded piece of paper. It was yellow now and ripped in places from the many times I'd held it.

When I passed Graham's room on my way down, sure enough my mom was in there. She sat on the edge of his bed, clutching his pillow. I hated hearing her cry. She'd cried every day at least once since the police showed up at our house. You'd think by now she would've run out of tears. But as long as you have something to cry about, they never dry up.

Back in the kitchen I handed Rowan the note.

I'd read it so many times I had it memorized.

Hi Tatie. I know you'll be the one to find this. I don't have any words right now other than I'm sorry. I'm sorry I wasn't strong enough. I'm sorry I wasn't a better brother and son. I'm sorry I couldn't be perfect. Now, Tatie, stop looking like that—I'm sure right about now you have your face screwed up in disbelief. But you know better than anyone else that I'm not perfect. I try so hard to be, but it's an impossible mission and I'm sick of trying.

What happened with Kaitlin broke my heart. I loved her, but apparently not enough. What she did showed me that life is a bunch of bullshit and I don't want to deal with this anymore.

Yeah, yeah, I know. This is the coward's way out.

But Tatie, we both know that's exactly what I am.

I've let mom and dad plan out my whole life and I'm not happy. I haven't been happy in a long time.

I'm sick of living a life that doesn't feel like mine.

Maybe I'll get lucky and I'll come back as someone else.

If that happens, I hope you'll be my sister in every life.

I can't say it enough, but I'm sorry. Don't hate me. Please.

And whatever you do, don't let mom and dad dictate your life like they did mine. Live your dreams, not theirs.

—Graham

Tears swam in my eyes when Rowan put the note aside.

"Tate," she said my name slowly, like it was a grenade she was afraid might detonate the moment the vibrations registered as sounds in my ear. She set the letter down and scooted closer to me, reaching for my hand, which I did not give her. "This doesn't sound like it has anything to do with Jude."

"It has everything to do with him!" My voice rose and my body with it—one second I was sitting and the next I was standing, glowering down at Rowan like she was the source of all my problems. "Read it again! You'll see!" I pointed at the letter like it held the answers to everything, which to me it did.

"Tatum."

I couldn't stand to hear the sadness in her voice. I wanted to cover my ears like a child and start humming so I didn't have to hear whatever she was going to say next.

"It sounds to me like," she began, picking up the letter, scanning it once more, "Graham had more of a problem with your parents than with what happened with his girlfriend."

"That's not true." My bottom lip quivered. "It's there, read it again. You have to see it. I'm not crazy. This is Jude's fault! It's his fault! If he hadn't fucked Kaitlin, Graham would be here right now! He wouldn't have killed himself! Please, read it again!"

"Sweetie." I flinched at the name. I didn't want Rowan or anyone else calling me *sweetie*. It had such a condescending tone to it. "It sounds like that was a part of it, but in this letter, he seems more pissed about your parents. Like they're the source of his problems."

"My parents are good people." My voice was quiet, no more than a whisper.

"Good people do horrible things." She bowed her head, her lips turning down in a frown. I knew she was thinking about how she kept her son a secret from Trenton.

I picked up the letter from where it had been left on the counter and flattened it against my chest.

"I think you should go now," I whispered, unable to meet her gaze.

"I know you don't care what I have to say, but you need to realize that your brother's death is no one's fault. Not yours. Not your parents'. And certainly not Jude's. He made his choice, Tate. Stop living in the past, it's holding you back. You deserve to be happy and not ... this." She waved a hand at my morose expression.

She didn't say anything more, just walked out of the kitchen and then out of the house. The sound of the front door closing felt like a slap to my face.

With a sigh, I looked toward the bowl of ice cream.

It was completely melted now.

Apparently, today was not my day for sweets—or anything for that matter.

I FELT his eyes on me before I saw him. It was like my body was always acutely aware anytime Jude was near. I didn't like it one bit.

I looked up from where I pushed my lunch around on the tray.

"Mind if I sit?" he asked, reaching up to adjust the beanie he wore.

"Something tells me that if I say no you're going to sit anyway," I mumbled, not bothering to lift my eyes to look at him.

"That's true." He shrugged, dropping his backpack on the ground and sitting across from me. Rowan was suspiciously absent. Something told me they'd orchestrated this. In fact, I probably didn't want to know how much those two talked about me. "What happened yesterday? I can't figure it out. I've been racking my brain and I honestly don't know what I did that could have anything to do with your brother's death. His death was an accident. It was a freak thing and it had nothing to do with me." His brown eyes pleaded with me to understand him as he looked at me through a veil of thick lashes.

"It wasn't an accident," I mumbled, glaring at my half-eaten food.

"Yes, it was." He sighed, clearly exasperated with me. He removed the beanie he wore, ran his fingers through his unruly brown hair, and replaced it. I think he just wanted to do something to busy himself. I'd been around Jude enough to know that he didn't like to sit still. He was a doer.

I shook my head. "Graham killed himself. He crashed his car because he couldn't deal with what you'd done." I was becoming more heated by the second and I might just throw my food at him. My mom always told me that as a child I was the queen of temper tantrums. Apparently, I never outgrew that.

"What the fuck did I *do*?" He spread his arms wide. "I'm so confused! I didn't even know your brother."

"You knew his girlfriend," I spat, my cheeks growing red with anger.

"Ohhhh," he drew the word out and his eyes lit with recognition. "*That's* what this is about." Smirking like he always did, he said, "Tater Tot's jealous. This is cute."

I blanched, unable to reply. "That's not what this is about at all. God, you're so fucking conceited it's sickening." Narrowing my eyes, I said, "Still think you can father a child after that kick I gave you?"

Jude was unfazed by my words. "Want to find out?"

"Ugh." I stood, gathering my bag and leaving my food on the table. "I don't have to deal with this," I muttered, and did what I did best, which was to walk away.

"I'm sorry, I'm sorry, I'm sorry," he chanted, running after me and cornering me in an alcove.

I rolled my eyes, looking down at the ground and away from his eyes.

"I shouldn't have said that," he continued. "It was a joke, I swear. You shouldn't take most of the things that come out of my mouth seriously."

I sighed, still not looking at him. I was never in the mood to deal with Jude.

His hands came up to rest against the wall beside my head. If he thought I was oblivious to the movement, he was wrong. It put his body closer to mine and I had nowhere to escape. Well played, Brooks. Well fucking played.

"You can think whatever you want of me, Tatum, but the

fact of the matter is what I did had nothing to do with what happened to your brother. You're acting like a child, trying to find someone to blame. I won't be your scapegoat." He lowered his voice and leaned in, his lips brushing my ear. I shivered from the contact. "Stop fighting what you feel for me."

"I'm not fighting anything," I panted.

He pulled away slightly, tilting his head so that strands of his hair tickled my forehead. "That's all you do, Tate. You fight everything." He straightened and lowered his arms to his side. "Now, this is the last time I'm going to extend my help with your paper. Think of it as a three strikes and you're out kinda deal." He winked. There was nothing playful in his gaze, though. He was dead serious. If I told him to leave me alone, he would, and then I'd be screwed. I didn't have the time to think up a whole new paper and go that route, so I was stuck.

"I accept your help," I mumbled, barely audible. I stared down at the scuffed ends of my Nike sneakers.

"What was that?" He turned an ear toward me. "I didn't quite hear you. Speak up."

"I accept your help," I said it louder this time, squaring my shoulders and holding my head high.

"Good." He smiled, rocking back on his heels. He started to walk away but turned back around to where I still stood against the wall. "Oh, and Tate?"

I nodded for him to continue.

"Try smiling sometime."

"Huh?" That was *not* what I had expected to come out of his mouth.

"You're always beautiful, but you light up when you smile. I'd like to see you do it more often."

"Maybe you shouldn't piss me off then," I countered, unable to hold back the words.

He chuckled, scratching his jaw. His smile was crooked when he said, "See you later, Tater Tot."

———

WHEN I CLIMBED into bed that night, I felt so confused.

For the last seven years I'd blamed Jude for Graham's death. I'd built this hatred up inside me. Now, between what he and Rowan said, I felt lost, like maybe it really wasn't his fault.

But if I didn't hate Jude, what was I supposed to do with all this anger inside of me?

CHAPTER SIX

Even though it was chilly, I sat outside on one of the many benches that dotted the campus grounds eating a banana. I didn't want to get caught out with Jude while I was hungry again. I might hurl another McFlurry at his head and that would be a real shame.

"You know," the voice sounded right beside me, "I could make a really dirty joke right now about you and that banana, but I'd like to live to see tomorrow so I'll keep quiet."

I looked over at Jude, continuing to chew happily on my banana. I wouldn't let him faze me. "Are you ready?" I asked.

He nodded. "I think the better question is are *you* ready?"

"I have to be," I replied. I stood and slung my backpack over one shoulder as I followed Jude to his truck. If there was one thing I knew Jude loved, it was that truck. It was an older model Ford with a shiny blue paint job. No matter the weather, it always sparkled like it had just been washed. Maybe it had.

He opened the truck door for me and I climbed inside.

I didn't thank him.

Rowan had made me feel crazy for hating Jude. I thought for sure after she read the letter she'd be on my side, but she still defended him. Then after my talk with Jude I felt unsure about the whole thing. I still didn't like him, I probably never would, but the overwhelming burn of hate was mysteriously gone from me. Well, maybe not *gone*, but redirected ... at the people I probably should've been angry at from the beginning.

"You look tired," Jude commented, taking in the bruise like shadows under my eyes.

Jude may have been a womanizer, but he also noticed more than most guys. I'd hoped I'd be able to hide them, but no such luck. Even Rowan had asked about them. I'd given her a mumbled answer that made no sense, but with Jude I found myself saying, "That'll happen when you're up all night thinking about the last seven years of your life."

"Tatum—"

"No," I cut him off. "I really don't need to hear whatever it is you think you have to say. You didn't lose your brother. You didn't have to find that note. You don't have to live with this constant *pain*." My breath stuttered and I looked away, hoping to get a better grip on my emotions. "Please, leave it alone."

He sighed heavily, not at all pleased with my request. "For now," he reluctantly agreed and I felt relieved to be let off the hook, even if it was only temporary.

"Is our bet still on?" he asked, filling the silence that loomed like a stormy cloud in the truck.

"Sure." I shrugged. At least the bet would give me something to think about other than Graham and the fact that his suicide really wasn't Jude's fault and the people I should blame were the ones living in my house.

"Why don't you ask me a question first?" he suggested, adjusting his grip on the steering wheel.

I leaned my head against the headrest, trying to think of a good question. So far, our questions had been relatively useless and silly. I wanted to know something personal about him. So, I asked the question that had been bugging me the longest. "Why do you want to be a nurse?"

He chuckled, but there was no humor in the sound. I wasn't sure if he was mad about the question or what. His eyes flicked my way for a moment and then back to the road. "I should have known you'd ask me that one eventually." He scrubbed a hand over his face.

"You don't have to answer it if you really don't want to," I said softly. I knew what it was like to be asked something that you didn't want to talk about and it sucked. I might not have liked Jude but I was really working on at least tolerating him.

"You're not the first person to ask me that question," he whispered, squinting against the sun, "but you are the first one I've ever wanted to tell the truth to."

His words caused my heart to stop momentarily. I didn't know whether I was excited about knowing something about Jude that no one else knew or terrified. Probably terrified.

He looked at the clock on the dashboard and said, "I'm never late, so if I call the nursing home they'll understand, but there's something I need to show you to make you understand *why*."

"Oookay," I drew out the word. "You're not kidnapping me, are you?"

"No," he laughed. "You'd only find a way to escape if I tried that."

"True," I agreed.

Jude pulled out his cellphone and called the nursing home. I was surprised by how easily they let him off the hook.

"They love me." He shrugged when I stared at him incredulously. "They gave me the whole evening off. I'll just put in some extra time for a few days to make up for it."

"Man." I shook my head, stifling a laugh. "You are quite the charmer."

He glanced at me with a wide smile, displaying his perfect white teeth. "Except my charms don't work on this one girl that I really, *really* like. It kinda sucks."

"I'm sure you're terribly sad," I played along, looking out the window. "I bet you cry yourself to sleep every night."

"I do. I use my teddy bear to mop up my tears and I also suck on my thumb," he rambled, not missing a beat.

"Now *that*," I couldn't help laughing, "is something I'd love to see."

"You can come over anytime." He grinned. "There's plenty of room in my bed for an extra snuggle buddy. But you already knew that." He winked, laughing under his breath.

I had no comeback for that one and he knew it.

We grew quiet as he turned off the highway and drove along. The town soon disappeared, replaced by the country and a dirt road. A wooden fence kept cattle from crossing into the road and trees were everywhere, blanketing the sky around us.

"Where are we going?" I asked, unable to handle the suspense a moment longer.

"To answer your question."

"I really hate show and tell," I muttered under my breath. "You better not take me to a whorehouse or something."

He let out a belly laugh and smiled crookedly. "You're funny."

"I was being serious," I replied.

"I know you were, that's why it was funny."

The dirt road narrowed into a driveway and I stared around in awe at all the animals. There were goats, cows, sheep, llamas, and the most beautiful horses I'd ever seen. "Wow," I breathed, unable to keep myself from uttering the word.

"I know, right," Jude agreed. "It's beautiful here. My favorite place in the world," he whispered the last part.

"I've never seen anything like this before," I admitted, still in awe of the spectacular property.

"You've never been on a farm?" he asked, his tone of voice incredulous. "Isn't that like a prerequisite to live here?"

"My parents are pretty city-fied," I mumbled. "My mom would've complained that she was getting her shoes dirty and my dad wouldn't have set foot at a place like this. Did you grow up here?" I realized immediately that maybe I shouldn't have asked the question since our deal was one question a day, but I couldn't help myself.

He answered anyway, despite my slipup in our plan. "Yes and no."

"What does that mean?" I asked, my nose crinkling in confusion.

He shrugged and I let it drop. I didn't want him prying into my life, so I wouldn't do the same to him.

The trees pulled away, hanging in a way that they almost framed the two-story white house. A porch wrapped around the front and sides. I could tell the home was old, and in need of a lot of work, but no less beautiful. A large red barn sat behind the house, looking exactly like I'd imagined one to look. If I peered far enough, I could see at least two more barns on the property. In the distance, there were rows upon rows of cleared land, ready for the planting season.

Jude killed the engine on his truck and hopped out. I was left to follow.

He bounced up the rickety steps to the front door.

I was much slower, a bit afraid that the steps might cave in.

He opened the door and waved me inside ahead of him.

Like the exterior, the interior was obviously old and in need of repairs. Flowery pink wallpaper in the foyer peeled down and the wood floors needed to be sanded and re-stained. I still thought it was beautiful in a rustic, homey sort of way.

"Pap?" he called out. "Where are you?"

"Back here, boy!" sounded a gruff voice from the back of the house.

Jude nodded his head for me to follow him.

We rounded the hallway into a kitchen and the first thing I noticed was that it was covered with dirty dishes. It was also covered with at least ten baskets of eggs. I had never seen so many eggs in my life. Not even at Easter brunch as a child when we had an Easter egg hunt with family.

In the corner of the room, sitting at a small wood table, was an older man. His gray hair was thinning but there was a sparkle in his brown eyes—the same shade of brown as Jude's. His face was heavily wrinkled, and he looked *tired*—like a man that had worked hard his whole life. Upon seeing us, he smiled and it lit up his face.

It didn't escape my noticed that despite the fact that it was the evening, the man was reading the newspaper, a plate of bacon and eggs in front of him. A cup of coffee and orange juice sat at the side of the plate.

"Pap," Jude groaned, "what have I told you about the eggs?" Not waiting for the man to respond, he continued, "They *spoil*. You either need to sell them, or toss them. You can't eat all these."

Lowering the newspaper, the older man responded. "Andrew, I've taken care of myself this long, I think I'm fine."

Andrew?

"Pap—?"

"The yard needs to be mowed, do you think you can do that?" he talked right over Jude.

Jude shook his head. "You know I will, but not—"

"Today, please. It's looking shabby." His eyes landed on me. "Who's this? Oh ... is this Julia? She's lovely, Andrew. Your description didn't do her justice. She's stunning."

I shot Jude a questioning gaze.

"Pap, we'll be right back." Jude reached for my hand and pulled me from the room.

"All right, I'll finish my breakfast while y'all talk," the man said from the other room.

Once we were in the living room away from the kitchen, Jude released my hand. "I should've explained before we walked in here. I don't know what I was thinking," he muttered, shoving his fingers through his hair so it stuck up wildly. "That's my grandpa, which I'm sure you've figured out. He has Alzheimer's. Some days are good, some days are bad. Very bad. Like today. He was fine yesterday, so I thought he'd be okay today."

"So, Andrew is ...?" I prompted, my gaze travelling around the room. An old piano sat in the corner with an even older couch. One of those giant Grandfather clocks took up space against the wall. I'd never seen one in person. This house was screaming to be fixed up.

"My dad," Jude clarified.

"And Julia?" I tilted my head to the side.

"I don't know." He frowned. "My mom's name is Karen. When he gets like this, I've found it's best to play along. He gets mad if I contradict him." Jude's eyes grew sad. Normally, he always smiled or laughed, to see him like this was a new experience for me. Jude loved his grandpa. That was obvious.

"I don't understand what any of this has to do with answering my question," I muttered, suddenly feeling even more uncomfortable. It had to be a terrible thing to lose your memories.

"It has everything to do with it," Jude said simply. Pointing in the direction of the kitchen, he explained, "That man in there practically raised me. He was more of a dad to me than mine ever was. Watching him slowly start forgetting things hurt more than anything. When I started college, I knew I wanted to be a nurse and work in a nursing home. I wanted to work with people like my grandpa and maybe make their day a little nicer. I want to *help*, because watching someone you love slip away day by day is a terrible thing. If I can ease the burden for another family, I'm glad to do so."

I think my mouth fell off at one point during his speech and currently rolled around on the floor.

Jude Brooks had a heart.

Hell must have frozen over. Between this, and my conflicted feelings over Graham's death, today was proving overwhelming.

"You don't need to say anything, but that's the truth."

I shut my mouth, because if I spoke I might say something nice to him and that would not be good. Instead, I nodded.

"Are you okay to go back in there?" he asked, appearing nervous—like he believed I'd be afraid of his grandpa.

"Of course," I replied. "He's not a rabid animal."

Jude threw his head back and laughed merrily about that. He laughed a lot. Most guys didn't. It would be refreshing if he wasn't, well, *Jude*.

Back in the kitchen, his grandpa said, "Son, get the yard mowed. You've got all day to flirt with the pretty girl."

I looked out the kitchen window at the sky beyond. It was getting dark now, too dark to mow.

"I'm going, I'm going," Jude chanted.

"You can't mow in the dark!" I cried. I don't know why I was coming to Jude's defense, but I knew I couldn't let him do that. On a property this large, it would be impossible to mow in the dark.

He leaned into me, brushing strands of my blonde hair off my shoulder with a single flick of his fingers. Whispering in my ear, he said, "I installed a headlight on it. I'll be fine. Besides, I won't do it all. Just enough to make him happy."

"But—" I gaped.

"You'll be okay?" he framed it as a question.

I looked from his grandpa to him and nodded.

"Just play along," Jude reminded me.

His steps thumped against the old floors as he headed outside. The screen door creaked shut and I was left alone with the eldest Brooks.

"Lovely morning, isn't it?" He nodded toward the window.

"Beautiful," I agreed.

"Are you hungry?" he asked. "I made plenty. Grab a plate for yourself."

"I already ate," I assured him. "But thank you for asking."

He nodded. "I see you have manners. I like that. You're a pretty girl, Julia."

"Thank you," I said again.

"You're too good for Andrew," he continued. "That boy's trouble."

"Is that so?" I asked, pulling out a chair and sitting down across from him. The table and chair set looked like it was made in the seventies. The chairs were a pukey green color and the table was a dark wood. "Tell me more about Andrew."

The man smiled, his eyes lighting up. He lapsed into a tale about a wild boy and all the shenanigans he pulled. I wondered if Jude's dad was really like that, or if his grandpa's Alzheimers had caused him to combine Andrew and Jude's childhood.

I found myself intrigued by everything the man said. I didn't want him to stop telling me stories of his and Andrew's past. I wanted to ask him about Jude, but since I was "playing along" I knew that was strictly forbidden and I didn't want to make his grandpa mad by asking something he didn't remember.

"Come with me." The man stood. "I'm Jerry, by the way. I'm so sorry I didn't introduce myself. My rude son should have made the introduction for us."

"Sometimes Andrew forgets his manners," I said. It felt weird to call Jude by a name that wasn't his.

"That he does," Jerry agreed, leading me through the house. "I raised him better than that. Sometimes, you do all the right things, and they turn out to be the wrong things."

I nodded in agreement, mulling over his words. "That's very true."

"I grew up in this house, and my father before me," he said, looking around with nostalgia written on his face. "It's been in my family for generations."

"It's a beautiful home." Despite the fact that it was falling apart, it had good bones. With enough money and manpower, it could sparkle like new again.

"I wish Andrew thought that. He hates this place. He can't wait to get away," Jerry rambled. "He doesn't want to live a farmer's life. I can't say I blame him. It's hard work."

"I'm sure he'll change his mind," I assured Jerry.

He shook his head. "No. Once Andrew sets his mind to something, he doesn't change it." Smiling at me, he added, "He's like me. Stubborn to a fault."

I couldn't help laughing. The same things had been said about me more times than I could count.

"I should stop rambling about Andrew and show you the place. This is obviously the living room."

I'd already seen this room when I was with Jude, but I didn't say that. Instead, I looked around and told him how nice it was. "Do you play the piano?" I asked, nodding to the upright in the corner.

He shook his head. "That's Mae's. My wife," he added. Looking around, he said, "I haven't seen her this morning. I wonder where she is."

"I'm sure she's around here somewhere." I patted his arm. Jude hadn't mentioned a grandma, so I assumed she was gone. It broke my heart that Jerry was so clearly stuck in the past—in a time when his wife was alive and his son was still home.

He led me upstairs, showing me the bedrooms and bathrooms. The upstairs was a little more updated than the rest of the house.

The last room he showed me was 'Andrew's' but from what I saw in there, it had Jude written all over it.

The walls were painted a dark blue and the furniture was old and well-worn. The bedspread was blue and gray stripes and gray curtains hung beside the windows. A calendar with scantily-clad women hung on the wall. There were some clothes strewn around and enough odds and ends to tell me that someone still occasionally used this room.

Jerry took me downstairs again and showed me a sunroom. I was sure it was beautiful during the daytime.

"Huh." Jerry tilted his head as he looked out the wall of windows, "it got dark fast. I forgot lunch ... and dinner."

I frowned, but didn't say anything.

"Are you hungry, Julia?" he asked me.

I shook my head. "No."

"Well, I am. I'm going to make something for Andrew and me to have when he comes in. You can stay out here if you want. Or go out on the porch. There's blankets in a basket beside the couch in the living room."

While he went back in the kitchen, I decided to listen to his suggestion to sit out on the porch. I grabbed a blanket, which was right where he said it would be, and found a rocking chair on the front porch.

It was completely dark now, but there were small solar lights dotting the walkway leading up to the front of the house. They provided enough light to illuminate the fence and some of the animals.

I shivered and wrapped the blanket tighter around my body.

The day was shaping up to be interesting. I didn't know quite what to make of it.

Jude was beginning to break down the wall of cinderblocks I'd built around my heart and myself. I didn't want to be his girlfriend, or even his friend, but he was weaseling his way into my life and I didn't like it one bit. Or maybe I did like it and that's why it scared me so much.

"I thought you might want something to drink."

I jumped at the sound of the voice. Jerry stood beside me with a glass of water. I hadn't heard him approach. My heart gradually slowed and returned to its normal pace. "Thank you." I took the proffered glass from him. He didn't reply as he turned and disappeared inside once more.

I took a sip of the ice-cold water. I was thirsty and hadn't realized it. I drank every last drop and set the glass on the ground beside me.

I rocked slowly in the chair, letting my eyes drift closed as I hummed softly under my breath.

It was nice here and I really liked Jerry, even if he didn't know who I was.

Somewhere in the distance, the sound of the tractor cut off.

A few minutes later, a sweaty Jude bound up the steps.

"Tired?" I asked.

He jumped at the sound of my voice, pushing damp hair from his eyes. "I'll live." He winked.

"Your grandpa's making dinner," I told him.

"He was eating when we got here," Jude groaned. "I'd joke that the man's lost his mind, but that would be the truth." He shrugged, sighing heavily. "And the truth makes for a pretty shitty joke."

"Do you stay here with him often?" I asked, unable to help myself as I remembered the room Jerry had shown me earlier.

"A few times a week," Jude admitted. "It depends on classes and how much time I have. This place isn't exactly that close to school." He shrugged.

"No one else takes care of him?" I asked. I was full of questions today.

Jude shook his head. "Only me." Muttering under his breath, with venom lacing his words, he said, "No one else cares."

Something in my heart shifted.

I was beginning to realize that I'd misjudged Jude.

I'd hated him for the stunt he pulled with Graham's girlfriend and the part I'd believed it played in Graham's death.

I'd hated his whole playboy demeanor.

I'd hated the way he always seemed to use women.

But, the fact of the matter was, I didn't really know him.

Right now, this man in front of me, was the *real* Jude and he just might be worth getting to know.

"I'm going to shower before we go," he informed me. "Pap will be mad if we don't stay for dinner. I hope you don't mind." He appeared almost sheepish.

"I don't mind at all." It was true. I liked Jerry and I hated to think of him sitting in this house eating dinner alone. In fact, I'm pretty sure it broke my heart.

"Good." Jude's smile was wide, his eyes crinkling at the corners.

With that, he disappeared inside and through the screen door. I could hear his boots slamming against the steps.

I stayed outside for a moment longer, admiring the way the stars sparkled like new diamonds and the sounds of nature weren't masked by car horns and chaos.

Maybe there was a little bit of a country girl inside me.

I stood and folded the blanket, draping it over my arm. I placed it back inside the basket I got it from and joined Jerry in the kitchen.

"Can I help?" I asked, leaning against the doorway. My stomach came alive at the smell of whatever he was cooking.

He turned to look over his shoulder at me. "Of course, sweetheart."

I smiled at the term of endearment. I might not like Jude, but I was kind of falling in love with his grandpa.

As I approached, I noticed he was stirring something in a large pot with a wooden spoon. "You take over with this," he told me. "I'll get the table set."

I leaned closer to the pot and smelled. "Mmmm," I couldn't contain my hum of approval. I hadn't had a home-cooked meal like this in a long time. I could cook, but nothing I made could ever compare to how this *smelled* and I hadn't even *tasted* it yet.

Jerry chuckled from somewhere behind me. "You like the smell of that."

"It smells so yummy," I told him, stirring the mixture carefully.

"That's my mama's world-famous chili. That recipe has been passed down for generations," he explained, setting bowls and napkins on the table. Returning to my side he said, "That should be done now." He peered down at the mixture and nodded. "It's perfect."

He reached in front of me and turned off the stove eye. He picked up the pot, carrying it over to the table and placing it on a trivet.

"Julia, there's some cornbread in the oven, could you grab that for me?" he asked.

"Absolutely," I replied, slipping an oven mitt on and reaching inside to pull out the pan. I placed it beside the chili and put the mitt back where I found it.

Before I could sit down, Jude strode into the kitchen. "Something smells good." He sniffed the air, reaching above his head to clasp the top of the doorway leading into the kitchen. I swore he did it on purpose because the gesture did amazing things for his muscular arms and the way his shirt pulled taut over his chest hinted at a six-pack.

And oh, my God, I was *staring*—and not just at anyone, but at Jude-freakin'-Brooks.

Had my brain taken a vacation?

I cleared my throat and hastily turned my head away. From the telltale smirk on his face he hadn't missed the fact that I had checked him out. I was never going to live this down.

"Andrew, stop gawking at the pretty girl and sit down and eat."

"Aye, aye, sir," he saluted his grandpa.

Jude and I sat side by side, facing his grandpa. He ladled out chili into all of our bowls and then bowed his head to say grace. Jude and I hastily followed suit, mimicking his position.

Once that was done, we all ate like we were starved to death. I could understand why Jude and I were hungry, but his grandpa had eaten "breakfast" when we got here. It broke my heart that the man was basically losing his mind. It was horrible—something no one should have to go through, and no loved one should have to watch.

I glanced at Jude out of the corner of my eye. He watched his grandpa carefully, his jaw clenched and his eyes lined with worry. If there was one person in the world that Jude loved, it was his grandpa. Today showed me that there was a depth to Jude anyone rarely saw. I might not like him, but I'd take this small gift he'd given me by showing his true colors.

"This is delicious, Jerry," I spoke up.

He smiled widely, pleased that I enjoyed it. "I'm happy to hear that. You should come over one day and I'll teach you to make it."

"Really?" I lit up at the same time that Jude said, "Quiet, Pap."

"Certainly." Jerry nodded at me. He narrowed his eyes at Jude. "Manners, boy."

"Sorry," Jude bowed his head like a small child who'd just been scolded.

It was so weird to see Jude cave so easily to everything his grandpa said. He respected and admired the man.

Once dinner was done, Jude and I stayed to clean the

dishes. On his way out of the room, Jerry said, "Make sure to fix a bowl of leftovers for her to take home."

"Will do," Jude chimed, turning on the hot water and taking the bowls from my hands. "I'll wash, you dry."

We stood side by side, cleaning and putting away the dishes used.

If someone had told me a week ago that I would be in Jude's grandpa's house cleaning dishes I would have told them they were batshit crazy, flipped them the bird, and strode away.

But right then, there was no place I'd rather be.

I'd forgotten what it was like to sit down with other people and eat a meal. But it was more than that. There was a comfort present in this home that had long been absent from mine—even before Graham died.

Sometimes, I think the mind has the ability to make you forget traumatic things, at least temporarily. I wondered what all I might have blocked myself from remembering.

"I hope he wasn't too bad," Jude murmured under his breath in case his grandpa still lurked near us. "I didn't want to leave you alone with him, but I knew he wouldn't quit asking me to mow and I if I didn't do it, he'd try to and—"

I surprised us both by reaching up and placing a finger against his lips. It effectively ceased his rambling, but now we were locked in a staring contest and I wasn't sure who would look away first.

Of course, it was me.

Swallowing thickly, I continued to dry the already pristine bowl in my hands. "You had nothing to worry about," I told him. "Your grandpa is pretty amazing."

He chuckled. "You might be the only person that thinks so."

"Besides you," I added, because we both knew it was true. He didn't need to say it.

"Yeah, I think he's pretty amazing." He looked over his shoulder, as if his grandpa was standing there, but I'd heard his footsteps ascend the steps a few minutes earlier. "I worry about him," he whispered under his breath, then looked at me with soft brown eyes.

I didn't know how to handle this Jude. He was a stranger to me.

None of my normal bitchy comments would be appropriate right now. Jude was being oddly serious, and I needed to do the same. It was hard, though, because I was afraid of being played.

"I'm sure you do." I gave him a reassuring smile. Because he'd opened up about why he wanted to be a nurse, and showed me a vulnerable side of himself that I hadn't known existed before, I added, "I worry about my mom."

"Your mom? Why?" His thick brows furrowed together.

I let out a heavy sigh. My shoulders drooped with heaviness. "It's a long story."

"I like stories." His voice was soft with none of his normal joking tone.

"This isn't a story I want to tell." I shrugged, setting the dish aside and taking the next one he offered me. Since it was the last, he pulled the plug from the sink and the soapy water swirled away.

He leaned a hip against the counter and crossed his arms over his chest. The action caused his short-sleeve shirt to ride up a bit, exposing the smooth planes of his stomach and the dents that disappeared underneath the band of his jeans.

Annnnd, I was staring. Again.

Jude noticed where my eyes lingered and a smirk lifted his full lips. "It's okay to look, Tatum."

A blush stained my cheeks and I hastily turned away. I hated being flustered but I was beginning to feel like that's all I ever was around Jude.

"We better go," he said, grabbing up two plastic containers full of chili—one for me and one for him. "It's getting pretty late."

For the first time since we arrived on the farm I thought of my mother home alone with no one to take care of her. I couldn't believe I'd completely forgotten her. What was wrong with me?

Jude pulled on a sweatshirt and held the front door open for me.

The small lights outside didn't provide enough clarity for walking, so Jude guided me to his truck with a hand balanced above my waist. He held the door open for me as I climbed inside and then handed me the containers to hold on the ride home.

Neither of us said much, and it wasn't until he dropped me off at campus to get my car that I realized he'd never asked me a question today.

CHAPTER SEVEN

"Hey, Mr. Jenkins, how are you doing?" Jude asked the man lying in the bed as he glanced down at a chart.

"I'm doing better now that you're here." The man coughed, his entire small frame shaking with the movement. "None of these women ever want to talk about sports. It's annoying."

Jude chuckled and pulled out a chair, sitting beside the man. He reached for his arm and started taking his pulse. "What do you want to talk about today?"

"Baseball," he responded.

As Jude took the man's vitals he immediately lapsed into an easy conversation about different teams, stats, and a bunch of other things that sounded like he was speaking Martian. I'd been a cheerleader for a short time before Graham died, and I knew a *little* about football, but not enough to brag about.

As Jude quieted, taking notes, the man asked, "Who's this pretty lady? Your girlfriend?"

"I'm *not* his girlfriend," I spat before Jude could respond and I said it like it was the grossest thing imaginable.

"She doesn't know it yet," Jude's grin lifted his cheeks as he spoke, looking at Mr. Jenkins, "but one day I'm going to marry that girl."

"Over my dead body," I grumbled, rolling my eyes as I stood in the corner jotting down notes for my paper.

"I'm a nurse. I could revive you," he quipped without a second of thought. Jude had an answer for everything. Turning toward the man lying in the bed, he told him, "She thinks she's immune to my charm, but she's not. No one is." Looking back at me he winked.

I shook my head, feigning that I was disgusted, but I really wasn't. With as much time as I'd spent with Jude in the past week of shadowing him, I'd gotten to the point that I could tolerate him. I was trying to watch what I said and not be rude, because I really hoped he'd take me back to his grandpa's farm. I was dying to see it during the day.

"Don't worry," Mr. Jenkins said as he reached over and patted Jude's hand, "she'll come around one day."

Smiling at me with his brown eyes sparkling, he said, "I know."

"So, if you're not his girlfriend, why are you here?" Mr. Jenkins addressed me.

I wanted to laugh at his girlfriend comments. It seemed he, and everyone else, was convinced that we were dating.

"I'm writing a paper on nurses and how much work they have to do. It'll cover more than that, but that's just the gist of it." I shrugged, twirling my pencil between my fingers from nerves.

"Interesting," he commented, and then turned to Jude and started talking about sports again.

In my time at the nursing home with Jude, I'd quickly learned that he took the time to get to know everyone. He knew personal details about each person he dealt with and spent time talking to them. I'd seen several patients light up as soon as he entered their room.

I'd never known Jude had this side to him. I'd seen a glimmer of it the day at his grandpa's, but with each additional day I spent with him a new layer of Jude was exposed. There was far more to Jude than I or anyone else ever knew. I think he *wanted* people to think he was dumb and nothing but a playboy because that was what was *expected* of him. In actuality, the man had more of a heart than anyone I knew. He surprised me with his kindness toward the patients he dealt with. Even when he had to deal with someone being fussy he stayed calm and kept a genuine smile on his face. It was obvious to me that he was doing what he loved by taking care of people. I hated to admit it, but I admired that about him.

After talking to Mr. Jenkins for at least twenty minutes, Jude stood and with apology written in his voice he said, "I'm sorry, Mr. Jenkins, but I have to go. I'll see you again soon, though."

"Take care." Mr. Jenkins smiled at me, and then Jude. To Jude he whispered, but loud enough for me to hear him, "Don't let that one get away."

"I don't plan on it," Jude assured him.

I followed Jude out of the room and cornered him in the hallway. "Are nursing home patients performing some kind of matchmaking service for us or something?"

Jude's laugh bellowed around the hallway. "Why don't you just admit that there's something between us?" He smiled crookedly. "Everyone can see it, so why can't you?"

"I have twenty/twenty vision," I replied easily, "clearly everyone else is simply seeing things."

"You have an answer for everything," he muttered as he turned down the hallway to visit another patient.

For the rest of the evening, I took notes and asked Jude questions. He always surprised me with his long, thought-provoking answers. I wondered if he'd ever stop shocking me.

Later that evening, we were getting into his truck when his cellphone beeped with a text message. Jude smiled at whatever the message said.

"What is it?" I asked curiously. I couldn't seem to stop the words from tumbling out of my mouth.

"Rowan wants to know if we'd like to come over for dinner."

"How does she know we're together tonight?" I frowned.

"It's Rowan," he chuckled, "she knows everything. You want to or not?"

I thought of my mother sitting at home by herself, staring listlessly around at nothing.

A good daughter would refuse the invitation and go home to take care of her.

But I was tired of being good.

"Sounds like fun," I replied, buckling my seatbelt.

Jude smiled widely. He hadn't believed I would agree. Was I really that predictable?

We were quiet on the drive to the townhouse Rowan and Trent shared. A few minutes before we arrived, Jude said, "My grandpa has been asking about you."

"He has?" I don't know why that fact made me light up so much.

"Yeah, he misses you. He still thinks you're this mysterious Julia person, though." He chuckled.

Even if to his grandpa I was simply a girl named Julia, that may or may not have ever existed, it still warmed my heart that he missed me. No one had missed me for a long time.

"I'd like to see him again sometime," I told him, my soft voice betraying a shyness I didn't normally feel.

"Really?" Jude seemed genuinely surprised by my admission.

"Absolutely." I nodded as we rounded the corner and the row of townhouses came into view.

He didn't say anything but the way his lips were pursed I knew he was mulling over my reply.

He parked the truck in front of the house and I hopped out before we could have another heart to heart.

I jogged up the front steps and rang the doorbell.

Rowan let us inside and led us back through the house toward the kitchen.

I screamed when I saw something furry scurry across the floor. Somehow, I ended up grabbing ahold of Jude's arm and hiding half-behind him. As soon as I realized what I'd done I released him and stepped away, my cheeks tinged pink.

"That's just Bartholomew," Rowan explained. At my continued befuddled appearance, she added, "Trent's ferret."

"Oh, the ferret. Of course. I thought it was a mouse," I mumbled under my breath.

"Dinner's almost ready," Rowan continued, "the table's set, so you guys can sit down with the kids. Trent and I have this covered."

She didn't wait for us to reply; with a swish of her long light brown hair she was gone.

Jude nodded his head toward the table. We didn't make it very far before we heard, "Hey, Jude!" in a sing-song voice.

"The kid never gets tired of that." He chuckled.

"At least he has good taste in music for a six-year-old." I smiled.

Tristan, Rowan and Trent's son, appeared at the top of the stairs running down them toward us. Well, not *us*, but to Jude.

Jude lowered so that the small boy crashed into his waiting arms, giving him a giant bear hug. Standing, Jude spun Tristan around, his high-pitched shrieks of delight echoing through the space.

"Don't kill my son!" Rowan called from the kitchen.

"Fun sucker," Jude and Tristan said at the same time.

I shook my head, looking around for Ivy—Rowan's nine-year-old little sister that lived with them. She came down the steps too, although not as enthusiastically as Tristan. Ivy was a sweet girl, but I knew the last year or so had been rough on her emotionally. With her morose expression and overall melancholy appearance I wanted nothing more than to reach out and hug her.

"Hi, Ivy, how are you?" I asked, suppressing a laugh as Jude ran around with Tristan's arms wrapped around his neck, the boy hanging down his back like a cape.

"I'm good," she replied softly, tucking a stray curl behind her ear. She looked up at me with wide, doll-like, eyes. "How are you?"

Ivy was always so polite, sounding more like someone middle-aged than the young girl she really was.

"I'm doing okay. Your hair looks pretty like that," I commented, noticing she had two strands pulled back in a braid, secured with an elastic.

"Thank you." She smiled, maneuvering around me to get to the table.

I sat down too, while Jude and Tristan continued to play.

Trent carried out a large dish, the scent of garlic and marinara lingering in the air. My stomach rumbled and I longed to dig in.

"Be careful with him," Trenton warned Jude.

As soon as Trent was gone, Jude looked at me and rolled his eyes. He mouthed, "Overprotective."

A few minutes later we were all seated, ready to eat.

Trent cooked most of their meals because he really enjoyed it. Tonight, he'd made homemade lasagna. My mouth watered at the heavenly aroma. Between Jude's grandpa and now this, I was getting spoiled.

Jude cut a piece and set it on my plate. I gaped at him and he shrugged, a small smile threatening to tug up his lips. His gesture didn't go unnoticed by Rowan and she watched us sharply. She didn't miss anything.

I took a bite and flavors exploded across my tongue. Taking a sip of ice water, I told Trent, "This is delicious. Thanks for having us over."

Trent set his fork down, looking across at where Jude and I sat. "Wait ..." His head swiveled toward Rowan. "Are they together now?"

I snorted, not only at his question, but at how he addressed Rowan instead of us.

Rowan lifted a single brow, tilting her head toward Jude and me. "Well?"

"No," I said at the same time Jude replied with, "I wish."

"Hmm," she mused, sitting back in her chair. She watched us closely, like we were a map she was trying to decipher.

Clearing my throat, I went back to eating my food. I tried my hardest to ignore the heat infusing my cheeks.

Trent, obviously, didn't understand that I'd like the subject dropped because the next thing out of his mouth was, "I think you guys would make a great couple."

Is no one on my side?

I felt like everyone was rooting for Jude and I to end up together and, frankly, all I could think about was graduating college and the enormity of life as an adult. The last thing I needed to add into the mix was any sort of relationship, especially one with *him*.

"I think so too." Jude smirked, tossing an arm over my shoulders. I shrugged off his touch like he carried some disease I might contract if he got too close. Yeah, I was totally acting like a little kid freaking out at the thought of *cooties* but I didn't care. Ignoring my gesture, Jude leaned his face toward mine, but looked at Trent and Row. "Don't we look so *hawt* together." He flipped his hand in the air, making his voice sound high and over exaggerating his words. "*Like* we'd have the most *adorable* babies *ever*." Despite myself, I couldn't help giggling.

Tristan started to laugh too, and then everyone was laughing. Leave it to Jude to make me feel better by turning it into a joke.

Once our laughter dulled, Rowan moved the topic to more neutral grounds. "How's your paper going?"

I shrugged. "Okay, I guess." I'd only rewritten it like ten times. It was my final paper and I wanted it to not only be perfect, but to *mean* something. I wanted to make an impact with the story and my words.

"Come on, Tater Tot, give us more than that," Jude chimed in.

"Tater Tot?" Tristan giggled, marinara sauce spread over his cheeks. "That's a funny nickname."

I elbowed Jude in the ribs and mumbled, "Stop calling me that."

"Mommy says hitting isn't nice." Tristan's eyes widened as

he witnessed the gesture. "You should say you're sorry and kiss it to make it better."

Jude leaned back in the chair so that only two legs rested on the ground. His brown eyes sparkled with barely contained laughter. I was in trouble now. Crap. "Yeah, Tate, kiss it and make it better. It hurts really bad." He pouted his full lips and proceeded to pull his shirt up so that his side was exposed.

I narrowed my eyes, opening my mouth to retort. Before I could say anything, Rowan slapped her palms against the table. "God, you two are worse than children. I wish you'd just do it already to alleviate the tension!"

Ivy giggled and Tristan looked from his mom and dad to us. "What do you want them to do, Mommy?"

Rowan's eyes widened and her cheeks colored.

Trent saved her by leaning his elbows on the table and peering at his son. "She wants them to play Scrabble."

"Scrabble?" Tristan's nose scrunched with confusion. "What's that?"

"It's a board game," Trent explained.

"Oh, I think we have that one. I'll get it." He wiped his small hands on a napkin, climbed off the chair, and ran into the living room.

We all swiveled to look at Trenton. "What?" He shrugged, using his hand to cover his smile. "It was all I could think of."

A moment later Tristan called from the living room, "I can't find it!"

Rowan started to stand, but Trent urged her to sit. "I've got this," he assured her, gazing at her lovingly. She instantly relaxed as his lips pressed tenderly against her forehead. Sometimes they were too much to handle, but I was truly happy for them. They had the kind of love that comes once in a lifetime, and I only hoped I was lucky enough to find that one day.

Trent brought Tristan back into the dining room sans the board game. "Sorry," Tristan said with a frown, "we don't have it."

"That's too bad," I said, reaching for the glass of water. I suddenly felt parched.

We finished eating and the guys were relegated to babysitting duty while Rowan and I cleaned the dishes. I knew the real reason she stuck the guys together. She wanted to talk.

Almost immediately, she hissed under her breath, "What the hell is going on with you two?"

"Honestly?" I asked, turning on the sink.

"Of course."

"Nothing." I shrugged simply.

"Nothing?" she repeated. "That did not look like *nothing* in there."

"Trust me, it is," I mumbled, adding soap to the water.

She cocked her hip to the side and stared me down. I squirmed beneath her penetrating gaze, wondering what she saw. Finally, she turned away, taking a dish from me so she could rinse and dry it. "You don't see it, do you?" she finally asked after a minute or so had passed.

"See what?" I replied in confusion.

"The way he looks at you."

My head shot up to look at her. "See how *who* looks at me?"

She rolled her eyes. "Don't play dumb with me, Tatum. We both know you're not stupid."

"He looks at me in no particular way," I mumbled, looking back down at the white plate in my hand.

"Did you know that since he started helping you with your paper he hasn't been with any other girl?" I was shocked by her words but didn't show it.

"What do you mean by, 'been with'?" I asked, scrubbing the same plate that already sparkled.

She sighed dramatically and I knew she wanted to smack the back of my head. "If you want me to say it I will." Before I could reply she said, "Jude hasn't had sex with anyone since he started helping you." She crossed her arms over her chest and leaned her hip against the counter. "I know Jude well and Jude *loves* to tell me all about his exploits, even though I'd rather he didn't." Muttering under her breath she added, "I think he just likes to watch me freak out. Anyway," she drew out the word, "my point is he's been strangely quiet toward me. Are you guys …?" she trailed off, waiting for me to fill in the blanks.

"No!" I cried, almost dropping the plate in the sink. Blowing a piece of hair out of my eyes I said, "You know how I feel about him."

"I do," she agreed. "But I also know that your reasons for feeling that way are completely idiotic. I know he tends to act like a playboy and sometimes the biggest douche on the planet, but I wouldn't be friends with him if I didn't know he was a good guy."

Feeling angry, I snapped, "Can you leave it alone? Seriously, how I feel about him or anyone is none of your business. I have a right to not like him. I don't care what you or anyone else says, he *is* the reason my brother is dead. I'm stuck with him until this paper is done and that's it. Nothing more is going to happen."

She appeared hurt by my words but the cloudiness quickly cleared from her eyes. Sighing, she quirked a brow and snapped, "You keep telling yourself that, Tate. One day the sexual tension between you two is going to burst and I'm going to be able to say I told you so."

"What's going on in here?" Jude asked, appearing in the

doorway with Tristan hanging onto his leg crying for him not to leave.

"Nothing," I answered before Rowan could speak. "Are you ready to go?"

"Yeah, if this guy here will decide to let me go." He reached down, ruffling Tristan's sandy hair.

"Tristan," Rowan sighed, pinching the bridge of her nose. "Let him go. You can't keep him here forever."

"Don't leave!" Tristan cried, tightening his hold on Jude's leg.

Jude chuckled. "I've got to get Tater Tot over there home and it's time for me to go to bed. Isn't it time for you to go to bed too?"

"I don't wanna!" Tristan shrieked.

Rowan shook her head and mouthed, "I'm so sorry," at Jude.

"I have an idea." Jude looked down at the little boy. "What if I read you a bedtime story before I go?"

Almost immediately Tristan released his hold and scurried for the steps.

"Brush your teeth and get in your pajamas!" Rowan called after her son.

"I've got it," Jude assured her with a smile as he took off after the kid.

Looking at me, Rowan sighed heavily showcasing how tired she was. "Kids are hard work."

"That they are," Trent agreed, breezing into the kitchen and wrapping his arms around her, "but they're worth it." Nuzzling her neck, he murmured, "Let's have another baby."

I laughed as she hastily wiggled out of his hold. "How about we try being married for the next one?" Pausing, she added, "For like three years."

His mouth fell open. "But Tristan will be nine then! He deserves to have another sibling while he's young enough to enjoy it."

Rowan rolled her eyes. "Talk to me again after we're married."

She started to walk away and he called after her, "If it was up to me we'd already be married!"

She laughed, turning her head to smile at him. "You would've married me when we were sixteen years old, Trenton Wentworth."

"Damn straight." He grinned crookedly, his eyes sparkling with happiness. "Even then I knew I'd found the love of my life."

"Bleh," I pretended to gag. "Y'all are getting too sappy for me."

Trent chuckled. "One day it will be you, Tate."

"Not likely," I replied. "Love makes things complicated."

"No," Trent disagreed, his eyes growing serious, "love makes life worth living for. No matter how bad your day is, or what kind of horrible shit you go through, loving someone completes you."

Cracking a smile, I joked, "Have you been reading poetry?"

He chuckled, brushing his fingers through his dark, nearly black hair. "No." Sobering he looked from Row to me, "We both just want you to find someone. Don't hold yourself back from falling in love. Yeah, it's scary as fuck, but it's worth it. No matter what." He looked significantly at Rowan. "It's always worth fighting for."

"Seriously," I assured them, "you don't need to worry about me. It's not like I'm anti-love. I'm just not at a place in my life where I'm ready for a serious relationship."

"Love doesn't wait till you're ready," Rowan piped in.

God, those two weren't ever going to let it rest.

"I haven't found 'the one' yet," I mumbled.

"That's not true," Rowan whispered, looking at me sadly, "you're just too stubborn to see what's standing right in front of you."

"I think you're too caught up in seeing something that isn't really there," I countered, jutting my chin in the air haughtily. Between the two of them I felt cornered. I wanted nothing more than to run out the door, but once again, Jude was my ride.

Neither of them said anything more, because Jude returned at that moment. I had never been more thankful to see him in my entire life.

"You ready?" he asked, looking at me first and then glancing at the other two. He could sense the tension in the air but chose not to mention it.

"Yeah," I told him, breezing past Trent and Row.

I didn't say goodbye.

CHAPTER EIGHT

I BIT INTO THE APPLE, SCANNING THE PIECE OF PAPER in front of me. It was instructions for another paper due the next week. The professors were throwing the work at us the closer we came to graduation. Spring break was coming up and I wanted to have everything done before I left for the beach with Trent and Row.

"Afternoon, Tater Tot." Jude slid into the seat across from me, his heavy bag thumping against the table.

"What do you want?" I asked, never bothering to lift my head from the piece of paper in my hand. I took another bite of apple, chewing loudly.

Out of my peripheral vision, I saw Jude lean across the table and clasp his hands together. "I'm not at the nursing home tonight, as you know, but I thought we could do something anyway."

I set the apple down slowly, like it was a bomb, and let the piece of paper in my hand drift onto the surface of the table. "Like ... hang out? With *you* for *fun?*"

He chuckled, lowering his head so his dark hair swept into his eyes. "Well, you don't have to make it sound like a death sentence. There's something I want to show you, and I thought we could have dinner with Pap again. He's been begging to see you." Placing a hand over his chest, he pouted, "Don't make me break my grandpa's heart. He's already in a fragile state."

Oh, he was guilt tripping me big time. I did want to see his grandpa again, though. "Fine," I agreed, "but I have to go home first before we go."

"Deal. I'll pick you up at five-thirty."

"Yay," I mumbled, feigning excitement.

He smacked his hand lightly against the table. "By the end of the evening I promise I'll have you smiling."

I rolled my eyes as he stood, grabbed his bag and left.

A moment later Rowan took the seat beside me. "What was that about?"

I groaned loudly, causing a few heads to turn my way. "Did you watch the whole thing?"

"It didn't seem like I should interrupt." She shrugged casually, unwrapping a sandwich she'd brought from home.

"I know you wish that there was something going on between us, but there's absolutely *nothing*. We're just ... I really don't know what we are," I muttered. Jude and I were far from friends, but I didn't quite feel like we were enemies anymore. The more I read Graham's letter, it became clearer to me that Jude really didn't have anything to do with his suicide. But I'd probably always associate Jude with that God-awful day and the pain it caused me. That wasn't something you got over easily.

She sighed heavily and, before she could launch into a lengthy speech, I interrupted her.

"I don't need to hear it, Rowan. There's a lot about me that you and no one else knows. The last thing I need is the baggage of a relationship with *anyone* especially Jude. Please, let it go," I begged, pleading with my eyes for her to stop bugging me about it.

She took a bite of her sandwich and I relaxed, thinking I was off the hook. Wrong.

"I think I understand more than most people about how baggage can keep you from letting someone into your heart, but eventually you have to stop fighting it. Love is a beautiful thing, don't let your past rule your future. I missed out on so much time with Trent, because I fought so hard against what I felt for him. I'd give anything to get that time back, but I can't. I don't want to see you make my mistakes."

"How very motherly sounding of you," I muttered.

She laughed, "I am a mom, I guess it shows in everything I say." Sobering, she frowned. "I worry about you a lot, Tate."

That made me feel bad. I didn't want Rowan worrying about me. I was fine. I forced a smile and told her, "Honestly, you don't need to worry about me."

"All right," she sighed again, "I won't bring it up anymore."

I doubted that, but I didn't say it out loud.

"Are you excited for spring break?" she asked, brushing breadcrumbs off her lap.

"Definitely." I nodded, finishing my apple. "I'm ready to get away."

I wasn't sure what would happen to my mom while I was gone, and maybe it was selfish of me, but I couldn't take being in that broken house for much longer. Besides, it wasn't like I could live there forever. She needed to snap out of it, and maybe my dad could try being a concerned husband and actually take care of her for a change. Too much responsibility had been on my shoulders for too long. I guessed I was rebelling as an adult, not a teenager. It was bound to happen eventually—and maybe that made me a shitty person for giving up on my mom, but it had been seven long, hard years. I'd reached my limit and I couldn't take it anymore. I had to stop making choices based on everyone else and start living my own life.

"I'm worried about leaving the kids, but I know Trent's mom will take good care of them. It's hard, though. We rarely leave them."

Sometimes I really felt bad for Rowan and all the responsibility she had on her shoulders at such a young age, but she never, not once, complained about any of it. I admired her for that fact.

"They'll be fine. Lily's awesome," I assured her. I'd only met Trent's family on a few occasions but they were some of the nicest people I had ever met.

"You're right, but it's impossible not to worry."

I stood, slinging my backpack on, and gathering my trash. "I've got to get to class. I'll see you later."

"Are you going to the library tonight?" she asked before I could get away.

"No," I answered, "but I think you already knew that."

SINCE I WAS HAVING dinner with Jude's grandpa, I only made enough dinner for my mom and dad—if he decided to come home tonight. He was gone more and more. I couldn't even recall the last time I saw him.

I set the plate in front of my mom where I'd seated her at the kitchen table.

She stared at the food like she had no idea what it was. "Mom, it's spaghetti. Your favorite."

Her vacant green eyes that were the same shade as mine, peered up at me. "Please, eat," I begged.

Her head lowered to look at the food once more.

I wanted to take the plate and smash it against the floor. I wanted to yell and scream and pull my hair. I wanted to cause a scene. I'd only ever done it once, but it had done no good, and I knew now would be no different.

My mom was gone and she was never coming back. All I had left was this shell.

I groaned and muttered, "Whatever. I don't care anymore."

With my words still lingering in the air, I left the kitchen and headed upstairs to my room. I changed my clothes, but kept it simple in jeans and a loose gray sweatshirt. I pulled my hair to the side and braided it before sweeping a pale pink gloss across my lips. I wasn't trying to look nice for Jude, I wasn't even getting that dressed up, but for once I wanted to feel like a normal girl going out for a while instead of the hermit I'd become. Life had been passing me by for far too long and it was time for me to take control again. I held the reins of my future and I was doing an about-face. It was time for me and everyone else to discover the real Tatum O'Connor.

My phone beeped from my pocket and I pulled it out to see a text from Jude telling me he was waiting outside. I bound down the steps and to the front door. Just before I opened it, I called, "Bye, Mom!" Although, she probably didn't even hear me.

Jude stood beside his truck, leaning against the passenger door. As I approached, he opened the door and I hopped inside. He slid into the driver's seat and said, "Someone seems eager to see me." His grin spread across his face, lightening his eyes to a golden color.

"More like eager to get out of the house," I mumbled.

He nodded his head sympathetically like he understood.

Buckling the seatbelt, I asked, "Where are we going?"

He snorted, driving out of the neighborhood. All the houses looked the same, blending together. I wondered if the people living behind the walls were aware of how bad things were for me, or were they oblivious to everything but their own lives? Probably the latter.

"Where's the fun in telling you?" he responded.

I should've known to expect that kind of answer from him.

I sat back in the seat and brought my feet up against the dashboard, resolving not to ask him any more questions.

Surprisingly, he grew quiet. I didn't know he could go a minute without filling a void with the sound of his voice.

A little while later, he turned down a familiar dirt road. "I thought we were doing something before we went to your grandpa's?" I asked, as the trees grew plentiful. They were only beginning to bud, but there were so many of them that they provided a decent amount of shade.

"We are."

That's all he said on the matter and I knew I wouldn't get anything else out of him.

Suddenly, he stopped the truck, putting it in park.

I looked around, waiting to see something profound. "Why are we stopping here?" I asked, when I didn't see anything but grass and trees.

"I hope you don't mind walking." He smiled, reaching into the back of his truck for something. "It's about a mile walk to get where we're going."

"I'll be fine," I assured him just as he dropped whatever he'd been looking for into my lap. I picked up the Shenandoah University sweatshirt and stared at it. "Why do I need this? I'm already wearing a sweatshirt."

He narrowed his eyes at what I wore. "Uh, yeah, that thin thing isn't going to do anything to keep you warm. Put the sweatshirt on and don't argue with me. I won't have you getting sick on my conscience."

"Do you even have a conscious?" I countered, pulling the sweatshirt on. It was warm from the heat of the car and smelled woodsy and masculine with something else that I couldn't put my finger on that was inherently Jude.

He grabbed another sweatshirt from the back and shrugged it on before climbing out of the truck with a blanket tucked under his arm. I did the same, standing by the fence as he came around. He tossed the blanket over the fence and grabbed ahold of the top part of the fence and hoisted himself over with one easy jump. Um, yeah ... there was no way I could do that in these jeans. It wasn't that the fence was that high or anything, but I wasn't sure I was graceful enough not to make a fool of myself. I'm sure Jude would find it absolutely hysterical if I fell on my face.

He held out a hand for me. "Just put your feet on the bottom piece and lift your leg over. I'll help you."

I looked at him hesitantly.

He thrust his hand toward me again. "Come on, Tater Tot, just take my hand. I would never let you fall."

I reluctantly did what he asked and let him help me over. Somehow, on my way to the other side I lost my balance and my body slammed into his. We fell to the ground but somehow Jude maneuvered us so that he took the brunt of the fall. He grunted from the impact and then again when my elbow hit his ribs by accident.

"I'm so sorry!" I immediately jumped to my feet.

Jude was sprawled on the ground with brown pieces of grass stuck in his hair. He seemed stunned, but then he started to laugh. "I said I wouldn't let you fall and then you went and tackled me. I wasn't prepared for that, pretty girl."

"I'm so sorry," I repeated, heat infusing my cheeks at my clumsiness. I was so mortified that I was even able to overlook him calling me 'pretty girl'.

He sat up, rubbing the back of his head. "I'm okay."

He clambered to his feet, dusting dirt and grass from his clothes. He picked up the blanket that had fallen to the ground and started walking. I had no choice but to follow him.

The dead grass crunched beneath my feet as we trudged through the field. It was crazy to think that in a few short weeks spring would be here and the grass would soon be green. Spring was my favorite time of year. I loved the colors and flowers, even the smells. There was something so promising about spring—a new beginning.

Jude stopped in the middle of the field and spread the blanket out on the ground. "Sit," he instructed.

With a reluctant sigh, I did as he told me. "Why are we out here?" I asked, drawing his sweatshirt closer to me as I shivered.

"I want you to see something."

"Thanks for the non-answer," I mumbled as he sat down beside me. He wiggled around until he got comfortable.

He chuckled, sweeping his hair from his eyes. "There's something I want you to see," he repeated, "be patient."

You'd think Jude would know by now that I was the least

patient person on the planet. Only a few minutes had passed when I asked, "What are we waiting for?"

"Oh, Tate." He chuckled, his eyes crinkling as he lay back, propping his body up with his elbows. "You're something else." Tilting his head, he continued, "Look around you, appreciate what's right in front of you for a change. You need to slow down and enjoy life."

"Look at you sounding so wise," I commented, resisting the sudden urge to smile. I wanted to smile a lot around Jude and that scared me a bit.

He gasped, his eyes brightening. "I am wise." He sat up and drew his knees up, draping his arms on top. "Now watch, here comes the surprise."

For a moment, I wondered what he was talking about and then I realized we were watching the sunset. The sky deepened with hues of orange and red as the sun descended. My mouth fell open in awe as the meadow around us became awash with golden light. I didn't speak and neither did he. For once, I was living in the moment, and maybe this moment wasn't such a bad place to be.

There was calmness in the air around us as the last of sun's rays fanned across the land. It didn't take long for the sun to disappear and for the stars and moon to twinkle above us.

Without saying anything, we both lay back on the blanket, staring up at the sky above.

"Beautiful, isn't it?" he whispered, his fingers brushing lightly against mine where we rested side by side.

"What?" I asked, trying to pick out any of the constellations.

"Nature ... everything ... *you*."

I felt his eyes staring at the side of my face and I turned to look at him. "Jude—"

He placed a warm finger on my lips. "Don't say anything. Please, don't ruin this moment for me."

I shivered, but it wasn't from the cold. "I don't know you at all," I admitted, feeling ashamed of all the judgments I'd made of him. Knowing Jude in high school, and after what happened with Graham, I'd turned him into this horrible person in my mind but he really wasn't the guy I thought he was. People are always spouting about not judging one another, but we all do it, and I'd been completely unfair with my assumptions of the man looking at me. I'd held onto childish notions making him into the bad guy, when he really wasn't. It was so much easier to blame him, though. But easier doesn't always mean better.

"No, you don't," he breathed, scooting closer to me so that there was barely any space between our bodies. He turned away from me to look back up at the night sky. "We didn't ask any questions today."

"No, we didn't."

"I don't even know what to ask."

"I'll go first then." I smiled, even though he didn't see it. I racked my brain for something to ask him. I didn't want it to be something stupid or irrelevant. Finally, I breathed, "Why me? Why am I different?"

He chuckled, turning to look at me again. His gaze was intense as he grinned. "That was two questions, Tater Tot."

"They're similar, so it counts as one." I stuck my tongue out at him.

Sobering, his eyes darkened as he gazed at me. I saw a million different things in his eyes, none of which I could figure out. "Because you just are."

I laughed. "That's a really sucky answer and you know it."

"It's the truth." He lifted his shoulders in a small shrug.

"Even in high school there was always something about you that caught my eye." Chuckling, he pinched the bridge of his nose. "I think you carved a permanent spot in my heart when you kicked me in the balls. You were so beautiful and fierce."

"You're a strange guy, Jude Brooks." I shook my head. "Most guys would be turned off if a girl did that to them."

"What can I say?" He smirked. "I've always been different." He shifted so he hovered above me. My breath stuttered at his proximity. "You wanna know what I think is the most attractive thing about you?"

"What?" I whispered, scared to move.

"That you're completely unaware of how beautiful you are."

I didn't know how to respond, so I didn't. He lowered his head, and my heart rate picked up, convinced that he was going to kiss me.

I turned my head away before he could try anything and he sank down beside me, letting out a heavy sigh.

Wanting to alleviate the awkward tension hanging in the air, I said, "Your turn."

He bit his lip, thinking carefully before searing me with his dark brown eyes. "Do you think you'll ever stop hating me?"

I wasn't expecting that question and was unprepared with how to answer. After a moment, I replied honestly. "I don't know." I knew that wasn't the answer he wanted, but it was all I had.

He scrubbed a hand over his face. "At least that's better than no."

With a groan, he stood and held out a hand to help me up. I reluctantly placed my hand in his, ignoring how my whole body zinged at the touch.

He draped the blanket over his arm and we headed back to

the truck. It didn't take long for the house to appear and it was just as beautiful as I remembered it.

"I know it's not the nicest place—" Jude started but I quickly cut him off.

"It's magical." Before I could feel embarrassed by my words I jumped out of the truck.

His grandpa was expecting us and opened the door before I could step up onto the porch. His smile widened and then he asked, "Jude, who's this pretty girl? Have you finally settled down?"

Jude chuckled, shoving his hands in his pockets. "This is Tatum, she's a ... " He peered at me, tilting his head. "Friend from school."

His grandpa snorted. "I'm old, not blind." Turning to head inside, he kept a hand on the door and said, "Come on in, Tatum."

"Play along," Jude mouthed unnecessarily.

"You know," his grandpa said with a chuckle as he headed to the kitchen, "I should've known you weren't his girlfriend. You're too pretty for him."

I laughed at the same time Jude groaned, "Pap!"

"What?" Jerry shrugged innocently. "It's true."

Jude shook his head, muttering under his breath before asking, "What did you make for dinner? Something smells delicious."

"Pulled pork," Jerry replied, setting a platter on the table and waving his hand for us to sit.

We had no more than started to eat until he asked me, "Jude said you were a friend from school, what are you studying?"

"Journalism," I answered, waiting for the dirty look.

Anytime I told people what I was studying they would cringe and tell me, "Good luck with that."

Jerry didn't do that.

His smile widened. "Good for you."

As we ate, he lapsed into tales of Jude and all the shenanigans he'd pulled on the farm. Like trying to ride a cow, falling off the tractor when he was ten and breaking his arm, and skinny dipping with the girl on the next farm over at fourteen. Jude shrugged sheepishly at that one.

"Always a ladies' man, that one." Jerry chuckled. "I'd like to see him settle down before I die."

"Pap!" Jude groaned, setting his fork down. "How many times have I told you not to talk about that?"

"Face it, boy, we all die someday and it's looking like my someday is around the corner. Between my age and my mind, I'm a ticking bomb."

Jude frowned, his shoulders slumping with sadness. "I don't like to think about it," he mumbled.

"I ain't going to live forever." Jerry tried to get Jude to look at him. "Might as well accept that fact."

"I'm not very hungry anymore." Jude pushed away from the table and stormed from the room without looking at either of us. I heard his boots pound against the steps.

Jerry sighed and looked at me sadly. "I practically raised him. He looks at me like I'm his father, and that makes it that much harder for him to accept that I won't be here much longer."

"Jude isn't close with his dad?" I questioned. I'd picked up on some animosity there, but I hadn't wanted to ask him about it.

"No." Jerry shook his head sadly. "Andrew, my son, was

never a real father to him. My wife and I took him in and practically raised him. It was hard on him when my wife, Mae, died a few years ago." His brows furrowed together and I was sure he was trying to remember exactly how long it had been since she passed. "Jude doesn't have much to do with either of his parents. I love my son, but let's just say he and his wife weren't cut out to be parents. Jude was merely an accessory for them."

"That's horrible." Something in my heart shifted, a small piece filling with compassion for the man I'd blamed for the worst event in my life. I hated myself for making so many assumptions about him. I'd never given him a fair shot and that made me a pretty sucky person.

"It is," Jerry agreed.

Sliding my plate away, I said, "Would you mind if I went and checked on him?"

"Not at all." He smiled. I started to leave, but his next words stopped me in my tracks and I leaned against the doorway for support. "Be kind to him, Tatum. He needs someone in his life besides me to care about him."

I swallowed thickly and didn't look back at Jerry as I headed out of the room and up the steps.

I found Jude in his room, sitting on the bed with his back to me. His shoulders shook and I frowned, realizing that he was crying. Jude Brooks had feelings. Who knew?

I took a hesitant step into the room. I wasn't sure if I'd be welcome.

"Jude," I said his name softly as I reached out and put my hand on his shoulder, "are you okay?"

"No." He looked up at me with red-rimmed eyes. "I'm not."

I sat down beside him and laid my head on his shoulder. Air escaped his lips in a sigh.

"Do you want to talk about it?" I whispered, gazing out the window at the night sky.

"Yes. No. I don't know," he mumbled, rubbing his face tiredly. "It really fucking sucks to know he isn't going to be here for much longer and there's nothing I can do about it. I hate being helpless."

"It's okay to be sad or angry or whatever it is you need to feel, but he isn't gone yet. Enjoy every moment you have left with him, that way you'll never have any regrets."

"You make it sound so simple, but there's nothing simple about watching someone you love disappear right before your eyes ...," he paused, gathering his thoughts. "It's not even the thought of his death that upsets me, it's the thought of what comes before ... how he'll completely forget me and I'll cease to exist in his mind."

"We can't live our lives worrying about the unknown," I stated. "Every day and what it brings is a mystery, a gift to be unwrapped and treasured. All we can do is find happiness in the little things and peace in the chaos."

He was quiet, absorbing my words. "I can so tell you're a writer."

I laughed. "It's not about being a writer, I'm just a deep thinker."

We sat like that for a while, side by side with my head on his shoulder.

Eventually, we headed back downstairs and helped Jerry clean the dishes. I gave the man a hug before we left, holding him tight.

"You come back now," he told me, walking out onto the porch as Jude and I headed toward his truck.

"I will," I assured him, wondering when I returned whether I'd be Tatum or Julia.

JUDE PARKED his truck in front of my driveway, and turned to face me. "Thank you for coming with me tonight."

"Thanks for inviting me." I smiled, grabbing the handle to open the door.

"Tate?"

"Yeah?" I looked back at him.

"Goodnight," he murmured, his eyes darkening. He leaned closer, and pressed his lips against my cheek in a kiss that was so light it didn't even seem real.

My eyes fluttered closed and I sighed breathlessly. I hoped he didn't notice but based on his smirk my reaction hadn't gone unnoticed.

I forced my Jell-O-like limbs from the truck and watched his taillights disappear as he left.

I brought shaking fingers up to my cheek and swore my skin felt heated where his lips had seared it like a brand.

It wasn't until I was inside and getting in my pajamas that I realized I still wore his sweatshirt and I had no intentions of giving it back.

CHAPTER NINE

I strode across campus, looking for Jude. He hadn't been waiting for me by the fountain like he said, so I figured he was at his truck.

I heard shouting up ahead and slowed my steps.

I wasn't sure if I should turn around and haul ass away from whatever was going on or check it out.

Since I wasn't ever one to back down from anything, I strode forward with my shoulders squared. If some idiots were fighting, I figured I could either break it up, find someone to help, or ignore it if need be.

When I rounded the side of the building and the parking lot came into view, I saw two large figures arguing on the sidewalk. Hairs on the back of my spine stood up as I recognized one of the guys was Jude. No wonder he hadn't been at the fountain. He was clearly occupied trying to defend himself against the mammoth hovering above him.

The guy swung out, and his fist connected with Jude's face, causing him to stagger a few steps back.

Without thinking, I dropped my books on the ground and ran toward the guy. "What the hell is your problem?" I screamed at him.

"My *problem*—" he shoved a finger in Jude's direction where he hovered behind me "—is that prick sleeping with my girlfriend."

"I didn't fucking sleep with her!" Jude cried.

I didn't care whether he had or not, something inside me felt the need to defend him.

The guy tried to lunge for Jude again, and I cocked my leg back to kick him. My foot connected sharply with his kneecap and he dropped to the ground. I think he was more stunned than hurt.

I stood there, my mouth hanging open in shock that I'd actually managed to bring a guy of his size to the ground. *That was pretty damn awesome, if I did say so myself.*

Jude busted out laughing.

I still stood rooted to the ground in disbelief at the lump on the ground. The guy growled, trying to stand.

Jude grabbed my hand and screamed, "Run!"

Like two little kids we ran across campus, laughing heartily at what had transpired. When my legs threatened to give out, Jude opened a random door to one of the buildings and we tumbled inside. We were both out of breath, our cheeks flushed.

"That was fun," he panted.

"Fun?" I questioned, unable to keep the smile from my voice. "I think he wanted to kill us." The hallway was dark, everyone having gone home, but I tilted my head trying to see what was on his face. "Oh, my God! Jude! You're bleeding!"

His brows pulled together, like he hadn't even noticed it. He reached up, touching above his upper lip and then staring at the red now coating his fingers. "It's just a little bit of blood, Tate."

I rolled my eyes. "Don't be macho. Come on." I grabbed his clean hand and started towing him down the hall, "I have a First-Aid kit in my bag."

"Of course you do," he laughed. "What else do you have in there?"

I looked over my shoulder at him and shrugged. "You'll never know."

There was a bathroom at the end of the hall and I pulled him into it. He looked around and grinned. "So, this is what the girls' bathroom looks like."

"Oh, please," I snorted. "I'm sure you've had sex in plenty of bathrooms."

He hopped up on the counter, letting his feet dangle and his laugh bellowed around us. "First off, just because I like to have sex doesn't mean I want to do it in public places. Secondly, if I did have sex in the bathroom, it's not like I'd be paying much attention to my surroundings." My mouth fell open and his grin widened. "Just sayin'." He held his hands up innocently.

"You're disgusting," I mumbled, rifling through my bag.

"Hey, you're the one that kicked a guy for me," he defended. Chuckling, he scratched his chin. "That was pretty badass of you."

"I'm not a princess."

"No, you're not," he agreed.

I finally located my First-Aid kit. I set it on the counter and began rifling through it for what I needed. I pulled out a wad of cotton balls and dampened them with rubbing alcohol. I wasn't sure if he was cut, or if the blood was from his nose, but I wanted to be on the safe side and try to avoid any sort of infection.

"This might sting," I warned.

"I know. I'm a nurse, remember?"

"Of course." I laughed, my hair falling forward as I reached up to wipe away the blood. Even with him sitting on the counter he was still a lot taller than me and I had to stretch up on my tiptoes to reach. I noticed his eyes flick down and he swallowed thickly. "If you're trying to look down my shirt I will punch you."

His eyes immediately flew up to look at the ceiling. "Sorry," he mumbled. "I'm a guy. You put boobs right in my face and I have to look. I'm pretty sure it's a law or something."

I wanted to be mad, but I couldn't help but laugh. I couldn't remember the last time I'd laughed so much. It seemed weird that of all people it would be Jude that made me laugh again, but then again maybe it was appropriate.

Wiping away all traces of blood, I inspected his face.

"You know," he started, "it's kind of funny that *I'm* the nurse and you're the one taking care of me."

"I'm not the one that got punched," I replied easily. "Everything looks fine. You might bruise, though."

"Tate," he whispered my name and I found myself held in his brown-eyed gaze. It was like I was hypnotized—caught in his trap.

Before I could reply, or do *anything*, one of his hands cupped the nape of my neck and drew me close. My breath fanned out of my lips and my heart beat rapidly. It was like everything was moving super fast, but super slow at the same time. It was weird.

He closed the distance between us and sealed my lips with his.

I lost control of my body, leaning into him as he devoured me. I let out a small moan and my fingers tangled in the soft strands of his brown hair. I never wanted to let go. His tongue pressed against my lips, seeking entrance. Nothing had ever felt this good. This was so much more than a kiss. I couldn't get close enough to him. Our bodies lined up perfectly and my chest pressed against his as I leaned closer.

"Tate," he breathed my name in the space between our lips.

I startled at the sound of his voice, jolting away from him, breaking the kiss. It was like my hand had a mind of its own as it flew out and smacked his cheek. His head swiveled to the side, stunned by my action.

I used the same hand to cover my mouth as I gasped, "I'm sorry! I-I don't know what made me do that!"

"Jesus Christ." He rubbed his cheek. "What is today? Everyone-smack-Jude-in-the-face-day?" He started to laugh, and I was tempted to hit him again.

"It's not funny."

"You're right, it's hysterical," he countered.

I felt defensive so I took a few steps back and straightened my clothes. "Never kiss me ever again." I turned hastily, pushing open the bathroom door and ran out into the hallway. I couldn't get out of there fast enough.

"Aw, come on, Tate!" Jude called after me. "You know you liked it!"

Didn't he know that was the problem?

"It was gross," I called over my shoulder. "I felt like I was drowning in saliva."

"Oh, Tater Tot, that's a new one. Most people *love* my kisses." He grinned. He caught up to me easily, slinging his arm over my shoulders as I pushed the door open and stepped outside. I hoped that guy had left. I'd hate to run into him again.

"I'm not most people," I retorted.

"You're not," he agreed.

"Oh, crap!" I exclaimed suddenly, stopping in my tracks.

"What is it?" Jude asked, stopping as well and looking at me quizzically.

"My books!" I cried, burying my face in my hands.

"Don't worry about them, we'll just go back and get them." He turned, ready to head back in the direction of the bathrooms.

"They're not there." I put a hand on his arm to halt him. "I threw them down on the ground when I jumped between you and that guy."

Jude gasped dramatically, placing a hand over his heart. "You mean that you threw those poor defenseless books so you could help me? I'm honored."

"You're such an ass." I groaned, looking around to get my bearings on campus so I could head back in the direction we came from. I really hoped they were still there. Nibbling my lower lip, I looked up at Jude. "What if someone took them?"

He shrugged. "So what? It's not the worst thing that could happen. At least you're alive."

"Thanks," I grumbled. "That makes me feel loads better."

A grin spread across his face. "Glad I could be of assistance." When I headed in the wrong direction, he grabbed my arm. "Nuh-uh, pretty girl, it's this way."

"Oh," I mumbled, with eyes downcast.

"You know, I think I need to change your nickname to Rambo."

I rolled my eyes. "How about no nicknames?"

"Where's the fun in that?" he countered.

We approached the area where I'd seen him arguing with the guy and I scanned the ground for my books. Luckily, they were there. Albeit, covered in dirt. I picked them up, brushing off the debris.

"You ready to go?" Jude asked as he pulled his keys from his pocket.

After the kiss, I thought maybe I should back out, but this was for my paper and Jude would know what was up if I said I needed to go home. "Yeah."

He seemed surprised. "Good, let's go. We're running late and I didn't have time to change into my scrubs."

We rode in silence on the way to the nursing home—neither of us acknowledging the kiss. I knew it wouldn't be long until Jude had to say something. He wasn't the kind of guy to keep quiet about something like that.

JUDE DIDN'T BRING up the kiss until we were almost back to campus so I could get my car.

"We haven't asked any questions today." He smiled. "You first."

"Did you really sleep with that guy's girlfriend?" I asked immediately. It had been bugging me. Even though Jude had denied it to the guy, he could've been lying. The answer shouldn't have mattered to me, but for some reason it did.

"I didn't," he assured me, sincerity shining in the depths of his eyes. "I don't know why he thinks I did, but I didn't. In fact —" he looked at me significantly "—I haven't slept with anyone for weeks." I blanched at his words. Was he saying that he'd given up his man-whore ways because he was spending time with me? I couldn't even begin to process that information. Rowan had said as much but it still baffled me. "My turn," he said, straightening in his seat. I waited for him to ask his question, but after a long moment of silence I figured he couldn't think of anything. Finally, his voice filled the cab of the truck, and the next words he spoke echoed around my skull. "Can I kiss you again?"

Jude Brooks was asking me for *permission?* This was new.

"I thought you were the kind of guy who takes what he wants and doesn't ask questions?" I replied.

"You're right." He grinned, and I knew I was in trouble.

As the truck came to a stop at a red light he grabbed the back of my neck and tugged my body against his, sealing his lips over mine. Every time his lips touched mine it was like he stole a piece of my soul and made it his.

This time, I didn't pull away—or slap him like I should have. Instead, I let myself *feel*. I'd closed myself off from my emotions for so long that I'd forgotten what it felt like to have this scary, stirring of butterflies feeling in my stomach. I couldn't believe it was Jude of all people making me feel this way, but a kiss was innocent enough, right? Well, maybe not this kiss, 'cause it was pretty freakin' hot.

The cars honking behind us was what finally tore us apart.

"I'm going to do that again sometime," he murmured, brushing his thumb over my lips before pressing the gas and taking off.

I felt giddy, almost high, from the kiss. I wanted to hate it, God, I really did, but I couldn't.

I didn't know the exact moment that Jude paved a way into my heart, all that mattered was he did, and I was never going to be the same once I gave in completely.

I WAS SURPRISED to see my dad's car in the driveway. While it was late, it wasn't *that* late and even before Graham died he'd never been home at this time. Nowadays he rarely even bothered to come home to sleep. I didn't know where he stayed most nights. My guess was that it wasn't at his office. I didn't like to think about the possibility of my dad cheating on my mom, but I wasn't naïve enough to think he hadn't.

I stepped inside, looking around for him. I didn't see him, though. He was probably only home to grab something before leaving once more. It was what I'd come to expect. In the last six months, I'd only seen him a handful of times. There were other times I'd known he'd been home, the evidence left sitting around in the form of mugs of coffee and packets of sugar.

My mom sat on the family room couch. I stepped into the room and kissed her forehead. "I'll make dinner, Mom."

She didn't acknowledge my words; I didn't expect her to. It would shock me if I ever heard her voice again. I honestly wondered why my dad had never tried to get her help. Maybe he knew it was hopeless.

In the kitchen, I pulled out ingredients to make fettuccine alfredo. I loved pasta and would live off the stuff if I weren't afraid of clogging my arteries.

I grabbed my iPod, set it on the docking station, and let the music filter into the too-quiet kitchen. I didn't think it would ever stop bothering me that so few words were spoken in this house anymore.

I was humming along to a song, when I heard, "Tatum."

I jumped, letting out a squeal. The spoon I'd been using to stir the sauce went flying through the air and landed on the floor, sauce splattering everywhere.

"Hi, Dad," I squeaked, taking in the tall man in front of me. He was slimmer than the last time I saw him, his light hair mostly gray now. Lines that weren't there a few months ago turned his mouth down in a permanent frown. My dad had never been a happy man anyway.

"It's nice to see you." His voice was low and gravelly.

"Uh, yeah." I tucked a piece of blonde hair behind my ear, feeling über awkward. "It's nice to see you too?" For some reason, it came out sounding like a question.

"What are you making?" he asked, peering around me to get a look at the pots on the stove.

"Fettuccine alfredo," I replied.

He nodded. "Oh."

"Are you staying for dinner?" I dared to ask.

"No."

Of course. I expected it, but it still hurt.

"All right," I sighed, picking the spoon off the floor and tossing it in the sink. I grabbed another from the drawer and returned to making dinner after cleaning up the mess. "I'll see you later, Dad." And by later I meant a month from now.

"Bye, kiddo," he said from the doorway. Minutes passed, and I thought he'd left, but then he said, "You seem happy."

By the time I'd whipped around, he was gone and I was left mulling over his words.

I was happy, and that was all thanks to the guy I was hell-bent on hating.

They always said hate was as passionate as love. I was starting to see how true that was.

CHAPTER TEN

"Twizzlers, milady," Jude sing-songed, dropping a plastic bag from Sheetz in front of me.

I looked in the plastic green bag and pulled out the pack of Twizzlers. "You're awesome." I tore open the wrapping and pulled out one of the red pieces of licorice.

"You look like you need a pick me up." He shrugged, sliding out the chair across from me. "I wanted some gummy bears, so when I saw those I thought I'd get them for you."

"Thank you," I told him, taking another bite. I stared at the computer screen in front of me, wishing the words would magically appear. I was still having trouble with my paper—the one Jude was helping me with. I couldn't seem to find the proper words to convey what I needed to say. I wanted my words to be powerful, and everything I wrote sounded weak to me.

"Where's Rowan?" he asked, looking around the library.

"She must be running late." I shrugged, glaring at the

damn blinking cursor on my word document. I swore the thin black line was mocking me.

"Having trouble?" he asked, opening the bag of gummy bears and popping a green one in his mouth. I detested the green ones. And the yellow ones. Actually, I hated all gummy bears after my last incident with them. Nasty little things. They looked so cute and innocent with their tiny bodies and little faces. Douse them in vodka and they could take out anyone.

"Can you get those away from me?" I pointed at the bag of gummy bears, fighting my gag reflex. He slid the bag on his lap, chuckling under his breath. "And yes, I'm having trouble. I can't get my paper to sound right." I frowned. "I feel like I can't convey the proper emotions."

"Well," he started, chewing on an orange gummy bear, "why don't you try not overthinking it?"

"It's not that simple," I mumbled, musing my hair—I was sure it looked like a rat's nest with as many times as I had ruffled it in the last hour.

"Yes, it is," he argued, propping his feet up on the table. "You have to let yourself *feel*."

"Feeling gets me in trouble," I mumbled. Like letting Jude kiss me again in his truck. I shouldn't have let him do that. But I did and it was amazing, but now I felt conflicted.

He was breaking down all the walls I'd spent the last seven years building around my heart. He was forging a special place in there for himself and I didn't know what I'd do when he inevitably screwed it up. A person could only be hurt so many times before they fell apart completely, and I thought I'd met my quota.

"Is it that it gets you in trouble?" he repeated my words. "Or that it scares you?" He tapped his fingers along the wooden tabletop. "Never let fear dictate your life."

"Why do I feel like we're no longer talking about my paper?" I breathed.

"Because, we're not." He took off the beanie he wore, tousled his hair, and replaced it.

"You don't scare me," I stated, tilting my head slightly to the side.

"I know I don't," he replied immediately. He leaned forward and his voice dropped low, like he was letting me in on a secret. "But what you feel for me ... *that's* what scares you."

I squirmed in my seat. "That's not true."

"You're such a bad liar, I almost feel sorry for you," he replied, returning to his previous position with his legs perched on the table.

I ignored him and went back to staring at my computer screen. With a groan of frustration, I saved what I had written and slammed the lid closed. "This is pointless."

"Want to go get ice cream?" he suggested. "I hear that makes everything better."

"Didn't you just eat a whole bag of gummy bears?"

"It was *half* a bag. Big difference." He grinned, letting his feet drop to the ground. He stood and stretched his arms above his head. The movement caused his shirt to ride up, exposing the bottom of his smooth stomach. I wished I wasn't staring, but I was. I was looking at him a lot lately, and not with hate in my eyes. What had become of me? "What do you say? Ice cream?"

He must've known I could never say no to ice cream.

"Sure." I stood, packing up my stuff. It wasn't like I'd been getting a lot accomplished anyway.

On our way out of the library we ran into Rowan. She

paused in her steps and her grin said it all—she was excited at the idea of Jude and me spending time alone.

"Where are you guys going?" she asked, adjusting her hold on her books.

"To get ice cream," Jude replied.

"Ice cream?" With her smile widening, she said, "I notice you didn't invite me."

Jude's smile mirrored hers. Looking from me to Rowan, he shrugged. "You wanna get ice cream? I'm buying."

"No, but thanks anyway." She suppressed a laugh, hiding her growing smile behind her free hand.

"See you later, Row." Jude lowered his head and kissed her cheek before running out the doors.

Shaking her head Rowan looked at me and muttered, "That boy."

Those two words summed up Jude perfectly.

With a quick wave, I mumbled goodbye to Rowan.

Jude waited outside on the steps for me. His hands were shoved in the pockets of his jeans and he looked out toward the parking lot. The sun created a golden halo around him. If I was honest with myself, he took my breath away. I think maybe he always had. Even before Graham died, I'd always been one to deny my feelings. I bottled them up and stored them away carefully in neat little drawers, never to be peeked at again. I always did whatever it took not to get hurt. Even if it meant holding myself back.

I didn't bother suggesting that we take separate cars; I knew Jude would veto that idea immediately.

Once in his old blue truck, he turned the heat on and glanced at me before backing out. "Do I get to ask you a question today?"

"You just did."

"Ha. Ha. Ha," he chanted. "You're so clever, Tater Tot."

"I detect sarcasm in your tone." I did my best to keep from smiling. I failed.

"You do indeed. *But* I do actually think you're the smartest person I know." His tone was serious.

"Thank you," I told him, a bit taken aback.

"You're also the prettiest."

I held up a hand. "Quit while you're ahead, Brooks."

He chuckled, scratching his lightly stubbled jaw. "Okay, okay. But you never *actually* answered my question."

"You can ask me whatever you want." I shrugged. "I don't care."

"Hmm." He tapped his fingers against the steering wheel, driving into the old part of town. "Why do you want to be a journalist?"

"Because I want to write about things that matter," I replied immediately, without a second of thought. "If I can make a difference with something I wrote ... Well, that would be the best feeling in the world." A small smile touched my lips. "You know, I think you're the first person to ask me that."

"I think that's a pretty amazing answer," he whispered, his eyes a dark stormy brown when he looked at me out of the corner of his eye.

I racked my brain for a question to ask him. I finally settled on, "When can I go back to the farm?"

He glanced at me, adjusting his hold on the steering wheel. I expected him to laugh or say something mocking, but he did neither. Jude Brooks was full of surprises.

"Whenever you want, pretty girl." He smiled over at me—a genuine smile too, not one of the cocky ones he always seemed to wear. "I'm surprised you like it there."

"I love it," I whispered. "It feels like home," I whispered under my breath, but of course he heard.

"It is home."

I STARED open-mouthed at all the ice cream flavors before me. This was the equivalent of heaven to sugar lovers like myself.

"I can't believe you've never been here before." Jude shook his head incredulously. "That's a real shame."

"I'm here now." I scanned the selections for the tenth time.

"With me," he added unnecessarily. "I like having you with me."

I ignored his comment, before I either said something rude or overly gooey and affectionate, because dammit I was really starting to like the guy and I mean *like, like* him, and I'd really hate to get myself in trouble.

The girl working behind the counter tapped her fingers impatiently. "Have you decided yet?"

Rude, much? Didn't she know choosing ice cream flavors was a monumental decision, not to be taken so lightly?

I didn't say any of that, though. Instead, I answered, "A scoop of the fresh strawberry and banana."

"In a cone or a cup?" she droned, clearly bored with her job as she picked at invisible dirt under her nails.

"A cup," I replied. She grabbed a scoop and got my ice cream. Before she could hand it over I clapped my hands. "Ooh, ooh! I want rainbow sprinkles too!"

Jude chortled beside me. When I glared at him, he asked, "What are you, five?"

I stuck my tongue out at him as she handed me the cup.

Jude ordered three scoops of chocolate on a cone. When the girl finished and handed it to him, my eyes threatened to bug out of my head. The thing was massive. Like, as long as my arm, and he was going to *eat* it? Looking at his light gray shirt and tan colored pants I really hoped he didn't let it drip on his clothes. That would be unpleasant. And then, knowing Jude, he'd probably try to give me a striptease as he removed the soiled clothes. Okay, now I was picturing him getting naked and I liked that image a little too much ... or a lot too much. *Crap*. I was in deep.

Looking over at Jude as he paid the bill, I realized that there was no reason for us to continue with this silly "bet". He'd already won. I wasn't telling him that yet, though. I needed to drag this out for as long as I could. If he found out I had *feelings* for him, it wouldn't be good. I didn't see what was so different about me that he'd change his womanizing ways, and I didn't want to deal with the pain of heartbreak.

"What are you thinking about so deeply?" Jude asked, with a light hand on my waist as he guided me to the table. He licked at the rapidly melting cone as he slid into the chair across from me.

"Nothing," I replied hastily.

"That look did not mean 'nothing'." He eyed me, giving me a look that said I was stupid if I thought I could pull something over on him. I'd always been good about hiding my feelings and keeping things bottled up inside, but Jude not only saw right through me, but he also tended to get me to spill my guts. I wasn't going to let that happen this time.

"I was staring off into space." I shrugged easily, lifting a spoonful of ice cream to my mouth. "Oh, my God," I moaned embarrassingly loud. "That's the best ice cream I've ever had." Sweet baby Jesus, I was pretty sure I could live off this stuff.

This was more than ice cream ... It was like a treasure chest of buried gold—rare and amazing.

Jude cleared his throat and wiggled in his seat.

"What?" I asked, taking another bite.

"You really shouldn't make noises like that in public."

I glanced around and out of the handful of people in the shop they all stared. Fantastic.

My cheeks heated with color and I looked down at my ice cream. "Sorry. It tasted good."

"Don't apologize." He grinned and I knew something naughty was about to come out of his lips. "I quite enjoyed that. Although, I'd enjoy it even more if we were in my bed. And naked. And—"

"Shut up!" I groaned, shaking my head so that my long blonde hair shielded my face. I wasn't one to easily embarrass, but Jude? Yeah, he embarrassed me all the time. It was like some special talent he had.

Suddenly, his warm fingers were on my chin, guiding my head up. "Don't get shy on me now, Tate." He rubbed his large thumb in soothing circles over the apple of my cheek. "Where's that feisty girl who kicks me and punches me when I do stupid shit?"

"Kissing me wasn't stupid." My lips thinned into a hard line as I realized the words that had tumbled from my mouth.

He let his hand drop and sat back, taking a lick of the dripping chocolate ice cream. "I knew you liked it, and you liked it even more when I kissed you in my truck."

I didn't have a rebuttal, because he was right. I had enjoyed it, enough so that I wouldn't mind it happening again. But I kept that tidbit of information a secret. The longer Jude stayed oblivious to my growing feelings, the better. Actually, it wasn't even that. The longer *I* could pretend my feelings didn't exist, the better.

"For the record," he continued, licking ice cream off his upper lip, "I like kissing you too. A lot."

I was convinced that Jude liked to say things to make me uncomfortable. It was like he got some kind of pleasure from watching me squirm.

As if he sensed that he'd made me uncomfortable, Jude cracked a smile. "Hey, look at us enjoying ice cream and no one's gotten covered in it yet."

I didn't want to, but I laughed. And laughed some more until my sides hurt. I couldn't remember when I'd laughed that hard. Probably before Graham died. I couldn't believe it was the guy I blamed for my brother's death that made me so undeniably ... happy. It wasn't fair, but life rarely is.

CHAPTER ELEVEN

On Sunday morning, I awoke to someone banging pots and pans in the kitchen. I jolted out of bed, stumbling down the steps as I wiped sleep from my eyes. Who the hell was in the kitchen? My mom never got out of bed before twelve in the afternoon, unless I made her, and when I'd went to bed at one in the morning my dad still hadn't come home.

But if there was an intruder in the house, why the hell were they going for the pots and pans? I was pretty sure they weren't worth much.

I skidded to a halt in front of the archway leading to the kitchen. My socks spun me around on the slick floor and I grabbed the doorframe for support so I didn't fall on my butt. No one wanted a bruise on their ass.

"Dad?" I gasped at the form huddled over the stove making breakfast.

I rubbed my eyes, then blinked them rapidly when the image in front of me didn't change.

Holy shitake mushrooms. I couldn't believe my eyes. My dad hadn't cooked any sort of meal in this kitchen since before Graham died. Man, there was so much in my life that existed in *Before Graham Died* and *After Graham Died*. It was sort of pathetic.

"Dad?" I took a hesitant step into the kitchen. "What are you doing?"

"Making breakfast, Tatie. You want chocolate chip pancakes, right?"

Tears welled in my eyes at the sound of my nickname. I hadn't heard it in so long, and my God it felt so good to hear, but strange at the same time. I couldn't figure out what he thought was going to happen by making breakfast. He'd stopped being my dad a long time ago and I wasn't sure the damage could be undone.

"Um, sure." I took a seat at one of the barstools and placed my hands flat on the cool granite countertop. "Dad? I hope you don't mind my asking, but what do you expect to accomplish with this?"

He set the mixing bowl aside and put his hands on his hips. He let out a loud sigh and then ruffled his hair. It was getting a bit too long, like he'd forgotten to get it cut in a while.

"I'm just making breakfast."

I wasn't trying to start an argument with him, but I couldn't sit back and not say anything about this. "Dad, you haven't made breakfast in a long time. Hell, you haven't even been sleeping at home. I don't think there's anything wrong with me being curious."

"God, Tatum!" he yelled, slamming his hand against the mixing bowl. It went flying through the air and batter splattered all over the kitchen. I was startled. Stunned. Unable to move. To even breathe. "Why do you always have to question everything?" His chest heaved up and down like he'd run a marathon.

There was so much I wanted to say, but I was silent.

More than that, I was *scared*.

I pushed away from the counter, went up the steps, and closed my bedroom door. I leaned my head against its surface and breathed deeply out through my mouth.

I wanted to pretend that didn't happen.

But I couldn't, because when I went downstairs later the mess was still there and a chill lingered in the air.

I was starting to realize that the parents I remembered might have been figments of my own imagination.

I SAT down at the table, holding the warm cup of coffee between my hands. Eyeing all the magazines covering the surface of the table, I asked Rowan, "Do you really need all of this to plan a wedding?"

"Ugh!" she groaned, pulling her long hair away from her face and securing it in a high bun. "I hate this! I'm about to tell Trent to forget all this wedding crap and just go to Vegas."

I laughed, removing the plastic lid from my coffee and blowing the steaming surface. "Isn't it the guy that's supposed to hate all this big wedding crap, while the girl oohs and ahhs over everything?"

"I never realized how much thought and planning went into a wedding. This is *hard*. Trent's mom and grandma have helped a lot, and his mom offered to hire a wedding planner. But I refused. I didn't want to lose control."

Looking at the mess on the table and her overall frazzled

appearance, I said, "Maybe losing control wouldn't be such a bad thing."

"No," she stated flatly. Rowan Sinclair—soon to be Rowan Wentworth—was the most stubborn person I knew, besides myself, of course. "What do you think of this color for bridesmaid's dresses?" She pointed to a pale blue color.

"It's pretty."

"You hate it." She threw the magazine to the side.

"No." I picked it back up and flipped to the page she'd shown me. "I said it was pretty. Since when did that mean I hated something?"

"It was your tone."

I rolled my eyes. Sometimes Row could be the most impossible person to deal with. "I *love* the blue," I replied. Batting my eyelashes, I leaned across the table toward her. "It'll make my eyes pop and the men won't be able to resist me."

"Men? Or Jude?" She smiled wryly.

"There's nothing going on with us," I replied, putting the lid back on my cup of coffee and taking a sip. It was the truth. Well, maybe a half-truth. There was something between us, but there were no labels to describe our relationship. "So, are you going with the blue?"

"Yeah," she sighed, marking the page. "It'll be pretty on you and Olivia." Olivia was Rowan's other bridesmaid and she happened to be Trent's sister-in-law. I'd only met her a handful of times. She was sweet and really pretty. I could tell she and Trace, her husband, were crazy about each other. It made me a little envious. I wanted that kind of love, I just didn't want the pain, suffering, and heartache that could come from it. Let's face it, I was going to die alone surrounded by cats.

"I can't wait to leave for spring break and have an actual,

you know, break." She propped her head up on her hand. "I still hate the thought of leaving the kids, but I need this."

Judging from the dark circles under her eyes, I'd say she definitely needed this. With school winding down and the impending approach of graduation, every senior on campus was stressed out.

I needed this break just as much.

This coming week couldn't be over fast enough.

Taking one of the magazines, I flipped through it until I found the sluttiest wedding gown imaginable. Rowan was too stressed and I wanted to make her laugh. "There you go." I slid it across to her, tapping my finger on the glossy page. "It's perfect."

She snorted when she saw what I'd picked. "While I'm sure Trent would love it, I'm not sure I want every guest to practically see my goods."

"In all seriousness," I said, "what do you want for a wedding dress?"

She shrugged her slender shoulders. "I'm not sure. I know that's a sucky answer but it's the honest one. I was thinking maybe something more old-fashioned."

Looking at Rowan, with her long, light-brown hair pulled back, her fine features and sculpted cheekbones, I was pretty sure she could wear anything she wanted and look gorgeous in it. "If that's what you want, you should go for it."

"I really need to try on dresses." She bit her lip. "Do you want to come with me?"

"Of course," I replied immediately. "When?"

"Now."

"Now?" I sat up straighter, taking a large gulp of coffee. "Why now?"

"There's a shop on the next block. I might not try on

anything, but I'd like to look. Get an idea, you know?" She gave me an uncertain look and bit her lip nervously.

I stood and slung my purse on my shoulder. "Let's go."

"Are you sure?" She appeared hesitant, like she thought she'd made me mad. Rowan had nothing to do with my current pissed off state. That was all thanks to the man I occasionally called Dad when he bothered to come home.

"Absolutely," I told her, walking away to toss my now empty coffee cup in the trash.

As if she was afraid I'd change my mind, she hurried after me.

It was a warmer day and I reveled in the feel of the sun on my skin. I'd always loved the outdoors and being stuck inside all winter had really taken a toll on me.

We stepped into the shop and it looked like tulle had exploded in there. I batted my way through, hoping I didn't get scolded for touching the dresses.

A woman came out of the backroom, smiling warmly. "Hello, ladies, what can I help you with today?" she asked, clasping her hands together in front of her black pencil skirt. Her dark hair was perfectly coifed. I'd never be able to get my hair slicked back that tight unless I used superglue. I tended to let my hair do its own thing.

"She's looking for a wedding dress," I told the saleslady when Rowan didn't speak up. I looked over my shoulder to see her standing there, her face as white as the dresses. I guessed it was hitting her that this was real.

The lady began asking Rowan a thousand and one questions that made my head hurt. Another saleslady came to help me with bridesmaid's dresses. She pulled a few for Rowan to look over that could be ordered in the color she'd decided on.

I sat in an uncomfortable white chair, waiting for Rowan to

come out of the dressing room. The space was decorated in white and pale pink. The furniture was a bit too frilly for my taste. In fact, I found the whole space to be very prissy. I was tempted to throw some gum wrappers I had wadded up in my purse on the ground, just to mess it up a bit.

When Rowan stepped out of the dressing room and onto the platform, my mouth hung open. She twirled around, letting me see the dress from all angles. It was a mermaid-style lace gown with a sweetheart neckline, capped sleeves, and an opening in the back. It was absolutely stunning on her.

"Rowan, I think this is your dress," I breathed in awe, itching to reach out and touch the fabric. "It's gorgeous."

"You think so? I mean, it's the first one I tried on, so ..."

"No, don't second guess it. Sometimes you get things right on the first try, and this ... *this* is your dress. It's like it was made for you." I almost felt jealous as she smiled at her reflection. My best friend was marrying her dream guy, having her dream wedding, and going to live happily ever after. I didn't see a future for myself past graduation and that was really scary.

"You're right," Rowan agreed. "This is my dress."

The saleslady helped her off the platform and into the other room. The lady that had helped me find the bridesmaid's dresses ushered me into a room and helped me changed into one of the dresses.

I'd already told her it was an outdoor wedding, so all of the dresses she'd pulled were on the more casual side.

The first one she put me in was really shiny and itchy. I prayed Rowan hated it. If I had to wear this thing through her whole wedding I'd end up having a special burning of the hideous dress ceremony afterwards.

I was already standing on the platform when Rowan came

out of the dressing room from changing back into her clothes. Her face screwed up with complete and utter distaste. "That's awful."

I let out a sigh of relief. "I'm glad we agree."

After two more, I was about to give up. But then the saleslady put me in a floor-length flowy dress. It was strapless but had a sweetheart neckline to match the one on Row's. The one I wore was in a peachy color. It draped beautifully on my body and I wasn't worried about my boobs popping out, so that was a plus.

Rowan gasped when she saw me. "It's beautiful!" She clapped her hands. "Perfect! The color too!"

"What about the blue?" I asked, turning around so she could see the back.

"Forget blue, this is so much better and more elegant."

Well, for someone that had been so stressed earlier she'd made these decisions relatively easily.

She ordered the dresses, as well as one for Olivia, and we left.

Since we hadn't gotten anything to eat when we met for coffee, we decided to get lunch. It was nice to spend some time with her. We hadn't had much girl time in months. Life had a tendency to get in the way.

CHAPTER TWELVE

It was late when Jude and I pulled up to the old farmhouse after he'd finished volunteering. I was leaving for spring break with Trent and Row the next day, so this was my last chance to see his grandpa for a good week or more.

The last week I'd been able to steer clear of Jude's advances and there'd been no more kissing, but my God did I want to. I hated myself for liking him, and I hated him even more for causing me to have such conflicting feelings. I didn't know how much longer my defenses would last against him. I was hoping my week away would help me to fortify my walls to ensure that he didn't break through.

"Pap?" Jude called out as we walked inside. "Pap?" he called again when there was no answer.

He looked at me worriedly and my stomach dropped. Oh, no, he couldn't have …

"Pap!" Jude ran up the steps, taking them two at a time. "He's not here!" he called down a moment later.

I frantically started to search the bottom level but Jerry wasn't there, either. This was bad.

I was terrified he was having one of his episodes and had wandered off. On a property this large the chances of finding him in the dark ... Yeah, it didn't look good.

In the sunroom, I caught sight of him out the window. I let out a sigh of relief.

"Found him!" I called out to Jude. I wasn't sure where he had gone to look. "He's outside!" Not bothering to wait for him I darted outside, running toward Jerry. He just stood there in the middle of knee-high grass looking up at the stars.

"Hello, Tatum," he said, not even looking at me.

"Jerry," I said as I tugged on his arm, "it's cold out, you should come inside."

"I wonder if she's up there," he murmured, like I wasn't even there. "I wonder if each star is someone that was on this Earth once—a person that shined brighter than others. My Mae—" he clucked his tongue, laughing softly "—she shined brighter than anyone I've ever known."

I leaned my head on his shoulder and my racing heart calmed. "I bet she's right there then." I pointed at the brightest star I could see. It sparkled in the moonlight. "Look at that, she's winking at you."

He reached up and blindly patted my cheek. "Jude didn't tell me you were coming."

"I begged him." I grinned up at the sky.

"He doesn't want you around me," Jerry stated, "he's afraid I'll tell you something embarrassing."

"Like what?" I laughed.

"That boy cares more for you than he'd like to admit," he told me.

"That's not true. He doesn't even know me." Although, that

wasn't really true. While we'd never been friends, we had grown up in the same town all our lives, and with this little question game we had going on we knew each other pretty dang well now.

"How do you ever really know someone?" Jerry countered. "People are always changing. Sometimes, it's about how you feel them."

"Feel them?" I questioned, my brows drawing together.

He nodded, placing a hand on his heart. "It's what you feel in here and recognize in the other person, that matters. There's good and bad in everyone. No one's perfect, Tatum. Definitely not my grandson, but he has a big heart to offer you." I wanted to tell him that I didn't want Jude's heart, but that would be rude and untrue, because a part of me yearned strongly for the brown-eyed man I was desperate to hate. But the thing about hate is eventually it disappears and I think I'd just about used all mine up.

Jerry and I stood looking up at the stars for a few minutes longer. When we turned to go back inside, Jude was a few feet behind us watching us curiously.

"Pap, why were you out here by yourself? That's not safe." Jude frowned, looking his grandpa over carefully to make sure he was unharmed.

"I'm fine, boy." Jerry waved a hand dismissively as he headed for the back door. "You worry too much."

"Of course I worry." Jude sighed, pinching the bridge of his nose. "Have you eaten dinner?"

"Yes, I didn't know you two were coming," Jerry said, holding the door open for us to follow. "It's a nice surprise. There are leftovers in the refrigerator if you're hungry."

My stomach rumbled at the mention of food. Besides a

Special K bar after my last class I hadn't eaten anything in hours. Jude chuckled, having heard the noise. *Great.*

Jerry headed to the den and a moment later we heard the sounds of the TV.

Jude opened the fridge and pulled out a plastic container. Popping the lid off, he inhaled the scent, and breathed happily, "Mmm, meatloaf. Pap makes the best meatloaf."

"I'm pretty sure your Pap makes the best everything," I commented as he found plates and cut a square out for each of us. "Are you as talented in the kitchen as he is?"

"No."

"He's lying!" Jerry called from the other room, eavesdropping on our conversation.

I quirked a brow at Jude. "Is that true?"

He shrugged. "I can cook, just not this good."

"Lies!" came Jerry's voice again.

I couldn't help laughing. The way Jude and his grandpa behaved around each other, well it was heartwarming. They liked to pick on each other, but there was a bond there that was indestructible. It was obvious that his grandpa was his father figure, and I wondered if his grandma had been more like his mom than his own. I was dying to know why Jude didn't have much to do with his parents, but that was none of my business so I was keeping my mouth shut, for now.

Jude set the warmed plates of food on the table and I got us cups of ice water. It felt weird to be sitting at a table just the two of us enjoying a meal. It was so simple, so easy. I never thought I'd use either of those words to describe Jude and myself. Wow, we'd come a long way in a few short weeks in the sense that I didn't contemplate all the ways I could kill him with my bare hands every time I was in a room with him.

I studied his strong chin and brow, his full lips that had felt like heaven against mine, and something I'd never felt before stirred inside me.

"Why are you looking at me like that?"

I shook my head forcefully, bowing my head so my hair hid my face and concealed the embarrassment staining my cheeks. "I didn't know I was," I muttered.

Suddenly, his fingers smoothed my hair back and my chin was forced up so I had to look at him. His eyes were such a warm brown, like melted chocolate. "You can look all you want, pretty girl. I don't mind."

Of course he didn't, but *I* did. Jude Brooks was the last person I should have these ... these ... *fluttery* feelings about. It wasn't okay with me. But the heart wants what it wants, and mine very clearly yearned for Jude. I didn't understand how I could go from hating someone with every fiber of my being to wanting them. Actually, it was more than a simple want. I *craved* him. But I was determined to deny my feelings until either they went away, or he gave up on waiting for me, because he would give up on me eventually. Everyone did.

"Hey," he said, his voice deepening with seriousness, "what's wrong?"

"I'm fine," I assured him.

"That look on your face doesn't seem fine to me," he commented, tilting his head slightly as he studied me.

I bit my lip, letting out a heavy sigh. "I think I'm just really tired."

He nodded his head, like that was answer enough.

We finished eating in silence, cleaned the dishes, and joined Jerry in the living room to watch some TV before we left for the evening.

When we said our goodbyes, Jerry called me Julia and Jude had become Andrew. It broke my heart, seeing Jerry regress into his mind and into a time that was no more. I knew it had to be even more painful for Jude.

Back on campus, Jude parked his truck in the empty spot beside my old red Mazda. I didn't say anything as I got out and headed to my car. I jumped in surprise when I heard the driver's side door of the truck close. Jude had never gotten out of his truck before when he dropped me off.

He came around to where I stood by my car, leaning so close to me that you couldn't fit a sheet of paper between us.

My breath faltered as he stared into my eyes. His look was intense, searing me straight to my core.

A few weeks ago, I would've pushed him away and cussed him out for standing this close. I did neither of those things.

My heart raced dangerously fast as he lowered his head. I thought for sure he was going to kiss me, but he didn't. I was learning that Jude was full of surprises.

He brushed my hair back over my shoulder and nuzzled my neck. The light stubble on his cheeks and chin grazed my skin, causing me to shiver. "I just want to see you happy," he breathed against my skin. Then his lips were on my cheek, oh so close to my mouth, but he pulled away from me before it went any further. He turned hastily and strode to his truck. I watched him get in and pull out of the parking lot while I was left standing there, panting like I'd run a marathon, wondering what the hell had just happened.

CHAPTER THIRTEEN

"Oh, hell to the no!" I seethed, standing on my front porch at six in the morning with two suitcases by my side. "No one told me he was coming!" I pointed an accusing finger at Jude.

Rowan rolled her eyes as Trent grabbed one of the suitcases and Jude got the other. "I knew you wouldn't come if I told you Jude was coming too."

"You're right," I agreed. "This feels like a setup," I accused her. Rowan, Trent, Jude and me? Yeah, that was a bit too cozy for my liking. I'd been the third wheel when I thought it was only the three of us, but I'd never had a problem doing things on my own before. But now ... I was going to be stuck with Jude. I'd been hoping to use this time to get over my *crush*—I cringed at the word—on him. Stuck in a house 24/7 with him was going to prove futile to my plan. I was so screwed. Unless I didn't go. "I think I'm going to stay home."

"Tatum, don't make me get Trent to drag you into this car," she warned. "You know I will."

Judging from her serious tone and the look in her eyes, I believed her, and I knew Trent would do whatever she told him.

"Fine, I'll go, but I won't enjoy a minute of this *vacation*," I spat venomously as I passed her on my way to the car. Staring up at Jude, I warned, "Don't try anything."

He chuckled and raised his hands in surrender. "I'll try, but no promises."

Great.

Jude opened one of the back passenger doors and waved a hand for me to get inside. With a bunch of grumbling, I finally did. I heard him laugh as the door closed and he jogged around to the other side, sitting so close to me that our knees grazed.

The car we were in was some kind of fancy SUV that I knew didn't belong to Trent or Row. I figured Trent had borrowed it from his mom, since neither of their cars were made for long distance traveling.

I hated that our spring break was so early in April, so the weather was always cool. I really hoped it would be much warmer at the beach, but on the east coast you never knew.

Jude tapped his fingers along his jean-clad thigh to the beat of the song playing on the radio. I let out a sigh and turned to look out the window.

It was going to be a long drive.

"This is your beach house," I gasped when we pulled up to the gate blocking the entrance. It wasn't huge, but it certainly wasn't small, either. I'd been picturing a cottage. This looked like something you'd see in the movies. The siding was navy blue with white shutters, a deck, and stairs leading up to the dark wood door. The gate swung open and Trent drove through, pushing a button to open the garage door—which he didn't park in because there were two dune buggies and two Jet Skis.

"Yeaaaah!" Jude clapped his hands. "This is going to be awesome!"

We eased from the car and got our luggage from the trunk.

Jude took one of my suitcases and started wheeling it away before I could protest. I got the other, following behind him.

Trent passed us, pulling a key out of his pocket to unlock the door in the garage that led into the house.

I gasped again when I saw the interior. Everything was done in pale yellows and whites with pops of blue here and there. It didn't sound like it would work together, but it did.

"Welcome home." Trent grinned, tossing his keys on the marble countertop in the kitchen. Everything was so sparkly, shiny, and new.

"This is beautiful," I told him, looking around in awe. Before Graham's passing, we'd vacationed twice a year but we'd never stayed anywhere this nice.

"Come on, guys, I'll show you your room." Trent took my suitcase from my hand, starting up the steps.

"Wait." I shook my head, stunned. "I notice you said *room* not room*s*."

"There's two beds." He winked, jogging up with my suitcase like it weighed nothing.

"Rowan!" I screamed at the top of my lungs when she

came into the room. "I hate you!" I stomped up the steps, Jude following behind as he laughed hysterically. I was pissed. Actually, I was beyond pissed. I was whatever came after pissed. Livid, maybe? I was too mad to even think of the right word.

Trent opened a door and motioned me inside.

Sure enough, there were two queen-sized beds, so at least there was that. But it didn't make up for the fact that I was sharing a room with Jude. I couldn't escape him.

"Please, tell me you're messing with me?" I begged Trent.

He shook his head. "Sorry, Tate. This is all there is right now. There's another bedroom, but it's used as an office. Trace and I shared this room growing up."

I let out a heavy sigh. This was okay. I was okay. I was strong, I could make it through this week. I nodded my head and Trent left with an apologetic shake of his head.

I sat on the bed closest to the window, claiming it as my own. I drew my knees up and rested my head on top.

Out of the corner of my eye I saw Jude remove his beanie and toss it on the other bed. He ruffled his brown hair and turned to look at me. I couldn't read his expression to know whether he was happy about our sleeping arrangements or not.

"I'll sleep on the couch," he told me.

While that would certainly make me feel better, I didn't want Jude to be uncomfortable for the whole vacation. After all, this was his break too, and I wasn't *that* mean of a person.

"No." I shook my head, and his eyes widened in surprise. "That would be silly."

He looked like he was going to argue, but the sight of the comfy bed deterred him. He jumped on the one beside me and bounced up and down a few times before settling. "Hey, roomie, I don't sleep with any clothes on, in case you were wondering." He waggled his brows.

And now, I regretted my decision not to let him sleep on the couch. This was going to be the longest week of my life.

"Don't worry, I'll leave my boxers on to shield your sensitive eyes," he continued, his lips turned up in a wry smile.

"You better," I groaned, rolling onto my back and crooking my arm over my eyes.

I hadn't gotten much sleep last night, worried over my decision to leave my mom alone for a week, and hadn't slept in the car. So, I was exhausted.

"Tired?" Jude asked, no doubt catching my eyes threatening to drift closed.

"Mhmm," I hummed, counting sheep—it was something I'd always done since I was a child before I went to sleep.

"Me too," he yawned.

We got up an hour later and ate a late lunch. Everyone wanted to head to the beach, and I cringed at the thought of Jude checking me out in my bikini.

I changed in the bathroom connected to the room we shared. I knew he was just on the other side of the door changing too and for some reason that thought made my heart speed up.

I adjusted the straps of my white bikini with yellow daisies on it to make sure nothing came popping out. The last thing I wanted was to give Jude or any of the other beachgoers a show.

Thankfully, I'd been smart enough to bring a pullover with me so I wouldn't be completely exposed. Only, I'd left it in the other room ... where Jude was ... which meant he'd watch me walk out of here all awkward-like as I tried to hide my body from him. It wasn't that I was shy or had body image issues, I just didn't like being stared at.

To stall for time, I braided my hair to the side, letting it hang down. I added a bit of waterproof mascara to my lashes and pale pink gloss to my lips.

I sighed, knowing I couldn't hide in the bathroom forever.

I knocked on the door before I opened it. I didn't want to get an eyeful.

"I'm decent." Jude chuckled. "Took you long enough," he grumbled, reclining on the bed. His eyes instantly widened, zeroing in on my chest and then to the soft swell of my hips. I held my head high and willed my cheeks not to flush.

"Yeah, well, I'm a girl. With as many as you've been with you should know it takes us a while to get ready," I retorted.

"Not that long." He winked, tossing his beanie up and then catching it.

"Oh, ew!" I wrinkled my nose once I got his meaning.

I opened my suitcase and searched through it for the heather-gray pullover I wanted. It was more like a sweatshirt, but I thought I would need it.

When I turned around from putting on the sweatshirt, it was obvious Jude had been looking at my butt. I narrowed my eyes and he chuckled in response. He wasn't at all ashamed at having been caught.

"You ready?" he asked.

"Hold on." I held up a finger as I gathered more stuff in my beach bag. I pulled a pair of shorts out of my suitcase and put those on as well. They didn't cover that much skin, but they did cover more than the bikini bottoms and I didn't like the way Jude was looking at my long legs like he wanted to lick them or something.

Sliding sunglasses on top of my head, I slung my bag over my shoulder and said, "Now I'm ready."

Jude slid lithely off the bed and stretched his arms above his head. He tapped the top of the doorway on our way out.

Trent and Row were already waiting downstairs by the backdoor. Trent had his arms wrapped around her from behind and whispered something in her ear, which made her giggle.

She looked up, her cheeks flushed with warmth and smiled when she saw us.

"Y'all ready?" Trent asked, then nibbled on her earlobe. She giggled and pulled away. Rowan might've been madly in love with Trent, but she still struggled with public displays of affection. I had to admit that she was much better now than she had been a year ago.

We nodded, and Trent opened the door.

I don't know how it had escaped my notice, maybe because I'd been too busy gawking at everything else, but the beach was literally right outside. Yeah, it was a beach house, but I'd still thought we'd have to walk a few blocks to get there. Oh, no. It was right there. I ran outside like a crazy person, kicking off my flip-flops and twirling in the sand. My bag dropped somewhere behind me but I didn't care. I was on the beach!

I heard them laughing at my display.

I was letting loose and I was determined to have fun on this trip, even if I had a roommate. I wasn't paying attention and let out a squeal when my feet were swept out from under me. At first, I thought I was falling, but then my stomach hit against a muscular shoulder. Jude's familiar scent swam around me as he ran toward the ocean.

"Jude!" I screamed, laughing despite myself. "Put me down! It's going to be freezing and I have my clothes on!" My protests didn't matter, we both went in the water. A wave swelled around us, knocking him off his feet.

We went under and the icy water shocked me. I came up sputtering, wiping my eyes. I slapped at his hard chest, which was on full display in his drenched white shirt. Getting a good look at him, I swallowed thickly. I itched to reach out and touch his abs, but I clenched my hands together so I could do no such thing.

We stood staring at each other, drenched in water, panting —and it wasn't from lack of oxygen. The air was thick with sexual tension. It was like a palpable thing between us, wrapping around us with snaky tendrils drawing us closer.

I don't know who moved first, and it didn't matter.

Suddenly, his arms were wrapped around me, one holding my body and the other on the nape of my neck. Our lips collided together and I wanted to sigh in relief.

I hated him.
I wanted him.
I cursed him.
I craved him.

We were like fire and water—two opposites that should never come together, but somehow when we collided it was perfect. His mouth moved over mine with the skill of an artists' hand on a canvas. I breathed him in, savoring this moment. With each gentle press of his lips against mine, my resolve to avoid him crumbled. There was no staying away from Jude. I could run, hide, and deny my feelings for as long as I wanted, but they weren't going anywhere. I needed to get

Jude out of my system. At least that's what I told myself as I kissed him deeply, fisting his wet shirt in my hands. I couldn't hate him anymore, not after seeing the real, genuine Jude. The fact of the matter was I let go of my hatred when I'd seen what a remarkable person he was and I couldn't stay away. I'd always been a fighter, and I'd been fighting my thoughts and feelings for weeks now. There was a part of me that still fought hard to hate him, to *blame* him, because that was easy, but it wasn't working anymore. I saw now that no one was to blame. Not really, anyway. But humans long to find fault in someone else. It's so much easier to hold onto pain, to despise someone, than it is to let go and choose to be happy. I was letting go of my pain, letting it fly away like a balloon I'd once released from my grasp as a child. I'd watched it fly higher and higher, crying at first at the loss, but then marveling at its beauty as it spun through the air, travelling to lands unknown. The balloon was my pain leaving, but it also symbolized me. Free. Floating. Discovering a life I'd never bothered to imagine. One with love and happiness.

"Don't break my heart," I breathed when he pulled away, nipping my lower lip.

He kissed the edge of my nose. "Never," he vowed.

CHAPTER FOURTEEN

Jude and I ended up back on the beach, lying on towels side by side. I'd been surprised by the words that left my mouth after our kiss, but even more shocked by his reply. Rowan had watched us emerge from the ocean with a knowing smirk before moving aways down the beach with Trent.

It was still only Jude and me in this spot. From the lack of activity on the beach, I'd guessed it was private and reserved only for the people who lived here.

Jude reached over, lightly guiding his finger down my nose. "Still cold?"

I shivered. "What do you think?"

He chuckled, ducking his head. "I didn't expect it to be that cold, I'm sorry."

Closing my eyes, I let the sun's rays warm me. "It's okay."

In fact, what had transpired between us once we were in the water made it more than okay. Just this morning I'd been livid to find out Jude was coming with us, then mad we had to share a room, but now that I'd given in to the feelings I'd been denying I felt ... happy.

Happiness had been absent from my emotions for a long time. On the surface, I wore a smile and never showed the struggles I dealt with on the inside. The fact of the matter was, I'd been hurt. I was damaged goods, and I hadn't believed I was the kind of girl worthy of love—of being *saved*. But I was beginning to see that everyone is worth saving. It was strangely appropriate that the man I'd let break me was the one to put me back together.

I didn't know what tomorrow, or next week, or even the following month might hold for us, and I wasn't going to let myself overthink it. I was going to live in the moment.

Jude lay on his back, staring up at the clear-blue sky. "Tatum?"

"Yeah," I replied when he didn't continue immediately.

"Can I hold your hand, or are you going to hit me for that?"

I turned my head and laughed at his serious expression. "I think that would be all right, and I really am sorry about that. It was an automatic reaction."

"So ..." he started, a slow grin appearing on his face. "Your first response to a guy kissing you is to slap him? Interesting."

He was never going to let me live this down. I really hadn't meant to hit him. He knew that, but he also enjoyed my pain. *Douche*.

"Only one guy."

He brightened. "I'm the only guy to ever kiss you?"

"No!" I immediately shut him down. "I've kissed other guys, but you're the only one that I ... you know ..."

"Slapped?" he supplied. "Should I be honored that you like to hit me?" He winked.

"You make me sound like I'm abusive." I pouted, feeling ashamed of myself and my behavior.

"Nah." He propped his head up on his hand and stared down at me. "You're just a tough girl."

"Tough?" I wrinkled my nose. "That doesn't sound very appealing."

"Oh, trust me, it is. It's hot as hell, actually. But you want to know a secret, Tate?"

I nodded and he lowered his head so his mouth was pressed against my ear. My body shuddered at the close proximity and the heavenly feel of his breath ghosting against my skin. "Even tough girls need saving."

"Is that what you're going to do, Jude?" I quirked my head and squinted from the sun shining in my eyes. "Are you going to save me?"

"No." He shook his head, his dark hair brushing my forehead. "You're going to save yourself."

He said the words with such surety that I couldn't help but believe him. When I didn't say anything, he rolled onto his back and finally entwined our hands together. Peace flooded my body and I didn't understand it. How could the man that had filled me with such torment not long ago calm my body with a simple touch? It was mind-boggling.

I rolled my head slightly to the side, studying his profile—the elegant slope of his nose and the slant of his lips. I couldn't believe I was thinking this, and he'd probably kill me if I said it out loud, but he was beautiful—inside and out. It was a shame that I was just now noticing it. I think a lot of people never saw what a magnificent person he was. He hid his true self behind cocky smiles and flirtatious come-ons.

"You're staring at me."

"I'm not," I hastily turned my head away.

"I felt your eyes," he continued. "You were totally staring. It's okay, look all you want. I know I'm quite the feast for your eyes."

With my free hand, I smacked his stomach. My God he had abs of steel. I think I hurt my hand more than I did any damage to him. Not that I was really trying to hurt him. Although, I thought he needed a nice blow to his ego.

I squealed as he rolled on top of me and I found my arms pinned above me, pushed into the sand. His tongue slowly snaked out between his plump lips to moisten their surface. I thought he was going to kiss me, but he didn't. I was learning that Jude rarely did what I expected of him. In many ways, he was a mystery.

His dark eyes grew serious as he stared down at me and I found myself squirming as his hips dug into mine. I felt my body responding to the position—muscles tightening, pulse racing, and an overwhelming ache building inside me.

"Are you sure about this?" he breathed softly. There was a vulnerability in his eyes that I'd only ever seen when he was around his grandpa. "About us? Or am I going to wake up in the morning and find that you're gone?"

"You really think I'd run away?" I replied, wiggling my hips, which caused him to hiss sharply between his teeth.

"Honestly? It wouldn't surprise me. You're afraid of your own feelings." He lowered his head, brushing his nose against my neck. My eyes closed and a pleased hum resounded in my throat. There was still a voice in my head telling me to push him away, but I was done listening to it. "It's okay to be scared, Tate." He nipped my earlobe, the heat of his body wrapping around mine like a blanket. "I'm scared too."

"You are?" I breathed, my voice so soft the wind nearly carried it away.

I felt him nod, his hair tickling my neck. "I've never felt this way about anyone, but you," he confessed. "It's always been you."

His behavior with other girls suggested otherwise, but I didn't say any of that. While my problems had caused me to isolate myself, it was clear whatever haunted Jude caused him to seek comfort in the arms of another—a naked female, specifically.

His words made me wonder if maybe he really did see something different in me.

Maybe a part of me hoped I *was* different. It wasn't about taming the bad boy or any nonsense like that, but it was nice to feel ... I don't know ... special. I'd never been the girl to stand out, not even during my brief stint as a cheerleader. I'd always been okay with blending in with the crowd. But the way Jude looked at me sometimes made me want to be anything but a wallflower. He awakened something inside me I'd never thought existed. I wasn't quite sure what it was. I just knew he made me feel alive.

"I haven't scared you, have I?" he asked when I was quiet for a while. His finger twisted in the long locks of my long hair, which had fallen loose from the confines of the braid.

"A little," I admitted.

"Don't be afraid." His lips brushed my forehead and my lashes fluttered. "Let's just explore this crazy thing between us for a while and see where it goes."

"You mean, until you get sick of me," I stated.

"Pretty girl ..." His lips descended lower, closer to my mouth but mostly on my cheek. "I could never tire of you. If I was going to get bored with you, don't you think it would've happened long before now?"

He was right. Jude had been making advances toward me

since we were in high school. Our college campus was large enough that I'd thought he'd gone away for school and hadn't seen him on campus the first two years. It probably helped that we studied two completely different majors. In fact, I wouldn't have encountered him again if he hadn't become friends with Rowan. I'd been beyond livid when he'd shown up at the library one day where Row and I had been studying. From that moment on, he'd picked right up where he'd left off in high school with trying to get in my pants.

"That's a good point," I agreed, curling into his side. He was so warm and comforting and I almost never wanted to leave his arms.

I'd always been fiercely independent and it scared me to be falling so hard and fast for someone. Especially Jude.

"If I'd really only wanted to fuck you all this time I'm pretty sure you slapping me would've been a *huuuuuge* turn off," he continued, laughing so his chest shook, causing my head to bobble up and down where it rested on his shoulder.

"My mom would shove soap into your mouth for that statement," I dead-panned, refusing to laugh or acknowledge yet another mention of the slapping incident.

"Sounds like a kinky lady, must run in the family." He rose above me, smirking.

"Juuude!" I shrilled his name and reached up to lightly beat my fists against his chest in jest. He caught my hands before they could any damage.

I found my hands pinned above my head once more. "Do you want me to spank you, Tatum?" There was a hint of amusement in his eyes, but his tone was almost stern.

"Only if you want me to cut your balls off while you sleep." I smiled sweetly.

Something changed in his eyes and he opened his mouth to

say something, but promptly shut it. He released my hands and stood up, offering me a hand. "What do you say we go for a walk?"

A walk with Jude on the beach? It sounded grossly romantic, but I guess we were a couple now ... Wait, *were* we a couple? It was all so confusing.

He kicked off his shoes, letting his feet dig into the sand. I did the same and then took his outstretched hand. We started walking down the beach and everything about the moment felt strange to me. Jude hummed pleasantly under his breath, a small happy smile on his face. Every once in a while, he'd look down at me and his smile would widen. Shouldn't that have been me? Shouldn't I have been the one looking foolishly ... I shut down that thought. Love and Jude in the same sentence was not something that should ever be used. Regardless, I felt like I should've been the one beaming. Not that I wasn't happy, but let's face it. This was *Jude.* He could have any girl he wanted. Heck, he'd *had* every girl he wanted, but he was suddenly choosing *me* to have a relationship with? *Me?* The *me* who had hated him for the last seven years. It honestly made no sense, but I couldn't help believing that the most confusing things can turn out to be the simplest things in the world. I hoped that's what being with Jude would be like. Simple. Easy. Uncomplicated.

"You look like you're worrying," Jude spoke, his voice husky and deep like his throat was dry.

"I'm not," I said quickly.

"Come on, Tater Tot. I know you better than that."

I stopped suddenly and he did too. He loomed over me from his towering height. Even though I wasn't short by most people's standards Jude still made me feel small and dainty.

"Do you know me?" I asked, shielding my eyes from the sun. "Tell me Jude, do you really *know* me?"

His jaw clenched painfully tight, and a muscle ticked. Something about my question had made him angry. "I know that you say your favorite color changes depending on the day and where you are, so right now I'm going to venture to guess that it's blue." He nodded his head toward the ocean. He was right. "I know that your eyes light up at the mention of my Pap. I know that you love that house more than you'd care to admit." He thrust his fingers in his hair, getting heated. "I know things about you that you haven't even told me." I opened my mouth to protest, because what could he possibly know, but he plowed on. "I know that you want to ride one of the horses on the farm—I've seen the way your eyes linger on them when they're grazing. I know you loved your brother and wanted to blame me for every bad thing to happen to you, but you also know in your heart I had nothing to do with it." His chest heaved as he struggled to get enough air. "I know from the far-off look you get in your eyes sometimes that there's a lot you keep inside. I know you struggle to feel accepted, to feel like you belong. I know that you never talk about your mom and dad. I know you watch me when you think I'm not looking, but Tate—" he cupped my cheek "—I'm always looking at you."

I swallowed thickly and my body leaned into his touch. My heart raced and my palms dampened with sweat.

I felt like a frightened, cornered animal.

And then I did what I did best.

I ran away.

CHAPTER FIFTEEN

Sand kicked out behind me as I ran. My feet sunk down into it making it hard to run fast, but I tried.

It wasn't good enough.

Jude caught up to me easily and we fell to the ground as he tackled—yeah, he full-on tackled me to the ground like we were playing football. Sand got all over our clothes as we rolled around. There was nothing sexy or playful about the motion.

"Let me go," I protested, trying to wiggle away from his grasp.

"No." His tone was stern. He was bigger and stronger than me, so it didn't take much effort on his part to subdue me. "Look at me," he growled when I turned my head away from him. I could feel moisture stinging my eyes and the last thing I wanted was for Jude to see me cry. Talk about mortifying. "Tatum, *look at me*." His voice softened, pleading with me. I couldn't stop my head from turning. "That's my girl." He smiled. My heart still raced in my chest, but its beats were slowing. "I told you I was afraid of you running away, and then you go and do it. Way to bruise a guy's ego," he teased, but there was an uneasiness in his eyes like he was still worried if he released me I'd flee. All fight was leaving my body. I hadn't even been trying to get away from *him*. It was my feelings I was running from. They were a jumbled, twisted knot inside me. I couldn't untangle them and even begin to sort the mess. I didn't understand what he saw in me. I'd seen enough of his true colors to know he was an amazing man, but me? I had no clue who I was or what I wanted. I dwelled on the past too much and didn't talk about my feelings. I kept everything bottled inside me until I exploded—like when I threw the McFlurry at Jude. *May that Oreo McFlurry rest in peace.*

I took a shuddering breath as he said, "Talk to me, Tate."

"I don't know how to talk to you," I breathed, my chest rising heavily with each breath. "I don't know how to talk to *anyone*."

His dark brows furrowed together. "You're talking right now."

"Smart ass," I muttered.

"I'm not asking you to tell me every secret you've hidden away in that pretty head of yours." He smiled, like he was trying to reassure me. "I'm just asking you not to run away when your feelings get to be too much."

"You sound like a girl," I stated, glaring at him.

He bellowed a laugh at that. "Well, one of us has to be the level-headed, honest one in this relationship, and since you're clearly not ready to share a lot of things with me, I guess I'm that person."

"There are things you're not telling me," I stated, because I knew it was true deep down in my gut.

He bowed his head, strands of dark hair falling in his eyes.

"That's true, but at least I don't run from what I feel."

I winced. "Touché."

"If there's anything Pap taught me it was that being a man doesn't mean burying your feelings. Yes, it means being a leader and protecting the ones you love—" he smoothed my hair off my forehead "—but it also means you embrace what you feel in your heart. He taught me not to hide my emotions, to accept them all."

"Your grandpa is a wise man."

"He is," Jude agreed. "So, what do you say, are you ready to accept your feelings? To embrace this unknown rocky road ahead of us?"

No. That wasn't the word that left my mouth, though. "Yes."

His smile widened. "No. More. Running." He reinforced each word with a kiss to my forehead, the end of my nose, and finally a light kiss to my lips. He jumped up and pulled me up with him. "That walk was shaping up to be a bad idea, but I think we had a good talk." He slung an arm over my shoulders.

My heart skipped a beat. "I'm scared," I admitted, needing to tell him. "I'm scared to death of what I feel for you, of how you affect me. I feel like I'm falling."

"Ah," he breathed, "don't you know, falling is the best part of flying."

ROWAN CORNERED me in the bathroom before I could get it locked and jump in the shower. I knew it was only a matter of time before she sought me out. She found me sooner than I expected, and I'd been planning to use the time in the shower to figure out what to tell her.

"What the hell happened today?" she whispered just in case someone was listening. She lowered the lid of the toilet seat and sat down.

I shrugged.

"Tatum," she said my name sternly, the same way she said her son's when he was in trouble. "Tell me. I'm your best friend."

"I-I don't know," I shrugged, again. "We kissed and …"

"And?" she prompted.

"It was amazing." Those darn butterflies erupted in my tummy again as I relived the kiss in the ocean. I was convinced no man could kiss like Jude. He was a master.

"I need more than that." She waved her hand in a gesture for me to go on.

"We laid on the beach, talked for a while. That was about it." No way was I telling her I'd freaked and Jude had chased me down. Besides, I felt like everything we'd talked about should be kept between the two of us.

"Are you guys dating now?"

She wasn't going to leave this alone, but I hadn't expected her to. I knew she'd wanted something to happen between the two of us for a while. Nothing would have ever happened between us if it wasn't for my paper, and being forced to work with him. I was beginning to think Rowan had turned me down on purpose so that Jude would volunteer and we'd be forced to spend hours alone together. If that had been her plan, it had worked magnificently.

"I don't know what we are." I nibbled on my bottom lip nervously. We certainly weren't boyfriend and girlfriend, and we'd never been friends. "I don't think there's any label out there to describe us."

"Well, I knew that already." She laughed, pulling her long

hair over her shoulder. "You and Jude ... That has unique written all over it. In a good way," she assured me. She stood and patted my shoulder. "Well, I enjoyed our chat."

Before I could reply, she opened the bathroom door and was gone. Almost immediately it opened again. Jude stuck his head in and narrowed his eyes. "Was I missing out on some smoking hot girl on girl action?"

My mouth dropped open and my short fuse got the best of me. I bonked him on the forehead with the heel of my hand and his head disappeared. I slammed the door closed before he could finagle a way back inside. "You're disgusting!" I called through the door.

A cackling laugh was his only reply.

THAT EVENING, Trent decided he wanted to have a bonfire. It seemed really silly to go through all the trouble if it was only the four of us, but everyone else thought it was a great idea. I had to admit once it was done it was really pretty. I liked watching the way the fire moved, like it was dancing.

As the four of us sat around the bonfire huddled under blankets—Trenton and Rowan under one, and Jude and me under another—I felt relaxed. None of my worries and stress from the afternoon lingered. Poof. It was gone. The delicious s'more I was eating might have something to do that, as well as the soothing motion of Jude's hand rubbing up and down my arm to keep me warm.

"You know—" I looked around the empty beach "—it's really weird that we're like the only ones here."

"It's private," Trent explained, confirming my earlier belief. "People coming for spring break haven't arrived yet, it's still a bit too early." Shivering from the cool air, I agreed with the "too early" part.

Jude brought me closer against his warm body. He was like my own personal space heater.

"You want another?" he asked, leaning over to grab the box of graham crackers.

"I'm still eating this one!" I protested, trying to wipe marshmallow from my mouth.

Jude's eyes zeroed in on my mouth. Before I could guess what he was about to do his mouth was on mine, sucking it away. He let my lip go with a pop and then licked his. "Got it."

Sweet baby Jesus. One minute I wanted to slap him silly and the next my hormones were in overdrive. I'm pretty sure *I* wanted to lick him in that moment. Could you get drunk off sugar? Because there was definitely no alcohol in my system, but I was feeling loopy.

I managed to keep my tongue to myself and finished my s'more as Jude warmed a marshmallow until it was golden, then slathered the goo on the waiting graham cracker. He added the chocolate and top cracker before taking a huge bite.

A bit of chocolate sat in the corner of his lip and I reached over, wiping it away with my finger. I popped my finger in my mouth, licking the sweetness away. Jude watched me with hooded eyes, clearly getting turned on.

Yep, you could definitely get drunk on sugar. At least that's what I was going to blame my actions on. It was easier than accepting them.

I felt like we were in our own little bubble, like the blanket wrapped around us was our shield. "This is nice," I admitted, laying my head on his sturdy shoulder.

"It's more than nice, it's amazing," he breathed and his sticky lips pressed against the top of my head.

I was falling hard and fast for Jude Brooks. It was scary. I was also fighting it tooth and nail.

I didn't want to fall in love, and certainly not with him.

But matters of the heart aren't easily won by the brain. In fact, they're never won.

"Tatum?"

My name echoed through the dark room. When I didn't reply, it was joined by, "Are you awake?"

"Yes," I breathed, my voice almost shaky.

A moment later the sheet of the bed I slept in was lifted and a warm body pressed in behind me.

"What are you doing?" I asked, but didn't move.

He wrapped an arm tightly around my body. "Sleeping."

"Sounds more like talking," I whispered, snuggling closer to him. He felt so good wrapped around me.

"Always the sarcastic one." His lips pressed a kiss to my neck where the skin met my shoulder. "I couldn't sleep by myself knowing you were in the bed beside me. It felt like cruel punishment not to sleep with you in my arms."

"I'm tired," I yawned, snuggling closer against him.

"Then go to sleep," he whispered against my skin and I felt his smile rather than saw it.

"Then stop talking," I growled as he wound one of his legs around mine.

"Night, Tater Tot."

"Night, Jude."

I finally fell asleep, and it was without a doubt the best night of sleep I'd ever had.

WHEN I WOKE UP, I thought I was suffocating. I couldn't breathe from the body wrapped around mine like a boa constrictor. Jude was literally holding me so tight that my airways were blocked. I elbowed him in the ribs, and he released me ... a little.

I hadn't moved more than an inch until his arms were wrapped around me once more and I was glued to his chest.

"Jude?"

No reply.

"Jude?"

A grunt.

"Juuuuude?"

"What?" he growled, his voice thick with sleep. He was kind of delicious sounding first thing in the morning.

"You're squishing me and there's something poking me."

"He's just happy to see you." He chuckled. "I'm happy to see you too. You're pretty in the mornings. I was a bit afraid you might look monstrous," he said as he released me and propped his head up to look at me.

"That first comment was uncalled for." My cheeks flamed. I couldn't help it that I'd never slept the whole night with a guy and I didn't know these things. "Secondly, I'm offended that you'd think I'd be anything but a beaming ray of sunshine in the mornings."

He laughed, using his other hand to wipe sleep from his eyes. "You're so cute when you get mad." Cute? I didn't think any girl on the planet liked to be called cute. "You know, I'm really starting to think you're a virgin."

I bristled at that. It wasn't that there was anything wrong with being a virgin, it was just that ... I don't know ... Jude had certainly been around and I didn't want him to think that I was waiting for someone special. That *he* was someone special.

"I'm not a virgin," I growled. I might as well have been. I'd only slept with one guy and that had been in high school. We hadn't really dated, just fooled around. It wasn't one of my prouder moments. I'd been young and without anyone and found myself seeking comfort in the arms of a guy. A guy that turned out to be a real prick. Thank God he had gone away for school and I didn't have to look at him anymore.

"I wish you were." His eyes darkened. "I'm a selfish bastard and I want to be the only one to kiss you—" he reinforced his words by pressing his soft lips to the skin of my shoulder "—to touch you—" he glided a finger over my cheek "—to see you—" his eyes dropped to the swell of my breasts peeking out from the top of the tank I wore. "To hear you," he murmured, his hands ghosting along my stomach, causing me to let out a soft moan.

The feelings he stirred inside me were indescribable. I felt like we were moving way too fast, and we were, but my God, I didn't care anymore. Sensible Tatum was gone and in her place was a girl I didn't recognize, but I kind of liked her. I liked feeling happy and wanted. I'd just never thought it would be Jude to make me feel that way. Life never goes according to plan, though.

"You're right," I breathed, blinking up at him. "You do sound selfish."

He snickered. "Leave it to you to ruin the moment." He eased from the bed, stretching his muscles. I forced my eyes to the ceiling so I didn't stare at the rippling muscles concealed behind smooth, tanned skin. He slipped on a pair of jeans and a t-shirt, running his fingers through his hair to tame it. I think I preferred his sexy bedhead look.

"I'm going to go brush my teeth and see what we're doing about breakfast." He smiled, bending down to kiss my cheek before leaving.

Jude completely baffled me. I wondered when I'd get used to his sweet side. Well, it wasn't even a side, he was just genuinely that way, but he kept it hidden from everyone else. With me, he let his guard down. I was going to have to do a better job of that myself. I stood, staring in the mirror that hung above the dresser. My long blonde hair hung down in a tangled mess. My eyes were a bleak blue, not the happy blue they'd been as a child. They were regaining a little bit of their sparkle, and I knew that was all thanks to the guy who'd just left the room. I rubbed my chest where my heart lay shattered to pieces. I wanted to believe the pieces were big enough to be put back together, but something told me the shards more closely resembled dust.

I turned away from the mirror before I could get disgusted with myself. I had a lot of issues I needed to work through. Realistically, I knew I probably needed to talk to someone, like a therapist, but I was too prideful for that.

I changed into a pair of shorts and a plain white t-shirt then I brushed my teeth, and hair, tying the strands away from my face in a bun on top of my head.

Downstairs, I found Jude and Trent watching TV. Rowan sat in the kitchen drinking her morning cup of coffee. I was pretty sure she was addicted to the stuff.

I hopped up onto the counter beside her, swishing my legs. "Morning," she yawned. "Want some?" She pointed to the cup of coffee.

I shook my head. "No, thanks." I liked coffee, but unlike her I didn't need a shot of caffeine when I woke up. "Are we having breakfast here?"

She shook her head. "No, after I call and check on the kids Trent wants us to have breakfast at some diner here."

"Sounds good. What's this?" I asked, my eyes landing on a tiny vase. It was one of those that only fit a single stem, but instead of a flower inside there was a Twizzler.

She shrugged. "Ask Jude. I was just as confused as you are."

Overhearing our conversation, Jude strode into the kitchen. Grinning, he said, "I'm determined to show you that I'm serious about us, and that means treating you differently. Flowers are overrated, so I decided on something I know you love." He pointed to the Twizzler in the vase. "I think Twizzler bouquets will be all the rage from now on. I'm a trendsetter." He plucked the Twizzler out of the vase and waved it in front of my face. "Smells good, huh? It tastes even better."

I snatched the candy from his hand and took a bite. He grinned. Finishing it off, I said, "I never knew you could be so cheesy."

My words didn't faze him. "I'm a romantic guy and wear my heart on my sleeve when it comes to you, Tater Tot. Get used to it. Real men aren't afraid to show a girl they care."

"Aw, that was really sweet." Rowan patted him on the shoulder as she passed by, heading for the stairs. "I almost believed you for a second."

Jude chuckled. "You wound me."

"Yeah, yeah. I'm still not convinced you're a nursing major. I think you're playing us all and you're really studying drama," Rowan replied, crossing her arms over her chest as she stared him down.

"Sorry to disappoint you, Row, but I'm a sexy man nurse all the way."

I snorted at that and Row and I dissolved into a fit of giggles.

"Don't laugh." Jude smirked, watching me. Something told me I was in trouble with whatever he said next. "You're the one that was checking out my ass in my scrubs."

I groaned, cheeks flaming. My reaction prevented me from retorting. It was pointless anyway.

"While this conversation has been ... enlightening, I better go change so we can eat and call the kids."

"I notice you didn't deny it." Jude placed his hands on either side of me, leaning close, his head bowed so his hair tickled my forehead.

"You have a nice ass." I shrugged. "No point in denying it."

He laughed, rubbing his nose against mine. "I like this side of you." His lips quirked, and I couldn't contain my own smile.

"What side?" I questioned.

"The real one."

I started to squirm, feeling uncomfortable from his words. He stilled me by rubbing his warm hands up and down my arms in a soothing gesture. Without telling him, he always knew the best thing to do for me. It was like he could read my mind.

Instead of pushing him away, I did something that surprised us both. I laid my head against his solid chest and let my body sink into his. He folded me into his arms and held me against him. I loved how he felt wrapped around me, like we were made for each other. I let out a shaky breath. This whole letting myself *feel* thing was going to be hard. Real hard. But I was trying and that was something.

"I'm ready!" Rowan called, bounding down the steps.

Jude stepped back and I hopped off the counter. Trent was oddly quiet, watching Jude and me with careful appraisal. I wondered what he thought of the two of us together.

We piled into the SUV and it didn't take us long to get to

the diner. It was nothing fancy, but it was clean so that was something.

"They have the best milkshakes here," Trent informed us, not bothering to pick up his menu.

Rowan laughed beside him. "Trent, it's like ten in the morning. No one wants a milkshake at this time."

"Anytime is the perfect time for a milkshake," he murmured, nuzzling her neck and then kissing it.

"Annnd there they go with the gross public displays of affection." Jude coughed beside me as our friends completely lost themselves in each other. I might not have wanted to watch, but I did want to give Rowan a round of applause for opening herself up to Trenton. "Maybe we should get a different table?" he suggested.

"No, no," Rowan replied before I could, extracting herself from Trent's arms and swatting him away before he could continue. "We're here to have breakfast together. There's time for *that* later." She glared at Trent. He was completely unaffected by her threatening gaze. He'd put up with enough from her before that this didn't faze him.

"Whatever you say." He grinned at her, wrapping a strand of her hair around his finger.

"Annnnyway." Jude picked up a menu. "Trent's right, it's never too early for a milkshake. Ooh!" he exclaimed like an excited little boy. "They have chocolate peanut butter. Mmm, I love peanut butter." He licked his lips like he could already taste it.

"I'm with Rowan on this one." I picked up my own menu, perusing the breakfast items. "And I *love* ice cream, anything sweet, really, so that's saying something."

"Whatever." Jude shrugged. "You'll regret that decision when you see me drinking my milkshake."

He was probably right but I wasn't telling him that.

A waitress came by and we placed our orders. Since we were out, we decided to hang around town for a little while longer before heading back to the beach house. Once there, the guys decided to get out the Jet Skis. I changed into a black bikini and grabbed my beach bag. Once the Jet Skis were ready, the guys headed inside to change. Rowan and I relaxed on the beach while we waited for them.

They returned with four life jackets and I rolled my eyes as I took the one Jude offered me. I could swim and didn't feel I needed one, but "safety first".

Heading out to the Jet Skis, Trent hopped on one, Rowan climbing on behind him.

Jude tried to get in the driver's seat of ours, but I wasn't having that. "Whoa, bud, what do you think you're doing?"

"Bud?" He quirked a brow. "Did you seriously call me bud?"

"I seriously did, bud," I said it again just to irritate him. "I'm driving."

He put his hands on his slender hips. "And why is that?"

"Because, I am." I squared my shoulders, not backing down. Growing up with an older brother, I'd been quite the tomboy. No way in hell was I letting him drive. The Jet Ski was calling my name and my hands were itching to get on it.

He sighed and handed me the key. The child in me jumped with glee. "I expect some sort of payment later," he whispered gruffly in my ear, making me shiver as his finger glided over my collarbone. "I accept payment in the form of sexual favors."

I pushed him away. "Keep talking like that," I warned him, "and I'll throw you off of this thing and let the sharks eat you."

"I love sharks," he replied, smirking. "I was thinking of getting one as pet. I think I'd name him Herbert. That sounds like a good, non-threatening name for a shark, don't you think?"

Instead of replying, I climbed on the Jet Ski. I started it up, listening to it purr to life. I looked over my shoulder at him. "You coming?"

He sighed and climbed on behind me. "Too bad you have this life vest on. From this position, I could totally grope your tits."

I swatted his hand away as it inched under the vest. "I'm still not against making you shark bait," I warned.

"A shark would never eat me." He chuckled. "I don't taste good. You, on the other hand ..." He nipped my shoulder, and then licked the same spot. "Mmm, you taste real good."

Before he could say anything more, I floored the Jet Ski and we took off, bobbing up and down on the waves. I could hear Trent and Row laughing somewhere.

Jude's thumbs rubbed slow, smooth circles over the skin of my back. It felt good, relaxing. He felt *right* against me. Like my body was made for his.

The wind whipped my hair in my face and I'm sure Jude kept getting a mouthful of the blonde strands, but he never, not once, complained. I think he knew I needed this moment of freedom. I couldn't wipe the smile off my face. By the time we returned to the beach my cheeks hurt. I'd take that pain any day, though.

"My turn." Jude grinned, rubbing his hands together excitedly.

This time, I didn't complain and climbed on behind him.

As he drove, I wrapped my arms around his sun-warmed chest and laid my head against his back.

This felt good.

More than good, it felt *right*.

CHAPTER SIXTEEN

By the time Jude and I finished with our fun, Trent and Row had long since left.

Jude stretched out on a towel and crooked an elbow over his eyes.

"I'll be right back," I told him.

"I'll be here."

Most of the day had passed, and the two of us had completely forgotten lunch. It was closer to dinnertime now. I wanted to get a quick shower to rinse the ocean water off my body and make us sandwiches for a snack.

By the time I got upstairs, I regretted my decision to come inside.

"Oh, Trent! Yes! Harder!"

I backed into a wall, slamming a hand over my eyes, which was stupid since I didn't *see* anything. Oh, no, I *heard* it.

I scurried into the guestroom, feeling like an intruder. I had to get out of there. Now.

I grabbed a change of clothes and left as quietly as possible, so hopefully they'd never know I'd been there. Food would have to wait.

There was an outdoor shower, so I decided to make do with that. I laid my clean clothes on a chair and went to tell Jude about the change of plans.

"Hey." I shook his shoulder and he raised his arm off his face. Clearly, he'd fallen asleep.

"What's up?"

"Um." I bit my lip, embarrassed to say the words out loud. "I kind of walked in on Trent and Row having sex, not that I saw anything," I hastened to add. "I just ... uh ... heard it." Great, now my cheeks were heating. He really was going to think I was a virgin now. "So, I'm going to take a shower out here." I pointed over my shoulder in the general vicinity of the outdoor shower.

He nodded. "Okay ... but do you really need a shower? It's still kind of early."

"I feel gross," I replied. "I want a shower."

"Women," he muttered, before covering his face with his arm once more.

I shook my head and went to the shower. Since the showerhead was only blocked from the view of others by fence paneling—where there were large enough cracks to see through—I left my bikini on and figured I'd sit in one of the chairs and read a book while I dried. It didn't seem like the people that owned the homes on either side were even there, but I wanted to be on the safe side. Public nudity didn't seem like a good way to introduce myself.

I turned on the water, letting it warm before stepping beneath the spray. I instantly felt it rinsing the salt and sand from my body. I'd brought soap out to wash my body—figuring

I'd do my hair later when I had access to an indoor shower. I'd just begun to lather my body when the shower door opened and I let out a yelp. The soap bottle went clattering to the pebbled floor.

"Jude!" I shrieked. "What the hell?!"

His eyes were hooded, dazed. "I couldn't get the thought of you in this shower out of my head." He looked me up down, causing goosebumps to break out across my skin from the intensity of his heated look.

"I could've been naked," I hissed, covering my body even though it was completely unnecessary.

"I'm aware of that, and I wouldn't have minded one bit."

Before I could shoo him away, his mouth was on mine. With one kiss, he consumed me.

His mouth moved over mine like a skillful dancer. I struggled to keep up.

His tongue slipped past my lips and I gasped, drawing him in even more. He grabbed my thighs and my legs wrapped around his waist. My back was pushed against the fence wall as his hips dug into mine. My heart raced like a caged bird threatening to break free. Jude made me crazy—that was the only word for it.

"Tatum," he growled my name, biting at my lower lip.

I whimpered in response.

I could feel him growing hard between my legs and I wanted—no, *needed*—more.

"Jude, please." I tore at his shirt. I was tempted to rip it off him.

He set me down long enough to tear his soaked shirt off his body. It fell to the ground with a wet thump. He picked me up once more and my hands sought his chest, exploring the smooth hard planes.

His fingers found the string of my bikini top and tugged. I felt the fabric begin to fall away from my body. The only thing keeping it from falling off completely was our chests pressed together.

I wrenched my mouth from his. I needed to get the words out of my mouth before he kissed me silly and I changed my mind. "I'm not ready."

"I know you're not, but I need to feel you against me. Skin to skin. That's it. I promise."

He pulled back far enough to see my eyes. I gave him a single nod.

He grinned and grabbed the scrap of black fabric, tossing it away.

His eyes feasted on the sight of my chest laid bare to him. I suddenly felt shy and nervous. I wondered if I measured up to the other girls he'd been with. My chest wasn't huge, but it wasn't small, either.

"Perfect," he growled, almost as if he'd read my mind. His lips covered mine once more. One hand supported my body against the wall, while the other kneaded my breast. I soon found myself panting embarrassingly loud. The things he could make me feel ... The man had skills.

"You were fucking made for me," he informed me between kisses. "You're mine, do you understand me?"

In the past, the über Alpha male attitude had turned me off, but coming from Jude? It was hot.

"Yes," I gasped, seeking his lips once more. "And you're mine."

That's right, I, Tatum Elizabeth O'Connor, was staking claim to Jude Brooks. From this moment on he was mine. Bitches beware. I had claws and I wasn't afraid to cut a bitch if she got too close to my man.

"You know it, baby." He kissed me passionately, absorbing all my worries and concerns. As his lips moved against mine it was like I became a new person ... No, not *new*. I just became me again. I'd missed *me*. With every stroke of his lips and play of his fingers against my breasts, I felt my happiness returning in full force. My pain and suffering and all the anger I'd lived with—a lot of it directed at him—melted away and swished down the drain along with the shower water. Jude could work magic—or at least his lips and fingers could.

I'd been holding myself back from him, even after I'd resolved to an *us*. Running away on the beach proved that, along with my constant need to snap at him.

But I was really and truly giving myself over to him now. I wasn't holding myself back any longer. I wanted this. I wanted him. I wanted us.

My fingers tangled in the wet strands of his hair, tugging lightly to draw him closer.

Our chests slid against each other and both of his hands now cupped my butt to hold me up. We were drenched from the shower, but neither of us seemed to mind. My wet hair clung to my face and he moved a strand away.

He didn't try to remove my bottoms, which I was thankful for. He was respecting my boundaries and it made me appreciate him even more.

His lips slid down my neck, placing gentle kisses. "I could kiss you forever," he breathed, raising his head so his brown eyes connected with mine.

I nodded in agreement, because right then he'd stolen my ability to speak.

He placed one last lingering kiss on my lips before pulling away. He picked up my bikini top and instead of handing it to me he proceeded to help me put it back on—taking extra time to cup my breasts. I thought it was safe to say that Jude was a boob man.

"Why'd you stop?" I panted, still out of breath from our activities.

"Because—" he pressed his forehead to mine, his gaze searing me with its intensity "—you aren't ready for more yet and if we kept at it we might've gotten in trouble. I never want to do anything you'd regret." He smoothed his fingers down my cheeks, causing my lashes to flutter. Great, I'd turned into one of those girls that swooned. I was in too good of a mood to care, though.

Jude picked up his drenched shirt and headed for the shower door—which was really more like a flimsy gate.

He turned back and looked at me with dark, serious eyes. "Every time I kiss you I never think the next one can top it, but it does."

He let the gate close and I was left standing there in a daze. I wasn't sure if it was what had transpired between us, or his words that had left me so jumbled. I was going to guess that it was a mix of both.

I turned the water off and tried to smooth my fingers through my sopping hair since it was now a tangled mess.

When I came out of the shower, Jude was sitting in one of the Adirondack chairs drinking a beer. There was another one sitting by the other chair, waiting for me. I didn't drink at all, but right then I felt like I needed five beers to calm my shaking nerves. That boy could wind me up like no other. He knew all the right things to do and say.

I sat down in the empty chair and brought my knees up to my chest, wrapping my arms around them.

"I got you a beer." He nodded at the bottle sitting on the ground.

I gave him a weak smile. "I don't drink, not after what happened to Graham." I'd never said the words aloud, but it felt good to tell him. I found that Jude made me want to be honest. I didn't want to hide myself from him. I wanted to give it all to him.

"Ah, I see." He nodded in understanding. He brought the beer bottle to his lips, taking a small sip. "I don't think I've ever told you, but I'm really sorry about your brother." His eyes sparkled with sincerity. "When you talk about him ... I know you loved him a lot."

My smile cracked and I looked out to the ocean. "Even though he's been gone a long time, I still love him and miss him," I admitted, tucking a stray hair behind my ear, and squinting from the sunlight. "Sometimes I wake up and think it was a nightmare, but then I realize it was real and it all comes crashing down on me again." I found myself opening up to him further, telling him even more things I'd never told another soul. "My mom kind of lost it when Graham died. And when I say lost it, I don't mean in a violent way." I sighed. "She retreated into herself. It's what I wanted to do. Escape," I said the word softly. "But I couldn't. I had to carry on and be strong. Since she shut down I had to be the one to keep moving. I had to run the house and keep her fed and my clothes washed. It was all on me. My dad ... " I shook my head, laughing humorlessly. "He buried himself in work and Lord knows what else. My mom and I ... we ceased to matter to him. He started working later and later, and sometimes he doesn't even come home at all." I bit my lip, wondering if I should continue, but then I did, unable to stop myself. "The other day I woke up to the sounds of someone in the kitchen. I thought someone had broken into the house." I scrubbed a hand over my face and peeked at Jude out of the corner of my eye. He still sat, listening intently. He didn't look bored or irritated with my tale. "It was my dad. He was home making breakfast. He got mad when I asked him why and we got in a fight. It pissed him off because I was curious as to why he was making breakfast. After him being absent for so long, I thought it was weird. Anyway, I stormed off to my room, and when I came out he was gone." I felt my lip begin to tremble with the threat of tears. I turned my head to look at Jude. "When I lost my brother, I lost my parents too. I even lost my friends because I couldn't deal. I lost everyone and I've been so alone for so long. Having Rowan has made it better, but being with you makes me feel alive in a way I haven't been in a long time."

He reached over, wiping away my tears with his thumb. "Thank you."

"Thank you?" It seemed like such an odd response to everything I'd told him. Granted, it was probably better than him running away like a crazy person. "Why are you thanking me?"

"Because, I know it took a lot of courage for you to share that with me. You're not an open person, Tate. It's hard to get to know you. So, thank you." He wiped the last of my tears away and sat back. "I guess I should tell you something personal now too, huh?"

"Like our question game?" I forced a laugh.

"Sort of." He shrugged. He finished off his beer, slapping his hands on his thighs as he looked out at the ocean and away from me. "My mom wasn't much of a mom. She left when I was fourteen. Kind of messed with my head." He shrugged, picking up the bottle of beer I had neglected to drink. He tilted his head toward me and smiled slowly. "I guess that's what sent me into my man-whore ways. Like your dad, mine's a workaholic. Never home. Never willing to talk when he is. Before my mom left, she was pretty shitty anyway. As you already know, I ended up spending a lot of time at my grandparents' farm. They practically raised me from the time I was five until I started college. They're the reason I'm not a complete asshole." He winked at me. "My parents never really wanted a kid. If I could have a dollar for every time I was told that I was mistake ..." He chuckled but there was no humor in it. He took another gulp of beer, wiping his mouth with the back of his hand. "They didn't beat me, so I guess there's that." For some reason, I flinched and a long buried memory of my dad's fist connecting with Graham's cheek entered my mind. "Luckily, I had Pap and Grams. The farm gave me a much-needed peace. I loved it there ... I *love* it there," he amended. "They helped me to see that even though I had shitty parents, it didn't mean I was a shitty person."

I scooted my chair over to his. "Jude?"

"Yeah?" He set the beer aside.

"We're quite a pair, aren't we?"

His chuckle was the only answer.

CHAPTER SEVENTEEN

"This is nice, right?" Trent asked, spreading his arms wide as we walked into the fancy restaurant. Once he and Rowan finally finished their sexcapade, they'd been starving.

Now, the four of us stood in the entrance of a very fancy seafood restaurant. So fancy, in fact, that we'd had to dress up. Rowan and I both wore dresses. Trent was in a pair of designer jeans and button-down shirt. Jude wore a pair of his favorite tan pants and a blue polo shirt. I wanted to lick him. He wore blue so well. I was close to telling him that he could only wear blue from now on.

"Very nice," I agreed.

I felt out of my element in a place like this. I could tell Rowan and Jude felt the same way. Trenton, however, was completely at ease. I guess growing up a billionaire will do that to you. Surprisingly, though, Trent and his family acted like they were completely normal. It was refreshing.

The hostess returned to her station and Trent spoke with her.

Since it was a chilly evening we couldn't sit outside. Instead, we were seated in a room with windows all the way around. There was only the one table and I certainly appreciated the privacy it provided, although I was beginning to wonder how much this meal was going to cost.

Trent pulled out a chair for Row. I sat down before Jude could even think of pulling out mine.

"Don't worry about the price," Trent spoke up, as if he could hear my internal babbling, "it's on me." His words didn't make me feel better. I didn't want my best friend's boyfriend—fiancé—paying for my meal.

"No, don't do that," I said quickly, picking up a menu. My eyes bugged out at the prices. Oh, dear lord. I was positive one meal here cost more than my car.

"I insist. I wouldn't have come here if I wasn't paying." He waved his hand dismissively, taking a sip of the ice water a waiter had brought while I was freaking out over the prices.

I cracked a smile. "Thanks."

Suddenly, I felt Jude's warm hand on my leg, rising higher and higher. I didn't get mad like I should have. Instead, I found myself biting my lip to stifle my moan. Just when his hand was almost where I wanted, he let go. I whimpered from its absence but he'd had his desired effect in distracting me.

I planned on ordering the cheapest meal on the menu, but that proved futile since nothing was cheap.

I felt guilty through the entire meal, but it was worth every penny Trent was spending on it. I'd never tasted anything so delicious. The seafood was cooked to perfection and the flavors zinged in my mouth. I wished I could cook something that delicious.

After the meal, we headed back to the beach house. It was late so we all headed straight for bed.

I'd showered before we ate, but Jude hadn't so he locked himself in the bathroom. I guess I wouldn't be interrupting his shower like he had mine earlier. I got all tingly just thinking about what happened between us in the shower this afternoon.

While he was showering, I took off my makeup and changed into my pajamas—which was just a t-shirt long enough to cover my thighs. I didn't bother with pants. The room was on the warm side and if Jude slept with his body plastered against mine again tonight I'd end up drenched in sweat. So, no pants was my solution. I wondered what Jude would think once he discovered I wasn't wearing any. I wasn't trying to tease him, or tempt him.

Okay, maybe a teeny bit.

I turned off the lights and lay down in the bed. I was exhausted from all the fun I'd had today, but I was determined not to fall asleep until he came to bed.

Five minutes later, the door cracked open.

From the glow of a nightlight shoved in one of the outlets I could see the beads of water clinging to his abs. One of the droplets of water I stared at disappeared into the top of the white towel wrapped around his waist. I swallowed thickly, my eyes never leaving him as he stepped over to his suitcase and bent to grab a pair of clean boxers. I didn't even look away when he dropped the towel. I swallowed thickly at the sight. The man was perfect, of that I was sure. "I can feel you watching me," he stated, pulling his boxers in place and hiding his ass from my greedy eyes.

I didn't look away when he turned around to face me. I could hear my pulse racing as he approached, his eyes hungry.

"You know, I never collected on the sexual favor you owed me for letting you drive the Jet Ski first."

"Wasn't that what happened in the shower?" My voice cracked as he hovered above me. His body was large and when he was above me like this I felt so small but protected. I knew he'd never hurt me. At least not physically. Now, my heart? That was a whole other matter. He definitely had the power to break me that way.

"*That*, my dear Tate," he began. He flexed his arms in a push up position, his mouth sucking on my neck. "Was merely a warm-up. You ain't seen nothing yet."

I swallowed thickly and felt my body start to break out in a sweat. I wasn't sure if my body's response was because I was scared, or turned on. Probably turned on. Yeah, definitely that. My back bowed when his hips dug into mine. Despite my declaration of no sex this afternoon, I was about two seconds away from throwing my underwear across the room.

His fingers found the edge of my shirt and raised it up. He explored my stomach with a soft touch before finding the band of my panties. "I really like that you're not wearing pants. I think that should be a rule between us."

"What? Not to wear pants? That would be awfully inconvenient when we had to be in public." My words should have had a sarcastic biting edge, but instead they came out as a pant.

"No." He nuzzled my neck, the slight stubble on his cheeks and jaw chafing my skin, but in the most delicious way. "Only when it's the two of us should the pants come off. I don't want anyone else seeing what's mine, and this—" I gasped when his hand clasped me below "—belongs to me." He kissed my collarbone, up my neck, over my chin, and finally my lips. He pulled away enough to whisper, "I want to touch you, Tatum. That's all. I swear. I won't push you for more."

I swallowed thickly, unable to breathe for a moment as his stare penetrated me. With his body heat warming me and that look in his eyes, I was a goner. I nodded my head slowly, almost imperceptibly at first and then with more surety.

"I want to make you feel good, baby," he growled, nipping at my skin.

I closed my eyes, heat rushing through my body as he parted my panties. I'd never been one for silly nicknames, but I was really starting to like every name Jude had for me. Even Tater Tot. It was our thing.

Even more than nicknames, I was *really* enjoying what his skilled fingers were doing to me. I probably should've been irritated by just how good he was, but I was too far-gone. I was too wrapped up in him now to get scared for stupid reasons.

I clung to his shoulders as he rubbed his fingers against me. No one had ever touched me there like he was and I'd had no idea it could feel so good.

My breath soon turned to pants echoing against his ear.

His hair brushed against my chin and then his eyes met mine in a questioning manner.

"It feels good," I assured him.

There was a nervous edge to him, like he was determined to show me a good time.

He wasn't disappointing.

"Please, Jude," I begged. "More."

He kissed me deeply, still moving his hand against me. Two fingers slipped inside me and I gasped, clawing at him. It was tight, but felt amazing.

As he moved his fingers, the pressure built but my tension eased. My body began to relax and it felt even better.

My whole body began to curl in on itself and my eyes closed. My heart sounded like thunder in my ears and I saw sparks behind my closed lids. I knew something monumental was about to happen to me—something I'd never been able to experience with my other sexual encounters.

And then, I gasped loudly chanting his name over and over as I reached my peak and fell down.

Down.

Down.

Down.

But then Jude was there to catch me.

I shook against him. I couldn't believe that had just happened and I felt mildly embarrassed.

I opened my eyes slowly, suddenly feeling shy.

He was watching me with a look of reverence.

"God, you're amazing." His voice thrummed through me. I still felt like I was floating.

"Kiss me," I pleaded.

And, boy, did he kiss me.

Even though his lips were pressed against mine, it felt like he was kissing me everywhere—branding me as his.

There was no coming back from this. My heart—that treacherous beast—was all wrapped up in Jude. He was quickly becoming all I could think about.

Like his grandpa said, I *felt* him. He was all around me. Not in the physical sense. His presence was just that potent. Even when he was nowhere near me, my mind and body yearned for him. He'd placed a permanent mark on my heart, carving out a space for himself. I don't how he did it—I'd long ago believed that organ to be frozen and unmoving—but he did, and there was no going back. Something told me I was only going to end up hurt and broken, but I couldn't find the sense to care anymore. Once the heart gets involved, the mind can't win.

"You're so beautiful," he murmured. He smoothed his fingers through my hair. "Fucking amazing and you don't even know it. I wish you could see yourself the way I see you."

"I'm nothing special." I swallowed thickly. It was true. I was just a girl and he was just a boy. We weren't extraordinary we were just ... us.

"You're everything."

He kissed me again—and my God I would never get used to his kisses.

His hips ground into mine and I could feel him. All of him.

My hands skittered down his chest as he kissed me and before he knew what I was doing, my hands were around him. His body quaked as I ran my hand up and down his hard length. Holy hell. He was huge. There was no way that was fitting inside me, ever. And by *that* I meant his cock. Even thinking the word made me squirm. I needed to grow up and stop freaking out. I wasn't sixteen. I was a twenty-two-year-old *woman*. There was nothing wrong with me having sex or *wanting* to have sex. But growing up in a strict household, sex had always been made to feel dirty and wrong.

Looking at the pleasure on Jude's face ... there was nothing dirty or wrong about that. It was magnificent.

I ran my thumb along the tip and his eyes shot open. He grabbed my hands and fisted them in his own, pulling them away.

Hurt filled me and my lips turned down.

"Jude? What'd I do?" My voice shook with the threat of tears. Had I done something wrong? While I'd had sex, I was pretty inexperienced and I'd never had any desire to get up and personal with a guy's—

His words cut off my racing thoughts. "You didn't do anything wrong," he panted, swallowing so hard his Adam's apple bobbed. "God that felt fucking amazing. But what I did was for *you*. I didn't want you to feel like you had to return the favor." He kissed my forehead and rolled over so he was behind me. He pulled my body against his so that there was no space between us.

"I want to."

"No, Tate, tonight is for you and only you."

I grew quiet, clasping my hands beneath my head. Finally, when I couldn't stand the silence another second, I asked, "Isn't that painful?" I rubbed my butt against his still blatantly present hard-on.

"Some pains are worth the reward, and seeing you come apart like that, screaming my name ... that was worth everything."

With those words, I fell asleep with a satisfied smile.

CHAPTER EIGHTEEN

"Juuuuuuuude!" I shrieked as he ran down the beach with me on his back piggyback style. It was safe to say we were acting like five-year-olds, but I couldn't wipe the smile off my face. "You're going to drop me!"

"I'd never drop you!" he declared, spinning me around.

"Picture!" Rowan called out, holding her phone up.

Jude stopped spinning, teetering to the side a bit as he regained his balance.

"Smile," Rowan declared.

"I am smiling," Jude and I replied simultaneously. He lifted his head to look at me and we burst out laughing. All the while Rowan snapped away, taking pictures of our moment.

Our spring break was coming to an end. Tomorrow morning we had to head back home to the real world. But all four of us were determined to enjoy our last day, and by some miracle we'd been blessed with warm weather. The ocean was still nippy, but I wasn't opposed to putting my toes in it.

"Text those to me." Jude told Rowan after she'd taken all the photos she wanted.

"I will," she laughed, running over to Trent.

There were more people on the beach today, a few even our age.

When Rowan had invited me, I'd expected crowds of college kids, but that hadn't happened thanks to the private beach. I preferred it that way. I didn't like being surrounded by lots of people or noise.

Last night Jude and I had hung out on the beach, just talking for a while, and then I decided to read. I hadn't read a book for fun since, well, probably before I started college. My studies left little time for relaxation. Soon I'd have no time, because I knew once we graduated I needed to find a job and move out on my own.

I climbed off Jude's back and we collapsed in the sand, rolling around.

"Hey." He smiled down at me.

"Hi." I smiled back.

"You know—" he poked my cheek "—when you smile really big, you have this dimple right here." He poked me again for good measure. "I like it. I think I need to kiss it."

"Oh, really?" I giggled.

"Mhmm," he murmured, kissing my cheek where just a moment ago he'd poked me. "I love your smile. Have I told you that?"

"Only a few times." I wrapped my arms around his neck.

He looked down at me, his stare intense. I shivered, despite the warmth of the sand against my back and the heat of the air.

My lips parted, expecting him to kiss me, but he didn't.

He curled his fingers in my hair. "I love your smile," he

repeated. "Your laugh. The way your eyes light up when you're happy. The way you say my name. I love it all."

"My, Jude Brooks, it sounds like you love me," I took on an overly dramatic Southern accent.

My words were like a bucket of ice water to the both of us.

He rolled out of my hold and sat in the sand, staring out at the ocean.

Oh, shit.

"Jude," I gasped, fear at my own words consuming me, "I didn't mean it like that. I mean, how could you love me?" I rambled. "I'm kind of a bitch," I muttered. "I'm really quite a mess, actually. I honestly meant it as a joke."

"Hey." He turned to me, his gaze instantly shutting me up. "Don't talk about yourself like that. You're not a bitch and you're not a mess. A little lost? Maybe. But who isn't?" His shoulders sagged. "I just wasn't expecting that is all. You surprised me. I'm sorry."

"Please, don't apologize to me." I scooted over beside him.

"I know you didn't mean it like that, but I want you to know … I might not be able to say the words yet, and I know you're nowhere near ready to hear them, but I'm well on my way to being in love with you."

"Jude." My heart did this nervous fluttery thing inside my chest. If he kept this up I was going to have a heart attack before we graduated.

"Please, don't be scared. The last thing I want is to scare you away, but I just want you to know where this is heading for me. I know a part of you still thinks this is a fling for me, but it's not, Tate. When I look at you, I see my future."

Tears glimmered in my eyes. I wasn't sure if they were happy, sad, or scared-out-of-my-mind tears. I was going with scared.

"How can you say that?" I asked. I needed to know what made him so sure. Why could *he*, Jude Man-Whore Brooks, see us together but I couldn't?

"It's the truth," he said it simply with a small shrug, like it was no big deal, but it was a huge deal. At least to me.

A few days ago, I would've been mad over his words, but now I was simply stunned. The person in this relationship that should've been fighting us tooth and nail was Jude. He was the one that couldn't stay with a girl and settle down. But instead it was me that was scared shitless while he was probably sitting there picturing a wedding and babies and all that jazz. Wow. What a freaking role reversal. This was insane. *We* were insane.

"Don't be scared, Tate."

"I'm not," I said quickly.

"You're a really bad liar." He chuckled. "Whatever you're imagining, I promise my thoughts aren't that bad." He started to laugh harder. "I haven't named our kids past Jude Jr. I figured I'd let you pick the other five."

"*Six?*" I screamed. "You want *six* kids?" I was pretty close to passing out. Someone grab the smelling salts. *Stat.*

Jude fell back in the sand laughing so hard he clutched his stomach. "Oh, my God! Your face!" He wiped tears from his eyes. "You should've seen your face! That was priceless. I wish I'd gotten a picture."

As he rolled around, still laughing at my expense, I grabbed a handful of sand and threw it at him. He was unperturbed by the projectile. I needed something larger. Like a rock. Or a missile.

"Stop laughing at me!" I scolded.

He didn't listen.

Finally, I just gave up and started laughing with him. It was pretty funny after all.

Well played, Jude Brooks. Well freakin' played.

"You're kind of an ass," I told him when we sobered.

"Ah, but I'm *your* ass." He grinned. "And face it, you really, really like me."

"I do," I concurred.

"I'm a likable guy."

"When you're not being annoying."

He fake gasped. "I am *never* annoying."

"You wish." I patted his shoulder.

He looked at where my hand was. "Did you just *pat* my shoulder like we're *friends*?"

"I did." I nodded.

He did the gasping thing again.

Before I could blink he had me pinned on the ground, the sand sticking to my skin. He had quite the knack for pinning me down. I kind of liked it actually, but I was never telling him that.

"Oh, we are so far past friends, Tate."

"Are we now?" I quirked a brow.

"Mhmm." He nodded. "Friends don't kiss like this." And then he lowered his mouth to demonstrate. He kissed me leisurely, like we had all the time in the world, and I was happy to let him. When he pulled away I mewled in protest, causing him to chuckle. It wasn't my fault his kisses were mind-blowing. "And I don't think you let your friends touch you here." His fingers glided over the tops of my breasts, which heaved behind the confines of my bikini top. "Or here." His hand went lower, cupping me over my shorts.

"Jude!" I gasped. "People can see you!"

"I don't care," he said simply.

"I do!"

"Well ..." He kissed my cheek, rolling off me. "You shouldn't care so much what people think. People's opinions of you don't change a thing." He stared out at the dark blue ocean and sighed. His face grew serious. "I don't want to go home."

"Me either."

He continued on like I hadn't even spoken. "I'm afraid that when we go home, everything will go back to the way it was before. That this will have all been a dream and you'll hate me again. I don't like you hating me, Tate." He glanced at me and I could see the *hurt* etched into his face. He really meant what he said.

"That's not going to happen, Jude," I assured him, but he didn't relax. I laid my head on his shoulder.

"I'll believe it when I see it," he muttered, almost like he hadn't meant to say the words out loud.

I realized then that Jude had been doing nothing but trying to prove to me he cared for a while. I hadn't been nearly so open with my thoughts or feelings for him. I was closed off and sheltered. Jude said he wore his heart on his sleeve, and he was right. But I kept mine guarded.

"I'll just have to prove it to you," I murmured. I meant it too.

Jude had shown he was different with me.

Now, it was my turn to show that I was different with him —that we were two halves of a whole. A fucked up whole, but a whole nonetheless.

THE STARS SPARKLED above me and the ocean roared as it crashed against the sand. The night had grown cold, but I wore a sweatshirt and had a blanket wrapped around my shoulders to protect against the wind.

I'd found myself unable to sleep.

My mind wouldn't shut up.

When the clock read one in the morning, I gave up and came out here. I'd hoped the sound of the ocean would make me sleepy, but so far it hadn't. I was sure it was closer to two now. Maybe I'd be able to sleep in the car. Trent wanted to get an early start home. I could tell that he and Rowan wanted to get back home to Tristan and Ivy. It was weird to think that my best friend was a mom. Crazy, really. We were so young.

I sighed, stretching my legs out in front of me.

I startled when a body sank down next to me.

Jude.

I should've known he'd show up.

In fact, I was actually surprised that it took him this long to come find me.

He had a sweatshirt and sweatpants on, but he still reached for the blanket. I thought he was cold and moved closer, but when he wrapped his arms around me I knew he was only trying to get me warm. Oh, Jude, ever the thoughtful one. Tears pricked my eyes. I'd always believed Jude to be the villain, but he wasn't at all. He was amazing in so many ways. He was by far a better person than me. He was the hero of this tale and I was the wicked witch. I'd been so incredibly wrong about him and I'd hate myself for the rest of my life for that fact.

"What are you doing out here, Tate? You're going to get sick. Look at you, you're freezing," he admonished. I shivered as if my body needed to drive home his point.

"I couldn't sleep."

"So, you could've watched TV or something. You didn't need to come out here," he continued, his voice carrying a tinge of worry.

I shrugged. "I thought the ocean would soothe me."

He put a hand to my forehead, his nurse instincts kicking in. "Please, come inside."

"Not yet." I lay back on the ground, staring up at the stars. They sparkled above me, so pretty. Surprisingly, they weren't as clear as they'd been on his grandpa's farm. As a little girl, I'd loved stargazing. Graham and I used to camp out on the trampoline and look at the stars until the wee hours of the morning. I wondered if, like Jerry said, one of those stars up there was Graham. He'd certainly shone brighter than most people. I'd lost my best friend, not just my brother, when he died. I was learning that I'd always feel his absence, but I'd have to find a way to deal with it. Pain doesn't have to shut you down.

Jude lay down beside me and entwined our hands together. He gave mine a reassuring squeeze.

I felt tears coat my cheeks. They weren't necessarily tears of sadness, although there was a little of that. Instead, they were tears of acceptance.

Jude's finger brushed against my cheek and he startled at the wetness.

"Why are you crying?"

"Because," I started as my lower lip trembled, "he's gone and I'm here and I handled everything wrong." I turned my head toward Jude, taking a deep breath. "I'm so sorry for how mean I've been to you." I grasped the soft cotton of his sweatshirt in my hands and drew myself closer to his body, curling into him. "I see now how wrong I was for everything. Not just with you, but with everybody. I distanced myself, even from

Rowan, because I never wanted to feel the pain of losing another person ever again. It hurt too much. But what's life without a little pain, right?" He wiped my cheeks free of tears. "I'm accepting that he's gone and I can't change the past, but I can change my future." I clung to him, like my grasp on his sweatshirt could hold me together. "You make me happy," I whispered. I needed him to hear the words, to grasp the meaning. "What I feel for you scares me so much. *So much*," I reiterated. "Love is a messy, complicated thing that I wanted to avoid. But you, Jude Brooks, are unavoidable. Please, be patient with me. You know how stubborn I can be. Don't lose faith in what we have. Wait for me, please."

"Always." He cupped my cheek. "You're worth it." He pressed his lips tenderly against my forehead and I sighed in relief. In his arms, I didn't just feel at peace.

I was home.

CHAPTER NINETEEN

We eventually went back inside and got a few hours of sleep but, soon, Trent and Row were demanding we get up.

Rowan smiled with satisfaction when she opened the bedroom door and found us in the same bed with Jude's arms wrapped firmly around my body.

I dressed in comfy clothes for the journey home and Trent came in to get one of my bags. Jude grabbed the other. Just like when we got there.

When I stepped out of the room, the door across from our room was open. It had been closed the whole time we'd been here and I hadn't ventured to explore. This wasn't my house and I didn't want to be nosy.

My mouth fell to my toes when I saw what lay beyond.

A single queen-sized bed.

Those liars. I just *knew* there had to be three bedrooms in a home this large.

Trent caught my expression and smiled sheepishly as he started down the steps. "She made me lie."

Jude peeked over my shoulder to see what had caused me to stand still in the doorway. He began to snicker. "Remind me to thank her later."

"Will do!" Trenton called as he ran down the rest of the steps as fast he could.

I started to laugh. A small part of me wanted to be mad, but it was pointless. I'd enjoyed sharing a room—and bed—with Jude far too much to get angry about it now. Rowan the Matchmaker. Who knew? She'd been so against loving Trenton, but now she wanted everyone else to have love too.

I finally got my feet moving and we piled in the car.

In the backseat, I laid my head upon Jude's shoulder and soon I fell asleep. I was awakened two hours later when we stopped for breakfast. It had been dark when we left, but now the sun was shining in the sky.

For the rest of the drive I slept off and on.

Jude awakened me gently when we arrived at my house.

"Hey, sleepyhead," he murmured, kissing the corner of my mouth.

I rubbed my eyes, blinking at the large house in front of us. I almost didn't recognize it.

Jude reached up and tucked a stray piece of hair back into place behind my ear. There was a sadness in his eyes, like he was afraid to part ways. I was too, so I was glad I wasn't alone.

"Time to go home," he said forlornly.

I nodded, unable to find my voice.

We both clamored out and he grabbed my suitcases, taking them to the door and sitting them down.

Rowan and Trent waited in the car for him to return, but were kind enough to give us a moment.

"So, I was thinking …" He shoved his hands in his pockets. "Tomorrow's Sunday …"

"Yeah?" I prompted when he trailed off.

He shook his head and returned to reality. "I was thinking maybe we could go to Pap's for the day. It's supposed to be nice. and I know he'd love to see you."

I nodded. "That sounds great."

"Good." He grinned, appearing relieved.

I was beginning to realize that when it came to me, Jude had a lot of insecurities. I guess my rude comments over the years had had more affect than I ever realized. Good or bad, words were powerful.

He kissed me quickly, not wanting to give our audience a show.

"I'll see you tomorrow," he called, jumping off the porch steps.

"Show off," I muttered, to which he grinned.

"I'll text you later with a time I'll be by to pick you up," he told me.

I nodded, digging my house key out of my pocket.

I took a deep breath, bracing myself, before I opened the door.

"Tatum Elizabeth O'Connor!" My name was shouted at the top of my dad's lungs. I hadn't known he was there since he parked in the garage, and I hadn't expected him so I was beyond shocked to hear him yelling my name.

"Dad?" My voice cracked and my whole body shook.

He came storming out of the back area of the house, where his home office lay. I couldn't remember the last time he set foot in there.

"Where the hell have you been?" He was still yelling even though I was in front of him. His voice was so loud that it made my ears ring. His face was red, veins bulging, and spittle clung to his lips.

For the first time in my life I felt real fear.

"I-I-I was at t-the beach with my f-friends," I stuttered. I was scared out of my mind. I was tempted to open the door and run outside to see if my friends still lingered, but I feared what would happen if they were ... more so if they *weren't* there.

"The beach? The fucking beach? For a week? You have school, Tatum! And your mom! How could you be so irresponsible!"

I wanted to scream back, but fright kept my voice eerily soft. "It was spring break, Dad," I whispered. I was going into survival mode. Talking to him like he was suicidal and standing on a ledge.

"Spring break? You should've cleared this with me!" he yelled, slamming a fist against his chest.

"I'm twenty-two, Dad." I held my hands up in a calming motion. "I can go on spring break with my friends if I want. I don't need your permission."

His breathing was labored and his face was still red. He kind of reminded me of a bull.

"I saw you with that Brooks boy! He's bad fucking news, Tatum! Not the kind of boy for a girl like you!"

What the hell? There was no way he could've seen us if he'd been in his office.

"H-how do you know about that?" I was stammering again. Great.

"I had cameras installed while you were away. Lord knows what you're up to in *my* house." He pounded his chest again. "Got one on the door and I saw you pull up and get out with him. A boy like that ..." He shook his head. "Oh, Tate, what have you done?" His anger started rising again as his thoughts headed in a dangerous direction. "Have you fucked him in my house?"

"*What?*" I was stunned. "No! Of course not, Dad!"

"You're nothing but a useless whore spreading your legs for that boy!" He looked me up and down, with a sneer on his face. I could smell the stench of alcohol on his breath. The glare on his face made me feel like trash. "You're nothing but a disgrace like your brother!"

And then he slapped me.

He'd never hit me before, but now I could remember times where I'd caught him hitting Graham.

Tears stung my eyes, and my cheek felt like it was on fire.

Silence hung heavy in the air.

I didn't move, and neither did he.

We just stood there, staring at each other, waiting for the other person to make a move.

I was frozen, afraid that if I moved he'd come after me. I'd never dealt with a situation like this. What was I supposed to do?

After what felt like an hour, but was really more like seconds, he turned away. He walked at a leisurely pace back to his office. To a casual observer he seemed unaffected, but I knew my dad, and I could tell from the rigid curve of his shoulders that he was still mad. Mad at me? Or himself? I wasn't sure.

When I knew he wasn't coming back I grabbed my suitcases and dragged them up the steps behind me.

I was shaken, but I refused to cry.

I would not be beaten down.

I stood in the doorway of my bedroom, looking toward the closed door of my parents' room where I was sure my mom lay.

It pissed me off that she had done nothing to protect Graham from that monster. What kind of mother didn't protect her children? The answer was easy. The kind that was scared.

I closed my bedroom door and locked it.

I heard the garage door open a few minutes later and I knew he was gone.

I tore my room apart, searching for a camera. I was convinced he'd put one in my room too, if he was crazy enough to have one on the front door. I didn't find it though. If there was one in there, it was well hidden. I stood in the middle of my room, hands on my hips, staring at the destruction. It kind of looked like my life. A chaotic, out of control, mess.

God.

I sunk to the floor.

My butt landed on a shoe and I flinched. I picked it up and threw it across my room. It dented the wall, but I didn't care.

I pulled at my hair, letting out a scream of frustration. I was so done with this. With my life. When did it all get so fucked up? Simple—it always was.

But as a child I'd looked the other way, thinking it was normal.

And it wasn't that my dad was *always* a bad person. He had his good moments. But all I could see now was the bad moments. He had a temper and he wasn't afraid to raise his voice or use his fists.

Rowan had been right.

Graham's suicide had nothing at all to do with Jude.

It was all *them*.

My parents.

Mom and Dad.

The two people that should've loved and cared for us unconditionally.

What a load of bullshit.

Even my mom, when she wasn't in her catatonic state, hadn't been all rainbows and sunshine. I couldn't remember seeing her hit Graham like my dad did, but she did yell a lot. Graham and I were expected to succeed and when we failed … Well, the repercussions weren't pretty.

I had to get out of this house.

But with no job and no money I was screwed.

I knew if I asked Rowan and Trent they would take me in. They were nice people like that. Heck, Trent's brother and sister-in-law didn't even really know me, but I knew they'd never let me sleep in my car or on the street. And then there was Jude. I knew if I told him about this he'd be determined to protect me, and probably pick a fight with my dad in the process.

I couldn't tell him, or any of them.

This had to stay my secret for a while longer until I could make it on my own.

THE CHIME DINGED PLEASANTLY ABOVE the door when I walked into the shop.

Jude had text me earlier and I still had two hours before he picked me up to go to his grandpa's. I was utilizing my time by going in and out of stores and applying for jobs. I'd been unsuccessful with anything close to school or my house, so I'd ventured to the next town over. Almost immediately, a quaint little cupcake shop called my name.

A guy about my age, maybe a little younger, was working at the counter. Floppy brown hair fell into his bright unnaturally blue eyes. He was good looking sure, but there was something different about him that I couldn't quite put my finger on. He seemed wise behind his years, but wit sparkled in his eyes and his lips were turned up in a playful smile. I could tell this guy was going to be a handful if I got the job.

"Hi, I'm Tatum," I said politely, giving him a small smile. "I saw the sign on the door saying you were hiring."

He adjusted his black baseball cap, which was emblazoned with the cupcake store's name. *Lucinda's*.

"Yeah, let me grab Lucinda." He started for the back but turned back to me and stopped. He reached his hand over the counter. "How dare me forget my manners with such a pretty girl." He winked. I took his hand and shook it. "I'm Bryce." He nodded his head toward the tables. "Have a seat and she'll be right out."

"Wait—" I called and he paused before heading in the back. "Is she going to interview me now? I'm hardly dressed for an interview." I looked down at my jeans and t-shirt. "I just wanted to apply."

Bryce held his hands up in surrender. "Just doing what the boss would want."

I forced a smile. "Great."

There was no way I'd get hired like this.

A moment later, an older lady breezed out of the swinging door and headed my way. My nerves skyrocketed.

I stood, shaking her hand. "Hello, I'm Tatum."

She smiled pleasantly, smoothing her wavy gray hair away from her face. While she was older, the age of a grandparent, there was a timeless beauty to her. Few wrinkles lined her face and there was a twinkle in her eyes. "I'm Lucinda, the owner. Bryce said you were looking for a job?"

I nodded.

She began to ask me more questions and I answered them

as best I could. I was nervous but I didn't think I was doing too bad.

Finally, when she was done, I looked around. The walls were painted hot pink and there was an overall vibe in the place that could only be described as funky. It didn't seem like the kind of place a grandma would own.

"Your shop is adorable," I told her in all honesty.

"Thank you." She smiled, and appeared to be thinking over everything we'd discussed. "How soon can you start?" she asked.

I bit my lip, thinking. After this week I was done shadowing Jude and I had no commitments that extended beyond that. "The week after this one," I answered.

"That's perfect!" She clapped her hands together in excitement. "Bryce and I will train you." She leaned in close to me. "He's quite a mess, that one. Don't believe a thing he says."

I laughed. "I'll remember that."

She lowered her voice further. "He's the brother of my granddaughter's husband, so I have to keep him around."

"I heard that!" Bryce called from the counter. I turned to look at him and shook my head. There was no way he heard that with as softly as Lucinda spoke.

Lucinda laughed and shook her head. "See what I mean?" She stood, extending her hand one last time. "I'll see you next Monday, Tatum. Leave your information with Bryce and I'll contact you when I have the schedule ready."

"Thank you so much." I meant it, too. Lucinda had taken a huge weight off my shoulders by giving me a job. This was one less thing I had to worry about.

"You're welcome, dear." She smiled sweetly.

I thought I would really like working there, and then I turned to see a grinning Bryce. Yep, that one was trouble.

"Give me those digits, pretty lady." He licked his lips suggestively and held a pen to the palm of his hand.

I narrowed my eyes and tore the pen from his hands. "No way. You'll lose it like that and I need this job."

"You tell him!" Lucinda cackled from the back. "Oh, Bryce, I think you've met your match! He's scared every other employee away!" Lucinda continued to holler through the door. How did these people hear these things? Jesus.

Bryce gave me a sheepish shrug and handed me a piece of paper.

I wrote my information down and handed it to him. "This better not get 'lost'." I made sure to put emphasis on the word "lost" so he'd know I was on to him.

He chuckled. "I like you."

"See you next Monday," I called over my shoulder as I left the shop, choosing to ignore Bryce's comment.

His laughter carried behind me as the door swung closed.

I headed back home, taking my time since I really didn't want to be at home. I still had thirty minutes before Jude was supposed to pick me up, but when I got home his truck was parked in front of the house.

I shut my car off and jogged over to the driver's side of the truck.

He rolled the window down and smiled at me.

"You missed me so much you just couldn't wait to get me?" I asked, not bothering to hide my smile. I was pleased.

"Sounds right. Hop in." He nodded to the empty seat.

I jogged around the truck with a pep in my step that was normally missing.

As soon as I was in the car, Jude leaned over and seized the back of my neck, drawing my lips to his. He took his time, kissing me slowly. He didn't rush things with me and I was appreciative of that. His tongue skated against my lips and my mouth parted for him.

When he broke the kiss, we were both panting. He kissed my forehead tenderly before pulling away from my house.

"I missed you," he admitted.

I'd never known three simple words could make you feel so happy. A smile lifted my lips. "I missed you too," I confessed. The words didn't weigh me down like I'd feared. I'd spent so long avoiding commitment that it was strange to face it head on. It was funny, Jude and I had both avoided long-term relationships for completely different reasons, and we'd both approached it differently. I avoided everyone, and he went from one girl to the next.

"You did?" he asked, and surprise colored his tone.

I nodded. "I had trouble sleeping," I admitted.

Although, that could've been in part because of what happened with my dad and the subsequent hours spent cleaning my room once I destroyed it. I'd like to think my restlessness had more to do with not sleeping with Jude beside me. It made it not seem so bad.

He groaned low in his throat. "Keep talking like that and I'll climb through your window at night like a sixteen-year-old boy."

I laughed. "I wouldn't complain."

He groaned again. "You're killing me. Seriously, you'll be the death of me, but what a sweet death it'll be."

"I'm very sweet," I concurred. "It's all the ice cream and Twizzlers. I'm full of sugar."

"Tatum," he said my name low and slow, drawing it out, "did you just make a joke?" He turned stunned brown eyes my way.

I shrugged, leaning back against the gray leather seats. "I guess I did."

"Wow. I didn't know you had it in you," he scratched his chin.

"Hey," I cried, giving his shoulder a slight push—I was trying to watch myself with the hitting and smacking, even in jest. The last thing I wanted was to turn into my dad. Maybe that wasn't the kind of thing most girls worried about, but I wasn't most girls. "I can be funny."

"Anyone can be funny," he agreed, "but you're always so serious."

I frowned. He was right. I spent far too much time being a Debbie Downer.

"I'm trying," I whispered, playing with my fingers instead of looking at his face. My voice was soft, almost scared sounding.

"I know." He reached over, smoothing a finger over my cheek with his eyes still on the road. "And it makes me undeniably happy that you are."

Jude turned down the road that led to the farm and parked his truck. "We're going to hang out on the farm for a while, but I figured you'd want to see Pap first."

"Of course!" I cried, hopping out of the truck and running toward the door.

In the short time I'd known him I'd already begun to think of Jerry as my own grandpa.

We found Jerry sitting in a recliner watching TV. He grinned happily when he saw us. "Andrew! Julia!"

My smile fell a bit.

"Hi, Jerry," I chimed, determined not to let the hurt show.

He reached out and clasped my hand, patting it. "It's been quiet around here without you two. I've missed ya."

"Missed you, Pap." Jude ruffled the old man's hair playfully.

"Boy," Jerry scolded, "don't mess with the hair."

Jude chuckled. "Pap. I'm just going to show ... Julia ... around the farm for a while. We'll see you later."

"Do you want me to make lunch? Dinner?" Jerry made as if to rise from the chair.

"Why don't you leave that up to us?" Jude suggested. "You do so much for me. Let me take care of you for a change."

"Nonsense." Jerry waved a hand dismissively. "It's not like it's that big of a deal."

Jude sighed and pinched the bridge of his nose. He knew he'd never win an argument against Jerry. "All right, Pap. Make whatever you want."

"How about spaghetti with homemade meatballs?" His eyes brightened.

"Sounds delicious," Jude agreed. "We'll see you later," he said again, but this time we actually made it out the door.

Jude didn't say anything as we walked toward the big red barn. I could see the worry etched onto his face, though. I knew him well enough now to see that. Jude worried immensely about what he'd do once his grandpa was gone. It broke my heart. His grandpa was the only real family he had left.

"Hey." I stopped him just outside the barn. "It's okay."

He looked down at the ground, kicking his boot against the dirt. "It's really not." He swallowed thickly. "It tears me apart when he doesn't remember who I am. The last person I want him to think I am is my father. That man ..." Jude shook his head and trailed off. "Before and after my mom left, I was treated as a play thing. Something shiny and bright to help their image. My mom told me all the time that they never wanted kids, but when she got pregnant they decided to use me to their advantage." He kicked the ground harder, a cloud of dirt puffing up. "I was a *thing* to them, not a person. I was only wanted when I was useful and banished when they were through with me. Having Pap call me by my dad's name ..." He glared out toward the meadow beyond. "I hate it, but I can't say anything. I have to play along. I used to fight him on it, tell him I was Jude, but he would get frustrated and think I was messing with him. I learned early on it was best to pretend I was who he thought I was." Jude sighed, his dark eyes haunted. "The things we do for the ones we love."

With a shake of his head, he turned and opened the barn doors, effectively dropping the conversation.

I chose not to say anything about what he'd just told me. His rigid stance told me he didn't want to talk about it.

"What are we doing?" I asked, and I could see him visibly relax with the knowledge that I wasn't going to batter him with questions.

"We, my lovely Tate, are going horseback riding." He turned and saw my grin. "God, I love it when you smile like that. You light up the whole room."

"Smile like what?" I asked, covering my mouth since I suddenly felt bashful.

"Like I've given you everything you could possibly want," he whispered, staring at me fiercely.

I walked up to him and wrapped my arms around his neck. I loved that he was a good six inches taller than me. I felt so small and dainty when he held me.

He wrapped his arms around my waist, holding me close so that there was no space between us.

His nose rubbed against mine. "What are you doing to me?" His voice was almost pained sounding.

I laid my head against his chest, listening to the steady beat of his heart. I had no answer, because I had the same question for him.

We stood like that a few minutes longer before breaking apart.

"Come on." He entwined our hands together and led me over to one of the stalls. "This is Seraphina," he introduced me to the white horse. "Have you ever ridden a horse before?"

I shook my head.

"You can pet her," he assured me. "She won't hurt you."

I hesitantly reached out to the large horse. She was absolutely stunning. I wasn't afraid of her, not at all. I was in awe.

I placed my hand against the center of her head, above her nose. She snorted and I giggled in response. She came closer, nuzzling her head against my outstretched palm.

"I think she likes you." Jude grinned widely.

"I like her too." I smiled at the horse.

I knew it sounded crazy, but I instantly felt a connection with the creature. Maybe I should've been afraid that I was going to be riding this ginormous horse, but I wasn't. Not at all. I felt comfortable, peaceful almost. I didn't feel afraid or like she'd hurt me.

"Move back," Jude told me, and I hated to stop petting the horse.

He opened the gate to her stall and guided her out. He grabbed an apple from a nearby bag and tossed it to me. "Feed her this while I get Gimpy."

"Gimpy?" I giggled.

"Hey," he said as he started laughing, "don't diss the name. I was five and thought it was super cool."

"Why didn't you name him something like, Michelangelo or Batman?"

"*Because* ..." He walked backward, further into the barn. "Michelangelo is a *turtle* and Batman, well, that one speaks for itself."

"But Gimpy? Seriously, where'd that come from?" I asked, truly curious now.

He shrugged, opening a stall a few down from Seraphina's. "I made it up. I was a weird child."

I let the subject drop before we started talking about messed up childhoods again. I wanted to enjoy our day and not make it an emotion filled mess. After last night, I needed to do something fun.

While Jude got Gimpy—I snickered at the name again—I fed Seraphina the apple. Her breath blew against my hand that held the apple. With my free hand, I rubbed her gently and whispered how pretty she was. I'd always had a connection with animals, but we'd never been allowed to have pets.

"Seraphina was my grandma's horse," Jude explained, walking Gimpy over to where I stood. Gimpy was even larger than Seraphina and while she was all white, he was jet black. The name definitely didn't suit him, but I guessed he was stuck with it now. Poor horse. "She got her three years before she died ... breast cancer." He shrugged, looking down at his shoes. "It was bad. Took her quickly, so I guess there's that. She didn't have to suffer for long." Brightening, he reached out and rubbed Seraphina's body. "If she was alive today she'd still be trying to ride this beauty. She was a stubborn woman like that. She reminds me of someone I know now." He winked at me.

"She sounds wonderful." I smiled. "I wish I could've met her."

"You would've loved her." Jude smiled proudly. "She and Pap ... they're the best people in the world. She would've loved you too, you know." He shook his head and scratched his stubbled jaw as he chuckled under his breath. "She would've thought it was hilarious how you don't take any shit from me. She was feisty." He reached over and played with a strand of my hair. My heart swelled in my chest. "Sometimes I think Pap got Alzheimer's just so he wouldn't have to deal with the pain of losing her. I'm not saying he got it on purpose, not that that's even possible," he stammered. "I just wonder sometimes if God knew I needed Pap to stick around a little while longer, and the man couldn't do that if he remembered she was gone."

"Crazier things have happened." I reached up, smoothing my fingers through his brown hair. It was unfair that a guy's hair was that soft. He even had ridiculously long eyelashes too. He was beautiful, inside and out, and he was mine. I needed to appreciate that fact more and not take it for granted. A part of me was still scared that we'd go back to school tomorrow and this would all be a dream. I was strong enough now to accept that I didn't want to lose Jude.

"True," he agreed. He grabbed my hand, placing a long, lingering kiss to the palm before letting it go.

He went about fixing both horses for riding and then we led them out into the meadow. He tied Gimpy's reins around the fence and reached out for me. Before I knew what he was doing, he had his hands on my waist and lifted me onto the horse. I let out a small squeal of fright. I hadn't expected that.

I swung my leg over the other side of Seraphina and grabbed the reins. I was scared for only a few seconds before I started to appreciate the beauty of seeing the world around me from the back of a horse.

"Wow," I gasped, "this is amazing."

Jude chuckled and started to lead the horse. "I want you to get used to being on a horse before we try riding. Let me guide you and just ..."

"Just what?" I gazed down at him, an emotion I didn't even begin to comprehend filling me when I looked at him.

"Just let yourself feel."

I continued to look around at the green grass, the trees, and the flowers blooming. Spring was here and with it came the promise of new things and new beginnings, like Jude and me.

Eventually, I closed my eyes, holding on tight to Seraphina, and trusted Jude not to let anything happen to me.

A few minutes later I felt him nudge my arm. I smiled down at him and he handed me the reins. "It's time for you to try walking her."

He instructed me on what to do and I listened carefully.

"Okay, try now."

Seraphina started forward at a slow pace. It felt weird at first, almost like I might slip off, but I soon found my rhythm and when he saw I had the hang of it he helped me bring her to a trot.

"You're a natural." He grinned proudly. I was happy that I pleased him.

Seraphina came to a stop and Jude told me to wait while he jogged back to get Gimpy.

The horse and rider barreled toward us. "He's such a show off," I muttered to Seraphina.

She huffed in reply, like she too was disturbed by the display.

Coming to a stop beside me, Jude grinned proudly. I tried to pretend that I was completely unaffected by him, but it was futile.

He pushed dark strands of hair from his eyes and then raised up slightly, pulling his trusty beanie from his back pocket. He put it on and grinned boyishly. "That's better." Straightening, he said, "You think you're ready for this?"

I rolled my eyes. "I'll be fine. If I fall off I expect you to tend to my wounds."

He began to laugh. "Like you took care of mine? Something tells me you wouldn't take too kindly to being slapped."

My cheeks colored. Just when I'd begun to forget that he decided to bring it up again.

"Slapping would not be appreciated," I muttered.

He chuckled. My God, he loved to torture me. "Lucky for you, I'm a real nurse, and I know what I'm doing. You're in capable hands."

"I don't plan on getting hurt," I assured him.

"Hey." He raised his hands in surrender. "You're the one that brought it up. You know what heals scrapes and bruises really fast?"

"What?" I asked.

"Kisses. Particularly *my* kisses. You're very lucky in the fact that you're the only person I would ever suggest this method to. It's quite radical, really. In some countries it's even illegal," he said in a hush, like he was letting me in on something top secret.

"Oh, really?" I quirked a brow as we started to trot down the path.

He nodded. "My kisses save lives."

I snorted, and once I started laughing I couldn't stop.

I finally regained control of myself and wiped tears of laughter from my eyes. Only Jude could make me laugh that hard and over something so stupid.

"You thought that was funny?" he asked.

"Hysterical," I responded, fighting my lips natural urge to quirk up.

His face sobered. "I was serious."

"I'm sure you were." My hands tightened on the reins as I

tried to regain my balance. Riding a horse wasn't as easy as it looked. It took balance and grace. Balance, I had, grace ... not so much.

"Do I need to give you a demonstration of the miracles it can perform?"

I shook my head. "How about another time? Right now, I'd like to enjoy myself."

"Sure, sure," he agreed.

We grew quiet and I enjoyed the peace nature brought.

The birds chirping.

Bugs buzzing.

The clopping of the horse's hooves.

It was all so simple, but it centered me. I felt at home here on the farm with Jude and his grandpa. More than that, I felt like I belonged.

I turned my face up toward the sun, soaking in the warmth.

I was strong enough now to admit to myself that I loved it here and never wanted to leave. I wanted to be a part of Jude Brooks' life for forever. It scared me to death, but it was the truth that lived in my heart. I'd never believed in love at first sight, and that certainly hadn't been the case with us, but something had forced us together—not even my stubbornness could overcome us. Destiny? Fate? I didn't know, and I didn't care. All that mattered was that we'd happened and I was so incredibly thankful for that. I'd fought hard against him and my feelings, but it was a fight I could never win. The heart wants what it wants, and mine beat for Jude.

"There's a field up ahead." Jude pointed, interrupting my thoughts. "I thought we could stop there and sit for a while."

"Uh ..." I looked around us, feeling stupid. "Aren't we in a field?"

He laughed heartily. "Yes, but this one's a bit different. You'll see what I mean."

Sure enough, a few minutes later I did see what he meant.

This field was full of flowers like the other one, but there was a huge pond with a dock. It was surrounded by trees on three sides, but cleared from where we approached. The grass was getting high and in need of a mow, but it was beautiful. A dragonfly flew by my shoulder heading for the water.

"This is beautiful," I gasped. "I didn't know this was here."

"No one does." He shrugged. "It's our property and we don't want word getting out about it. It wouldn't be fun having to chase people off our property every day. Besides, Pap is too old to deal with that crap." Jude jumped off Gimpy with ease. I knew there was no way I could dismount Seraphina with such poise. Luckily, I didn't have to. Jude reached up and helped me down. Once I was off the horse he kept ahold of me, like he didn't want to let go. He stared into my eyes, resting his forehead against mine. "I wanted to share it with you, though. This is my sanctuary." He looked away from me and out toward the water. "When the weather's nice, I spend a lot of time here. It's …"

"Magical," I supplied.

"Not the word I was going for, but it works." He laughed. His thumb found the belt loop on my jeans and we walked forward to the water's edge. "The water is a bit too cold still, but soon it'll be warm enough to swim in. You can even fish."

"Do you normally ride Gimpy out here? It seems like it was pretty far from the farm."

"Honestly, I usually drive my truck out here. This terrain is nothing a Ford can't handle." He winked, pinching my side.

"Poor Gimpy." I wrinkled my nose in distaste at the name. "He probably hates being locked up all the time."

"You really hate that name." Jude's laughter filled the air. God, I loved the sound of it and he laughed a lot. I liked that Jude wasn't afraid to show his emotions, whatever they may be. "Once again, I was *five* and I thought it sounded cool. I don't even know what it's from."

I reached up and tapped his forehead. "It's from this strange brain of yours."

He captured my hand and held it. "This strange brain comes up with some pretty amazing ideas."

"Like what?" I asked, smiling.

"Hmm," he thought. "Well, first there was the vodka-soaked gummy bears I set out that led to the first night I got to sleep with you in my arms. If that doesn't have brilliant idea written all over it, I don't know what does."

"And I also threw them up," I stated.

"That was merely a minor hiccup." He shrugged, grinning crookedly.

"What other brilliant ideas have you had?" I challenged, quirking my head to the side as my lips threatened to turn up in a smile.

He tapped his chin, thinking. "There was the time when I kissed you in the shower ... You know, we should really do that again, for research purposes, of course."

"Oh, yes, of course," I agreed, but he was already talking again.

His voice grew low and gravelly in my ear. "Then there was the night you let me touch you," he groaned, his fingers digging into my hips almost painfully. "God, you felt fucking amazing. *You're* amazing." He nuzzled my neck. My eyes closed as his arms wrapped around me. "I want you in ways I've never wanted anyone else," he whispered so softly I wasn't even sure I heard him correctly, "it scares the crap out of me, but in the best way possible. You tear me apart and build me back up. You make me better without even trying." He looked into my eyes, smoothing his large thumbs over my cheeks.

He lowered his head and his lips formed a seal over mine in a soul-stealing kiss. His fingers tangled in my long hair and I grappled for something to hold, settling on the cotton of his shirt. He kissed me for so long that I began to feel lightheaded.

Panting with loss of breath, he ran his index finger over my bottom lip. "With others, kissing was never enough, but with you, everything is different. It's more important. I could kiss you forever and be a happy man."

"You sure about that?" Leave it to me to have a sarcastic reply to his deeply romantic words.

"Absolutely." He rubbed his nose against mine.

"Jude?" I asked. "What are we?"

He started to laugh. "What do you mean?"

"What are we?" I repeated. "We go back to school tomorrow and I want to know where we stand on our ... relationship." Basically, I wanted to know if I was going to have to watch him fawn over other girls.

He nipped my chin lightly with his teeth, almost as if he was punishing me for my question. "You're my girlfriend, Tate. Don't question that."

I let out a weak laugh. "I'm twenty-two years old and you're my first official boyfriend. I don't know what that says about me." I tucked a piece of hair behind my ear—I couldn't stand it being in my face.

He pressed his forehead against mine. "I'm the same age as you and you're my first girlfriend. I never cared about official titles until you." *Until you.* Those two words were the truth of our relationship. Until Jude I'd never imagined much of a future for myself. Until Jude my heart had been a frozen tundra.

Until.

Until.

Until.

I laid my head against his chest and he wrapped his arms around me, holding me close. I wanted him to heal all the parts of me that were still broken. I wanted him to make me better. But healing took time, and hopefully we had plenty of it.

Eventually, we broke apart and lay on the ground. I curled my body against his as his fingers lazily rubbed the skin of my arm. My eyes began to grow heavy from the heat of the sun and the feel of his fingers. Before I could drift off completely he interrupted the silence.

"You know," he started, then almost seemed unsure if he should continue, "we haven't played our question game in a while."

"Isn't it kind of pointless?" I asked, sitting up to gaze down at him.

He shook his head. "I just have one last very important question."

"All right." I shrugged, settling back down. "What is it?"

"Did I win the bet?"

Of course. I should've known that would be his question. I smiled to myself and sat up once more. I kissed him softly, letting my lips linger against his as I spoke. "You won the bet."

He won the bet.

He won my heart.

He won it all.

I was his.

CHAPTER TWENTY

"I honestly don't know if I'll ever get used to this." Rowan clapped her hands giddily, then pointed to where Jude and I sat across from her at the cafeteria table. "But I'm so incredibly happy you two finally got your shit straightened out."

"Um." I leaned toward her, propping my elbow on the table and my head in my hand. "If I recall, didn't you resist Trent for like ... *years*?"

Her cheeks colored slightly. "That was different." She pretended to pick lint off her shirt to avoid my eyes.

"Mhmm, sure it was," I laughed.

Beneath the table, Jude's hand found my thigh and gave it a slight squeeze. I'd been getting nasty looks all day from the female population. Even in college, there were still high-school-like antics and the women were *pissed* that Jude was off the market. I half expected one of them to grab me by my hair and try to throw me around. Jude acted like he didn't notice, but I knew he did. Even the guys on campus seemed surprised that Jude was holding my hand and we were acting like a ... Well, like a couple, because that's what we were.

I finished my lunch and pushed the uneaten portion over to Jude. I'd discovered the guy was a bottomless pit. He never seemed to get full.

"So," I said and smiled at Rowan, "graduation is in a month, and then your wedding is soon after. Are you ready?"

She took a deep breath. "I'm ready to be married, but not for the wedding itself. I feel so unprepared, and big parties aren't my thing anyway. We're trying to keep it small. But ... that isn't working out so well."

"You have nothing to be worried about," I assured her. "Everyone that meets you loves you. I wish you could see how amazing you are."

"Yeah," she groaned, biting into the sandwich she'd brought from home. "Maybe one day I'll view myself differently. I'm working on it."

I was beginning to think we were all always working on something to better ourselves. We all had our faults, and most of us were well-aware of them, even if we tended to ignore them.

I knew if I was a better friend I'd offer to help her out more with the wedding. But between finals and now a job, it left very little free time, and what time I had I wanted to spend with Jude. I was probably the most selfish person on the planet.

"Hey," Jude asked, rubbing my neck in a soothing manner, "why do you have that angry look on your face?"

I forced a smile. "No reason."

Jude didn't believe me, of course, but chose to ignore it. "Are you ready for your last week of shadowing me?" He asked. "I'll try to make it good for you," he joked with a wink.

He knew something had upset me and was trying to make me feel better.

"I'm ready to be done with my paper," I grumbled. I'd been struggling immensely to get it right. The day in the library where Jude and I went to get ice cream wasn't the first time I'd had to walk away from my laptop out of frustration. I needed it to be perfect and my words kept falling flat. "But I'm going to miss watching you work and interact with the patients. You're quite remarkable."

Jude grinned, then turned to Rowan. "She just likes to look at my ass in my scrubs."

"Do not!"

"Your cheeks are getting red, Tate. And I think—" he leaned closer "—yep, your nose just got a little longer."

My hand shot up to grab my nose, an involuntary reaction. "I'm not Pinocchio."

"Oh, I know you're definitely not Pinocchio." He nuzzled my neck, and then peppered light kisses along my chin and jaw.

"Ew." Rowan wrinkled her nose. "You guys are gross."

"You wanted this to happen," I admonished her. "It's too late to change your mind now."

"Yeah, yeah, yeah," she muttered. "I'm getting what I deserve. The disgusting public displays are worth it to see you guys happy." She cracked a smile.

"Are you happy with me?" Jude asked, playing with a strand of my hair.

I nodded. "Very happy."

We stared at each other for a moment before Rowan interrupted us. "I don't know which is worse, the PDA or staring lovingly into each other's eyes."

I picked up a leftover carrot and tossed it at her. It hit its mark, landing in her hair. She fished it out and dropped it on the table.

"No more complaining." I laughed at her.

She smiled and wadded up her trash. "See you guys later." She turned on her heel and her hair swished around her shoulders as she headed for the door.

"Well," Jude continued as he played with my hair, "we better get to class."

I nodded with a small smile. "Yeah, class."

After spending pretty much every moment with him the last week, it was weird to spend so much time apart. But class was necessary, and after this week I'd see him even less.

Oh, God. I'd turned into one of those clingy girls that never wanted to part from her boyfriend. Damn. What an about-face from who I'd been before. It was strange—especially after spending so long hating him—but once I saw that Jude wasn't the cause of all my problems it became impossible not to fall for him.

We tossed our trash in the closest trashcan and then he took my hand. His was warm and steady, clasping my smaller one. Even when he wasn't trying he made me feel protected.

Instead of going our separate ways, he walked me to class. Even in high school I'd never had a boy to walk me to class. It seemed Jude was making up for both of our lost time.

On the way, we passed the spot where the guy had hit Jude, which led to our first kiss. That was the beginning of the end for me. Although, I thought he probably already had me before then.

Jude released my hand when we reached the building my next class was held in. "See you soon." He lowered his head and lightly brushed his lips against mine. It wasn't even a real kiss, but my body didn't seem to know that. My fingers clasped his shirt and I leaned into him, letting out a soft moan. Jude made me crazy in the best possible way.

He chuckled and removed my fingers from his shirt. He kissed the tops of both of my hands before releasing them.

"Keep reacting to me like that," he leaned forward, growling low in my ear, "and I'll take you right here, right now."

Oh, God. A few weeks ago, I would've slapped him and run away for saying such a thing, but right now ... I was tempted to take him up on it.

"You're not protesting, I like that." He kissed the skin below my ear. "That's progress."

My blood roared in my ears. "Jude," I panted his name.

"Later," he said promisingly as he pulled away.

Immediately, I missed the warmth of his body.

I watched him walk away, a part of me in disbelief that he was mine.

"It'll never last." My head whipped toward the sound of the voice and found a gorgeous girl standing beside me. She had glossy, wavy black hair, dark eyes, and golden sun-kissed skin. "He'll fuck you and leave you just like the rest. It's what he does. And let's face it—" she looked me up and down with a sneer on her lips "—when he *does* settle down it won't be with someone like you."

Knowing she'd made her point, she flounced away before I could reply. I was tempted to run after and claw her eyes out, but I reigned in my anger. She was just a jealous bitch and nothing to me.

But that didn't stop the sting of her words or the pain I felt because of them.

Was she right? Would he leave me?

I'd avoided relationships for this very reason—I couldn't

bear the thought of having my heart broken—but I was in too deep now to turn tail and run.

But she made me wonder, would we get a fairytale ending, driving off into the sunset like those old movies, or were we destined to go up in flames?

"SOMETHING'S BOTHERING YOU," Jude commented as we walked to his truck.

"Just thinking about my paper." Lie. I was still obsessing over what that girl told me. I couldn't seem to get the words to stop playing on repeat inside my head.

"Oh." Jude shrugged. "Stop worrying so much about it. You'll get it right."

I forced a smile, trying my hardest to make it believable, and said, "I hope you're right." I had to play along the best I could. There was no way I was telling him what she told me.

Before either of us could say anything else, my feet went out from under me and I was down on the ground.

Jude surprised me by not laughing. Instead, he quickly bent down to make sure I was okay. "Tatum, are you hurt?" he asked, eyeing the knees of my now scuffed jeans. My hands were red and scratched from the concrete but I was otherwise unharmed.

"Oops, sorry." I looked up in time to see the girl from earlier breeze past us, laughing with her friends. "I didn't see you there."

Jude helped me up and didn't release his hold on me. "Brooke," Jude called after her. His chest heaved violently with barely contained anger. "Apologize."

Brooke paused, her glossy hair bouncing around her shoulders. "Why don't you call me when you're done playing house and then I'll apologize? All. Night. Long." The meaning in her words was clear.

Jude's hold on my hands tightened as he tried to restrain himself from going after her.

With a satisfied smirk, she flounced away with her friends.

Jude finally released me and I rubbed my hands on my jeans to displace the gravel clinging to the palms.

"I've never wanted to hit a woman until now," Jude growled, a muscle in his jaw twitching. "She had no right to talk to you like that." Intense brown eyes met mine.

I dipped my head and muttered, "It's fine."

"No." He lifted my chin. "It's most definitely not fine."

I shook my head. "This was bound happen." I sighed. "People aren't pleased to see the campus playboy settle down. I expected it." Not to this degree, but he didn't need to know about that.

Two confrontations with Brooke—at least I knew her name now—sounded a bit fishy to me. Was she really that desperate that she was purposely seeking me out? Were people that pathetic?

"Here, let me see your hands."

I reluctantly held out my hands for him to inspect.

"Good, nothing's cut. Just a few scrapes. They'll be tender, though." He met my eyes once more. "God, Tate, I'm so sorry."

I shrugged. "It wasn't your fault."

"Yeah, it was."

I suppose, in a way, he was responsible, but I didn't see it that way. "She's just jealous," I replied. "It's not a big deal." I tried my best to play it off. I didn't want him to see how much it affected me.

Jude put a guiding hand against my waist and we started

toward his truck. He hadn't changed into his scrubs yet. I wouldn't tell him, but he was right, I loved the way he wore those scrubs.

He opened the passenger door for me and I climbed inside.

He was quiet as we pulled out into traffic, but then he said, "We have time to stop and eat."

I shrugged. I didn't feel hungry.

"If I recall correctly, I owe you a McFlurry." He chuckled, reaching over to squeeze my knee. He was trying so hard to make me feel better.

"Only because I threw it at you."

"Logistics." He shrugged, pulling into the McDonald's drive-thru line.

He ordered our food and parked the truck. I figured we were eating in the truck, but he hopped out, grabbing a blanket that he kept behind his seat.

I followed him to the back of the truck where he pulled down the tailgate. I saw what he was trying to do and took the blanket from him before he dropped our food. I folded it so it was thicker and then spread it out so we could both sit.

So far, our April weather had been surprisingly warm. It was a nice change from cold, snowy, windy days.

Jude handed me the bag and I dished out our food. Two McFlurries sat between us. Hopefully, there would be no more McFlurry throwing—although, that would make an interesting sport. I could see it on the Olympics now.

"This is nice," Jude said around a mouthful of cheeseburger.

I nodded in agreement, dipping a fry in ketchup.

"Although," he continued, "this does not count as our real date."

"Huh?" I quirked a brow, eating another fry.

"You said I won the bet, which means we get to go on a date. This—" he pointed to the greasy fast food we ate "—is not a proper date."

"It isn't?" I asked. "What do you propose we do then?"

"Not sure yet." He shrugged, his face growing serious, "I've got to think of something good." He took a bite of his burger, staring out at the parking lot. "Are you free Saturday or Sunday?"

"I'm not doing anything." Except staring at my computer trying to write this paper. I should've had it halfway done by now, and this week of shadowing should have been unnecessary, but I only had two paragraphs written and knowing me I'd delete them the next time I opened my word document.

"Perfect." He grinned, bouncing with excitement like a little boy.

We finished eating, and moved on to the McFlurries.

"I have to say," Jude started, "this tastes much better going into my mouth than on my clothes. Do you have any idea how long it took me to lick those stains out of my scrubs?" He didn't give me a chance to reply. "In fact, they didn't come out at all. You, Tater Tot, owe me a new pair of scrubs. Should I tell you my size or do you have an idea? I mean, with as much as you stare at me you should know by—"

"Oh, shut up," I laughed, tempted to flick ice cream in his hair just for the heck of it.

"All right, I'll be quiet, but only because you have this look in your eyes that spells trouble." He licked ice cream from his top lip. "You know, you kind of remind me of a kitten. You look all cute and innocent, but you have claws."

I lightly scratched his arm. "And don't forget it."

"Miss O'Connor, did you just scratch me?" He pretended to

be shocked. "It's like you're staking a claim to tell all others to back off."

"Maybe I am." I smiled innocently.

"That's so hot." He leaned closer and pressed his forehead against mine. "But you don't need to stake a claim, baby. I'm yours."

Why did those words fill me with such relief?

I leaned my head on his shoulder, sucking the last remnants of Oreo McFlurry from the spoon. No one had ever made me feel as content as Jude did. He made me feel calm but I wasn't afraid to let my fiery side out. With him, I could just be ... me.

Jude finished his McFlurry and took the empty cup from my hands. "We've got to go or we'll be late. Go ahead and get in the truck, I'm going to change in the bathroom here."

I nodded as we both hopped off the tailgate. I grabbed the blanket and folded it as he threw away the trash and grabbed his bag from the truck.

I got in the truck and kicked off my flats, drawing my feet up to rest on the dash.

It didn't take Jude long to return. He tossed the bag behind his seat and we headed toward the nursing home.

By now everyone at the nursing home—workers and patients alike—were aware of who I was and didn't wonder why I was there.

Jude grabbed the chart from the receptionist and we headed through the building.

"Hey, Mr. Jenkins," Jude chimed, walking into the room. I'd been shadowing him long enough to know that Mr. Jenkins was his favorite patient, although Jude took the time to know bits and pieces about each of the people he worked with.

"Jude." Mr. Jenkins grinned. "I was beginning to think you

were never coming back."

"And not tell you?" Jude tsk'd. "Never."

Jude began checking over the man's vitals and asking him questions pertaining to that. I leaned against the wall with my trusty notebook and pen in hand.

Mr. Jenkins eyes found me. "You his girlfriend yet?" Before I could reply, the man looked to Jude. "You need to make that girl yours."

Jude chuckled, his dark hair brushing against his forehead. He looked to me, his eyes sparkling and something stirred in my stomach. "Don't worry, Mr. Jenkins. She's mine."

"Good." The man seemed to ease. "I better be invited to the wedding."

Jude and I both laughed at that. Jude turned to me. "Is tomorrow too soon for a wedding?"

"Probably." I shrugged. "And Vegas is a bit too far away."

"Well darn." He hung his head as if he was truly upset with this fact. "Looks like we're not getting married anytime soon Mr. Jenkins." Jude sighed. "I guess you better keep kicking so you can be there."

"Don't worry, boy," Mr. Jenkins stifled a cough, "if the war couldn't take me, this cold ain't, either."

Jude chuckled. "That's the right mindset to have." Turning to me, he said, "Mr. Jenkins fought in WWII."

"You did?" I asked, my interest piquing. I'd always been a closet history dork, even attending the local Civil War reenactments once a year. History Channel was my best friend when I was home alone.

The man nodded. "Yes, ma'am. I was a fighter pilot."

"That's amazing," I gasped. I completely forgot about Jude being there and sat down in one of the empty chairs. I proceeded to ask Mr. Jenkins any and all questions I could think of. I completely forgot about this being Jude's *job*. I was far too interested in learning facts straight from the source.

Eventually, though, Jude had to pull me away.

"I hope I get to see you again," I told Mr. Jenkins, waving from the doorway. Jude's rotation was almost always different, but he tended to see each patient at least twice a week.

"You take care now, sweetheart," Mr. Jenkins voice carried to me as the door closed.

Jude dragged me down the hall, opened a door, and pushed me inside. It was a storage closet. Lovely. He was probably pissed at me for taking so long to talk to Mr. Jenkins. Frankly I couldn't blame him, but—

My thoughts were cut off when his mouth covered mine. My back bumped into one of the shelves, knocking cleaning supplies to the ground with a crash. Jude didn't seem to mind, or to care about the attention it may draw.

He grasped my thighs, forcing my legs around his waist. "You're so fucking hot," he breathed between kisses.

"What'd I do?" I panted, my lips fighting to keep up with his.

"It's just you." He nipped my bottom lip. "You're amazing."

I was still lost as to what had prompted this kiss-a-thon but I decided not to think too much about it and enjoy myself instead.

"Fuck," he groaned, his hips bucking against mine, his hard length blatantly obvious. "I want you so bad. Only you. Only ever you."

We panted and clawed at each other like wild animals. It was like we couldn't get close enough.

I kissed him deeply, pushing forward and taking control. My fingers yanked at his hair and he growled low in his throat. God, I loved that sound.

He let me go and my feet connected with the floor. Then I was pushing him back and this time his back hit one of the shelves.

I'd never been so out of control and uncontained before.

His hands came up to cup my cheeks and he slowed the kiss to more gentle levels. I still knew my lips would be tender and swollen later, but it was worth it and I'd do it again in a heartbeat.

Somehow, my hands had found their way under his scrub shirt and his smooth skin was scorching against my palms.

I couldn't find it in me to be embarrassed, though.

I looked up at him, refusing to let any nervousness show. "I want you," I gasped, still out of breath from our kiss. "All of you," I added in case he didn't catch my meaning.

He kissed me soundly and then took a step back so there was plenty of space between us. "Soon." His tone made me squirm and the sparkle in his eyes promised delightful naughtiness.

We took a moment to straighten our clothes before he opened the closet door and poked his head out. "Coast is clear."

He took my hand and helped me out of the closet—which was now a mess thanks to our escapade.

"You really need to tell me exactly what that was about." I pried my hand from his. The last thing I wanted to do was get him in trouble here, but I guessed it was too late for that, what with making out in a closet.

He shrugged, smiling sheepishly. "It was so hot how excited you got talking to Mr. Jenkins. How could I not get turned on by that?"

"You're something else," I muttered. "I'm pretty sure you get turned on by everything." I stifled a laugh.

He chuckled, a grin turning up his lips. "I will neither confirm nor deny that accusation. Come on, this way." He grabbed my arm, pulling me down another hallway. Gone was the fun and now it was time for him to work again.

HE FINISHED out his volunteer hours and we headed back to campus. I hated to leave him and return to my shitty home life. I really had to get out of there. I was so done with all of it.

"Hey," he said before I got out of the truck.

"Yeah?" I perked up, hoping that maybe he'd decided to make a late-night visit to his grandpa's and wanted me to join.

"The guys and I are throwing a party this Friday ... Well, it's them, not me, that's having the party, but they want me to be there. So, I was hoping you'd consider coming."

"You know parties really aren't my thing." My excitement from a minute ago faded.

"Come on, Tate, I can't fend off the she-beasts by myself."

That was all he needed to say to change my mind. "I'll be there."

He laughed heartily. "I love it when you're jealous. Your face gets all red and your nose crinkles."

"How would you feel about guys flirting with me?" I countered. "I doubt you'd like it very much."

His brows scrunched together and he glared out the window. "You're right, I wouldn't. I'd probably punch them in the face."

I patted his shoulder. "There's no need to go all caveman possessive on me now. You know I can handle myself."

He chuckled at that, his face softening. "Yeah, you're right. You can certainly take care of it on your own."

"I'm glad you have faith in me." Staring out the window at the dark sky and few stars, I let out a breath. "I better get home."

"Yeah," he agreed, leaning over to give me a quick kiss. "See you tomorrow."

"Bye." I smiled, slipping out of the truck. Almost instantly I missed his presence.

I got in my car and gave him a quick wave before backing away and heading home, to the place that had become my prison.

MY DAD WASN'T there when I arrived. I was silently thankful for that.

I forced my mom to eat some dinner and helped her to bed. I once again found myself wanting to yell and scream at her to get her shit together, but I knew it would do no good. I'd long ago given up hope that she'd snap out of this.

After I'd gotten her in bed, I'd showered and worked on my paper for a while. I'd managed to get a good bit done and was quite happy with it. I'd changed the direction of it and I hoped Professor Taylor didn't mind. Instead of focusing on the struggles of being a student in the medical field, I'd chosen to write about the relationships healthcare providers formed with their long-term patients and with each other. How everyone banded together and became a, well, a family.

With this new direction, I was positive this paper would be the best thing I'd ever written.

Now, though, I was trying to go to sleep.

Tap.

Tap.

Tap.

Something smacked against my window.

I sat up and looked around my room as if the answer to the mysterious noise resided there.

Tap.

Tap.

Tap.

Eventually, I forced my tired body out of bed and went to the window. I looked down and saw Jude standing in the yard. When he saw me, he grinned and pointed to himself and then the window. He wanted to come up.

I nodded and then pointed my finger down to let him know I'd come downstairs to let him inside.

By the time I opened the front door he already waited there.

"What are you doing here?" I gasped, still surprised to see him.

"I couldn't sleep. I didn't have my teddy bear, and by teddy bear I mean you, of course."

I smiled at that and let him inside. He looked around, but not like he was taking in the place.

"You know you don't need to worry about my mom," I sighed heavily, "and my dad isn't home."

I closed and locked the door.

He grinned. "So, I don't have to worry about being shot by Papa Bear?"

"No," I laughed. "Come on." I nodded toward the stairs. "I'm sleepy."

He followed behind me and into my room. I closed and locked the door behind us just in case my dad did come home and decided to check on me. The chances were slim but I still wanted to be prepared.

I turned to find Jude grinning at me and then nodding at the closed door.

I rolled my eyes. "It's not for *that*. I wanted to be prepared in case my dad comes home."

His shoulders sagged. "Bummer. Things were just getting exciting in my head."

"I'm sure they were." I laughed, climbing in bed once more.

Jude kicked off his shoes and removed his jeans. He hooked his thumbs into the back of his shirt and took that off as well so he was left only in his boxers. My heart sped up at the sight.

He climbed into bed and wrapped his arms around me, cuddling me like, well, like a teddy bear.

I closed my eyes, wiggling around to get comfortable.

"Woman, if you keep doing that we're going to have a problem on our hands." He tickled my side.

I laughed as his fingers rubbed a ticklish spot. "Stop tickling me."

"You know ..." His fingers skated up my sleep shirt. "I really love the fact that you only sleep in a shirt and panties. It's fucking hot."

"Jude," I groaned, fighting a smile, "go to sleep."

He ignored my words.

"This isn't how I pictured your room," he stated.

I opened my eyes, taking in the pink walls and girly décor. I hadn't redecorated it since I was fourteen.

"What did you picture then?"

"Hmm," he thought, "a torture chamber with chains and whips."

I slapped a hand over my mouth to stifle my laugh. "A torture chamber? Really, Jude?" I rolled over to face him, cradling my hands under my head.

He shrugged. "You did kick me in the balls once and you slapped me when we kissed. Then there was the time—" I cut off anything further that he might say by putting my hand over his mouth. He retaliated by licking my hand.

"Ew." I wiped my hand on the sheets. "You're like a dog."

"Doggie style is one of my favorite positions," he stated flatly.

I rolled my eyes. "Go to sleep. I'm tired and now you're keeping me awake."

He chuckled. "Aw, don't get sassy on me now, Tater Tot. You know you love my wickedly inappropriate sense of humor. It keeps life interesting."

He was right about that.

I snuggled against him instead of replying. He smoothed his fingers through my hair and hummed a song under his breath. It sounded faintly like a lullaby. In no time, I was asleep.

WHEN I WOKE UP, I was more rested than I had been in days.

Jude was gone, and in his place was a note.

Heard your dad come in last night. I wish I could've seen your beautiful face when you woke up.

-Jude

P.S. Look on the nightstand

Immediately, I rolled over and started grinning like a fool. Sitting in a vase was not a single Twizzler like last time. Instead it was a whole "bouquet" of them, and they were even tied together to look like flowers. Only Jude.

The gesture warmed my heart and I knew nothing would dampen my good mood today.

CHAPTER TWENTY-ONE

THE WEEK PASSED QUICKER THAN I WOULD'VE LIKED and I started crying when we drove away from the nursing home.

Jude squirmed in his seat. "Uh, Tate, are you okay?"

The poor guy didn't know what to do with my sudden emotional outburst. I couldn't blame him. Even I hadn't anticipated this reaction.

"I'm sorry," I sniffled. "I don't even know why I'm crying." I wiped at my damp face, trying to get rid of the tears.

He reached for my hand, giving it a light squeeze.

"I'm just going to miss everyone so m-much," I sobbed. "Especially Mr. Jenkins."

"Aw, Tate." He squeezed my hand again, a little harder this time. "You don't need to be upset about it. You can always come visit. They allow volunteers to come in and spend time with the patients."

"I would like that." I rubbed my face again, wiping away black streaks of mascara.

"Good," he said.

By the time we got to Rowan's I'd managed to compose myself.

Trent and Row were coming to tonight's party too, and Rowan had insisted we get ready together

"I'll see you later." Jude leaned over, kissing my cheek. I loved all his kisses, but there was something so sweet about when he kissed my cheek. It was such an innocent gesture, but it made me feel special because I was sure he'd never treated one of his conquests with such tender care.

I didn't bother saying goodbye as I slipped from the truck since I'd be seeing him so soon.

Jude waited by the curb in his truck to make sure I got inside okay.

Before I could open the door, Tristan came running out, screaming, "Jude! Jude!"

I looked behind me and upon seeing the little boy running for him Jude had gotten out of his truck. He let Tristan tackle him to the ground and they rolled around playfully.

The door opened and Rowan poked her head out. "Tristan! Leave Jude alone! He has to go home!"

The boys stopped rolling around and I noticed a few strands of grass stuck in Jude's hair.

"I can stay for a few minutes," Jude told her. Then to Tristan he said, "I have to go home and shower, but we can play for a little while."

"Yay!" Tristan cried, throwing his arms around Jude. "You're the best! Wait till you see the remote control dinosaur Daddy got me. It's so cool." Tristan clapped his hands together excitedly and climbed off Jude's lap. He ran for the door, barreling by me and inside. "Come on, Jude!"

Jude chuckled, smiling as he headed past me after the boy.

Tristan led Jude upstairs to his bedroom, clasping Jude's large hand in his much smaller one. I had to admit, it was absolutely adorable watching them interact together.

Rowan closed and locked the door, shaking her head. "Boys," she muttered, as if that was the answer to everything. Maybe it was.

We headed upstairs to the bedroom she shared with Trent. When we passed Tristan's room we could hear them both making dinosaur noises. I happened to look inside and burst out laughing when I saw Jude impersonating a velociraptor. Day made.

Inside Rowan's room she dragged me to the bathroom and set about doing my hair. She curled my hair and braided the pieces that normally framed my face. She then took bobby pins and secured the braided pieces. I'd been nervous about letting her do my hair and makeup but, so far, she was doing a stellar job. She kept my makeup light and shimmery. When I looked in the mirror my skin appeared to glow.

"Dress time." She took my hand, leading me to her closet.

She searched through the racks for something suitable for me to wear.

"Hmm." She tapped a finger against her lips, thinking. She pulled one out and held it up for my inspection. I shook my head no. "What about this one?" she asked, grabbing another.

It was a pretty pale-yellow color, simple in cut but it would expose the barest peek of my breasts. She turned so I saw the back. My mouth fell open. The back was completely exposed except for a tiny strip of fabric at the top that connected the straps. The length was daringly short.

"Uh ..." I paused, searching for what to say. "I think that's so short my vagina would show."

Rowan laughed, shaking her head at me. She thrust the dress against my chest and I was forced to grab it. "At least try it on. The color would be so pretty with your hair and tan."

I sighed. There was no point arguing with Row. She always got her way.

I went back into the bathroom and closed the door, slipping into the dress. It was a little longer than I thought, but if I happened to bend over everyone would get a flash of my panties. That sounded like a great way to get everyone's attention and be the talk of the town.

I opened the door to show Rowan.

"Ooh! That looks so pretty!" She jumped up and down excitedly. "You have to wear it."

"Rowan," I groaned, tugging on the hem as if by sheer willpower alone I could make it longer. It wasn't working. "It's too short."

"No, it's not," she assured me.

I groaned. There was no way she was going to let me out of the dress now.

"Fine, I'll wear it," I agreed, "but if anyone that's not Jude sees my vagina then you better sleep with your eyes open."

She laughed so hard her face turned red. I wasn't trying to be funny. I was dead serious.

"Oh, Tate, you're something else."

"Mhmm, you tell me that when I'm in jail and you're missing an eye."

She started laughing again.

"I notice your dress isn't this short." I pointed to the pale pink dress she'd changed into. The top hugged her chest and flared out at the hips, stopping above the knees.

"I'm a mother," she answered simply.

I shook my head.

"Let me freshen my makeup and then we can go."

"Lily's already here?" I asked, referring to Trent's mom.

Rowan nodded. "Yeah, and Jude left."

My face fell, but I knew I'd see him soon. Besides, I knew he wanted to get home to shower and change before the party started. However, a part of me had hoped he might wait for me to get ready so we could leave together.

Rowan swiped mascara onto her lashes and a pink gloss on her lips. Fluffing her naturally straight hair she said, "Ready."

We headed downstairs where she said goodbye to Tristan and Ivy. Trent stood in the family room playing with his beloved ferret.

Rowan hugged Lily and thanked her for watching the kids.

It was amazing how easily Rowan had become a part of Trent's family. It had been a struggle on her end, but she'd finally allowed herself to embrace them completely. I knew she was particularly close with Trent's older brother, Trace, who'd helped her through a rocky situation when things had gone to shit between her and Trent.

Trenton put Bartholomew, the ferret, back in his cage and washed his hands. Running his fingers through his black hair he kissed Ivy on the cheek and hugged his son and mom. "Love you guys," he told them. Then he turned his gaze to Rowan. The love between them ... it never ceased to amaze me. They were perfect for each other.

We took Trent's Dodge Challenger again and like last time had to park a block away—and I was wearing heels. *Great*.

We entered the townhouse and my eyes immediately started searching for the only guy I wanted to see. I also steered clear of the bowl of gummy bears. I wasn't going to have an episode like last time.

I separated myself from Trent and Row, moving through the dancing bodies as I searched for Jude.

I squeaked in surprise when a hand grabbed my wrist. I was pushed against the wall before a large body blocked me in.

I smiled, thinking it was Jude. But the guy staring back at me wasn't Jude. Oh, no, because I had the best luck in the whole world I was staring at Tyler, the doucheknozzle I gave my virginity to. He was nothing but a jerk and piece of scum.

My heart sped up—not from fear, but from anger. Tyler was the last person on the planet I ever wanted to see again.

"Let me go." I squirmed against his hold but he was too strong.

"Nice to see you too, Tatum." He grinned, flicking his blond hair out of his eyes.

"There's nothing nice about seeing you," I spat venomously. I knew when he looked at me he could see the hate shimmering in my eyes. I'd never loved Tyler and our relationship had been based solely on sex—and it wasn't even like we'd done it that much—but it had ended on a sour note when I caught him having sex with another girl in his car. In retaliation, I'd taken a crowbar to his prized possession, a Chevrolet Camaro, and left a huge dent in the side. He could never prove it was me, but he knew anyway.

"Still got the same fiery personality, I see." He smirked, lowering his head as if to kiss me. I clawed at his chest, trying to get enough space between us that I could get away.

"Go away, Tyler," I growled. "I don't have time for your bullshit." I wondered why he was even back here. I thought he was away at one of the fancy state schools.

"Why don't we finish what we started so many years ago?" He sucked on my neck.

Oh, he was *so* getting kneed in the balls the minute I could get in proper position.

I decided to give him a warning though. "If you'd like to have children one day, I suggest you let me go right now."

He didn't listen.

I pretended to be giving into his touch so he'd relax his stance.

He believed it.

Idiot.

When he least suspected it, I brought my leg up and leveled my knee with his groin.

And down he went, howling like a wounded animal.

I crouched down and tilted my head, glaring at him. "If you ever put your hands on me again I will press charges, Tyler. I mean it."

He was too busy rolling around on the ground, clutching the family jewels, to pay attention to anything I said.

By now people were staring, and I really didn't care.

I straightened the dress I wore and when I looked up my eyes connected with furious brown ones. I froze in fear, unsure if he was pissed at me, or the crying mess on the ground.

Even in my frazzled state, I couldn't stop my eyes from perusing him. He wore a pair of tan pants with a simple white V-neck t-shirt that clung to his muscular chest and arms like a second skin. His dark hair was still damp from the shower and I itched to run my fingers through it.

He might've been pissed off, but he was still the most beautiful man I'd ever laid my eyes on.

Jude marched up to me and positioned my body behind his. I peeked around his shoulder to see him glare at Tyler.

"Don't you ever fucking touch my girlfriend ever again, Tyler. So help me God I will put you down like a dog."

Tyler didn't have the common sense to be afraid. Instead, around gasping breaths he grinned and said, "Fucking my sloppy seconds now, Jude? Interesting. She's a great lay, isn't she?"

I reached out, grabbing his arm, and dug my nails into Jude's flesh in an effort to hold him back. It was futile. He dropped to the ground and punched Tyler in the face. Tyler seemed to recover from his ball smashing and started to fight back.

Oh, shit.

"Jude!" I screamed.

People around us screamed, "Fight! Fight! Fight!" What was this? High school? Honestly. You'd think college kids would have enough maturity to stop this ridiculous display, but noooooo.

"Jude!" I kept yelling his name in the hope that my voice alone would break through to him.

He punched Tyler in the face and stomach, over and over again. Tyler got in a few punches too. They rolled around on the floor like wild animals.

I knew better than to try to break them apart. I'd only end up hurt in a scuffle like this.

"Jude! Stop it! He's not worth it!"

Either he couldn't hear me or he didn't care. I wasn't sure which.

I tore at my hair, groaning. What the hell was I supposed to do?

I finally looked up and saw Trent and Row breaking through the crowd.

"Oh, thank God," I sighed in relief. "Trent!" I called and his eyes connected with mine from across the hallway. "Can you stop them?"

No one else was going to do anything. Trent was my only hope.

He pushed to the front of the crowd gathered watching the two men fight. He reached down and got ahold of Jude's shoulder. Before he could yank him away Jude got another good punch in. Trent wrapped his arms around Jude, pulling him away from the writhing form on the ground. Jude was like a wild animal, clawing at Trent in an effort to get away.

"Calm down, man," I heard Trent tell Jude.

Jude breathed heavily, nostrils flaring. I'd never seen Jude lose his cool, ever, and he'd completely lost it now and over me of all things.

Tyler clutched his nose, rolling around. "Vuck! Vou vroke vy vose," Tyler said in a garbled voice.

"You're lucky I didn't break everything!" Jude yelled, pointing at Tyler. "Get the fuck out of my house and if you ever set foot in here again, so help me God I will rip you to shreds!"

Someone, one of Tyler's friends I assumed, came out of the crowd and picked him up, dragging him away.

When Trenton was sure Jude wasn't about to go after Tyler he released his hold on him.

Jude still breathed heavily and a bruise was forming on his cheek. Once everyone saw that the show was over the party returned to normal.

"Tate?" Jude turned to me and his eyes were full of worry. He was afraid I was mad, and I was to an extent.

"Thank you," I told Trent before grabbing Jude's hand. Jude said nothing as I dragged him upstairs and to his room.

Just like last time he unlocked the door, and then made sure to lock it behind us so no one could get in.

This time I felt giddy at the prospect of being alone in Jude's room.

I turned on a light and frowned at the bruise forming beneath his eye.

I went into the bathroom and he followed behind me, not saying a word.

I grabbed a washcloth and wet it with cold water since I didn't have access to an icepack.

Jude sat down on the closed toilet lid and I gently pressed the cold cloth to his eye.

"Are you mad?" he finally asked.

I twisted my lips, shrugging. "A little."

"A little is better than a lot." He reached up, putting his hand overtop the one I used to hold the cloth.

"I had it under control," I whispered, eyes lowering.

For some reason, my heart rate picked up at our closeness and the thought of the bed only a few feet away. My body craved his touch. It was like I was starved for him.

"I know you did," Jude agreed, "but then when he said that stuff about you I ... I lost it. Obviously." His shoulders sagged.

"I don't need you to defend me," I breathed. I ran the fingers of my free hand lightly over the side of his face that was uninjured. His eyes closed and a content sigh escaped his lips.

"I know," he agreed once more. He grew quiet and his eyes were angry and dark when he looked at me. "Was what he said true? Did you sleep with him?"

I flinched and that was all the answer he needed, but I still replied. "Yes."

He let out a growl. "I hate him."

"Me too."

"He's a jerk, Tate. Why would you be with someone like him?" he asked, his eyes pleading with me to explain.

I sighed, shaking my head. "I was young and stupid. I wanted to feel cared for. I just picked the wrong guy."

"What happened with you guys?"

I narrowed my eyes. "Is this something you *really* want to know?"

He nodded.

I took a deep breath. "We only had sex a few times, and that's all it ever was. I will admit to being stupid and hoping for more. It ended when I caught him in his car with another girl."

Jude's mouth fell open. "Are you the one that fucked up his car? You are, aren't you?"

I nodded. "Yeah, that was me."

I removed the cloth, dampened it with cold water once more and put it back to his eye.

Jude started to laugh.

"God, he complained about that for *months*. Everyone at school knew about it."

"He shouldn't have messed with me." I shrugged. Smiling, I said, "Pretty girls can be dangerous."

His voice grew low when he replied, "Oh, yes, they definitely can." His hands found my hips, running up my sides and back down to my ass.

"Jude," I said warningly.

"Tate."

The lust in his eyes nearly knocked me down. I knew he saw it reflected in my eyes too. I was trying not to act on it, what with him being hurt.

He startled me into dropping the cloth when he shot up

into a standing position.

"Tate ..." He grabbed my cheeks in his hands, kissing me slowly. "I need you," he breathed when he pulled away. His eyes were hooded and *want* shimmered there. I shivered from the intensity of his look.

My blood roared in my ears. I felt lightheaded and everything around me became sharper, clearer.

I nodded and it was all the answer he needed.

His lips crashed against mine. He sucked my bottom lip into his mouth and then his tongue played against mine. I'd never known a kiss could make you go weak in the knees, but this one certainly did. He backed me out of the bathroom and my legs hit the edge of his bed. I sunk down onto the mattress and he came with me.

I grabbed at his shirt and he yanked it off.

I was glad to have it out of my way.

My hands skated along his chest. His skin was so smooth and warm. His abs were hard against my hands and I found my fingers tracing the indent of them.

Our breaths filled the air and I could focus on nothing else but him. I completely forgot about the party raging around us. All that mattered was this. *Him*.

"Dress. Off," he growled.

Before I could remove it, he did it for me, tossing it off the bed and out of his way. He cupped my breasts in his large hands through the material of my bra.

His eyes were heated and I bit my lip nervously as he stared at my body. I'd never been scrutinized quite like this before. I should've hated it, but with Jude I couldn't help but love it. I felt beautiful beneath his gaze.

"God, Tate. I've never wanted someone like I want you. What have you done to me?" he groaned and, like he was a magician, my bra and panties disappeared.

He didn't wait for me to reply. He wasn't expecting an answer.

His eyes raked over my body and I started to feel shy, wondering if I measured up to the other girls he'd been with.

"You're perfect, Tate," he said, like he knew what I'd been thinking.

His hands roamed over my body going lower and lower.

He parted my thighs and his fingers found me. He let out a hiss. "You're so wet for me. Do you know how fucking hot that is?" His eyes found mine as he slipped a finger inside me.

I gasped, not expecting it, and clawed at the bedcovers.

"I want to taste you," he breathed. A moment later his mouth was on me and I gasped again, even louder this time.

"Jude," I panted his name, my hands flailing. I didn't know what to do or what to hold on to. I was pretty sure I was about to float away. His hands pushed against my stomach, rendering me immobile.

The sensations he created in my body caused sparks to glitter behind my closed lids.

My hips were desperate to move as pressure built in my body.

I could feel the pleasure in my body building to dangerous, soul-shattering levels.

He hummed low in his throat as his tongue lapped against me.

My limited sexual experience had never included this. I'd never believed it could feel this good. But *oh, my god.*

He sucked harder and I came undone, screaming his name. Or at least I thought it was his name. My mind seemed to have turned to mush.

I gulped down air, unable to get enough oxygen to my lungs.

Jude kissed his way up my stomach, over my breasts, before taking my lips with his. My fingers tangled in his hair, holding him to me. There was so much I needed to say to him that I just *couldn't*, so I showed him with that kiss.

His body shook and he seemed to understand.

"Are you sure you want to do this?" he asked, kissing the area where my neck met my shoulder.

"Yes," I gasped desperately. There was no way I wanted him to stop now. Was he crazy?

"Thank God." He kissed me again, sucking on my bottom lip. He undid his belt and kicked off his jeans and boxers.

My eyes roamed over his chest before looking lower. I swallowed thickly. Yeah, I was totally staring at him like a creeper, but I couldn't help myself. He was beautiful everywhere.

I reached out and ran my hand up and down his length. His hips bucked as his eyes closed.

A moment later he took my hands, pinning both above my head. Before I could be hurt by his actions, his hooded eyes met mine. "Later," he promised. "But right now, I need to be inside you."

He reached over to his nightstand to grab a condom. I put a hand on his arm to stop him.

"We don't need one of those," I told him.

His brows furrowed. "Unless you want little Jude Jr. in nine months, then yes, we do." He kissed the end of my nose.

I shook my head. "I'm on birth control. It's fine."

A shiver passed over his body. "Are you sure?" he asked and there was a look of awe in his eyes. "I've never had sex without one before."

"I'm sure." I nodded.

His body shook and he kissed me. He took his time too, memorizing the feel of my lips and tongue. Then, when he knew I was relaxed he slid inside me the tiniest bit. I gasped from the intrusion, fighting to get away. He grabbed my hips and looked into my eyes. "It's okay," he assured me. "We take this slow."

I nodded, swallowing thickly.

He slid inside a little further and I winced. He was too big. This was never going to work. I was pretty sure I was about to be split in half. For some reason, this seemed worse than when I'd lost my virginity.

"Tate," he gasped, like it pained him to speak. "Look at me."

I did.

"Just look at me," he repeated. "It's going to be okay."

I nodded, waiting for him to push in even further. He did, but instead of a little bit it was all the way. He silenced my cry with a kiss and I clawed at his back.

"I won't move until you're ready." He peppered sweet kisses to my jaw.

When I had adjusted to the feel of him, I nodded, letting him know he was okay to move.

He slid out slowly and back in. It hurt at first as he stretched me. My body wasn't used to such activities. It didn't take long for the pain to go away and pleasure like I'd never felt before replaced it.

Sex with Tyler had been dirty. I'd been a girl trying to escape.

With Jude ... it was magic. The look in his eyes spoke of such love that I almost wept. *This* was why you were supposed to wait to have sex with someone you cared about. The difference was astounding.

His movements were slow and steady and once I got the rhythm of it my hips joined his in a sensual dance. He held his weight off of me, but his chest was still pressed against mine. I loved feeling him skin to skin. I felt like I could sink inside him and get lost forever.

Everything about our coupling was slow and sweet. It was nothing like I expected. It was better. Perfect, even.

I came again, crying his name as I clung to his damp shoulders. Tears stung my eyes from the overwhelming sweetness of it all.

A moment later, Jude gasped my name over and over again in my ear as he found his release.

He rolled off me and onto his side.

He pulled my damp body against his and wrapped his arms around me.

His lips found the bare skin of my neck and placed a soft kiss there.

"That was amazing," he breathed, his breath tickling my skin.

"Amazing," I agreed.

My eyes drifted closed and I fell asleep with a smile on my face. With the arms of the one I loved wrapped around me.

Life didn't get better than this.

CHAPTER TWENTY-TWO

When I cracked my eyes open I couldn't help smiling at the sight of Jude snuggled against me. At some point in the night we'd grown cold and ended up getting under the covers.

He slept peacefully beside me, his breath even as it fanned over my face.

I reached out, unable to stop myself, and traced my finger lightly over the elegant slope of his nose. His eye didn't look nearly as bad this morning as I'd expected. There was a little swelling, but the coloring was non-existent. It made me wonder if Jude was used to being hit. If maybe his dad was like mine. He'd said his parents never beat him, but I knew from experience how easy it was to lie.

I chewed on my bottom lip worriedly as I pictured a small Jude, defenseless against his own father.

I never wanted this man to hurt or suffer.

That's what love did to you, and oh how I loved him.

I didn't know when I'd be able to find the strength to tell him. I was still too afraid of rejection—and frankly, it scared me that I felt so much for him in such a short amount of time. But I guess these things can't be controlled. You fall in love when it's right, not necessarily when you want to. It isn't a magic switch you can turn on and off. It just ... happens. Sometimes, it takes time, and sometimes, it happens overnight. I guess, technically speaking, this had been a long time coming for us—if you counted the seven years I spent hating him, and the last year and a half or so he spent pursuing me.

I shook my head free of my thoughts and reached my finger out to touch his lips. They were soft against the skin of my finger and plump. He had perfect pouty lips.

I jumped when he opened his mouth and lightly nipped my finger. I let out a cry of surprise and then started to laugh.

"How long have you been awake?" I asked, hiding my face behind my hands.

"Long enough." He rolled over onto his back and yawned as he stretched his arms above his head.

The sheet dropped down, exposing his chest and I couldn't help but stare and watch his muscles ripple.

"If you keep staring at me like that, Tater Tot, then we're going to have a problem."

I gasped as he rolled on top of me, the heat of his body warming mine.

"I wouldn't mind."

He hummed in the back of his throat. "God, I want you so bad all the damn time. Last night made it even worse." He lowered his head and nuzzled my neck. His hair tickled my skin and I giggled. "You're fucking amazing."

I took his face in my hands and forced him to look at me. "Can we do it again?"

He kissed me in answer.

In no time, he had me all worked up and just when I was ready to burst he thrust inside me. Things weren't as slow as they were last night, but it was still perfect in a different way.

We showered and I got dressed in my borrowed clothes. Out of the bed and in the light of day, I started to feel embarrassed about what we'd done. Jude took my worries away with quick kisses and heartfelt glances.

He led me to the kitchen and told me to sit down at one of the barstools. He then proceeded to make me breakfast.

He was scrambling eggs when one of his roommates walked in.

"Well, well, well, what do we have here?" the guy asked, looking me up and down.

I felt exposed in my revealing dress and my embarrassment returned. In this outfit, it was obvious I'd been at the party—which was long over. So the guy was privy to what Jude and I had done.

"Jacob, stop looking at her like that," Jude warned, despite the fact that he had his back turned to us.

Jacob gasped. "How do you even know I'm looking at her?"

"Because I know you," Jude said, still turned away from us as he cooked the eggs, "and you're definitely looking."

"You haven't minded in the past," Jacob countered, still checking me out. If he kept it up I wouldn't think twice about elbowing him in the gut.

"I mind now."

"I see." Jacob raised his hands in surrender despite the fact that Jude couldn't see him.

Jacob sat down on one of the three stools, leaving the empty one between us.

"I'm Jacob," he told me, grinning cockily. I supposed he

was good looking with his dark almost black hair, olive skin, and green eyes, but all men had lost appeal to me. There was only one that I wanted and he was currently sliding eggs onto a plate for me. Definitely a keeper.

"I gathered that." I propped my elbow on the counter and my head in my hand, giving him a look that said his charm wasn't going to work on me.

"You got a name?"

"Yeah," I replied. "But you don't need to know it." I smiled slowly.

He chuckled, and his hair flopped in his eyes. "I like her," he told Jude. Jude growled in reply, turning to glare at his roommate. "Hey," Jacob laughed. "I said I *liked* her, not that wanted her. There's no need to get so defensive. But I must say, Brooks, it looks like you've finally met your match."

"Go away," Jude growled. "You're getting on my nerves."

Jacob looked at me and shook his head, sighing loudly. "He's such a delight in the mornings." To Jude he said, "I'm hungry. I want some eggs too."

"I'm not your mom, make your own damn eggs," Jude replied.

"You made eggs for her!" Jacob cried, throwing his hands in the air.

Jude pulled two pieces of bread from the toaster and began to butter them. He raised a brow at Jacob. "*She's* my girlfriend. You're just a pain of my ass. I choose not to feed my problems. I find if I do that they just keep coming back for more instead of going off to die like they should."

"Asshole," Jacob grumbled, sliding off the stool. Instead of making eggs, he grabbed a bowl, dumped half a box of cereal in it and grabbed a gallon of milk. "I hope your PMS ends soon," he called over his shoulder to Jude as he left the room.

Jude slid a plate of food in front of me and then sat down a glass of orange juice. "Having roommates sucks."

"Seems like it," I agreed, picking up my fork and taking a bite. "Mmm," I hummed, "this is so good. I didn't realize I was so hungry."

Jude sat down beside me and leaned over to kiss my cheek. "Gotta keep your strength up, because I'm not done with you." His tone held the promise of delightful things to come. My body shook with excitement at the thought of all the things he could do to me.

"Your grandpa taught you to cook," I said as a statement, not a question.

"Pap and Grams." He shrugged. "They said it was important that I not starve to death. Plus, Grams was adamant that she wasn't going to feed me every time I was hungry, which was all the time when I was a teenager." He shoveled a heaping forkful of eggs into his mouth. "Turns out, I kind of like it."

I shook my head, a small smile lifting my lips. "Is there anything you can't do?"

"No, I'm Superman. When I'm not saving the world I make the best damn eggs you're ever going to eat. Now, eat up, woman, we have an exciting day ahead of us and," his voice lowered and he whispered in my ear, "I will have you again today and it's going to be even better than the other times."

I should've pushed him away and told him he was being presumptuous, but I couldn't. Instead, I leaned closer to him, swaying slightly. The effect he had on me was beyond unfair.

He turned back to his food, smirking. Arrogant jerk. He got me all worked up and left me hanging.

I finished my breakfast, feeling stuffed.

"I guess I better take you home," Jude said reluctantly as he gathered up our empty plates to wash them.

"Yeah," I sighed. "I'd like to at least change my clothes before we have a 'real' date." I smiled. I was insanely curious to know what he had up his sleeve but I knew better than to ask.

"You know," he said, turning away from the sink and crossing his arms over his chest, "we could make our date an all-day thing. Well, maybe the day part wouldn't be part of the actual date," he rambled. Frowning, he said, "I'm not making sense. Let me start over." He took a breath. "What would you say to visiting Pap before our date?"

"I'd say there's no other way I'd rather spend my day." I grinned, feeling excited.

"How did I get so lucky with you?" he asked.

I laughed. "Lucky? I'm the girl that kicked you in the balls, threw a McFlurry at your head, and slapped you when you kissed me. Nothing about that sounds like you should be lucky to have me."

His eyes darkened and he sobered. "You shouldn't underestimate yourself so much, Tate." Leaning forward, he placed his hands on the counter and stared into my eyes. "You make me better."

I nodded, losing my voice. Clearing my throat, I finally said, "You make me better too."

He grinned slowly, his brown eyes sparkling with happiness. "Now that we have that established, we should go. But first, I should change. This is hardly appropriate date attire." He plucked at his plain gray t-shirt and pointed to his black sweatpants. I thought he looked lickable but I wasn't saying that out loud. I knew he'd only use the information to torture me endlessly later on.

"I'll wait down here."

"Or," he drew out the word, "you could come upstairs with

me." He grabbed my hand, trying to pull me off the stool. "Please," he begged.

"Nice try," I laughed. "But I know what you have in mind and I need a break."

He sighed and put a hand to his heart. "You wound me, woman." Lowering his voice, he whispered in my ear, "Do you need me to kiss it and make it better? You know I will."

My cheeks flamed. "I'm good."

"You know you liked it," his voice was a throaty growl. "Admit it."

He brushed his lips against my jaw and I'm pretty sure I would've told him anything he wanted just to keep feeling his lips against my skin. "I liked it," I gasped.

"I knew it." He pulled away, grinning. My cheeks stung slightly where his stubble had scratched it.

I stood and headed toward the living room while he went to get dressed. Before we parted, his hand shot out and he slapped my ass.

"Jude!" I cried as he ran away.

His laugh echoed through the hall and down the stairs as he ran up them.

Oh, I was so getting him back for that one. I had to think of something good, though.

I found myself sitting on the couch by myself. Jacob must have gone to his room. I would've turned the TV on but there were about fifty remotes and I was afraid of breaking something.

A minute later, I startled when a half-naked guy walked in. He had shaggy light blond hair, was super tall, and had abs of steel. I was pretty sure he played on the college basketball team.

"Hi," he yawned. He picked up a remote, turned the TV on,

and sat down beside me. Well, not beside me, but on the couch. He was nice enough to leave a body's space between us. "I'm Dylan," he introduced himself.

"Tatum."

"I know," he replied, not looking at me but at the TV, "you're Jude's girl."

I was surprised he knew who I was.

"How do you know that?" I asked.

"I'm his best friend." Dylan shrugged. "He told me about you."

My mouth fell open in shock. First, from the fact that Jude had actually talked about me to someone whom he considered a friend *and* the guy was aware that I was "Jude's girl". As a smart, independent, woman, being called *his* girl should've made me mad, but I loved it. I was also surprised by the fact that this guy was apparently Jude's best friend. I couldn't recall ever seeing Jude talk to this guy on campus. But it wasn't like I made a conscious effort to look for Jude. Nope. Not at all. Okay, maybe I looked for him *sometimes*. Let's face it, even when I hated him a part of me couldn't resist the attraction I felt to him. How twisted was that?

As if conjured by my thoughts, Jude appeared in the doorway. His smile was blindingly bright.

I couldn't help staring at him. He looked strikingly handsome in khaki pants and an aqua t-shirt. He hadn't bothered to shave his stubble, and I thought it served to make him even more ruggedly handsome.

"I see you've met Dylan," he said as he stepped into the room. I noticed he wasn't pissed at the sight of Dylan and me like he had been when Jacob had come into the kitchen.

"Yes," I replied, "we were talking about the fact that apparently I'm your girl now."

Jude chuckled scratching his stubbled jaw. "That's right. Get used to it, because I'm never letting you go." He nodded toward the door. "We better go."

I smiled at Dylan. "Bye."

He nodded in reply. I got the idea he was a guy of few words.

Jude and I didn't speak much on the drive to my house. He did hold my hand the entire way, though. It amazed me how just being near him filled me with serenity. He soothed my broken soul. No, he didn't just soothe it. He mended it.

"Are you coming inside?" I asked him when he parked the truck on the street outside my house.

"Sure, why not." He shrugged, unbuckling his seatbelt.

I unlocked the front door and we headed inside, up to my room.

I closed the door behind us and looked through my closet for something to wear. I eyed what Jude wore and wrinkled my nose. "Do I have to get dressed up for this date?"

He bounced on the end of my bed. "I love how you say that like it's a bad thing, and no you don't need to dress up."

"Shorts okay?" I asked, holding up a pair.

He eyed the length and his eyes glowed. "Yeah, that's definitely all right with me."

I laughed. I took the dress off and tossed it at his head. He caught it easily.

I pulled on a tank top, my shorts, and grabbed a plaid shirt for extra warmth. It might've been spring, but that didn't mean it was warm all the time, and with the shorts I could use the extra layer of clothing.

Jude licked his lips, staring at my long legs. "God, you're gorgeous."

"If you keep telling me things like that I might end up

getting full of myself. A bit like someone else I know." I winked.

He chuckled and leaned back on my bed, resting on his elbows. "There's nothing wrong with being confident."

I walked over to him and climbed on the bed, straddling his lap. He grinned, thinking I was up to something. I really just wanted to see his injured eye up close. I reached out to tenderly stroke the skin and he flinched away from my touch. I frowned. "Does it hurt?"

He shrugged. "Not too bad."

I rolled my eyes. "You don't have to be such a guy. You can tell me if it hurts."

"It hurts," he sighed. Brightening, he grinned crookedly. "Are you going to kiss it and make it better?"

"Maybe." I smiled, and leaned in ever so slowly. I pressed my lips against the tender and swollen skin. His breath hissed out and I immediately pulled back. The last thing I wanted to do was hurt him. "Sorry." I frowned.

"It's okay," he sighed, smoothing his fingers through my hair. "You didn't mean to hurt me." He chuckled, grinning widely as his eyes flicked down. "I really like this position. Your breasts look great from here."

I rolled my eyes. Such a guy.

"Should I say thank you? Or hit you? Because I'm not quite sure."

He laughed heartily, but before he could reply the door to my room flew open. I hadn't bothered to lock it. I hadn't thought it was an issue. I was wrong.

"Tatum!" my dad bellowed. Standing in the doorway, he looked like a raging bull. His face was red, but it was quickly turning purple. A vein in his forehead throbbed, ready to burst. "What the hell do you think you're doing in my house with this boy?" His fists clenched so hard at his sides that the knuckles turned white.

I slid off Jude's lap and stood. He stood up too, positioning his body so that he was in front of me, protecting me.

"Sir—"

"You will not speak!" my dad yelled at Jude. "You are not welcome in my house! Get out!"

I couldn't figure out why he hated Jude so much, I guessed it really didn't matter, I just knew it wasn't for the same reason I'd hated Jude for so long. The man clearly wasn't in the right frame of mind. I didn't understand why he was suddenly coming home so often. It used to be rare for him to come home, and when he did he seemed to time it so he knew I wasn't home. It was like that day he told me I seemed happy something changed in him. Like, if he was still miserable, then I had to be too.

"Sir," Jude repeated, his tone calm. I could tell from his stance and the slope of his shoulders that he was anything but calm. I knew that if it came to it, he wouldn't hesitate to hit my father to protect me. "I'm not going anywhere."

"You're leaving! I'm a lawyer! I know my rights and you need to get out before I call the cops!"

"Then she's coming with me." Jude reached behind to grab onto my hand. He gave it a reassuring squeeze. I hadn't realized it until he touched me, but I was shaking.

My dad's face went from purple to blue. I thought he might pass out from lack of oxygen. He opened his mouth to start yelling again and this time I couldn't mistake the stench of alcohol on his breath. He reeked.

"I want you away from my daughter! You are a no-good son-of-a-bitch from the wrong side of the tracks! *She*—" my dad thrust a finger in my direction "—is an O'Connor! *She* will not end up with a scumbag like you!"

"Pardon me, *sir*," Jude sneered, "but who's the real scumbag here?" He looked my father up and down significantly. "The guy who cares about your daughter? Or the father who's yelling at her and looks like he'd love to put his fist to her face?"

"You!" my dad screamed rearing back to attack Jude. He was drunk, though, and therefore his movements were slow.

Jude beat him to it, tackling him to the ground. My dad was stunned by the turn of events and didn't seem to know what to do with himself.

"Come on." Jude reached for my hand. I gave it to him and he pulled me past my dad who still lay on the ground. He was starting to try to get up, though. "We've got to get out of here."

He all but pulled me down the steps. I couldn't seem to get my feet to move.

I was numb. Lost. Floating.

I didn't know how to handle what had transpired.

Jude sped out of the neighborhood, breaking at least ten traffic laws. "That man," he growled, clenching the steering wheel so tight I was surprised it didn't break off in his grasp, "is a piece of shit. *That's* what you live with, Tate? Why? Why don't you get out of there?"

The floodgates opened up then. "I'm trying!" I screamed at him. I wasn't even mad at him, but my God I needed to scream. I hadn't wanted him, or anyone else, to know how bad it had gotten recently with my dad, but now that he'd witnessed it firsthand I let all my emotions out. "I'm trying my hardest to get away from there!" I started to sob. "I'm trying," I repeated, over and over again for lack of anything else to say. I couldn't seem to stop my tears. My face was soaked with them and they fell from my chin to my shirt.

"Oh, baby," Jude's voice cracked. Suddenly, he pulled the truck off the side of the road. He parked the truck, undid his seatbelt, and pulled me into his arms. My elbow bumped into the horn and the sound of it reverberated around us. The tears kept coming and I was helpless to stop them. He wiped them away with his fingers as fast as they came. He even kissed some of them way, like he hoped maybe his kisses could heal the broken pieces of me. I was doing better, I was, but there always seemed to be something that knocked me down again. "I'm so sorry," he whispered, kissing the top of my head. "Let it out, baby."

I clung to him like he was the only thing holding me up and maybe he was. He was my strength. My rock. He kept me whole.

I tucked my head beneath his chin, my tears dampening his skin. I hadn't cried this hard since I lost Graham. I thought maybe I'd been keeping all the tears bottled inside me all these years. Now, the dam broke free.

Jude whispered sweet words to me, but I couldn't understand any of them. It was like my mind shut down all-together. It was the only way I could cope. It's what I always did: Pretend it wasn't happening. It was so much easier to ignore everything around me than to face it straight on. Maybe that made me weak, but I didn't care.

His lips brushed the top of my head. One of his hands wiped at my cheeks while the other rubbed my back in a soothing gesture.

I gasped for air. This was probably the most epic ugly cry in the entire universe, and Jude handled it as if he dealt with this kind of thing every day. Most guys would have run away from me, screaming their heads off. I was pretty sure it was a fact somewhere: Tears scared guys. But not Jude. He was different. I think deep down I'd always known it, but I'd clung to my hatred of him. I *needed* someone to hate and he became my scapegoat, but now that hate had nowhere to go but to my parents. I could feel the anger rising in my body to boiling levels. It would only take one more interaction with my dad and I'd lose my ever-loving mind.

"Let it out, Tate," Jude whispered, kissing my forehead in a tender gesture. "Let yourself feel."

I was letting myself feel. All of it. All the pain, and hate, and heartbreak, and a million other things I'd kept bottled inside for far too long. I felt it everywhere and it was the most painful thing in the world, but also the most healing.

I pushed away from Jude's arms and was out of the truck before he knew what I was doing.

We were on a back road and there were no cars or people for miles. Just animals, and I wasn't worried about them.

I walked aways, a hundred feet or so, and let my head fall back.

I opened my mouth, and I screamed.

I was doing what Jude told me. I was letting it all out and this was the only way I could truly do that.

I screamed again, because it felt so good the first time.

After another scream, I fell to the ground on my knees, my chest heaving as I gulped greedily at the air.

Jude had gotten out of the truck at some point and his arms wrapped around me.

He was quiet for a moment, just holding me, but finally he spoke.

"Feel better now?" he asked.

I nodded. I couldn't seem to find the words to speak.

"Good." He picked me up bridal style and I wrapped my arms around his neck, leaning my head against his chest. His heart thumped steadily against my ear. I decided in that moment that the sound of Jude's heart was my favorite sound in the whole world. It eased my pain and brought me comfort.

It was kind of funny actually, how falling in love with the wrong person could be the *rightest* thing in the world.

Everything about Jude was made for me and I was made for him. We completed each other in every way.

Jude set me in the truck like I was a doll.

He kissed me gently, as if he hoped his kiss alone could heal me. He looked down at me, his brown eyes full of warmth and caring. "It's okay to be sad, it isn't a bad thing, unless you let it be. When you're sad, you have to remember not to let it eat you up so that you can find happiness again." He traced his index finger lightly over my parted lips. "I used to be angry all the time, because of my parents, but my anger never solved anything. It just made me a miserable person. I don't want that for you, Tate. Don't let it eat you up. Find your happy."

"You're my happy." I whispered.

He grinned crookedly and cupped my cheek, rubbing his thumb against my skin. "And you're my happy."

To others our words might've seemed cheesy, but they were one-hundred percent true. Before Jude I hadn't realized how rarely I was happy. He gave that back to me. No, not just that. He gave me back *me*. He resurrected the Tatum who'd died with her brother. If that didn't make him special—*us* special—I didn't know what did.

I wrapped my arms around his neck, hugging him. He seemed surprised by the gesture and slowly wrapped his arms around me, which was hard since he was still standing outside the truck while I sat inside.

"Thank you," I whispered in his ear.

"For what?" he asked with surprise in his eyes.

"For you."

He smiled. "That's one thing you never need to thank me for, Tatum."

He backed out of the cab of the truck and closed the door. He jogged around to the driver's side and climbed inside.

"To Pap's?" he asked, seeming unsure if I still wanted to go or not.

I nodded. "Absolutely. I've missed that man."

Jude grinned, looking in the rearview mirror before pulling away. "I should be jealous. I'm pretty sure you're using me to get to my grandpa."

I laughed, flipping down the visor so I could check my makeup in the mirror. Wiping away streaks of mascara, I said, "You caught me. I'm in love with your grandpa."

"I knew it!" He laughed, tapping his fingers against the steering wheel to the beat of the song on the radio. "I'm cuter, though."

"Yeah, I'm not so sure about that." I smiled, and it was genuine. "Your grandpa is kind of hot."

He gasped and then we dissolved into fits of laughter.

It was amazing how one minute we could be having a serious conversation, involving buckets of tears on my part, and the next we could be happy and joking. I guessed when you found the right person that's what happened.

I tilted my head to the side, studying Jude's profile. From the slope of his forehead, to the arch of his nose, and down to his pouty lips he was perfect for me. But it wasn't just his looks. It was *him*. I was connected to him in a way I knew I'd never be with anyone else.

I hadn't been looking for *the one*, or anyone for that matter, but love doesn't wait till you think you're ready. It comes along when you least expect it and turns your life upside down. It sends you on a journey of epic proportions and changes the course of your life. It completes you.

WE SPENT the whole afternoon with Jude's grandpa, but when it came to be evening time, Jude made me wait in the living room while he did something in the kitchen.

I was desperate to know what he was up to, but I was sure it had something to do with our "date".

After my cry-fest, things had settled down and I let myself relax and have some fun.

"What's that grandson of mine up to?" Jerry asked me.

I shrugged. "Who knows?"

Jerry grew quiet and I could feel his eyes on me. I wondered what he was thinking.

"Jude is lucky to have a girl like you," he said.

I smiled, turning to face him better. "Thank you. I'm lucky to have him too."

"There's something I want to show you." Jerry stood slowly. His back creaked as he stretched.

"Uh ...," I started. "He might get mad if I leave the room and spoil his surprise."

Jerry waved a hand dismissively. "He'll have to go through me first to get to you. Don't worry."

I couldn't help laughing at that.

Jerry led me upstairs and into his bedroom. He shuffled stuff around on the dresser and looked through the drawers. "A-ha," he cried with joy when he found the box. He smiled proudly as he handed it to me. I lifted the lid and gasped at what I found inside. Nestled in the box was a silver bracelet with a single heart charm on it. "It was my Mae's." He smiled. "She'd want you to have it."

"I can't except this." I thrust the box back into Jerry's hands. "It isn't right."

"Yes, it is," Jerry said adamantly. "I see the way Jude looks at you. You're going to be in this family for a long time and I want you to have this. Please." He tried to hand me the box again, but I refused to take it.

"I can't take this, Jerry." I shook my head, backing a step away with my hands raised. "It was your wife's and I'm just Jude's girlfriend."

"Fine," Jerry huffed, and I thought he was going to put it away. Instead, he tried a different tactic. "Then accept it because you're my friend."

"Jerry," I whined desperately. "The bracelet is beautiful and I'd be honored to wear it, but it's special to you. I can't take it."

He shook his head. Stubborn old man. "Because it's special to me I want you to have it. It deserves to be worn, not sitting in this old box. Please." He handed me the box again and I took it. "It's yours now. I look at you as if you're my granddaughter and I want you to have something special. If it makes you feel better think of it as a graduation gift. You're graduating soon, right?"

I nodded in answer and was about two seconds away from crying again. "Are you sure?" I asked, cradling the box protectively against my chest.

"I'm sure." He smiled, patting my hand.

I set the box down and Jerry looked ready to argue with me again, but he closed his mouth when he saw that I was simply removing the bracelet to put it on my wrist. I stood on my tiptoes and kissed his wrinkled cheek. "Thank you."

He wrapped his arms around me in a bear hug. "You're welcome."

I picked up the box once more and held it carefully. The bracelet jingled against my wrist. I'd never worn a lot of jewelry but the bracelet felt like it belonged.

I started to walk out of the room, but something that had been bugging me for a while forced me to stop. I turned to Jerry and asked, "Do you remember a girl named Julia?"

Jerry's eyes filled with surprise. "I haven't heard that name in a long time, but yes."

"Did Andrew love her?" I asked. I don't know why, but it seemed important to know.

Jerry sighed, scratching his chin. "I'm not sure my son ever loved anyone but himself. Why are you asking?"

"Just wondering." I shrugged. I sucked on my bottom lip and decided to ask one last question. "Do you happen to remember Julia's last name?"

Jerry rolled his eyes in thought. After a moment, he answered, "Hansen. Julia Hansen."

"Thanks." I smiled.

We headed downstairs and found Jude waiting by the front door with a smile on his face. "What are you two up to?" he asked.

I held my wrist out. "He wanted to give me this."

"That was Grams." Jude smiled wistfully, his fingers brushing lightly against my wrist. "It looks beautiful on you, Tate."

I smiled. "Thank you."

Jude started to say goodbye to his grandpa, but Jerry interrupted him. "There's something I'd like to give you too." He nodded his head back up the steps.

"Oh." Jude sobered. "Yeah, okay."

I started to follow, but Jerry said, "Tatum, would you mind waiting down here?"

"Not at all." I smiled. I stood by the door, looking out the window.

They must have been having a long talk, because ten minutes had passed by the time Jude returned. Jude seemed oddly serious, and I worried that maybe Jerry had told him something that upset him. Something told me not to ask, though.

Shaking his head free of his thoughts, Jude smiled. "Date time."

"Bye, Jerry!" I called to the man who stood at the top of the steps. He nodded in acknowledgement, watching the two of us.

Once in the truck, I asked Jude, "Where are we going?"

"Not far," was his reply.

I knew Jude well enough to know that was all he was going to say on the matter.

A few minutes later, he was backing his truck up to the pond. I couldn't help grinning. I'd been picturing a restaurant or the movies for our first real date—something cliché—but leave it to Jude to surprise me.

He grabbed a blanket and hopped out of the truck. I followed.

He put the tailgate down and grabbed a picnic basket. I noticed the bed of the truck was covered in blankets and pillows.

He strolled over and found a spot he liked. He unfolded the blanket and fluffed it, spreading it down on the ground. I kicked off my shoes, grinning.

"A picnic?" I asked, although I already knew the answer.

He grinned. "Was it a good idea?"

"It was a great idea." I smiled back, my body filling with happiness. Only Jude could make me feel this happy without even trying.

I sat down on the soft blanket and he took the spot beside me, kicking off his boots.

"I wanted our first date to be special, something you'd always remember."

My heart swelled at his thoughtfulness.

Looking around the field and the pond in front of us, I smiled. "This is perfect." It was the truth, too. He couldn't have come up with anything better.

"Good." He leaned over and kissed my cheek.

My heart swelled. I'd never known someone could make you feel so ... *loved* without even saying it. But I guess that was the thing, love was more than just the words, you had to *feel* it, because at the end of the day, words weren't everything. They would've been nice to hear, but I knew neither of us was ready. So, for now, I was content in what I felt. Words could come later.

He grabbed the picnic basket and lifted the lid. He placed several different types of sandwiches, bottles of water, chips, and an assortment of fruit. He'd even packed paper plates, napkins, and forks. He hadn't forgotten anything.

I was so incredibly touched that tears pricked my eyes—and after my day, I was a tad over emotional.

Jude didn't seem to mind.

He unwrapped the sandwiches and said, "Those two are turkey and these two are chicken salad, and those two are ham. I wasn't sure what you'd prefer so I thought I'd give you some options."

I reached out and grabbed a plate with a turkey sandwich.

He chuckled. "I thought you might pick that one." He

handed me a small bag of chips and grabbed one for himself. He wiggled around, getting comfortable on the blanket. He set the bowl of fruit between us and handed me one of the forks. "I thought it would be easier if we shared," he explained. He picked up his own plate—one with a ham sandwich.

I took a bite of sandwich, staring ahead as the sun started to lower. Sunset was fast approaching and we were going to get to watch it. Out here, in the middle of a field and surrounded by nature, little things like a sunset seemed magnified. You were able to watch it in all its glory as it was meant to be seen. People tended to get too caught up in their lives and forgot to appreciate such simple beauty. Not Jude. He saw the beauty in everything, and that's why he picked this as our first official date.

"This is so amazing," I finally spoke, breaking the quiet. The sun bathed us in an orange glow.

"I'm glad you think so."

I grabbed my fork and stabbed a grape with it. It popped in my mouth, the juices exploding. Even though our meal was simple, I swore nothing had ever tasted this good before.

I speared a piece of watermelon next.

When my belly was full I gathered up my trash. Jude took it from me and set it in the basket. The only thing that would make it even better was—

"Dessert." Jude grinned, pulling another plate out of the basket. Two large slices of double chocolate cake sat atop it. "I know you love sweet things."

I laughed. "Yeah, my sweet tooth is quite a monster."

He took the Saran Wrap off and grabbed two clean forks from the basket. He set the plate between us, like he'd done with the fruit bowl, only this time he rolled onto his stomach. I mimicked his position.

We ate the cake and enjoyed the sunset. It wouldn't be long till darkness fell.

When the cake was gone—I finished off his piece as well—I asked, "Did you make this?"

He laughed. "I wish I could take credit, but no. I picked up the cake from a local bakery."

"It was fantastic."

"I'm glad you liked it." His voice lowered and his brown eyes darkened. He closed the distance between us quickly and kissed me. He grinned, licking his lips. "You had icing on your lips. I couldn't resist."

I bowed my head, smiling. "Jude?"

"Yeah?" he asked, watching me closely.

"I think it's safe to say this has been the best first date ever."

He grinned, his eyes brightening. "And it's not over yet."

"It's not?" I asked with a surprise.

He shook his head. "Oh, no, Tate, it's only getting started."

I narrowed my eyes. "What else do you have planned?"

He rolled onto his back and reached over, grabbing me around my waist. He moved me onto my back as well, and made sure my body was glued to his without a sliver of space between us. I tossed my leg over his and laid my head on his shoulder. I sighed with happiness and smiled.

The sun was a huge orange ball surrounding us. The air was growing cool, but the light from the sun swathed us in warmth. The flowers around us seemed to glow, as if the sun lit them like a candle. I'd never seen a more beautiful sight.

We didn't say anything. We didn't need to. Just being with each other was enough.

As if sensing that I was growing sleepy—from my full belly and the last of the days' warmth blanketing my body—

Jude jumped up and reached down to pull me up beside him.

"What are we doing?" I laughed.

"Hang on, you'll see." He pulled his iPhone out and music flowed around us. I recognized the song and couldn't help smiling. It was perfect. Jude didn't do anything halfway. He went all out. Even though I already thought our date was perfect, he wasn't done wowing me yet. He grabbed me around the waist with one hand and pulled my body against his. With his free hand, he entwined our fingers together. We began to sway to the music and he sang the lyrics softly in my ear. I closed my eyes, smiling, as I laid my head against his chest.

Happiness wasn't just one feeling. It was many, all combined, and Jude gave me that. I wasn't lying when I told him he was my happy. He made everything better without even trying. All he had to do was just be him. All the extra stuff was icing on the figurative cake—because I ate the real one.

I shivered as the sun went down and the air cooled even more. He stopped dancing long enough to grab the blanket from the ground and wrap it around us.

I looked up at him with heated eyes. What was he doing to me?

We started swaying again and the song changed to another. He sang along to that one too. When it finished, he leaned in close to me. "I'm going to kiss you now."

"'Bout time, Brooks." I grinned.

My eyes shut and he closed the distance between us. He kissed me slowly at first, then more deeply. He took his time, making sure I felt the kiss all the way down to the tips of my toes. He reached up to take my cheeks in his large hands and the blanket dropped to the ground.

His lips moved against mine and mine were more than happy to answer every stroke of his.

Every time we kissed it was exciting and different. He always found a way to make it even better than the last.

His tongue stroked mine and I gasped. My fingers tangled in the soft strands of his brown hair, drawing him closer.

His hand found my neck, tilting my head back. He kissed me slow. Then hard. Then fast. Then slow again. He deepened it, his tongue stroking lightly against mine. If kisses could make you dizzy, then this was one of those kisses.

With a grin, he broke the kiss. He smiled down at me like I was his world.

I squeaked in surprise when he turned me around so my back was to his front. His hand eased up my top and then under the edge of the tank I wore. His fingers stroked lightly against my skin in tantalizing circles. I reached up and tucked my hair behind my ear. He rubbed his nose against my cheek and then I felt his mouth against my ear.

"Want to know a secret?"

I smiled. "Yeah."

He chuckled warmly at my enthusiasm. "You're beautiful."

I reached behind me, wrapping my arms around his neck. I moved my hips to the beat of the song and his hands rose higher.

"You're a charmer, Jude Brooks."

He kissed the skin below my ear. "I'm no such thing."

"Mhmm." I closed my eyes, a small smile on my face.

He lowered his head, nuzzling my neck. His stubble scratched at my skin.

"The sun's going down," he whispered huskily in my ear. "Watch the stars with me?"

I couldn't seem to find my voice, so I nodded in reply.

He turned me around so I faced him once more and my eyes popped open. "I want you to know that you make me want things I've never wanted with anyone else." He swallowed thickly. "You should already know that." He cracked a smile and continued, "But I wanted to say the words out loud. I want you to know that you're more for me." He rubbed a strand of my hair between his fingers. "You've always been different, Tate. I used to watch you in high school and I couldn't believe how beautiful you were and, unlike other guys, I loved your tough girl attitude. You didn't take shit from anyone. You weren't afraid to speak your mind. I've always found that insanely attractive about you. But back then," he smoothed a finger over my cheek, "it wasn't our time. *This*, right now, is our time."

I nodded in agreement. "Our time."

He picked up the blanket and I thought it was to spread it back on the ground, but he didn't. Instead, he draped it over his arm and led me over to the truck. He put the tailgate down and grabbed me by my hips, lifting me up and onto the mountain of blankets and pillows.

I scooted back and found it surprisingly comfortable. He climbed in beside me and lay down on his back, fluffing a pillow behind his head.

We watched the last of the sun creep down below the line of the trees.

The sky became a pretty deep purple before darkening completely.

Under normal circumstances, I would've been scared to death out in the middle of nowhere in complete darkness, but with Jude I wasn't afraid at all. He made me feel comfortable and safe. I didn't fear him and I knew he'd protect me from anything hiding in the dark. I trusted him fully.

He spread the blanket over top of us and I rolled onto my side snuggling close to him. I laid my hand against his chest, rubbing my fingers in light circles over the thin cotton of his shirt.

I felt his lips brush my forehead in a barely-there kiss and then his fingers smoothed through my hair. "You always smell so good," he breathed.

I laughed, raising my head a bit to look in his eyes. "That was a strange thing to say."

"What's wrong with saying you smell good? Isn't that a good thing?"

I laughed again and laid my head down. "Yeah, it's a good thing."

"What perfume do you use? I can't figure out the scent." His fingers rubbed my back.

"I don't use perfume, just my shampoo and conditioner and that's jasmine scented, but I showered with you this morning, remember? So, I guess I smell like you."

His chuckle vibrated my body and without even looking I knew he was grinning. "That's why you smell even better today. I really like you smelling like me."

"Don't get all territorial man-beast on me now." I laughed, pinching his chest lightly and then rubbing my fingers soothingly over the area.

"Me? Territorial? Never," he gasped.

We both laughed at that.

"Tate," he said suddenly.

"Yeah?" I asked, stifling a yawn. Despite the fact that it wasn't that late, I felt exhausted after all of today's activities.

"We're supposed to be stargazing."

"Oh, right." I turned my head slightly and looked up at the night sky. Out here in the country you could see all the stars. There had to be hundreds, or thousands, maybe even more like a million. Regardless, they were stunning in their simplicity. They sparkled above us and almost seemed to be winking.

"Oh! Look a shooting star!" I pointed.

Jude started to laugh and I frowned.

"That was a plane, Tatum." His body shook as he continued to laugh.

"Oh," I mumbled. "My bad."

"You see that star up there?" He pointed.

I squinted, trying to see which one he was trying to show me. "I think so."

"That's the North Star."

"How can you tell?" I asked. I'd never been that into stars and knew very little about them. I wondered why Jude seemed so fascinated by them.

"Because, Tater Tot, I know everything."

I smacked his chest lightly in a playful manner. "That's a shitty answer, Brooks. You've got to give me something better than that."

"What's a better answer than that?" He chuckled. "I really do know everything. I'm kind of brilliant like that. Borderline genius."

"Mhmm, liar." I laughed, drawing random designs on his chest as I looked up at the sky.

"You wound me. My feelings are hurt now."

"Oh please." I rolled my eyes despite the fact that he couldn't see. "I know it would take a lot more than that to get to you."

"You're right," he sighed, sobering. "I grew a thick skin a long time ago."

"I hate that things were so awful for you," I whispered.

"Hey," he whispered, stroking his fingers gently through my hair, "things weren't so great for you either."

"You know," I started, drumming my fingers against his chest, "I think maybe we should try to find Julia."

"Julia?" he repeated in surprise. "The girl Pap thinks you are when he's having one of his episodes?"

I nodded and then said, "Yes. I don't know why, but I just have this feeling like it's important that we find her. It's weird." I squirmed a bit, thinking he'd tell me I was crazy and to let it drop. He didn't, though.

"Hmm." He tapped his fingers against my arm as he thought. "Let's do it then."

"You don't think I'm crazy?" I asked, sitting up. One hand was pressed against his chest and my other against the blankets. My hair fell forward, hiding my face. He pushed it back over my shoulder and cupped my cheek.

"Maybe a little." He grinned and I bowed my head. "How do we even go about finding her? She might not even be real you know."

"I asked your grandpa about her today." I shrugged before lying back down in my previous position.

"You did?" His tone was full of surprise. Obviously, he hadn't been at all curious about the girl named Julia, while I found it to be a mystery I was desperate to solve. Just call me Nancy Drew.

"I did," I replied. "He said her name was Julia Hansen. I didn't ask him anything else." I purposely left out the part where I *did* ask if Andrew, Jude's dad, had loved her. "Of course, she's probably married now, but it's a start."

"Look at you." He chuckled, tweaking my nose. "My little detective."

"Hey," I laughed. "If he's going to think I'm this Julia person half the time then I deserve to know who she is."

"I guess so." Suddenly, he pointed up at the sky. "Look, Tate! Now, *that's* a shooting star."

I gazed up in awe at the light streaking across the sky.

"Make a wish," he whispered.

I closed my eyes, but I didn't wish for anything. After all, I now had everything.

"What did you wish for?" he asked me.

"I can't tell you that. You know that would break the rules."

He rolled on top of me, pining me against the blankets with hands on either side of my head. "You make me want to break all the rules I made for myself," he confessed.

"And what would those rules be exactly?" I asked, tilting my head slightly to side.

He bit his lips, debating what he was going to say next. "I can't tell you yet."

"Can't or won't?" I countered.

"Won't," he answered immediately. "I'll tell you soon, though. When I'm ready."

I nodded. "Okay. As long as you promise not to forget. I'm really curious about all these rules you want to break with me."

"One day," he promised. His face grew serious, his eyes darkening to the point that they were nearly black. "Tate ..." He swallowed thickly, his eyes closing. They opened wide and he took a breath. "Will you make love with me under the stars?"

I smiled, wrapping my arms around his neck and brought him down to the point that our lips were almost touching, but not quite. Before I kissed him, I said, "Do you really need to ask?"

I didn't wait for him to reply. I closed that last millimeter between us and kissed him. He growled low in his throat. Jude initiated pretty much everything between us, but I was discovering that I could make him crazy by kissing him. I think it pleased him to know that he wasn't the only one that wanted this. I wished I could be as open with my feelings as him. I was getting better but I wasn't quite there yet.

So, I'd just have to show him instead.

"Tate," he breathed my name between our lips.

I kissed him leisurely, like we had all the time in the world. I put everything I had into that kiss so he'd *know* how I felt. I needed some way to express the depth of my feelings without saying them out loud.

His fingers found the buttons of my shirt, undoing them quickly. He pushed the fabric off my shoulders without breaking our kiss. It fell behind me.

I lightly bit his plump bottom lip and he let out a moan that had me squirming.

I pushed against him, deepening the kiss. Our tongues tangled together in a dance that only we knew.

My back rested on the soft blankets and my head was cradled by one of the many pillows. His lips broke away from mine and I gasped with longing. I wanted more. So much more.

His lips descended down my neck and he planted kisses over my breasts which heaved with every breath. I couldn't get enough oxygen—no, that was a lie. It was *Jude* I couldn't get enough of.

His fingers found the edge of my tank top. He didn't bother taking it off slowly. It was ripped from my body and tossed outside the confines of the truck bed. Something told me I might never find it, and I really didn't care.

I needed this.

I needed *him*.

"You're all I want." His breath tickled the skin of my stomach with his words. "You're it for me. Please, never doubt that."

Somehow, without even telling him, Jude was aware of my insecurities. But how could I not be insecure when I knew he was a player? No matter the depths of my feelings for him, there was still this nagging voice in the back of my head telling me this wouldn't last. Someone like Jude wasn't made to be tamed, so what made me different?

"I only want you," he continued, pressing soft kisses to my belly. His mouth ventured lower to the skin just above the top of my shorts and my hips bucked involuntarily.

I didn't have a reply. I was pretty sure my brain had shut down entirely and could only process the touch of his fingers and the sensations they created in my body.

He undid the button of my shorts, but I grabbed his hand to stop him.

He looked at me quizzically, his fingers twitching against my shorts as he tried to restrain himself from tearing them off my body. "Tate?" he prompted.

I swallowed thickly and reached out for his shirt. He let go of my shorts and lifted his arms to remove his t-shirt. Yes. That was so much better.

I sat up and kissed his chest, right over his heart and then put my hand over it. I lifted my head and looked into his eyes. We both breathed heavily and his eyes were a heated brown, dark with longing. I couldn't believe he was mine. It seemed surreal. I was so afraid that something was going to come along and rip him away from me. I wasn't sure I was strong enough to survive the loss of another person.

I looked away and said nothing as I went back to kissing his chest. His skin was so smooth and soft, but hard at the same time. He was going to have to let me watch him work out one of these days, because I really wanted to see what he did to get these muscles.

His hands skated up my back, oh so slowly, making me shiver.

He found the clasp of my bra and it fell between us. He pressed our chests together so we were skin to skin. I fit perfectly against him, like we'd been designed to come together like two puzzle pieces.

His lips found mine in the dark and he tilted my head back with one hand. His tongue pressed against my lips and my mouth opened for him.

Our hearts thumped in sync.

He lowered me once more as I fumbled with his belt and then the button of his pants. He kicked them off and then we were both left with only a single garment separating us.

I couldn't seem to catch my breath and neither could Jude.

We hadn't even gotten to the good part yet.

My body tensed with excitement. My legs wrapped around his waist and I pulled him down against me. We both let out a moan.

Something told me this was going to be even better than the last two times.

I rubbed my hands against his back and reveled in the feel of his muscles tensing and flexing as he restrained himself.

He pulled down my shorts and underwear and I lowered my legs so he could slip them off and then returned to my previous position.

His fingers rubbed against me, and my back arched as I let out a loud gasp that echoed through the night.

"Fuck, Tate," he gasped, lightly biting my shoulder, "I don't know if I can wait."

I swallowed and forced my breathing to slow so I could speak. "Then don't."

I reached for his boxers and he growled low in his throat. His eyes drifted closed and his too-long lashes fanned against his cheeks. It filled me with pleasure to know that I put that look on his face. I knew I was relatively inexperienced and I'd worried I wouldn't be good enough for him, but that clearly wasn't the case.

He fixed the blanket on top of us, but with the heat we generated we didn't need it to protect us from the cold. My skin was already feverish and dampened with a light sheen of sweat.

"Jude," I found my voice once more, "please, I need you. Now." I panted like a wild animal, but I couldn't make myself care. My desire to have him was far too great to worry about such silly things.

He growled and nipped at my chin before capturing my lips. I wrapped my arms around his neck and played with the short strands of his hair that reached his neck. He reached down, guiding himself inside me the barest inch. My body tensed at first, still not used to it.

"Relax, Tate," he murmured against my lips and kissed me again, and again, until my body melted and relaxed enough to let him slip inside.

When he was all the way in, he stopped. He grabbed my hips between his fingers, his hold nearly bruising. His head fell back and his mouth parted slightly. He shuddered all over and then looked at me.

"No one has ever felt as good as you. No one," he reiterated. His mouth found my breast and he took a nipple into his mouth. "It was always meant to be you." He said the words so quietly that I wouldn't have believed he said anything if I hadn't seen his lips move.

I nodded my head in agreement.

Jude Brooks was the last person on Earth I'd ever wanted, but there are some things you just can't fight. We were meant to be. I saw that now. Fighting on my end had been futile.

He slid in and out slowly, taking his time. My hips rose to meet his. There was nothing hurried about our movements. We both knew we had all the time in the world.

He sucked on my bottom lip, drawing it into his mouth and letting it go with an audible pop.

He cupped my breasts in his hands as if testing their fullness. Then, one of his hands headed lower and rubbed against me. My hips bucked and I clawed at his back. I couldn't even begin to describe the feelings he generated inside of me. It was like he knew exactly what to do to make my body sing. I wrapped my arms tightly around his neck, my fingers slipping against his damp skin, but I needed something to hold onto, because I was pretty sure I was about to fly away.

His fingers rubbed harder and my body tightened before relaxing. I gasped his name in his ear as I came down from my high.

He murmured something in my ear, but my brain couldn't process his words.

He moved in and out of me torturously slow.

"More, harder, please," I begged wantonly.

"No," he growled. "This is making love, Tate," he panted, "I'm not going to fuck you this time. We'll save that for later." There was a promising tone to his voice and my body shook.

His tongue laved against my neck, leaving a wet streak, and

then he lightly bit the same spot as if he was marking me. I didn't mind the territorial display.

He rubbed his thumbs over my nipples in a circular motion and my body arched back, giving him better access. He knew exactly what to do to make me crazy. He owned me, body and soul.

His mouth took my breast once more and my body clenched around him from the sensations he created. I'd never known I could experience such pleasure.

His jaw clenched and his eyes closed. I rubbed his cheek soothingly with a stroke of my fingers. "Jude," I pleaded, my words a breathy gasp, "look at me. *Please*." I didn't care if it sounded like I was begging. I *needed* to look in his eyes. I had to know if he was as affected by this as I was. I didn't know if I could survive if he didn't feel the same.

His eyes blinked open slowly, like it took a lot of effort.

My gut clenched at the look in his eyes. Oh, yeah, he felt it too.

At the same time, and staring into each other's eyes, we fell apart together as the stars twinkled above us.

Perfection?

I thought so.

CHAPTER TWENTY-THREE

I walked nervously through the back entrance of the cupcake shop. I'd been so consumed by school for so many years that I'd never had a real job. Just the random babysitting gig now and then.

"Tatum!" Lucinda smiled, breezing over to me.

"Hi." My voice shook with nerves.

She seemed to sense it and patted my cheek. "Don't be worried, dear. This job is easy peasy. Come on, let's get you a shirt and hat." She led me over to a closet and opened it up. Inside were several different styles of shirts and a hat like Bryce had been wearing the other day when I came to see about a job.

Lucinda looked me up and down and pulled out a shirt. She'd grabbed the right size. She handed me a hat and pointed to a door. "That's a bathroom. You can change in there and then we'll go over everything."

Inside the bathroom, I locked the door just in case Bryce

was here and tried to pull a prank on me. He struck me as the type to try something—not to be mean, but to have a laugh.

I removed my shirt and put it in my purse before shrugging into the Lucinda's shirt. It was black with pink writing on it.

I pulled my hair back into a ponytail and secured it with an elastic. I put the hat on and pulled my long hair through the opening in the back. I sighed, looking at my reflection. Here I was, about to graduate, and working at a cupcake shop. It wasn't the glamorous journalism career path I wanted for myself, but you had to start somewhere, and I needed the money. When I told Jude about my new job, he hadn't been thrilled about all the time it would tie up, but after experiencing my dad firsthand he knew this was what I had to do.

I opened the door and found Lucinda standing at one of the counters, dropping ingredients into the bowl. Upon seeing me, she wiped her hands on a dishrag and blew her hair out of her face with a breath.

"I thought we'd start you on the register for a while and work your way up to baking. Making cupcakes is an exact science, and until you know how to make them right, it can turn into a disaster." I laughed, nodding my head in agreement. "All right, come on, sweetie." She put a hand on my shoulder and guided me to the front.

Bryce was busy boxing cupcakes for a customer.

Lucinda decided to use this as the perfect opportunity to teach me how to work the register. When the customer was gone she pointed a finger at Bryce. "You. Back. Now." She tossed her thumb over her shoulder.

Bryce bowed his head. "You're so mean to me."

"Well," she called to his retreating form, "if you didn't do stupid stuff all the time, I wouldn't have to worry." Lucinda sighed with her hands on her hips. "I swear, if he wasn't family I would've killed him by now. He's a pain in my—"

"I can hear you!" Bryce yelled from the back and it sounded like a bowl dropped.

Lucinda shook her head, her gray hair falling forward to frame her face.

She took a breath and sobered, going back to my training. She was really nice and took her time explaining everything so that there was no chance that I would forget it.

Soon, she left me on my own. For the first few customers I dealt with on my own, I was insanely nervous and my fingers were clumsy, but I quickly calmed down. Most people seemed to be regulars and took the time to stop and chat with me since I was new.

At the end of the day, I was exhausted. My bed was calling my name, but I still needed to shower and work on my paper. It was due Friday, so there was no time to spare. Thankfully, I knew it was close to completion.

I drove home slowly, a part of me wanting to drive right by and go to Jude's or even Rowan's. I knew with every fiber of my being that I didn't want to set foot in that house. But I did, because it was what I had to do.

My mom was in the living room when I walked inside. Just sitting there, staring off into space.

My dad didn't seem to be home, unless he was in his office and I wasn't going to go in there to check. No way was I going to risk that with the way his temper had been lately.

But not just lately, I had to remind myself. I had to remember that he *had* been like this before. I just hadn't been the one dealing with the brunt of his temper.

I helped my mom up and sat her down at the kitchen table with a bowl of soup I warmed on the stove. I knew she'd eat eventually if I left her alone long enough. It was pretty sad that I couldn't even remember the last time my mom spoke. I knew she wasn't completely out of it, because she could still get around on her own if she wanted, and sometimes I'd find things moved when I knew she was the only one home. But whenever I was around, she just ... *stopped*. It was like it was too much effort for her to function around me.

I went upstairs and showered, changing into a pair of sweats and a tank top.

By the time I checked on her again, she'd eaten. I helped her into bed and turned off the light in her room.

I closed and locked the door to my room when I stepped inside. After what happened with my dad I wasn't going to chance leaving it unlocked again. Lesson learned.

I sat down on my bed with my laptop. I pulled up the word document, read over the last thing I'd written, and began to type. The words flowed easily now and I even found myself smiling as I typed.

After a good hour, exhaustion overcame me. I saved my paper and put my laptop in my backpack.

It took me a little while to fall asleep. I missed Jude's warmth surrounding me.

I FELL into a pattern that week.

School.

Homework.

Work.

Homework.

Sleep.

Finals were killing me and I wanted to curse myself for

getting a job now, instead of waiting till after graduation. At least I'd have almost a month's worth of pay saved up, so that was better than nothing, but it left little time for anything else. I barely saw Jude, which meant I hadn't seen his grandpa in a while and that made me immensely sad.

Luckily, all seniors were in the same boat. Jude was just as busy as me, cramming in as much study time as possible in-between tests.

Jude, Rowan, and I sat in the school's library at one of the tables with papers, books, and computers scattered around us. All of us had dark circles under our eyes and Jude looked like he hadn't shaved since last week. At this point my brain was so dead that I couldn't even remember when I showered last.

I'd gotten my paper done for Professor Taylor and I had two more to finish by next week, on top of tests.

I was pretty sure that when I took my last test I'd immediately fall over asleep ... or dead. One of the two, because I also couldn't remember the last time I ate. And I really needed a coffee. *Someone! Get me an IV of caffeine, stat!*

As if he heard my thoughts, Jude's head rose and he rubbed his tired eyes. "I'm going to Griffin's. Y'all want anything?"

"I'm coming with you!" I jumped up, stuffing everything into my backpack.

"I'm going home," Rowan yawned, standing up and packing her things away as well. "I'm so tired that I keep reading the same sentence over again. This isn't benefitting me. I just need some sleep at this point. See y'all later." She waved, heading away without a backwards glance.

Jude and I headed out to the parking lot, neither of us talking. We were both too tired to form sentences it seemed.

When I turned to head toward my car, he cried, "Whoa," and grabbed my hand.

"What?" I asked.

"You're riding with me," he stated, entwining our fingers together and leading me to his truck.

"I should really take my car," I told him, trying to get him to let go of my hand. "It'll be easier."

He stopped in the middle of the parking lot and looked down at me. "I've seen you barely any this week. Even if we don't talk, I just want to spend some time with you."

How could I resist that?

"Okay." I smiled. I understood where he was coming from. I felt the same way. Being in his presence was enough to make me happy. We didn't have to talk or do anything else. I thought that might be how you knew you'd found the one. It wasn't one single thing that attracted you to them. It was everything.

"Did you finish your paper?" Jude asked as he pulled out of the library parking lot. "The one you shadowed me for?"

"Yeah." I smiled, tucking my hair behind my ear. "I'm really happy with how it turned out."

His gaze flicked to me. "Do you think you might let me read it?"

I shrugged. "Sure." My cheeks started to heat. "I hope you like it."

"If you wrote it, I'll love it. I always love what you write."

"How do you know what I write?" I asked curiously.

Jude chuckled, scratching his jaw. "I happen to find reading the school paper highly entertaining."

"Really?" I asked, my eyes widening.

"No." He shook his head, and dark strands of hair fell into his eyes. "I only ever read the articles you write."

"You're messing with me," I stated, crossing my arms over my chest.

"No, I'm definitely not."

"Name an article I wrote," I countered. I still didn't believe him and wanted him to prove it. I didn't care if he read them or not, but since he claimed to, I was dying to know.

"Hmm," he thought, watching the road ahead of us, "last month you wrote an article about the merits of the plea bargain. Interesting topic choice, O'Connor." His grin was wide when he glanced at me.

"I can't believe you read my articles." I shook my head in disbelief.

"Hey, I might have a pretty face, but I'm not stupid."

"Definitely not," I agreed, not being the least bit sarcastic.

We arrived at Griffin's a few minutes later. "Want to study here for a while?" Jude asked.

"Sure, why not." I shrugged, grabbing my bag. If I didn't study here, I'd study at home since I didn't work today, and I really didn't want to go home. My dad had come home the past few nights, and while he hadn't said anything to me, his glances were chilling.

Jude and I ordered coffee and snacks. I found a quiet table in the back and sat down.

I pulled my computer and notes out, getting ready to study once more.

Study, study, study. That's all I seemed to do lately. Graduation couldn't come fast enough.

Jude appeared a few minutes later with our coffee and food. His grin was nearly infectious as he held the steaming cup of coffee out to me.

I grabbed my coffee from him and took a large gulp—not

caring that I probably scalded my throat in the process. I need the caffeine too much to care.

He chuckled and handed me a cupcake. I'd ordered a sandwich, so he'd added this.

I took the cupcake and devoured it like I'd never eat one again.

Caffeine and sugar? I was a happy camper ... until I looked at my computer and realized I was nowhere near done with my papers or studying. It never ended. At this rate, I'd be thirty before these papers were done and I only had five more days to finish them.

Jude leaned back in his chair, sipping slowly at his coffee. He appeared relaxed. I knew I should probably take a short break too, before delving in once more, but I didn't feel like I had time for that.

Before I had time to start typing, Jude asked, "So ... can I read your paper now?"

"Now?" I blanched. "As in *right now*? Where I have to watch you read it? Uh ..." I'd thought maybe I could email it to him later. I wasn't sure I could stomach watching him read the paper I'd so lovingly worked on. I was terrified that he'd think I hadn't done the medical field justice and he'd hate it.

"Come on, Tater Tot, it's not like I'm going to rip it apart and tell you it's horrible. After a month of helping you, I'd like to see where all that note taking on your part went."

I sighed, knowing no argument on my part would deter him, and brought up the correct word document on my computer. I turned my computer around to face him and slid it across the table.

My heart raced with nerves as his eyes scanned the screen. No one else had laid eyes on my paper yet, and since he was the one responsible, and the reason it took on a new direction, I thought I might pass out as he read it.

It was the longest five minutes of my life.

"Tate?" He slid my computer back across the table to me and a wrinkle marred his brow. My heart stopped and I bit down on my lip to the point that I tasted blood. He hated it. I knew it. "You know how you told me that you wanted to make a difference with something you wrote?" I nodded my head at his words. "I think you've done that with this." He tapped the open lid of my computer. "Your essay is absolutely beautiful." His brown eyes were warm. "Thank you for letting me be a part of this."

Relief flooded my veins.

Oh, thank God he didn't hate it.

He had me really worried there for a minute.

"You really like it?" I asked, needing to hear him say it again.

"I love it, Tate. You couldn't have written anything better." His voice rang with sincerity.

I let out a deep breath I hadn't realized I was holding in. "Thank you," I whispered, smiling bashfully. I always got shy after someone read what I'd written. No matter what I wrote, each paper held a part of my soul. I invested so much of myself in it and always feared that it would be rejected. I understood that rejection was a fact of life, but it's not always easy to handle when it comes to something so personal. "I'm really happy you love it, Jude."

"You know," he paused to take a sip of coffee. "I think you should print it off so I can take it to Mr. Jenkins. He asked me about you every time I saw him this week. He likes you and he'd want to read this."

"I can do that." I smiled, relaxing a bit and taking a bite of my sandwich—I probably should've saved my cupcake for after the sandwich, but my sweet tooth couldn't wait. "I really need to see about volunteering after graduation so I can visit him."

"Yes, you do," Jude agreed, stifling a yawn. "Man," he said as he scrubbed his hands over his face, "I'm so exhausted I feel like I'm starting to see things."

"I know what you mean," I agreed.

"No, seriously, that guy looks exactly like your dad, but—"

I whipped around in my seat to see my dad sitting at one of the tables, chatting with some woman who looked like she was barely thirty years old. He reached across the table, taking her hand in his. I cringed, bile rising in my throat. I turned back around before he could see me. "Yeah, that's my dad."

"Shiiiit," Jude cursed. "I really thought I was seeing things. Honest." He raised his hands in surrender.

"I'm not mad." I sighed tiredly. "I'm just ... done. I'm done with the whole thing. I'm mad at *him*, but not for that." I shook my head, taking a deep breath. "How dare he think he can lecture me on my love life when he's nothing but an asshole and a cheat," I spat.

"Tate ..." Jude said my name slowly, like he knew something bad was coming.

I could feel my anger rising inside me, boiling over to volcanic levels. Oh, yeah. I was about to lose it. It was bound to happen eventually. Too bad it couldn't have happened behind closed doors. Nope, instead I was about to go batshit crazy in public.

"Grab my stuff, and get out of here," I warned Jude.

"What are you going to do?" he asked, his face paling. "Tatum, he's not worth it."

I ignored Jude and picked up my coffee cup. I only had to hope he did as I asked, or I was screwed.

I marched over to my dad and the woman.

I forced the sweetest smile on my face I could muster. "Hi," I said, and both their heads whipped up to look at me. Confusion laced the woman's face, while my dad looked pissed. Gotcha.

"Uh ... do I know you?" the woman asked me. She had blonde hair, but unlike mine it was obviously fake, and judging from the size of her breasts those were fake too. *Great taste, Dad*, I thought to myself, *if you were going to cheat on your mental wife you could've picked someone a little more ... I don't know, real.*

"I'm his daughter." I grinned and nodded my head at daddy-dearest.

"Oh." Her mouth parted and she started spewing out all these silly excuses for why they were together.

"Look." I held up a hand to shut up her insane babbling. "I honestly don't care what y'all are doing, and it's obvious what that is, I just came over to tell my *daddy* that he's an asshole and he can choke on his tongue and die." I smiled maniacally and, before I lost my nerve, I threw my coffee at him. The lid flew off and coffee splattered all over his suit, the table, and Malibu Barbie—that was the nickname I'd given his mistress in my head.

"Bye, Daddy," I sing-songed before running for the door.

Jude stood there with both our bags in his hands, his mouth hanging open. He was shell-shocked.

I pushed his shoulder roughly. "Run!" I screamed.

That got him moving.

We ran as fast and hard as we could to his truck, not daring to look behind us.

When we were in the truck, he locked the doors, and sped out of the parking lot and down the street. We saw my dad standing on the street, chest heaving like a bull, and drenched in coffee.

I laughed until tears ran down my cheeks. "God, that felt so good!" I cried, looking out the back window at my dad's retreating form.

I knew I should've been fearful of how my dad would retaliate, and I would be later, but right now I felt giddy. Almost like I was high.

"I can't believe you did that." Jude laughed too. "Remind me to never piss you off."

I expected Jude to take me back to the library, but he didn't.

Fifteen minutes later, we pulled into the driveway of the townhouse he shared.

"What are we doing here?" I asked.

He looked at me like I'd lost my mind. "Do you really think I'm going to let you go home after that display? You need to give your dad a few days to cool off." His jaw clenched and he stared out the window for a moment before his gaze met mine. His eyes were dark and his face was shadowed with worry. "I'd never forgive myself if something happened to you."

"I can look out for myself," I whispered.

He picked up my folded hand and kissed the top. "You might be tough, Tate, but there are some things even you can't fight. I experienced your dad firsthand. He wouldn't think twice about hurting you. *Seriously* hurting you."

I grew quiet, nibbling on my bottom lip. "Fine, two days tops." I held up two fingers and waved them around. "Then I'm going back home and you're not to say anything. Deal?"

He clenched his teeth and a muscle in his jaw twitched. "I don't like it, but deal."

"I don't have any clothes." I frowned.

Jude's eyes brightened as he grinned. "That is not a problem."

I rolled my eyes. "I don't think you want me going to school naked."

"True," he agreed. "We'll figure something out. I'm sure Rowan would bring you some clothes to wear. Y'all are about the same size. I'm definitely not letting you go into that house tonight."

"Aww, look at you being all protective."

"This isn't a joke, Tatum," he sobered, "he could hurt you."

I bowed my head and my shoulders fell slack. "Yeah, I know." It was easier to make a joke and pretend the situation wasn't as serious as it was.

Jude hopped out of the truck and grabbed his backpack. I did the same, following him inside.

Inside, we found Dylan and a guy I hadn't met yet playing Xbox in the family room. Neither of them looked up when we entered the room.

"You've met Dylan," Jude said, "and that's Grant." He pointed at the other guy. Grant had a sweet face, floppy brown hair, and wore thick-framed black glasses on the end of his nose. "He lives here too." To the guys, he asked, "Where's Jacob?"

"Who knows?" Dylan replied with a shrug, his eyes never leaving the video game.

Jude shook his head and we headed upstairs to his room.

It was only eight o' clock in the evening, but I felt like I could sleep for years. All the studying, paper writing, and the event with my dad had zapped my energy.

"You want to call Rowan?" Jude asked, stripping his shirt

off and working on his belt buckle as he head toward the bathroom. "It's getting kind of late."

I shrugged. "Yeah, I guess so."

I pulled my phone out of my pocket and called her. The shower started and then Jude reappeared, kicking off his shoes and jeans.

His boxers soon joined them in a pile on the floor and I instantly became distracted by his naked body.

"Hello? Hello? Tatum? Are you there?"

I shook my head and turned away. Jude chuckled, knowing he'd succeeded in distracting me.

"Oh, sorry. Uh ..." I couldn't remember why I called. *Oh. Clothes. Right.* "I hate to ask you this, but I was wondering if I could borrow some of your clothes?"

"Of course, but why?" She sounded worried, not curious.

I bit my lip and mumbled, "Um, something happened with me and my dad so I'm staying with Jude for a few days while it blows over. He doesn't want me going home to grab any clothes, so you're kinda my only hope right now."

Rowan laughed. "I'll bring stuff over within an hour."

"Thank you so much," I told her, and meant it.

I didn't know what I'd do without Rowan as my best friend—my only friend, but when one friend was as amazing as her you didn't need anymore.

"You don't need to thank me, Tate, but you're welcome."

We hung up and I tossed my phone on the bed.

I jumped when a hand came around my stomach. I thought Jude had already gotten in the shower.

I was pulled against his body and I leaned my head back against his chest, letting out a happy sigh. He pulled my shirt off my shoulder and kissed the exposed skin there.

My body relaxed against him and my mind began to float

away. It was like with each kiss he took my breath away.

His hands slid underneath my shirt, pulling the fabric away from my body. He pulled it up and over my head and tossed it into the corner.

"Jude." I wasn't sure if I was pleading with him to stop, or to keep going. I guessed it didn't matter.

He drew lazy circles on my bare stomach, still kissing my neck.

His body was warm against mine and I found my eyes closing.

My bra fell to the ground and soon my shorts and panties joined them. I protested no more.

I needed him.

He turned me around so that we were front to front. His hot skin seared the palms of my hands where they rested against his chest.

He lowered his head and gave me a heated look before capturing my lips.

My legs went out from under me and he carried me into the bathroom.

"Screw the shower," he growled as he set me down.

He reached over and turned the water from the shower to the faucet. He reached down and pushed in the plug so the water would hold in the bathtub.

"Girls love baths, right?" he asked, his brows furrowing as if he suddenly seemed unsure.

I nodded, letting out a giggle. "Yeah."

"Good." He moved closer to me, as if he was going to start kissing me again, but stopped himself. "Bubbles. We need bubbles." He looked around the bathroom, coming up empty. "Shit," he cursed. "What's a romantic bubble bath without bubbles?" He put his hands on his hips, unembarrassed to be standing in front of me completely naked. Then again, I wasn't trying to hide my nakedness either. Jude made me comfortable in my own skin. I didn't feel like I needed to hide from him. Suddenly, he snapped his fingers together. "Grant's girlfriend stays here a lot. There might be some in his room."

He started to walk out of the bathroom, but I called him back. "Jude?"

"Yeah?" He turned around.

"You might want to grab a towel." I laughed.

He looked down at himself and grinned. "Oh, yeah. That might be a good idea."

I grabbed one of the fluffy white towels and tossed it at him. He tied it around his waist and it should've been illegal how good he made that towel look.

I closed the bathroom door just in case someone besides Jude showed up, and waited for him to return.

It didn't take long.

"A-ha!" he chanted, opening the bathroom door and holding up a bottle of lavender-scented bubbles proudly. "Found some."

He poured a generous amount into the steaming water and it started to foam. He hung the towel up and reached for my hand.

He climbed in first and I sat down in front of him. He pulled my back against his chest as the water sloshed around us.

"You know what would make this better?" I asked, suppressing a laugh.

"What?" he asked as his fingers glided over top of the skin on my shoulder.

"A rubber ducky."

He laughed heartily at that. "I'll remember that for next

time."

"Next time?" My brows rose in surprise.

"This is kind of nice. We should make it a rule that we take a bath together once a week, sort of like the no pants thing—which I have to add, we haven't done yet. What's up with that?"

"You are ..." I shook my head, at a loss for words. I finally settled on, "One of a kind, Jude Brooks."

"What's the point in being like everyone else?" he asked, leaning back and pressing a hand to my stomach so I went with him. Water sloshed out the side and I reached up with my foot to shut it off before we made an even bigger mess. "I like being me."

I tilted my head back and lifted to place a light kiss on his heavily stubbled jaw. "I like you too."

"You do, Tate?" He grinned, his hands sliding up my body to cup my breasts. "Do you *really* like me?" He gave them a squeeze and I let out a moan I couldn't contain.

I nodded my head.

"Say it," he growled, nipping my earlobe. "I want to hear you say it."

"I really like you," I panted, unable to catch my breath. It was completely unfair that with a few simple touches he could make me want him so much. In fact, it scared the crap out of me just how much he affected me.

"I really like you too, Tate," he whispered in my ear.

Suddenly, his hands were gone from my body and he started playing with my hair. "Let's talk," he said, bringing the blonde strands up and rubbing his fingers against the back of my neck.

"Talk? About what?" I asked.

"I don't know." I felt him shrug. "Anything. I haven't seen

you much this week, we've both been so busy. Don't get me wrong," he whispered low in my ear, "I love having sex with you, but you and I ... we're so much more than the physical."

His words made me feel giddy and I couldn't help smiling. "Well, for starters, I love my job."

"That's great." He started rubbing my shoulders, which were tight with tension from all the stress of the past week. "You should make me a cupcake with gummy bears."

I laughed. "Lucinda won't let me make cupcakes yet, I'm still learning that part, but they don't have a gummy bear cupcake anyway."

He tsked. "That's not cool. Gummy bears deserve a cupcake."

"I'll let her know." I relaxed my head against his chest and lifted my eyes to look at him. I reached up and ran a finger along the strong line of his jaw.

"You do that." He grinned down at me. "And I expect to be the test subject that gets to try every single one until you get it right. Gummy bears deserve no less than perfection."

"Deal." I smiled. "You know, this is really nice."

"I'm glad you think so," he agreed.

"Can you believe graduation is in two weeks?" I asked. "It seems so soon and finals aren't even over yet. I think they're trying to kill us."

Jude laughed. "Yeah, it feels that way. But it'll be worth it when we stride across that podium and get our diploma. It's time to start the rest of our lives."

"It scares me," I admitted, picking up some bubbles and blowing them away.

"What does?"

"Life," I whispered.

He chuckled. "I think everyone is scared of life, at least a little. Although, I think it's less about *life* and more about failing. We only have one chance to live our life and if we don't do it right, it's gone. That's a scary thing to think about."

"I'm scared I'm like my dad." The moment the words left my lips I started to cry as the fear consumed me. I was so terrified of being like him, of hurting the ones I loved, and letting my anger get the best of me.

"Oh, Tate." Jude wrapped his arms around me from behind and more water sloshed over the sides. We were going to have a mess to clean up. "You're nothing like that man. You're stubborn, true, but being stubborn is nothing like being an asshole and that's what he is. But you're so much more than that feisty, tough girl. You're brilliant. And kind. And caring. And loving. And beautiful. And a million other things that make you, you." He lowered his head and nuzzled my neck before kissing the skin there. "You're amazing. Don't ever doubt that. Everyone has faults, but that doesn't make you a bad person."

The tears came harder now and I flipped around so we were facing each other—and there went more water over the side.

I reached my arms up around his neck and clung to him. He wrapped his arms around me and let me cry, kissing the top of my head before resting his chin there.

When I'd cried all my tears, I pulled away and wiped at my damp face.

"Thank you. Thank you for always making me feel better when I'm at my worst."

He reached up and cupped my cheek. "I'd do anything for you, Tate.

Sincerity shown in his eyes and I knew his words were the truth.

"Back at ya, Brooks."

CHAPTER TWENTY-FOUR

The next day was spent going to class and studying. Study. Study. Study. If I never saw another textbook again, it would be too soon. I was tempted to chuck the one I was currently reading from at Jacob's head. I wasn't sure why Jude had thought studying at his place was such a great idea. As promised, I was staying there again tonight, but I swore I was going back home tomorrow. Jude had pouted at me when I told him I couldn't stay there forever. His adorable pouty lip had started to crumble my defenses, but I stood strong.

It was weird, though; while our relationship was new, I couldn't help feeling like I'd known him forever. Jude and I shared a soul deep connection that many never found. It was the kind of connection I'd been envious of Rowan and Trent having.

"Jacob, shut up," Jude slapped his hands against the kitchen table where we were gathered.

Grant and his girlfriend were in the living room and I heard the sounds of her giggles.

Dylan slammed the lid of his laptop closed and thrust his fingers through his hair so it stuck up wildly around his head. "Dude, we're all fucking exhausted. I think we should take a break and go out for a while. I'm so done with this."

"Yeah," Jacob agreed. "We can only study so much, and I swear after graduation I'm throwing the biggest party we've ever had. I need a little fun in my life."

Jude sighed and looked at me. "What do you say? Should we take a break?"

The sensible part of me knew I should keep studying until I fell over, but I honestly couldn't take another minute of it. "Let's go."

"Yes!" Dylan and Jacob high-fived.

We didn't waste any time in leaving. The guys wanted to go to a bar, so that's where we ended up.

I was finally introduced to Grant's girlfriend. Her same was Anna and she seemed nice enough, but maybe a bit of an airhead. Then again, maybe she only looked that way because she was googly-eyed over Grant. I looked over at Jude who sat beside me at the large booth. I really hoped I didn't act like that around him.

The guys ordered a bunch of food, everything from nachos to potato skins to barbeque wings. They dug in and I quickly grabbed enough for myself before it disappeared.

The bar was loud and the crowd was a mix of young and old. Most people looked a little ... rough, and I would've been uneasy if it wasn't for Jude and the guys.

Jude finished eating and wiped his hands on a napkin. Pointing across the room to an area I couldn't see from where I sat, he asked, "Wanna play a game of pool?"

I looked up at him and grinned. "Can we play against each other?"

"One on one?" he clarified and I nodded. "Sure, but do you know how to play?"

I tamped down my smile. "A little. I'm not that good, but I don't want you to use this as an opportunity to rub up on me while you pretend to teach me."

He chuckled. "I'd never do that to you, Tater Tot."

I snorted. "Yeah, right."

"Okay, maybe a *little* rubbing." He chuckled, lifting his thumb and forefinger up a centimeter apart. "But it's only because your ass is amazing."

I rolled my eyes and slid out of the booth. "I think we should make things interesting."

"How so?" He narrowed his eyes, and by this time the guys were listening with interest.

"A bet." I grinned. "You seem to like bets, Jude," I tilted my head to the side, waiting for a reaction. His eyes narrowed.

"Tell me about this bet." He stood and crossed his arms over his chest, his hip leaning against the side. "What do you get if you win?"

"Hmmm." I tapped a finger against my lip. "If I win the game … Well, I'll figure out what I want later. I mean, it's not like I'm going to win. I have no clue how to play this game. What do you want if you win?" I asked.

His lips quirked with interest. "I feel like I'm being played, sweetheart."

I shrugged. "I guess you'll have to play to find out."

He shook his head. "You're up to something."

"Come on, Jude, tell me what you want?" I grinned.

He chuckled, his lips quirking up. "No. If you're not telling me what you get if you win, then I'm not telling you."

"Fair enough," I agreed and followed him across the room to the pool tables. We had to wait a few minutes for one to free up.

Jacob, Grant, Dylan, and Anna watched from the sidelines with interest. Well, the guys did. Anna clung to Grant and looked like she'd rather be anywhere else. I couldn't blame her, the bar certainly wasn't the nicest place, but I was determined to have a good time.

Jude got everything set up and for my first few shots I pretended to have no clue what I was doing to put him at ease. Then, when he felt comfortable, I made quick work of sinking the balls into the nets. He had no idea what hit him.

When I was done I held the pool stick proudly and grinned at his mystified look. "And that, Brooks, is how you play pool."

The guys busted out laughing and clapped at the display. Other people in the bar came to investigate what had happened.

Jude's mouth hung open and he shook his head roughly. "I should be pissed, because you totally played me, but that was so fucking hot that I just want to throw you on this table and fuck you senseless."

I startled at his words. I hadn't been expecting that, but then when I started imagining what he could do to me on that table I got all kinds of excited.

He bowed down, to which I laughed, and then said, "Well, you won, tell me what you want."

"I just wanted to make you sweat." I strode forward and patted his chest as I gazed up at him. "The real reward was seeing your face when I won." Lowering my voice so that no one else could hear, I said, "Although, what you suggested sounded appealing."

He growled low in his throat and grabbed me around my

waist. "That can be arranged." He nipped at the skin where my neck met shoulder.

"Uh, guys," Dylan cleared his throat, snapping us back to reality. With Jude, it was all too easy to forget everything else and only think of him.

I took a step back from him in the hopes that it would clear my head.

I turned to the guys and said, "Y'all want to play teams?"

"Sure," they agreed.

It ended up with Jude and Jacob against Dylan and me. Grant and Anna decided to head out.

We played game after game and I couldn't remember the last time I had smiled or laughed with other people like that. I really liked Dylan and could even see myself becoming friends with him. I still wasn't that fond of Jacob, but he was growing on me. He was a bit of a loud mouth and that tended to get on my nerves.

As we headed out of the bar to return home Dylan put his arm around my shoulders and said to Jude, "I like her, don't fuck this up."

"Not a chance," Jude chuckled. Knocking his friend's arm off my shoulders, he narrowed his eyes. "Keep your hands off my girl."

Dylan chuckled and jogged ahead of us. He turned around to face us, walking backward. "Jude Brooks getting jealous because I touched his girl ... never thought I'd see the day." Dylan winked at me and I smiled back.

We'd gone in separate cars so I counted it as a blessing that I didn't have to listen to Jacob fill every second with the sound of his voice.

In the truck, I leaned my head on Jude's shoulder as he drove.

"Did you have fun?" he asked as headlights lit up the cab of the truck.

"Yeah. Your friends are cool," I yawned.

"Tired?"

"Exhausted," I amended, yawning again. Hanging out with the guys and getting a much-needed break had been fun, but now all I wanted to do was sleep.

He began to hum and in no time, I was asleep.

I was awakened a little while later by Jude grabbing me from the truck and carrying me inside.

"I can walk. I'm heavy," I protested, but instead of trying to pull out of his arms I snuggled closer. Why did he have to smell so delicious? And feel so good? Despite his muscular stature he was really quite cuddly.

Jude chuckled and his lips brushed against my ear. "You're not heavy, Tate."

My body jostled as he carried me upstairs.

He laid me down on his bed and proceeded to take my shoes, pants, and top off. He went to his dresser and grabbed one of his t-shirts. Returning to me, he unhooked my bra and slid the shirt on. He let out a satisfied growl when he stepped back to appraise me.

"My girl, in my bed, in my clothes ... I think we need to make a habit of this." His eyes grew dark with lust.

I laid down, stretching out my legs and drew the sheets over me. Snuggling against the Jude scented pillow I yawned, "Whatever you say." I was too tired to argue with him, and his shirt was so soft anyway that I doubted he'd ever get it back. He'd have to wrestle me for it. Now *that* had *fun* written all over it.

Jude stripped off his clothes and climbed into bed behind

me. He pulled my body against his, and I curled around him, entwining our legs together.

Never in a million years did I imagine I'd be sleeping in Jude Brooks' bed, but I'd guessed crazier stuff had happened.

"I'M NOT LETTING you go inside by yourself," Jude protested when we pulled up to my house.

I unbuckled my seatbelt and let out a sigh at his protective caveman demeanor. "I'll be fine."

"No way." He shook his head, dark strands of hair falling into his eyes. "I'm going in with you, or you're not going in at all."

So bossy.

"Fine." I slid out of the truck.

I pulled out my house key and headed inside. My mom stood in the living room, looking out the window at nothing, of course.

Jude followed behind me and stopped when he spotted her. After a momentary pause, he resumed his pace behind me and said nothing about what he saw. I was thankful for that. I'd already told him enough that he knew how she was, but it wasn't something I wanted to discuss. I'd only get upset ... or angry.

I went into the kitchen first and there he was, sitting at the kitchen table reading the morning paper and sipping coffee. He was the picture of ease and it pissed me off. My fists clenched at my sides.

Jude grabbed my hand, unfurling it and slipping his inside. Once his fingers were wrapped around mine he gave my hand a reassuring squeeze. I took a deep breath and braced my shoulders before squeezing his hand lightly in acknowledgement. I was strong. I could do this. I would not let this man get the best of me.

I sat down at the table across from my father and Jude took the seat beside me. The table was round and the way we sat Jude was between us. His presence alone acted as a buffer. My dad had already expressed his dislike of Jude, but after their last encounter in my room I thought maybe he knew better than to mess with him.

My dad had yet to look up from the newspaper, but from the visible tightness in his shoulders I knew he was very much aware of our presence.

When more time past and he refused to acknowledge either of us, I cleared my throat. "Hello, Dad."

"Tatum." The venom with which he said my name felt like a slap to the face. This was my *dad*—the man who'd read me bedtime stories and taught me to ride a bike. He looked like everyone else's dad. Nice. Normal. *Safe*. But a monster lurked behind his eyes. I'd pretended not to notice it before. It was so much easier to lie to myself than to face the truth, but I couldn't avoid it forever. I knew now that evil didn't lie in obvious places. It was anyone and anything. It hid behind pretty faces as much as ugly ones. It was everywhere and inescapable. "Have you come to apologize after your ... episode ... at the coffee shop the other day?" His tone was calm, but in his eyes, I could see the anger. He flattened his hands against the table, smoothing out a wrinkle in the paper. A single brow rose on his forehead as he waited for my answer. When I refused to speak, he added, "You owe me a new suit."

Beneath the table my hand tightened painfully around Jude's. I wouldn't have been surprised if my fingernails drew blood.

"I owe you *nothing*," I spat—and there went my anger getting the best of me once more. I couldn't control it, and maybe my father couldn't either.

He brought a hand to his face, tapping his chin. Slowly, he turned to look at Jude. "I think this ... young man," he said, and I got the impression he'd very much wanted to say something else, "has been a bad influence on you, Tatie. You used to be such a sweet little girl."

I flinched at the use of my old family nickname. It didn't feel right coming from my dad, not anymore—not after all the damage that had been done.

"I used to be naïve," I countered. "There's a difference."

He clucked his tongue. "The older you get, the more you act like your brother. He didn't know when to keep his mouth shut either."

"Do *not*," I hissed, coming to a stand so fast that the chair clattered to the floor, "talk about my brother like that."

He simply tilted his head, studying me. "I don't think there's a law against me talking about my own son."

I lost it.

Slapping my hand sharply against the table, I screamed, "*You* killed him! It's your fault! He killed himself because of you! You drove him to madness and now you're doing it to me too!" I tore at my hair, ripping some strands from my scalp.

"Tate—" Jude started.

My dad came to stand as well, glaring at me across the table. "Tatum," he growled harshly, "your brother was in a car accident. I had nothing to do with that."

"Yes, you did!" I screamed and it was so high-pitched sounding that I was surprised the glass in the windows didn't shatter. "He killed himself because of *you*."

Tears ran in a torrent down my face. I wiped them away, but they just kept coming.

"You're crazy, Tatum," my dad said in a surprisingly calm tone.

I wasn't crazy, and I was going to prove it.

I ran from the kitchen and up to my room to retrieve the letter.

Jude was behind me, not daring to let me go on my own.

"Tatum," he said once we were in my room and I opened the top drawer of my nightstand to grab the letter, "I think you need to grab stuff and let's get out of here. You can't stay here."

"I don't have a choice," I whispered.

"There's always a choice," he countered.

"What am I supposed to do?" I asked, clutching the letter against my heart. "Live with you? Become your burden? I refuse to do that." I shook my head harshly. "I'll figure it out on my own."

Jude blocked the door with his body so that I couldn't leave my room unless I drop kicked him, which I wasn't opposed to if he didn't move.

"Tate, you don't have to always do things on your own. You have people that care about you. *I* care about you. Why can't you believe that?"

My chest heaved as I struggled to get enough air. I didn't know when I'd ever been as mad or upset as I was now. "It's not about believing it. I know you care about me. I care about you too, but that isn't always enough. I'm not your responsibility."

"I want you to be, dammit!" he screamed. "Why do you have to be so fucking stubborn that you can't see what's standing right in front of you?!"

"And what's standing right in front of me, Jude? Enlighten me, please." I crossed my arms over my chest.

"A guy that cares about you so much that it scares him more than anything. A guy that only wants the best for you, no matter what that is. A guy that wants to protect you. A guy that just wants your heart," he whispered the last part, bowing his head.

"Jude," I begged, "please, don't do this. I can't hear this right now. I just can't."

He sighed and stepped away from the door. "I wish you'd stop being afraid of your own feelings," he groaned. "They're not going to blow up in your face."

I started out the door and turned back to face him. "I don't know that. There's no guarantee that someone else won't catch your interest tomorrow and I'll become a distant memory to you. You told me I had to save myself, and that's what I'm trying to do. I'm trying to be a better, stronger person. I'm trying to find *me*, before I allow myself to depend on someone else." I waved a hand at him. "Look at my family—" I spread my arms wide. "They've done nothing but let me down. I've been hurt, deeply. Please," I begged, "*please*, don't be mad at me for this, but I can't do this right now."

"It's not like you'd have to live with me forever," he whispered, "not if you didn't want to. It could be a temporary thing until you got your own place, or you could stay if you wanted. It would all be up to *you*. But you have to get out of this house, Tate. It's toxic. It's killing you, can't you see that?"

I nodded. "I know, but I can't leave yet."

His jaw clenched and he mumbled something about me being too stubborn for my own good. He was probably right.

I headed back downstairs and Jude followed. I half expected my dad to have left, but he was still there.

I threw the letter at him and warned, "So help me God if you ruin that letter I will kill you slowly and painfully."

Jude chuckled behind me, but I was dead serious. That letter was my last tie to my brother and I wouldn't let him destroy it.

He picked it up carefully and ran his fingers over the now yellowed pages. His eyes scanned every word, and then went back to read it again, and again.

"No," he whispered putting the letter down on the table. "No," he repeated, shaking his head.

His eyes were troubled and for the first time in a long time he looked human. There wasn't an angry snarl on his face, or a fake smile. Just ... shock.

"No," he whispered yet again. He pulled the chair out and sat down once more. "I ... I can't believe this. What have I done?"

"Believe it," I snapped.

He put his head in his hands and sobbed. Like gut-wrenching, body shaking, *sobs*.

I couldn't believe my eyes.

I even rubbed them and blinked several times to make sure it wasn't a mirage.

Nope.

The man was crying.

I hadn't heard him cry since the night the cops showed up to tell us Graham was dead.

I stood shell-shocked, clueless as to what I should do.

Jude came up behind me and wrapped his arms around me, laying his head on top of mine.

Minutes passed before my dad wiped his eyes and lifted his head to look at me. "I'm so sorry, Tatie."

An apology.

I hadn't expected that at all.

I didn't know what to do, so I nodded my head and that seemed to be enough for him.

He stood and pushed the chair into the table. He handed me back the letter and said, "I need a minute. Excuse me." He passed by us and headed down the hall to where his office sat.

Jude guided me into the living room and sat me down. My mom had moved from the window to one of the chairs and now stared at the ceiling.

I clutched the letter tightly between my fists like it was the only thing keeping me from falling to pieces.

Jude sat down beside me and brought my body into his arms. I wrapped mine around his neck. I didn't cry. I wasn't sure there were any tears left in me at this point, but I needed to be held. I needed the comfort another person's arms provided.

Jude murmured sweet things in my ear, but I couldn't comprehend any of them. I was in a state of shock from the events that had transpired. He rubbed my back soothingly, but the gesture did nothing to calm me.

From where I sat on his lap I could see my father approach.

I stood up hastily and smoothed down my shirt, just to have something to do with my hands. I felt fidgety and nervous. I had no idea what to expect from him, because his reaction hadn't been anything like I anticipated.

He stood in the doorway for a moment, rubbing his jaw absentmindedly.

Jude stood beside me and took my hand in a show of solidarity. He wasn't going anywhere, no matter what was said.

My dad nodded slowly, as if he was agreeing with his thoughts. He brought his head up and his eyes connected with my own. He took a deep breath before speaking. "I ... I ..." He seemed at a loss for words. "My anger has always been an issue for me, from the time I was a boy. I had good days, and bad days ... very bad days," he added, his voice dropping low. I was surprised by how calm he sounded, compared to all the yelling we'd done earlier. "Your brother's letter ... God, I can't even tell you what I felt reading that." He pinched the bridge of his nose. "It was a much-needed wake up call, I can tell you that much. I need help," he whispered, his eyes lowering. "I'm going to get help," he added with surety. He turned his head toward my mom. "I'm going to see what I can do for her too." Scratching his jaw, he said, "I don't really know what to say to you, Tate, except I'm sorry and I know that will never be good enough. Not for what happened with Graham, or what I've done to you, but I hope one day you can find it in your heart to forgive me."

My mouth fell open in shock. Was this a dream? He was going to try to get help?

"Wow, um—"

"You don't need to say anything." He shrugged, cutting me off. "I just wanted you to know. I already found a place, while I was on my computer, and I'm going to be checking in there tonight. It's sort of like rehab, but for people like me." He turned to leave and then stopped, turning back. His eyes grew sad. "I know you don't want to hear this, and hell, you might not even believe me, but I love you."

With that, he walked out of the room and back to his office.

"Tate?" Jude said my name softly.

I looked up at him with wide eyes. "Did that really just happen?"

"It really did," he assured me.

"Maybe ... maybe things will get better now?" I meant it as a statement, but it came out sounding like a question. I looked up at him with pleading eyes. I felt like a small child, needing someone to reassure me.

"Maybe." But the tone of his voice said that he didn't think so.

I had to hold on to hope, because somewhere inside me was a small little girl desperate to have her mom and dad back. I had to believe it would all be okay.

CHAPTER TWENTY-FIVE

The next week went by faster than I thought possible.

I stood in front of the mirror, staring at my reflection.

I'd waited my whole life for this one moment.

The moment I'd stride across the stage, grab my diploma, and become a college graduate.

From this moment on, I was out in the real world.

There was no more messing around.

This was the first day of the rest of my life.

I reached up and adjusted the black cap so that it sat straight on top of my head. I took a deep, steadying breath.

"You did it, Tate," I said to my reflection, forcing a smile.

Despite my excitement for graduation, I also felt an overwhelming sadness.

Anytime I'd pictured this day, my mom, dad, and brother were there in the audience cheering me on.

No one would be there for me today.

My mom was currently off somewhere getting counseling—I doubted it would help, though.

My dad was in anger management.

And my brother was dead.

I was all alone in this world.

Except for my friends and Jude.

Thank God for them.

I took the cap off and smoothed my hair down. I had to get to campus before I was late.

On my way out, I stopped in the doorway of Graham's room. I closed my eyes and took a deep breath, picturing him as I remembered. I hoped that wherever he was that he was watching over me today. I needed him to be there.

Opening my eyes, I said, "I love you, Graham."

Warmth filled my body, and maybe it was crazy, but I *knew* he was giving me a sign that he was there.

When I got to campus I texted Jude and he let me know where he was. When I found him, he stood with his roommates—who were also graduating—and Rowan. Trent was nowhere to be seen and I figured he'd already taken the kids and sat down for the ceremony.

"Hey, guys." I smiled as I approached. Despite my sadness, I refused to let that ruin my day. Today was meant for celebrating and that's what we were going to do—or at least that's what Jacob kept saying. He swore the party he and the guys were throwing tonight was going to be epic.

"Well, if it isn't my favorite girl." Dylan grabbed me around the waist and spun me around.

"Put her down," Jude growled warningly. "I won't hesitate to punch you."

Dylan chuckled and set me down. He whispered in my ear,

"He's just afraid you're going to wake up one day and realize you like me more."

"Shut up," Jude seethed, having heard what his friend said.

Dylan laughed and ran away. Jude didn't bother to run after him.

I'd discovered Dylan loved to get Jude riled up over me. I thought it might've become Dylan's new favorite hobby, and I had to admit that Jude's overreactions were often comical.

"He's pissing me off," Jude muttered, bringing me against his side.

I laughed, smiling up at him. "He's your best friend. He just likes to mess with you."

"Yeah, well two can play that game." Jude looked off into the distance where Dylan had disappeared. "Don't be surprised if he's sporting blue hair one day."

"Blue hair?" I asked, suppressing another laugh and failing. Leave it to the guys to make me feel better when I was having such a shitty day.

"Yeah." Jude nodded. "I'm putting hair dye in his shampoo tonight for that one. I think blue would be fitting."

"Pink would be better," I told him.

He chuckled, his eyes lightening. "I love the way you think. Pink it is."

"You're not really going to dye his hair?" I sobered.

Jude shrugged. "Just act surprised."

"Jude!" I shrieked, giving him a light smack against his ribs. "You better not."

He shrugged and mumbled, "He deserves it."

Oh, good Lord.

"You're terrible."

"Hey." He let go of me, raising his hands innocently. "The fucker is asking for it."

Rowan laughed, shaking her head at us. "You two are too much sometimes."

"What's that supposed to mean?" I asked.

She shrugged lightly, combing her fingers through her long, light brown hair. "Just that you two are absolutely perfect for each other. It's kinda creepy."

Jude chuckled and kissed the top of my head. "I bet you're regretting pushing us together now, aren't you?"

"Not at all." She smiled.

They called for us to start lining up, and my heart jolted.

This was it.

We walked together over to where they were putting us in alphabetical order.

"Hey," Jude said, his voice low.

"Yeah?" I looked up at him, and was once again struck by how crazy it was that he was mine. I hadn't wanted any guy, especially not Jude, but here we were and I was quickly finding myself unable to imagine my life without him. It was scary and exhilarating all at once.

"You never told me what grade you got on your paper."

I laughed, wondering what had made him think of that today. "An A of course." I shrugged. "Were you afraid I'd bomb?"

"Not at all. With my help how could you possibly fail?" he joked.

"Professor Taylor loved it," I assured him with a grin on my face. "In fact," my voice lowered, "I'm not supposed to tell anyone yet, but he knows someone who works at the city newspaper and they want me to shorten it for an article and they'll publish it."

Jude's eyes grew wide and his mouth fell open. "That's amazing, Tate!" he cried. "I'm so proud of you!"

I squealed, surprising the people around us, when he picked me up and hugged me tightly. When he lowered me, he dipped his head and captured my lips. The kiss started out sweet, but quickly escalated to dangerous levels.

"Get a room," someone coughed. I was pretty sure it was Jacob.

I broke the kiss and Jude placed a single light kiss on the end of my nose.

He had to leave me then, since they were calling for us to line up and with his last name he was at the beginning of the line.

It took a little while to get all of us in order. Once we were in a straight line, it was time for us to enter the lawn and take our seats.

Despite knowing no one was there for me, I couldn't help looking out to the crowd, searching.

I spotted Trent waving to Rowan, with Ivy and Tristan beside him, as well as his mom and grandma.

I didn't know what Jude's parents looked like so I didn't bother searching for them. Besides, they probably weren't even there.

I took my seat and settled in to listen to all the speeches. They all sounded the same. About how we were all going to leave here and do great things, change the world, blah, blah, and *blah*. I was tempted to stand up and scream, "Give me my diploma and let me leave!" But I didn't think that would go over too well, so I kept my mouth shut.

Our class was large so once they started calling names I knew we'd still be there a while.

When Jude's name was called I shot out of my seat and clapped like a maniac. The people beside me looked at me like

I'd lost my mind, but I didn't care one bit. Jude spotted me and dipped his head in acknowledgement, grinning crookedly.

Name after name was called out, and then I heard mine.

"Tatum Elizabeth O'Connor." Excitement and nerves filled my belly. I felt sick and high all at once.

I strode across the stage, my head held high. I shook the Dean's hand and accepted my diploma.

As I descended the steps, I heard someone yelling. When I looked up I saw Jude and I smiled instantly. But there was someone else yelling too. At first, I thought it was Trent, and he was clapping, but he wasn't doing the hollering. Looking farther into the crowd my eyes fell upon Jude's grandpa. Tears sprang to my eyes. I'd never imagined he'd be here and I hadn't heard him when Jude's name was called, but then I guessed I was yelling too loud myself to hear anything else.

I realized then, that I did have a family.

They might not have been blood-related, but they were family nonetheless. I took my seat once more with the biggest smile I'd ever worn plastered on my face.

The last name was called and the dean spoke some more before we tossed our caps in the air, just like we had four years prior in high school. Only this time, there was finality to it.

People went in search of their family and I fought against the crowd to find Jude.

"Tatum!" I heard my name called, but I couldn't see him.

Finally, I spotted him and ran into his arms.

"Whoa," he cried, rocking back on his heels as he caught me.

"We did it," I cried, "we really did it."

"Yes, we did." He chuckled, spinning me around, his excitement matching mine. "We're big kids now, Tater Tot."

I swayed dizzily when he set me down. He reached out a hand to steady me. "You okay?" he asked when I was righted.

"Yeah, never been better."

"I need to go find Pap," he told me as his eyes scanned the crowd.

"I saw him cheering for me." I grinned. "I didn't think he'd be here."

"I picked him up and brought him. No way was I going to let him miss this." Jude smiled down at me and reached out to stroke my cheek. The gesture seemed automatic for him. It wasn't to calm or soothe me. He was touching me simply because he wanted to.

"I'm really glad you did." I took his hand as we pushed our way through the thick crowd of bodies. "It made me happy to see him."

"He was mad at me when I picked him up, because you weren't with me." Jude chuckled huskily. "I told him I didn't want you to know that he'd be here, that you didn't have any family coming, and I wanted him being here to be a surprise. He was okay after that." Shaking his head, Jude grinned. "He started yelling at me, actually, when he didn't see you because he thought I'd done something to piss you off."

"Don't you visit him without me?" I asked, puzzled.

"Yeah, but he thought you'd be with me today. Crazy old man. I don't know what I'd do without him, though." He quickly sobered, his face growing somber.

"Hey ..." I reached up and took his cheek in my hand. "Let's not think about that today. Okay?"

He looked down at me and nodded slowly. "Yeah, you're right. Sorry." He cracked a smile.

"Jude!"

We both looked to our right and there was Jerry, standing

on top of a chair waving at us. "Pap!" Jude cried, running to his side with worry. "Get down from there! You're going to hurt yourself!"

"Nonsense, boy," Jerry grumbled when Jude tried to help him down. Jerry swatted Jude's hand away rather harshly and Jude glared up at him.

"Pap," he said warningly. "Get down before you break a hip."

"I'm old," Jerry grumbled, "not broken. I can get down just fine on my own. I got up here without your help," he pointed out.

Jude shook his head and stepped back, but held his hands out in case he needed to steady his grandpa.

Jerry lowered and stepped off the chair. Straightening, he looked at Jude. "See, I'm fine. No broken hip."

Jude let out a disgruntled sigh.

Jerry strode over to me and threw his arms around me. "I'm so proud of you."

"Thank you," I told him, tearing up a bit. Until he said the words I hadn't realized how much I needed to hear someone say them.

Jerry released me and turned to hug Jude. "I'm proud of you too." He lowered his head and whispered something in Jude's ear that made him smile.

Turning back to me, Jerry said, "Jude told me y'all are having a graduation party and I'm not invited, so I think I should at least be allowed to buy you a late lunch."

I looked at Jude and shrugged. "I don't mind."

"Lunch it is." Jerry clapped his hands together before Jude could say anything.

We started to head back to the parking lot, there was no point in lingering, when we heard, "Juuuuuuuuuuude."

Jude fell to the ground as Tristan crashed into him.

"That's my boy," I heard Trent say.

Rowan gasped. "Jude, are you okay? I'm so sorry!"

Jude rolled over and grabbed Tristan, lifting him in the air easily despite the fact that the boy wasn't that small anymore.

"I'm fine," Jude assured her, "he just took me by surprise is all." He set Tristan in the grass and sat up, ruffling the little boy's hair.

"I'm really sorry," Rowan said again as she approached and reached for her son's hand, "he wouldn't listen to me when I told him you were busy."

"It's fine." He waved a hand dismissively. He stood and dusted pieces of grass off his gown. "Rowan, this is my grandpa. Pap, this is Rowan, my best friend. Her fiancé, Trent, and their son, Tristan. And that beauty back there hiding—" he pointed to where Ivy stood a few feet away by a tree "—is Rowan's sister, Ivy."

"It's so nice to meet you." Rowan smiled at Jerry. She let out a squeak in surprise when he hugged her.

"We're heading to get lunch. Would you all like to join?" Jerry asked, nodding at Rowan and her family.

Her face fell. "I'd love to, but Trent's mom is having a meal for us at her house."

"Some other time then." Jerry smiled. "I must get to know you better."

"Yes, of course," she agreed. "I've got to go." Trent picked up Tristan and lifted him onto his shoulders as they walked away.

"Wait!" Jude called and Rowan turned back. "Are you coming to the party?"

"I'm not sure." She bit her lip. "We'll try."

Jude nodded and her answer seemed good enough for him.

Jerry, Jude, and I started to head toward the parking lot again. This time we made it without any interruptions. There wasn't enough room for all of us in Jude's truck, so I followed them to the restaurant in my car. That was fine by me, because I needed to go home and get ready for the party.

Our lunch was short and then it was time for Jude to take Jerry back home. He hugged me tight before leaving and told me he better see me soon for dinner. I agreed.

Since Rowan was busy and not sure if she was coming to the party, I was getting ready by myself tonight.

The house was eerily quiet around me as I scrambled around. I found myself speaking out loud just to fill the silence.

After spending most of the day in a nice dress, because we were required to dress formally for the graduation ceremony, I wanted nothing more than to wear shorts and a tank top. So, that's what I did. Jude wouldn't care and I had no reason to dress up for anyone else.

I left my hair down and touched up my makeup. I still had several hours to kill before leaving for the party. I ended up spending it cleaning the house, since I had nothing better to do.

It came time for me to leave and for the first time ever I was excited for a party. Maybe this time felt different since we were actually celebrating something worthwhile.

I parked my car down the street and sent Rowan a text as I walked toward the townhouse, asking if she was coming. She didn't reply immediately so I stuck my phone in my pocket.

I turned my head up to the sky. It was quickly becoming a dark, stormy gray. I wasn't too thrilled about the prospect of rain, but at least it had held off till after graduation.

I bound up the steps and opened the door into the townhouse.

The place was already packed.

If the guys had another party I was going to have to make sure to get my ass here early. I really hated pushing my way through the crowd. I was pretty sure someone elbowed me in the ribs and I'd have a bruise in the morning.

I saw Grant and Anna in the corner of the living room. I lifted my hand and waved, but they didn't see me.

I finally broke through the crowd and into the hallway. I didn't see Jude anywhere.

"Hey." I grabbed Dylan's arm when he went to pass me. "Have you seen Jude?"

"Oh, yeah." He smiled, a beer bottle clasped in his hand. "He went up to his room."

"Thanks."

I jogged up the steps, heading to Jude's room.

I was surprised when I saw it open, since he always kept it closed during parties, even when he was inside.

I stepped inside his room and froze.

Every surface was littered with white rose petals and tea candles he was in the process of lighting.

But that wasn't what had bile rising in the back of my throat.

Oh no, that was all because Jude's arms were wrapped around Brooke, their lips sealed together.

I stood shocked, unable to move.

I couldn't believe this was happening.

I wanted to pretend it wasn't real.

But it was.

Brooke opened her eyes and saw me and I could see the pleasure she felt at destroying my heart.

I stepped back and turned to run.

My foot got tangled in the laces of my sneakers and I fell down, smacking my knee roughly against the floor.

"Tatum—"

Hearing his voice was more than I could bear. Especially when I knew if I turned to look he'd be holding *her*. God, he could've had the decency to break up with me and not go behind my back. I was a big girl. I could handle it.

Without a backward glance, I took off down the steps.

I pushed people out of my way, not caring if I hurt them. I *had* to get out of there. I refused to cry until I was in the safety of my car. I wouldn't give the bastard the satisfaction of seeing my tears.

"Tatum!" I heard my name called. Not just by Jude this time, who I could tell was close behind me, but Dylan as well.

When Dylan saw that I was racing to get out of there and struggling to hold onto my composure, I heard him yell at Jude. "What the fuck did you do?"

"It wasn't what it looked like!" Jude cried. I wasn't sure if the words were meant for Dylan or me and I didn't care. I was almost to the door.

I heard a crash behind me, and people gasped. The disruption wasn't enough to get me to look. I opened the front door and slammed it behind me.

I ran down the street to my car.

"Tate—"

Rowan.

Great.

Now everyone was going to be a witness to me getting screwed over. I didn't stop to look or even acknowledge her. I just kept running. My desperation to get away was all consuming.

I reached my car and started it up as quickly as my fumbling fingers could manage.

I kept making the strangest sound I'd ever heard. It was half-gasp, half-cry.

Tears stung my eyes as I raced down the street. I saw Jude running down the sidewalk looking for me and—sick person that I was—I got satisfaction out of imagining running him over ... just like he had done to me.

I drove home as fast as I could, but it was still the longest fifteen minutes of my life.

I tore inside the empty house and my tears finally began to flood. I gasped for air as I blindly climbed the stairs.

I fell to my bed, burying my head in my pillow and sobbed.

But then I began to think of Jude being in my room, and in my bed, and I had to get away.

I wrenched out of the bed and grabbed the pillow. I threw it across the room and something shattered. I didn't know what and I didn't care.

I ran out of my room and into Graham's. It was one room that would never make me think of Jude, and I felt better in here anyway—like Graham was there to give me a hug and tell me it would be okay.

I sat on the floor with my back against his bed. I drew my knees up and wrapped my arms around them. My tears dripped from my chin onto my bare knees. I cried so hard that my whole body shook with the force. I hadn't cried this hard when Graham died—then, I'd been numb, but now I was cut open painfully.

I'd known my feelings for Jude were so intense that it would tear me apart if something happened to us. But I hadn't anticipated this kind of reaction. I'd hoped it would never come to this, but it had.

I'd been so stupid to trust him.

I wiped at my eyes, my hands coming away covered in streaks of black from my mascara.

The doorbell rang and my whole body stiffened.

I knew it was him.

It wouldn't be anyone else.

But it was more than that. My body was just that aware of him. I was tuned into the feel of him and I always knew when he was near.

I rose with shaky feet. I took several deep breaths and almost didn't go to the door.

But I needed to.

I took the steps slowly, dreading facing him.

When I opened the door he stood there, soaking wet from the rain. He shivered, water dripping off his nose and onto his chin.

"Tate," my name was no more than a whisper on his lips, and his brown eyes were pained, "I swear to God it wasn't what you think it was."

My breath shook with barely contained tears. "It was exactly what I saw. I'm not stupid Jude, so don't treat me like I am. I always figured you'd get bored with me and move on to someone else. I just figured you'd have the courtesy to break up with me first. I guess I was wrong." Nodding my head toward the road, I started to close the door. "You can leave now."

He slammed his hand against the door and pushed it open completely. He stormed around me and into my house. "I'm not leaving until I can get you to see the truth."

I snorted at that. "I saw the truth, that's why we're here in the first place. And if you won't leave, then I will."

I didn't have my car keys, but I didn't care.

I walked onto the porch, down the steps, and into the street.

It was pouring down rain and I was soaked in seconds.

My hair was plastered to my forehead and I could barely see in front of me the rain fell so hard, but I kept walking. The chill of the rain was nothing compared to the internal pain I felt at the moment. In fact, the harsh sting of the water brought clarity to my muddled brain.

I let out a scream when a hand clamped around my arm. Jude turned me around sharply and gripped my arms roughly in his hands. His fingers dug into my skin and he bared his teeth. He was angry. Pissed. Livid. Whatever you wanted to call it. He looked like he was two seconds away from shaking me.

"I fucking love you, Tatum!" he yelled and his words felt like ice on my skin, even colder than the rain.

"Why don't you try saying that without the *fucking* in the middle?" I sneered, trying to pull my arms from his grasp but it was futile. He was so much stronger than me and he was determined not to let me go.

He pulled me closer and lowered his forehead to mine. I hated that it felt so good. I wanted to hate everything about him, but I couldn't.

"I love you," he said again, his voice low. "I love you. Please." He swallowed thickly as the rain slicked off his skin, beading in his hair and the stubble on his cheeks. He smoothed his hand over my cheek causing me to sigh with pleasure—I couldn't stop the noise if I tried. His effect on me was too powerful to be ignored. "Don't do this to us."

I turned my head away and the tears started anew, but since they mixed with the rain and the sky was black he couldn't see them.

"I didn't do this to us. You did," I choked.

"Did you not hear me, Tate? I love you! *She* kissed me! She followed me into my room and kissed me!" His teeth clamped shut and his brows drew together as he willed me to believe him, but I knew what I saw and I couldn't get that image out of my head.

"I want to believe you," I whispered, biting my lip as the rain fell harder, "but I saw how you held her ..."

"Fuck, Tate!" He shoved his fingers through his wet hair so it stuck up. "That was me trying to push her *away!* What will it take to make you see that I only want *you?*" He spread his arms wide as the rain pelted his body.

I shook my head. "Jude, I ..." I looked down, unable to find the words I needed to say. "I *can't* do this."

"What is *this?*" he panted, spreading his arms wide. "You can't let me love you? You can't be with me? What is it that you can't fucking do, Tatum?"

"I can't be this girl!" I cried. "The one that turns into an emotional mess because of some guy! I need to be stronger than that!" I took several steps back, shivering from the cold and nearly fell over from a dip in the street. I wondered if my neighbors were watching the scene playing out before them in the middle of the road. Between the veil of the rain and night sky, I doubted anyone could even see us.

"What the hell is wrong with being upset? Huh? I'm hurt too, Tate! It tore me apart seeing that look on your face ... having you run away from me. But loving you makes me a better person. With you, I'm me." He beat his fist against his chest, as if trying to drive home the point that his heart belonged to me.

"Stop it, please," I sobbed. "Just stop." The rain felt like thousands of nails piercing my skin repeatedly, but the sting was nothing compared to the damage I felt to my heart. The way I felt right now had me convinced that being heartbroken was worse than any kind of physical torture I could ever be subjected to. I knew I never wanted to feel this way again. I'd been right to guard my heart all these years, and it figured that the guy I'd willingly given it to smashed it to bits.

"Why the fuck should I? It's the truth." His chest heaved and his wet shirt clung to every muscle. Despite my anger my fingers itched to reach out and touch him, but I couldn't. I was letting him go. He wasn't mine anymore.

"I need you to leave." I stared at my shoes, because I couldn't meet his eyes.

"No," he growled and I saw him take a step toward me. "I didn't fucking kiss her, Tate, and I'm not leaving here until I get you to understand that."

"Jude, *please*," I begged, finally forcing myself to look at him. Rain slid off his face, getting lost in the fabric of his wet t-shirt. "This—" I pointed to him and then myself "—isn't good for me. You need to go."

"I'm not going anywhere," he repeated as he closed the distance between us and took my cheek in one hand, pressing my waist against his with the other. "I love you and you're not getting rid of me that easy."

He lowered his head and captured my lips in a searing kiss that I felt all the way down to my toes. I let my fingers tangle in his hair as I kissed him back. The rain mingled with our kiss, clinging to our lips. I kissed him back with everything I had in me. *One last time*, I told myself.

He growled low in his throat and his hold on me relaxed.

He didn't know it, but this was me saying goodbye.

I broke away and stood on my tiptoes to kiss his cheek and whisper in his ear, "Goodbye, Jude."

Before he could react, I took off running for my house.

I slammed the door closed and locked it. My shoes squeaked against the hardwood floors as my back slid down to the floor. My butt hit it roughly and I knew my bottom would hurt later—but everything else hurt, so it didn't really matter.

I started to cry again and Jude rang the doorbell. When that didn't work he started smacking his fist against it.

"Tatum," he called through the door. "Please, don't do this," he begged. He sounded so torn up, but I couldn't open the door and comfort him. I couldn't tell him that it was okay and make all of this go away.

The fact of the matter was I realized now that I needed to get stronger on my own and I couldn't do that with Jude.

I wanted to believe that Brooke had kissed him and he hadn't meant for it to happen, but I knew what I saw and right now I was too upset to think logically.

Love made you crazy, and I was the craziest of them all.

"Tate," he cried, hitting his fist against the door again and again.

I didn't move for hours, and neither did he.

He stayed outside the door waiting for me to open it up—to change my mind—but I never did.

Eventually, I heard the sounds of his footsteps on the stairs of the porch.

I forced myself to stand and look out the window, watching him get in his truck and leave.

My heart broke all over again as I watched the taillights on his truck disappear down the street.

How had one of the best days of my life turned into the worst?

CHAPTER TWENTY-SIX

Somehow, I'd managed to get myself upstairs and climb in bed—Graham's bed, because I wasn't planning on going back in my room anytime soon. My mom probably would've snapped out of her ... Well, whatever strange in-between state she was in and had a conniption if she'd seen that I had disturbed the shrine my brother's room had become.

I was curled up in his bed, crying my eyes out, when Rowan found me.

"God, Tate, look at you," she sighed, standing beside the bed.

"How'd you get in?" I mumbled. My eyes were puffy and it made it hard to see her clearly.

She shrugged and crossed her arms over her chest. "Trent happens to come in handy for lots of things, like picking locks."

"Lovely," I grumbled.

"What the hell happened?" she asked, sitting on the edge of the bed by my feet.

I rolled onto my back and blinked bleary eyes at her. "Jude didn't tell you?" I asked.

"When I went to talk to him he was too busy destroying his room to answer." She sighed, looking up at the ceiling. "I'm sure whatever it was was silly and you two can work past this."

"He kissed another girl." Rowan's eyes grew wide at my words. "Or she kissed him. But does it really matter?"

"Of course that matters!" she gasped. "If she kissed him, it wasn't his fault, Tatum."

"But why didn't he push her away?" I cried, reaching over to the nightstand for yet another tissue. I was pretty sure in the past twenty-four hours I'd used up nearly every tissue in the house.

"Maybe he did and you just didn't see," she countered.

"It felt like I watched them forever." My lower lip trembled. "How would you feel if you saw Trent kissing another girl?"

Her lips thinned and she looked away. "I understand where you're coming from, Tate, but don't throw away something so great because of a misunderstanding. Life's too short for that."

I turned away from her and stared at one of the bookcases in my brother's room. It was covered with books, pictures of his friends and even some with me, and all his sports trophies. "I need time."

"Yeah, but how much time?"

I rubbed my eyes. "I don't know. Until it stops hurting, I guess," I mumbled, wrapping my arms around the pillow and hugging it to my chest.

Rowan laughed, but there was no humor in the sound. "It's never going to stop hurting, not if you love him. Do you love him?" Her eyes widened in surprise at her own question.

I nodded. "I do." My lip trembled.

"Oh, Tate." She climbed onto the bed beside me and wrapped her arms around me in a hug. "I'm so sorry. I know it hurts, but he's hurting too. Please, don't give up."

Sniffling, I wiped beneath my eyes. "It hurt so bad seeing him kiss her. It felt like my heart was ripped out of my chest and stomped on. I just need to regroup."

"How long will that take, though?" she asked. "A few days? A week? A month? Forever?"

"I don't know," I mumbled. "I just need to figure some things out."

She smoothed her fingers through my hair and then started to braid it. I'd seen her do something similar with her sister when she was trying to comfort her. "If you need to talk about it, or a shoulder to cry on, I'm here for you."

"Thank you," I said and meant it.

"No problem. That's what friends are for."

We grew quiet as she braided my hair. After a while, I asked, "Can you stay for a while?"

"Of course," she replied.

"I'm feeling a little hungry. Could we order pizza?"

"Pizza sounds great. I'll get it ordered while you shower."

"Is that your subtle way of telling me I stink?" I asked, rolling over to face her.

She laughed. "No, but you look like crap and a shower always makes me feel better. Come on—" she pushed my shoulder "—out of bed."

I rolled out of my brother's bed and stretched my arms above my head.

Looking around, Rowan said, "This is your brother's room."

I nodded, even though it hadn't been a question.

"Why the hell are you in here, and not in your room?" she asked.

I looked away and let out a sigh as sadness filled me once more. "My room reminded me too much of him."

Just saying the words made me remember the feel of his body wrapped around mine as we slept in my bed.

Rowan's eyes filled with pity. "I'm sorry, Tate."

"It's not your fault," I mumbled, heading for the bathroom. If it was anyone's fault, it was mine for believing I could be different. When it came down to it, Jude obviously thought I was another girl he could screw over easily. He'd used me until he'd grown tired of me and tossed me away like a broken toy the moment he kissed Brooke.

I turned the hot water on and stayed beneath the hot spray for as long as I could stand it. Rowan was right, it did make me feel better. I let the water soothe my tense muscles and washed my hair.

When I got out of the shower I brushed my hair and teeth. I was surprised to find clean clothes waiting for me when I opened the bathroom door. Rowan had grabbed them and set them out so I wouldn't have to go into my room.

I grabbed the clothes and closed the bathroom door once more as I changed into the sweatpants and t-shirt. Despite spending all of last night and most of the day in bed, I felt exhausted. My rest had been filled with troubled thoughts.

I forced my sluggish feet downstairs and found Rowan sitting in the family room, watching TV. "Hey, feeling better?"

"A little." I forced a smile, but it splintered and cracked. I began to cry as I sat down beside her. She grabbed a blanket, draped it around my shoulders, and pulled me into a hug.

"Shh," she comforted. "It's okay, Tate. Let it out."

"Why does it hurt so bad?" I sobbed. "It shouldn't be this

painful." I wiped my tears on the blanket. I was sick of crying over Jude, but I couldn't seem to stop. I was hurt and angry—at him and myself.

"Oh, honey," Rowan sighed, "love is painful. It tears you apart and puts you back together. It's not meant to be smooth sailing. Relationships are hard. They take time and effort."

"But that isn't the problem," I sniffled, my eyes stinging with even more tears. "He *kissed* her."

"Oh, Tatum," she sighed heavily and rested her chin on top of my head in a motherly gesture. "Do you really believe that?"

"I don't need to believe it," I choked. "I *saw* it."

Rowan let out an exasperated breath. "Tatum, I really believe it was a misunderstanding. Jude ... The way he looks at you ... Trust me, he wouldn't hurt you like this."

I slid away from her to put some distance between us. "Whose side are you on? His?"

Rowan blew out a breath, her hair swaying around her shoulders as she shook her head. "You're both my friends, so I'm on both of your sides. Not one or the other. I had no idea what happened when I saw you go running down the street, but then Jude came out ..." She bit her lip and her eyes filled with pain as if she was remembering something from her past. "That look on his face, was the look of a man in love and in pain. A man with that look would never try to hurt you on purpose." Rowan's face grew shadowed with anger. "Whoever this bitch is that fucked you two up, I want to punch her in the face. Or yank out her weave. Whichever would be more painful."

My tears stopped, and I laughed. I swore only Rowan could make me laugh in a situation like this when she wasn't even trying. I knew from her expression that she was dead serious.

"You know," she said as she leaned her head back against

the pillows, "I don't understand girls who want another girl's guy. Like, bitch, come on. There's other fish in the sea. Why do you need this particular fish, you know?" She turned her gaze to me and I laughed again. "It's so not cool, but you know, I think girls, or even guys, that pull stunts like that are just really insecure with themselves. Please, Tate, *please* don't let some bitch ruin the best thing that's ever happened to you." Unshed tears shimmered in her eyes. "In all the time we've been friends, I've never seen you happier than you have been these months you've been with Jude."

"It was only like two months," I grumbled.

"Love doesn't have a timeline." She severed me with a glare. "Love doesn't wait. When it's meant to be, then it is."

"Well, if it's meant to be I guess it'll work itself out." I used her words against her.

Her lips thinned. "That doesn't mean you don't have to *try*."

Luckily, I was saved from replying by the doorbell ringing.

At first my heart jolted behind my ribs as a part of me hoped it was Jude, but I quickly realized it was simply the pizza arriving.

Despite my current pissed off state where Jude was concerned, I still yearned to see him. I was pathetic.

Rowan jumped up from the couch, patting my knee as she passed me on her way to the front door. She paid the guy for the pizza and set the box on the coffee table.

Without saying anything to me, she disappeared into the kitchen and I heard cabinet doors slam as she searched for whatever she was looking for. She returned a few minutes later with plates and glasses of water.

We ate in silence and watched TV. Well, I didn't really watch it. I sort of stared at the TV as my mind wandered to thoughts of Jude. How he made me feel, how he could make me laugh, the feel of his fingers on my skin, how it felt when we made love. It was all there on an endless spin cycle in my head. No matter how hard I tried not to think of him, he was always there.

"Will it ever stop hurting?" I asked Rowan eventually.

She turned to me, and set her plate of pizza on her lap. "Honestly?" Her lips turned down in a frown. "When Trent and I were broken up, or whatever you want to call it, after he found out about Tristan, it never stopped hurting until he forgave me and took me back. The pain was suffocating at times. All I wanted was him and I knew he was the only man I'd ever want. I was so scared that I'd completely fucked us up and that we'd never be together …," she trailed off, her eyes sad.

"Is it wrong of me to feel like I need time to think things through?" I asked her.

She shrugged. "I don't know. I don't know what I would've done, or how I would've felt, if I saw Trenton kissing another girl … or a girl kissing him," she amended. "Since I haven't been in that spot, I don't feel like I can judge or pass an opinion." She frowned, her nose crinkling with thought. "You have to do what you have to do, but this, isn't the reaction of someone who can just move on easily. You … you love him."

"I do," I agreed, my lip trembling. "I love him so much." I'd never said the words out loud, but it felt good now that I had. But Rowan wasn't the one who should've heard them. Those words belonged to Jude.

"Then tell him that. Move past this. Don't let this bitch win. Go get your man back, Tate."

I shook my head and swiped tears from beneath my eyes. "I can't. Not yet." My body trembled with shaky breaths. "I … I need a few days." I couldn't forgive and forget so easily. Not while I still felt so hurt—the pain still raw and festering.

"What for?" she asked, tilting her head to the side.

"I don't know, to make sure I really forgive him, I guess. I can't expect him to take me back or for us to ever work if I can't let go of this anger." I sighed. "I don't want to think about that kiss every time I look at him. I have to get past it first."

"I think you're being stupid," Rowan spat, her eyes growing angry. "He loves you, you love him. It's as simple as that. Now, you're just coming up with excuses to talk yourself out of being with him because love is scary." She stood up, glaring down at me. I looked away, toward the wall. My shoulders shook with barely contained sobs. "I've got news for you, Tatum. *Life* is scary."

With her words hanging in the air, she stomped out of the room and out the door, letting it slam closed behind her.

My cries were all that could be heard in the silent house.

CHAPTER TWENTY-SEVEN

Ten days.

Ten days without Jude.

Ten days of being miserable.

Ten days of moping around the house, only leaving to go to work.

Ten days of complete and utter insanity.

I was pretty sure at this point I was going crazy, if I hadn't already.

I'd thought of going to him so many times and apologizing, but my stubbornness wouldn't let me.

I had spent hours hoping he'd come see me.

He didn't.

That scared me like nothing else could.

Between not seeing him and Rowan's disappearance—I hadn't seen her either since the day she walked out—I had myself convinced that Jude had moved on with Brooke. It was easier to believe he stayed away because he'd found something in her that he didn't have with me, than to accept responsibility for what happened—that I pushed him away.

"What did that pen ever do to you?"

I jumped at the sound of Bryce's voice. "Sorry." I put the pen down, the top chewed on. "I didn't realize I was doing it."

He stared at the crumpled top of the pen. "Well, keep it now. No one wants your germs," he joked, hopping up on the counter.

It was closing time and I should've been helping him wipe down the tables and clean the floors, but I was too lost in my thoughts.

"What's going on with you?" he asked. "You haven't been okay for a week now."

I sighed. "It's nothing."

"Boy troubles," he spoke over me. "It's definitely boy troubles. I can tell from the look in your eyes." He reached out and lifted my chin. "The guy's an idiot to leave you."

I pulled out of his grasp and his hand fell to his lap. "There ... there was a misunderstanding, and I made things worse," I admitted. It was the first time I'd accepted some of the responsibility.

"Talk to me," Bryce said as he hopped off the counter. He grabbed two rags and tossed one to me. I managed to catch it. "You clean those tables, and I'll take the ones over here."

I did as he told me, but didn't speak. I didn't know what to say.

"Come on, you can tell me whatever is. I might be able to impart some wisdom, or not."

I shrugged, wiping the table in circular motions. At the rate I was going, I was about to rub a hole into the surface. I let out a pent-up breath and told Bryce everything, from how I found Jude and Brooke, to how depressed I'd been the past ten days.

When I was done, I pulled out one of the chairs and put my head in my hands. "I've ruined everything."

The legs of the other chair squeaked against the tile floors as Bryce pulled it out and sat down. "You haven't ruined everything," he said softly, his voice oddly serious. "Everyone makes mistakes, but it's what you do after that matters."

"What do you mean?" I looked up at him, sniffling.

He shrugged. "I just mean, when you make a mistake you either have to own it, or suffer because of it. Apologize to him. If he really loves you he'll understand. Everyone makes mistakes and you both did in this situation. He shouldn't have let whatever-her-name-is into his room, and you shouldn't have pushed him away. Tell him you're sorry."

"I don't know if I can," I admitted.

"Apologizing isn't a weakness." Bryce stood, throwing the damp rag over his shoulder. "It's a strength."

Whistling, he headed to the back to clean up there while I finished out front.

I kept replaying his words over that evening and on the drive home.

I was surprised to see Rowan's car parked in the driveway when I arrived home.

I got out of the car and found her sitting on the top step of the porch. Her elbows rested on her knees with her head in her hands.

I approached hesitantly, like she was a rabid animal that might bite me at a moments' notice. After our last conversation, I had no idea where we stood.

"Hi." My voice was soft as I approached.

She looked up at me and let out a sigh. "Can I talk to you?"

"Sure." I nodded. I sat down on the step beside her, instead of inviting her inside. I figured if things got bad I had a better chance of running away if we were outdoors.

"I'm sorry for the things I said." She turned to look at me, and tears shown in her eyes. "I shouldn't have been such a bitch to you. You were hurting and I wasn't respectful of that."

I shook my head. "You were telling the truth. I was being stupid." I let out a pent-up breath.

"How have you been?" she asked.

"Miserable," I answered without any hesitation.

"He's—"

"I don't want to know about him," I stopped her.

"But—"

"No," I said sternly. "I don't want to know."

Rowan sighed and reached for me, putting her arm around me and coaxing my head onto her shoulder. "I hate seeing you like this."

I lifted my shoulders in a small shrug. "It is what is."

"You're not going to fix this, are you?" she whispered into the night air.

I stared out at the yard where lightning bugs glowed. "I still need more time. I need the hurt to go away." It was basically the same thing I'd told her the last time she was here.

"It's not going to stop hurting until you get your man back, Tate," she stated.

I scrubbed a hand over my tired face. "He hasn't tried to see me."

Rowan sighed heavily. "He thinks you hate him."

I pulled away from her, not even bothering to scold her for giving me information on him. "I could never hate him. I tried, but I can't."

I started to cry, for the thousandth time it seemed, and

Rowan stood up and helped me to stand as well. She led me to the front door and I pulled out my key to let us inside.

Rowan didn't say anything as she led me to the family room and disappeared into the kitchen. When she returned she held out a gallon of ice cream with two spoons stuck in the top. "Ice cream makes everything better, right?"

"Right," I replied.

But then before I could take a bite I started to cry harder, because now ice cream only made me think of Jude.

Jude.

Jude.

Jude.

He was every-fucking-where.

He'd invaded every aspect of my life without me even realizing that he had.

Rowan ignored my tears. I guessed she'd decided to let me cry it out.

After a few minutes where the only sound in the room was my hiccupping sobs, she said, "Trent's family is throwing a Memorial Day barbeque. I want you to come."

Composing myself, I choked, "Is h-he going to be there?" I knew she'd know which *he* I meant. After all, there could only be one I was referring to.

Rowan shrugged. "He's invited, but I don't know if he'll come or not."

I sighed, running my fingers through my hair. "I'll think about it."

"That's better than no." She smiled and set the ice cream aside when it was obvious that even its sugary goodness couldn't tempt me. "Let's go out."

"I don't want to." I frowned, my shoulders sagging with a sigh.

"Just for dinner," she pleaded. "You need to get out and you have to eat. It's a win-win."

I couldn't very well argue with that. Besides, I needed to push past my sadness over the situation with Jude and find that strong girl I used to be once more.

With startling clarity, I realized that Jude didn't take away my strength. He gave it to me. He lifted me up, and didn't drag me down. He pushed me to be better.

I began to toy with my bottom lip as my thoughts began to show me what I'd been too blinded by hurt and stubborn proudness to see.

Jude made me better.

He didn't change me, he just helped me improve upon the person I was.

I'd been too mad to see that and grasping at reasons to stay mad at him.

God, I'd been so *stupid*.

I stood hastily and my hand flew to my mouth. I thought I might be sick.

"Tatum—" Rowan started.

I lowered my hand and took a deep, steadying breath. "You were right," I gasped, "I've been so stupid. I … I … I was so *hurt* over seeing him with Brooke and pissed over my own reaction. I hated that I cared so much, but I can see now that if I hadn't got upset *that* would've been more disconcerting." I shook my head, my hair falling forward to frame my face. "What the fuck is wrong with me?" I lifted my head to look at her. "Why do I do this to myself? Why do I push everyone away?"

Rowan wrapped her arms around me in a tight hug. "You're so much like me," she whispered in my ear. "I did the same thing with Trenton. Over and over again I pushed him away because I was scared to love him." She stepped back but rested her hands on my shoulders. "But being without him was the worst kind of pain I've ever felt."

"I-I need to go to him," I stuttered, looking around for my purse and car keys. I couldn't remember where I'd laid them when we came inside.

Rowan reached out and grabbed my arm, halting my frantic search. "It's late, Tate. Wait till morning."

My face fell. "Has he moved on?"

"God, Tatum, don't be ridiculous."

"I feel like there's something you're not telling me." I frowned.

"I promise there's not, it's just late and ..."

"What?" I prompted when she didn't continue.

"I don't know. It just seems like you should do something nice to apologize. He's really torn up."

"*He's* torn up?" I snapped. "What about me?" I pointed to my chest. "What about what I feel? Huh? The past ten days have been hell for me."

"I'm not saying they haven't, but ... let's face it," she said as she played with the ends of her hair, a nervous gesture, "Jude pursued you, I think it's time for you to do a little chasing of your own."

I narrowed my eyes. "This 'chasing' you speak of sounds a lot like groveling. I won't beg him to take me back." It had nothing to do with pride, but I wasn't going to turn into a pathetic mess because he wouldn't take me back—at least not in front of him. In the comfort of my home? Now that was a different story.

"No," she laughed. "I just think he deserves a romantic gesture."

"What if he laughs at me?" I frowned.

Rowan sighed. "I'm not saying it needs to be something overly romantic and gooey. Do something from your heart. Something that will make him smile." She threw her arm over my shoulder. "Come on, we'll talk about it over dinner. I'm sure between the two of us we can come up with something brilliant to blow his mind."

CHAPTER TWENTY-EIGHT

"Lucinda." I walked up to my boss, nervously fiddling with my fingers.

She looked up from the cupcakes she was icing, arching her brow in question.

I decided not to mess around, because if I stalled too long I'd lose my nerve to ask for her help. "I ... uh ... I made a mistake."

"With the register?" she asked, flicking gray hair out of her eyes with a shake of her head.

"No," I laughed, but it came out nervous sounding. "With my boyfriend."

"Oh, I'm sorry." She stood up straight. "But I don't understand why you're telling me this."

"You see ..." I fidgeted restlessly with unease. "I want to apologize to him, but my friend says I need to do something romantic so I was thinking ..."

"Yeah?" she asked, icing more cupcakes while she waited for me to get on with it.

"I want to make him a cake, and I know how to make a cake, that isn't the problem ..."

"So, what's the problem?" she asked. "I'll help you in any way I can." She smiled, alleviating some of my stress.

"He loves gummy bears, so—"

"You want to make him a gummy bear cake." She chuckled, setting the bag of icing to the side. Wiping her hands on her apron she said, "I can do that, but you're helping. I have to head out of here in a little bit, but we can do it first thing in the morning and I'll give you the rest of the day off tomorrow so you can, hopefully, make up." She winked and picked up the icing bag once more.

"Thank you!" I cried. I was a bit upset I had to wait till tomorrow morning—probably the afternoon by the time the cake would be done and I could get it to him—but I would take this as a victory.

I returned to the front and Bryce stepped away from the register so I could take over.

"From the smile on your face, I'm going to guess it went well." I'd already told Bryce my idea and he'd thought it was great. His exact words had been, "No man can resist the temptation of a cake and a hot girl holding it." He'd looked me up and down then, grinning slowly before adding, "You should totally hide in his room and when he opens the door you'll be standing there naked holding the cake."

I'd responded by telling him to shut his mouth and that I bet his girlfriend wouldn't like hearing him say that. Having met his girlfriend, a pretty redhead named Charlotte, I couldn't help wondering how those two ended up together. While Bryce was loud and said whatever he wanted, Charlotte was quiet and barely spoke. Maybe that's why they worked. They did say opposites attract, and look how opposite Jude and I were and I loved him deeply.

"It did," I finally answered him, "she said she would help."

"Sweeeet." He rubbed his hands together. "I told you she'd be in."

"Why are you so excited?" I asked, leaning my hip against the counter. "It's not like you're getting any cake."

He chuckled, crossing his arms over his chest and leaned against the wall. His shaggy dark hair fell forward, shielding his face. He always reminded me of a dog for some reason when he did that. His personality was kind of dog like too—super friendly and frighteningly hyper.

"You've been super cranky during this whole lover's spat. I'm looking forward to getting the more pleasant version of Tatum back, although," he paused, his eyes sparkling with laughter, "you can still be kind of bitch when you're normal."

I grabbed the first thing I could get ahold of, which happened to be a pen, and threw it at his head.

He ducked so fast I swore his body blurred. My mouth fell open in surprise as the pen bounced off the wall. "Whoa," I breathed. "You're like Superman."

Bryce chuckled and bent to retrieve the pen. He placed it back on the counter and returned to his previous position. He snorted. "I'm way cooler than Superman. Everyone knows that."

I laughed and turned to face the register when I heard the bell on the door clang.

"Cusssssstommmmer," Bryce sing-songed. "Oh, cusssssstoooooommmmer," now he really started to sing, "whaaaaaat caaaaan weeeee heeeeeeeeeellllpppp yooooooooooooooooou wiiiiith?" My eyes widened in surprise at the sound of his voice. He could actually sing. Becoming serious, he stated, "Our cupcakes are fabulous. You should have one."

I laughed. "We only sell cupcakes."

"Yeah, but he doesn't know that," Bryce hissed, like he was letting me in on a secret. "What if he's here for pie and we don't have pie? I've got to play up the cupcakes."

I shook my head. I didn't think Bryce would ever cease to amaze me.

The customer looked from me to Bryce and busted out laughing. Extending his hand for me to shake I took it with a puzzled brow. "I'm Caeden, that thing's my brother," he released my hand and pointed at Bryce. "Don't worry, I'm used to his antics."

"Oh," I breathed, feeling relieved.

Now that I looked I was surprised I hadn't noticed the resemblance earlier. They were practically identical, with the exception that this guy was obviously a little older. His hair was a dark chocolate brown and his eyes a piercing blue. Like Bryce's they were so bright they didn't seem real.

I realized I'd never told him my name. "I'm Tatum, by the way."

He chuckled. "Nice to meet you, Tatum. I came by because I need to talk to Lucinda." He pointed toward the back.

"Oh, of course." I moved out of the way so he could come around the counter and go to the back.

"Thanks." He smiled as he brushed past me.

The door had no more than swung closed till Bryce narrowed his eyes and said, "I better see what's going on. Can you handle the front?"

"Yeah," I replied, but he'd already gone. "Huh," I huffed to myself, wondering what that was about.

Several customers trickled in then and my mind became distracted as I flitted around filling their orders.

Lucinda's was usually busy between the local high school, which hadn't let out yet, and working professionals in the area. It seemed that everyone wanted a cupcake from Lucinda's.

By the time we closed, Caeden and Lucinda had left and it was just Bryce and me.

We cleaned up, talking about random things before heading our separate ways.

I managed to get some sleep that night with the comfort that in the morning I would make my apology cake and set things right.

Hopefully.

Because there was always the chance that I had damaged things beyond repair and Jude wouldn't want to take me back.

LUCINDA REMOVED the two round pieces of chocolate cake from the pan to cool. With each passing second my body tightened a bit more with anticipation.

While the cake cooled I made the icing—a whipped buttercream that smelled so good that I couldn't resist dipping my finger in and tasting it. It was delicious.

Lucinda narrowed her eyes, having caught me, and smiled. "I saw that," she chuckled. "You know you're not supposed to do that."

I shrugged. "It's for Jude, he won't mind."

Together we iced the cake when it cooled enough. All right, I let her do most of the icing, but only because she did it so much better than I did.

Once all sides of the cake were covered in icing I grabbed

the bag of gummy bears and sprinkled them on top, as well as sticking some to the sides.

And that folks, was how you made a gummy bear cake.

Lucinda appraised our handy work with a small smile. "They say the way to a man's heart is through his stomach, if this doesn't work then I don't know what else would."

"Thank you so much for helping me with this, Lucinda," I hugged her.

Patting my back, she said, "It was no problem at all." Stepping back, she looked over my disheveled appearance; cake batter and icing covered my clothes and I felt something sticky on my cheek. "You better clean up and get out of here."

I'd brought a change of clothes with me so I wouldn't have to go home.

I cleaned up in the bathroom, wiping icing from cheek and freshening my makeup. I swiped on some mascara and put a red gloss on my lips. I fluffed my hair and changed into shorts and a t-shirt. Nothing fancy, but that wasn't me, and I knew no pretty dress would erase what I had done. Only I could do that with my words—and the gummy bear cake of course.

"Thank you, again!" I called to Lucinda as I dashed out of the bathroom.

"I hope it goes well." She turned on one of the beaters as she started making cupcakes for the morning crowd that would be arriving soon. I couldn't believe she'd offered to come in before opening time to help me. I really liked her, and Bryce too. I'd lucked out with this job.

I grabbed the cake up—which was fixed in a glass cake platter—and went out to my car. I prayed to the cake gods that nothing messed it up and it would make it to Jude in one piece. Even if he said he never wanted to see me again he should at least get to enjoy the cake. Although, with my fiery personality it was more likely I'd try to throw it at him.

I drove to Jude's townhouse, my heart thundering in my chest and my blood roaring in my ears. I was about two seconds away from breaking out in an all body nervous sweat. I was terrified to see him after twelve days apart. But I was even more terrified of living my life without him.

Jude was my future and I wasn't going to let my pride ruin that. It was time to stop running and hiding from my feelings. I had to accept them and give Jude my whole heart. Not part, not half. All of it.

No more holding back.

I was going to lay it all out there.

I parked on the street in front of the townhouse and turned off my car.

"You can do this, Tatum," I chanted quietly to myself. "Get out of the car and get your man back."

Repeating this mantra in my head I grabbed the cake and forced my stiff body out of the car.

I stepped onto the walkway and up the steps. I adjusted my hold on the cake so I could ring the doorbell.

I held my breath when I heard footsteps approaching. I lowered my head, not ready to face him.

The door swung open and I heard a gasp of, "Tatum?"

It wasn't the voice I longed to hear. My head rose slowly and my eyes connected with Dylan's.

His face darkened and he glared at me. I flinched. I wasn't expecting that kind of reaction from him, but he was Jude's best friend so of course he was mad at me.

"Why are you here?" he snapped, moving his body so that it was clear I wasn't invited inside.

My palms grew sweaty against the glass cake holder.

"I-I came to apologize." I stuttered, flicking hair from my eyes.

He narrowed his eyes. "Apologize? It's a bit late for that," he growled. "Don't you think?"

Tears pricked my eyes but I dammed them back. Squaring my shoulders, I held my head high. "I understand if he doesn't want to see me, or if he's moved on—" I swallowed the lump in my throat that my words had created "—but I need to see him. I have to let him know how sorry I am for overreacting. I should've listened to him and—"

Dylan cut me off with a heavy sigh and his eyes softened. "He's not here."

"He's not?" My face fell. "Oh," I mumbled as realization dawned on me. He was *out*. Probably with her.

I turned to leave, but Dylan called, "Wait!"

I stopped with my back to him. I didn't want him to see me break down.

"You really fucked him up," Dylan whispered and I heard his footsteps approach me on the walkway. His hand came down on my shoulder and he turned me around. "I've never seen Jude like that before. You broke his heart."

My eyes closed as pain lanced my body. "I saw them kissing and ... and ... I thought he didn't want me anymore."

"I know what you saw," Dylan said. When my eyes widened with surprise, he added, "Yeah, he told me. He also told me she kissed him, which I'm sure he told you." Dylan crossed his arms over his chest. "Jude's not a liar," he stated. "He wouldn't play you like that."

"I know." My voice came out as a squeak. "I fucked up, okay? I used that kiss as an excuse to push him away because what I feel for him is so powerful that it scares me more than

I'd care to admit. I love him, Dylan, I really do. With all my heart and soul."

Dylan's jaw clenched and he looked away. "I'm sorry for being a jerk." He took a step back. "But I've hated seeing my best friend so fucked up over you. That's not him."

"I understand," I whispered and started heading toward my car once more.

"He's at his grandpa's!" Dylan yelled, surprising me.

I closed the passenger door where I'd just set the cake down and turned to face Dylan where he stood just outside the door to the townhouse.

"He's at his grandpa's," he repeated when he knew he had my attention.

I nodded my head in thanks and circled around to the driver's side.

I was a bit nervous that I might get lost on the way to his grandpa's since it was hidden away and down an old country road.

But I knew if I didn't go to him now I never would.

I paid careful attention to everything I passed and crossed my fingers that I turned onto the right road.

I let out a sigh of relief when I spotted Seraphina grazing in the distance.

My heart fluttered in my throat.

Close.

So. Close.

I tried to mentally prepare myself to see him. Twelve days felt more like twelve years.

When the trees parted and the road opened up, the house came into view.

Jude was out front, up on a ladder painting the siding. It looked like he'd been working on the house. The steps were no longer leaning and since most of the house was freshly painted it looked fresh and new. He'd even fixed some of the broken shutters.

He heard my car approach and turned his head.

The ladder swayed as surprise hit him when he recognized my car.

He put the paintbrush on the top rung of the ladder and scrambled down.

He lifted his hands in front of his face to shield his eyes from the sun. As I got out of the car I could see his brows furrowed together.

I stood for a moment, just staring at him so I could soak him in.

His dark hair was damp with sweat and the white sleeveless shirt he wore clung to his chest and exposed his impressive arms. His jeans hung low on his hips, the bottoms rolled up. Paint stained their blue surface.

His face was the same, of course, but maybe a little tired looking. The bags under his eyes were nearly as bad as mine. A few days' worth of stubble dotted his cheeks and chin.

"Tatum?" he asked, his voice full of shock like he believed I was some kind of mirage that had appeared in front of him.

"It's me." I forced a smile, tucking a piece of hair behind my ear.

"What are you doing here?" he asked, lowering his hands from his face.

"D-Dylan told me where to find you," I admitted, hoping he wouldn't be pissed at Dylan for giving me his whereabouts.

"Is that so?" He shook his head, putting his hands on his hips. "I kind of had myself convinced I'd never see you again."

"I can go." I turned to head back to my car.

"No!" he cried and then I felt his hand on my wrist, spinning me around. He smoothed his fingers through my hair and my eyes fluttered closed, a happy sigh escaping my parted lips. "Don't go," he whispered, staring down at me with his warm brown eyes.

I got lost in his stare. "I came to tell you I'm sorry."

"You're sorry?" He cracked a smile, tracing his fingers over the curve of my cheek. It was like he had to touch me to convince himself I was real.

I nodded and bit my lip, my body shaking in his arms. "I should've believed you, but it was easier not to."

"Why?" he asked, sounding pained. "God, Tate, watching you run away from me in the pouring rain was the worst kind of torture you could put me through."

"I know and I'm so sorry." My breath caught and I fisted his shirt in my hands. I brought my eyes up to his. "I was so scared of my feelings for you that I pushed you away. It's what I do best, Jude. I hurt you and I hurt myself in the worst way imaginable. These twelve days without you have been the worst days of my life. Even worse than losing my brother." I swallowed thickly, trying to compose myself. "I felt like loving you was taking away my choices, but *you are my choice.* You don't ruin me. You make me better."

He leaned his forehead against mine, his breath fanning over my cheeks. "Only you could tear me apart and put me back together with a few words."

I tried to smile. I reached up and placed my hand over his—the one he held against my cheek. "You told me you couldn't save me, that I had to do it myself, but you were wrong, Jude. You did save me. We did it together. You healed me without even trying and I gave you my heart. All of it. It's yours, if you still want it."

He chuckled huskily, rubbing his thumb over my bottom lip. "Of course I still want it, silly girl. I want you. Always."

He lowered his head and I closed the distance between us. I let out a sigh of content as our lips collided. *Finally.* My hands wound around his neck, locking in his hair to hold him to me. Twelve days had been too long to go without him. I'd been crazy to think I could live without this.

Without him.

Without love.

He bit lightly on my bottom lip and my mouth parted. His tongue touched mine and I let out a moan I couldn't contain.

One hand cupped the nape of my neck, while his other slid down my back and settled on my waist before skimming up my shirt. The heat of his hand against my bare skin made me shiver.

He pulled back with a chuckle and nipped my bottom lip once more. Staring down at me, he warned, "You better not try to leave me again, pretty girl. I won't let you get away so easy next time."

"Don't worry." I stood on my tiptoes to whisper in his ear, "There won't be a next time. You're stuck with me now, Brooks."

He growled huskily and claimed my lips once more.

I had no clue how long we stood there kissing and I didn't care. I would never get my fill of Jude, no matter how many years we might have ahead of us.

He rubbed his nose against mine and stepped back. "Want to go to our spot?"

My smile was huge at his words. *Our spot.*

"That sounds perfect."

He started for his truck and I jumped. "Wait!" I ran to my car and pulled out the gummy bear cake. "Here." I held it out to him. "I made this for you ... Well, I *helped* make it for you. It's the thought that counts, right?" I laughed.

He grinned crookedly as he looked at the cake. "Did you make me an apology cake?"

I shrugged, laughing harder. "Um, yeah. It's your favorite ... gummy bear."

He chuckled and scratched his jaw as he reached for the cake. "I think you like me, Tate."

I stared into his warm eyes as I said the words I knew he needed to hear as much as I needed to say them. "I don't like you, Jude Brooks. I love you."

His smile fell and I feared he was mad, but then he cried, "Fuck the cake," and dropped it to the ground. By some minor miracle the glass didn't shatter, but the cake did get messed up. But then his lips were on mine and my legs were wrapped around his waist and I completely forgot about the cake—about everything.

All that existed was Jude.

My body, my mind, my heart—all of me—had been starved for him.

I owed many thanks to whatever god had listened to my prayers and let Jude forgive me.

I'd expected him to be angry with me—and I'm sure he was—and unforgiving.

Being back in his arms reminded me that my home was wherever he was.

I fought to catch my breath when he set me down.

He cupped my cheeks in his large hands and stared down at me. "You love me, Tate?"

"I love you," I said again.

He growled low in his throat and took my earlobe in his mouth. Letting the flesh go, he brushed his mouth against the curve of my ear. "I'll never get tired of hearing you say that for as long as I live. And Tate?"

"Yeah?" I breathed, my tongue slipping out to moisten my suddenly dry lips.

"I love you. I. Love. You. Do you hear me?" He narrowed his eyes, wanting to make sure his words penetrated my stubborn skull. "I love you and only you. It's only ever been *you*." He skimmed his fingers lightly over my cheek and down my neck. "Every part of me was made to love every part of you." His voice lowered and his eyes darkened. He wrapped his arms around me and held me close. "I've been in hell without you."

"Me too," I agreed. "I hate that I did this to you. To me. To *us*."

"It's okay, Tate." He cupped the nape of my neck and tilted my head back slightly. His eyes bored into mine. "It's over now, and I think we learned a valuable lesson from this."

"And what would that be?" I asked, trying to keep the laughter from my voice.

"That we're better together."

"Sounds about right." I smiled. "Now, are we going to our spot or not?"

He chuckled. "Let's go." He reached down to entwine our hands and his eyes landed on the cake lying on the ground. The glass might not have shattered, but there was a crack in it, and the cake inside lay smashed. "Well," he said, bending to retrieve it, "it's still edible."

Such a guy.

He handed me the cake and I held it on my lap as he drove us to our spot. As he drove, his hand rested possessively on my thigh and he continuously looked over at me, as if to make sure I was still in the truck.

Once we were at the meadow he led me over to the pond

and onto the dock. We kicked off our shoes and sat down, letting our feet dangle into the water.

The sun shone bright in the sky—glowing down upon us and casting a golden glow.

The cake sat untouched between us as we grew quiet.

"Are you mad at me?" I asked eventually, growing fearful that now he was second-guessing forgiving me.

He shook his head. "No. I was. But seeing you again, hearing you tell me that you love me ... That took all the anger and pain away. I'm just happy to have you back. You're not the kind of a girl a guy wants to lose. I don't mean that in a possessive way, just ..." He shrugged, letting his shoulders sag as he kicked at the water. "You're *my* girl, Tate. There's no one else I want. I'd be a fucking idiot not to forgive you." He ran his fingers through his dark hair and turned his head slightly to look at me. Squinting against the sunlight, he confessed, "With you, it's different."

I knew exactly what he meant.

"It is different," I whispered in agreement. "You know, I always thought relationships seemed like a lot of work, but I feel like with us it's effortless."

"Effortless?" he snorted, eyeing me. "It was hardly effortless."

I laughed. "Not in the beginning, and it certainly wasn't easy these past two weeks, but before that ... things were pretty dang perfect."

Jude smiled widely. "What we have, it's true love, baby. You can't fight destiny."

I opened my mouth to speak but he reached out and grabbed my hand, pulling me into the water.

I squealed in fright, expecting to get soaked, but surprisingly the water didn't even reach my knees.

Jude tightened his hold on me and I knew he was going to try to pull me into deeper water. "Jude!" I screamed, trudging through the water to get away from him. His hold slackened and I managed to get a few feet away.

I squealed, jumping up when he splashed me with water. I screamed his name again and splashed him back.

I tore my damp shirt off, throwing it as far as I could so it landed in the grass, before it ended up drenched.

Jude used that to his advantage and maneuvered in front of me.

He walked up real slow, smiling innocently. "Sorry, Tate, I couldn't resist. I'll stop. Forgive me?"

I opened my mouth to tell him to kiss my ass when he reached down and splashed more water at my face.

"Juuuude!" I shrieked yet again.

I cupped water in my hands and dropped it on his head in retaliation.

All the while, we both laughed.

Laughter had been missing from both our lives for too many days.

He swiped a long arc of water at me, drenching my legs and shorts. My hands flew up to cover my face. The water wasn't cold, but it definitely wasn't warm either.

Once I recovered from his onslaught, I splashed him back, and a full-on water war ensued. Both of us ended up drenched, but I was too happy to care.

Jude grabbed me around my waist, spinning me around. Both of us grinned like fools.

I'd missed him more than I thought it was possible to miss another person. I wasn't lying when I told him he was stuck with me. There was no way I was ever leaving him again. This man was mine, forever.

"I love you," he murmured in my ear, smoothing my hair out of my eyes.

"I love you too." I clasped arms around his neck, my legs wrapping around his waist as he held me up. I stared down at him, the sun shining on our faces. My damp hair clung to my chest, the ends dripping water onto his shoulders. Now that I had said the words, I realized they weren't that scary, and I just wanted to keep saying them over and over again, because they filled me with such joy. I lowered my head, a smile on my face. My lips grazed his ear and I murmured, "I love you, Jude Brooks. I love you with all my heart."

He kissed me slowly, deeply, savoring every touch of our lips.

He set me down and then crouched for me to climb onto him piggyback style. He lifted me up and tilted his head back to look at me. His eyes were serious as he stared me down. "You're the only girl for me, never forget that, Tate."

"Never," I agreed, burrowing my head against his neck with a smile on my face as he carried me out of the water.

I hated that I hadn't believed him when he told me about Brooke. I hated that I pushed him away and ran from my own feelings. I hated that I fought my heart so hard.

But all my fighting was futile; because love is one battle you can never overcome. Love always wins.

Jude put me down when we reached the grass. He pulled a beanie out of his back pocket and fixed it on, his damp hair sticking up in the front.

Growing serious, he leaned forward and his nose grazed mine. "Marry me, Tate."

"What?" I gasped with wide eyes.

"You heard me." He chuckled, and then like a typical guy his eyes dropped to the swell of my breasts barely contained behind my bra. "Marry me. Maybe not today or tomorrow, or next week or next month, or maybe so." He shrugged. "It doesn't matter to me, as long as you promise to marry me one day ..." he paused and cracked a grin. "And promise to have lots of my babies." His hand reached for my stomach, his fingers skimming my skin. "I want it all with you, Tate. Marriage, babies, a house, a *life*. None of it has any meaning without you. Please, say you'll marry me?"

I stood, mouth agape, and stared at him like he'd grown three heads. I hadn't been expecting that to come out of his mouth, especially since I'd shown up today to seek his forgiveness. I was shocked, to say the least, and didn't know what to say. I knew what I *wanted* to say, but I was scared. I closed my eyes and swallowed thickly, silently telling myself not to be so scared all the time. Pushing my fears and anxieties aside, I spoke, "One day?"

"One day," he promised. "When you're ready," he amended.

I nodded, and a slow smile lifted my lips. "Yes."

"Yes?" He stepped back with shock. Grinning, he gasped, "You said yes!"

He picked me up around my waist and spun me around. I had no choice but to hold on tight. When he set me down he kissed me soundly, humming low in his throat. He gripped my face between his large hands and pressed his forehead against mine. "We're getting married."

"One day," I repeated.

"One day soon," he whispered low. "I hope," he added, nibbling on my lips. I sank into his touch. I couldn't get enough of him. Why had I ever thought I could live without this? I was crazy.

He took my hand and sat down in the grass. I lay down beside him and he turned to look at me. "I have so much to tell you." He smiled, his eyes roaming greedily up and down my body.

"Like what?" I prompted.

Shrugging, he pulled his knees up to his chest and wrapped his arms around them. "Well, for starters, since you broke my heart—" his sad eyes slid to me and then he smiled jokingly "—I had to find ways to distract myself so I couldn't think about you. I spent a lot of time fixing things at Pap's house, which I'm sure you saw. But there's something else I did." His lips turned down in a frown and my heart stopped beating all together. Shit. He was going to tell me he slept with someone else. I knew it. Oh, God. I was going to be sick. "I found Julia."

Okay, that *so* was not what I'd been expecting.

"Julia? *The* Julia? The Julia your grandpa thinks I am during one of his bad days?" I couldn't get the words past my lips fast enough.

"Yeah." He nodded, his brown eyes sad.

"Have you talked to her?" I asked.

"Yep." He tapped his fingers against the top of his knees. "I've talked to her. She ... uh ... she thought my dad put me up to calling. I told her I hadn't talked to that fucking asshole since I moved out. I explained to her about Pap calling you Julia, and that we were curious." He shrugged, letting out a sigh.

"And?" I prompted. "Was she nice? What did she have to say? How was she involved with your dad?" I kept firing questions at him, curiosity eating me up.

"She said that her and my dad were high school sweethearts. They planned to get married after college and live happily ever after," he mumbled.

"Come on, Jude." I sat up, tucking my damp hair behind my ear. "I know there's more to the story than that."

He sighed, running his fingers through his hair. "She caught him cheating on her with my mom. My mommy's the best, ain't she?" He smiled but the happiness from minutes ago was gone. "Julia, uh," he cleared his throat and his jaw clenched, "she was pregnant at the time."

"What?" I gasped, almost falling over with shock.

Jude nodded. "Yeah, that was pretty much my reaction. I have a brother. He's three years older than me."

"Wow," I breathed. "You have a brother?"

He nodded. "Crazy, right?"

I couldn't believe what he was telling me. He'd not only found Julia, but a brother. Family he never knew he had. I knew since Jude didn't have a relationship with his mom and dad, that he worried about what would happen once his grandpa was gone. But now he wouldn't be alone. He had a brother.

"Do you know his name?" I asked.

"Archer," he answered. "Apparently, it's a family name on her side." He shrugged, squinting against the descending sun.

"Have you talked to him? Are you going to meet him? Them?"

He swallowed thickly and nodded. "Yeah, they're supposed to come up to the farm next week for lunch. Archer wants to meet Pap. Julia is coming too. It'll be nice to meet them, but I'm nervous. I hope you'll be there with me."

"Of course I'll be there," I gasped. "I want to meet them too."

"Thanks." He reached over and wrapped an arm around my shoulders, pulling me against him. His lips brushed against the top of my head. "God," his voice lowered, "I fucking hated not having you by my side."

"I felt the same," I agreed. "You'll never know how sorry I am for pushing you away and not believing you."

"Well, you have our whole lives to make it up to me. I accept payment in—"

"Sexual favors, I know, I know," I chanted with a laugh. I stood up and stretched my legs. "You'll have to catch me first before that happens."

Before he could respond, I took off running.

I didn't know where I was going, and I didn't care.

I let myself smile and laugh as I ran through the field of tall grass and flowers. Jude's laughter sounded behind me as his footsteps grew closer.

I closed my eyes as I ran, the setting sun warming my face.

I spread my arms out wide like I was flying.

His arm came around my waist and we tumbled to the ground. I ended up on top of him and his hands gripped my waist. My hips dug into his as I lowered my head to kiss him.

As the heat of the kiss grew to scorching temperatures our clothes melted away and we made love there in our meadow.

The sun disappeared beneath the line of trees and the stars soon shimmered above us.

My body curled against his, molding to the shape of him.

Never again would I ever leave this man's side, because I'd found the one, and he would *always* be worth fighting for.

CHAPTER TWENTY-NINE

"Ahhhhh!" Rowan screamed when Jude and I showed up to the Memorial Day party hand in hand. "Yes! Yes! Yes!" She fist-pumped. Sobering, she added, "You two had me worried there for a little while that you weren't going to work it out."

Jude chuckled, keeping his arm around me so I couldn't leave his side. "This one had me worried too." Looking down at me, he added, "If you hadn't come to me in a few more days I think I would've finally caved and gone after you. I wanted to come to you every day we were apart, but I knew you needed time, so I was giving you that."

"You're too perfect for me sometimes," I replied, trying to keep the dreamy sigh from my voice. I was young and in love, so sometimes it was hard not to act like a lovesick fool.

"Bleh," Rowan gagged. "Stop with the lovey dovey looks. You're making me ill."

Jude and I laughed. Smiling at my best friend, I said, "You

wear the same look around Trent all the time and if I recall, you're marrying him in two weeks."

Rowan smiled widely, looking around for Trent. "Yeah, I guess I do." With a gasp, she cried, "You will never believe what he did the other night!"

"What?" I asked, hoping it wasn't something that was going to gross me out and make me picture Trent naked, because that would be fucking weird.

A blush stained her cheeks as she spoke. "So, we were talking about our honeymoon, and then he started talking *again* about wanting another kid. I want to wait, he doesn't, blah, blah, blah. Anyway ..." She guided us over to a private side of the yard where there weren't so many guests—and let me tell you, since it was a Wentworth party there were at least a hundred people in attendance. "He got so mad at me for saying that I wasn't ready that he took all of the condoms and threw them out the window." Jude snickered. "Oh, that's not the best part." Rowan crossed her arms over her chest. "He refused to go outside and get them, so I wouldn't either. The next morning one of the neighbors is walking their dog, and the little hairy beast tries to eat one of the wrappers. The neighbor then finds all the condoms on the driveway, picks them up, and brings them to the door." She threw her hands in the air. "I've never been more embarrassed in all my life."

Jude and I dissolved into fits of laughter. "Oh, my God." I wiped tears away. "That's the funniest thing I've ever heard."

She shook her head. "If I didn't love him so much, I'd kill him for that stunt."

"So," Jude started, "does this mean we should expect a bouncing baby boy or girl in nine months?"

Rowan sighed and pinched the bridge of her nose. "Looks like it."

"Yes!" Jude cried. "I'm going to be an uncle again!"

Rowan laughed. "Don't get too excited just yet."

"I think," Jude said as he put a hand to his chest, "that I should be your children's godfather, since Tater Tot here refuses to let me have Jude Jr. for a few more years."

Rowan's lips quirked into a smile. "I think Trace would kill me if we didn't let him be the godfather."

"I heard my name!"

A moment later Trace, Trenton's older brother, appeared and slung his arm over Rowan's shoulder. "You called for me."

She laughed, pushing him away. "No, I just said your name. There's a difference."

"Usually, when someone says my name it's because they want me. I'm a very likable guy." He grinned at Jude and me. His dark hair fell messily over his forehead, shielding his green eyes. Heavy stubble dotted his cheeks and chin. He was dressed the same way he always was, jeans, a white shirt, and a plaid shirt over top.

"Trace!" his wife called, walking up to us. "Grace won't stop crying." She held their baby daughter. "She needs to go to sleep before the fireworks start in an hour or she'll get too upset to sleep." Olivia rocked the crying baby in her arms. The poor woman looked exhausted, but happy. Their son, Dean, the cutest three-year-old I'd ever seen, clung to her leg peeking shyly at us. He had a mop of dark wavy hair and green eyes like his dad. He was even dressed similarly in a plaid shirt.

Trace held out his arms for Grace and began to sing to the baby. Her cries ceased and she looked up at her daddy in awe. She was dressed in an adorable pink and purple flowered dress, with a white headband around her head. Like her brother, she had dark slightly curly hair.

"I'll see you guys later," Trace called, walking off and into the large mansion singing to his daughter.

Something about seeing Trace with his kids made me look up at Jude and think about him as a father one day. Our kids would be the luckiest kids on the planet.

Dean tugged on Olivia's jeans and she lowered to pick up the boy, grunting at his weight. Dean laid his head on her shoulder, blinking curious owlish eyes at all of us. "Where Daddy go?" he asked her.

"He went to put Gracie to bed." She kissed his cheek. He wiggled in her arms, wanting down now.

"Where Rent?" Dean asked, looking around.

Olivia held out her hand for him. "I don't know. Let's go find him."

Rowan nodded her head for us to follow Olivia and Dean.

We found Trent sitting at a table with Ivy and Tristan playing a card game. When Dean saw his uncle, he screamed, "Rent!" and took off running.

Olivia shook her head and smiled at us. "He's such a handful, but I love him so much."

"Believe me, I understand completely." Rowan nodded toward Tristan. "Kids are hard work, but worth every second of it."

Olivia nodded her head in agreement. "Grace makes our family feel complete ... although, Trace is already talking about wanting another baby. I think he'd be happy if I spent the next ten years of my life pregnant." She laughed. "He loves being a father." Her eyes grew misty, and at that moment he returned. When Dean saw his daddy, he forgot all about Trent and took off running once more. Trace pretended to fall to the ground when the little boy collided with his legs and the two tumbled to the ground. Trace picked up his son, tossing him in the air. "Seeing him with our children," Olivia sighed dreamily, watching her husband and son, "makes me love him even more and I never thought that was possible."

Trace picked up Dean, lifting the small boy onto his shoulders, and sauntered over to us. Dean pulled and plucked at Trace's hair, but he didn't seem to mind.

"When are we eating?" Trace asked. "I'm hungry." Catching sight of his mom, he yelled her over.

Lily Wentworth breezed over, her dark hair blowing around her shoulders and her blue eyes bright. "Yes?" she asked.

"I want to know when we're eating. I need food."

"Food! Food!" Dean cried, beating the top of Trace's head with his hands.

"Calm down, Dean." Trace reached up, grabbing the little boy's hands. "You're going to hurt Daddy."

Dean frowned and when Trace released his small hands the boy ceased his onslaught.

Lily smiled beautifully. She reminded me of an heiress or maybe a princess with her effortless beauty and kind personality. "You're always hungry." She laughed at her oldest son. "But the food is almost ready. Why don't you guys go ahead and get seated at one of the tables." She waved her hand to the many picnic tables littering the green lawn. Each table was covered with a checkered red and white tablecloth.

"Sounds good." Trace grinned, lifting Dean off from around his neck. Dean giggled in delight as Trace spun him through the air.

Trent and Jude pushed two of the picnic tables together so we'd all be able to sit together.

It didn't take long for waiters to start serving us. I expected some kind of fancy fare, but I was pleasantly surprised to see they served us normal backyard party food. Burgers, hotdogs, mac n' cheese, you name it and it was accounted for.

There were already plates in front of each of us and we were allowed to grab whatever we wanted to eat.

I chose a cheeseburger, some mac n' cheese, and assorted fruit. Jude grabbed a bit of everything and I had no doubt he would eat it all.

Across from me, Trace grabbed two hot dogs and drenched them in ketchup. He cut up a hot dog for Dean and covered that in ketchup as well.

"Trace," Olivia scolded, wrinkling her nose, "that's not necessary."

"Hey, you can't start them loving ketchup or Star Wars too young. You're the freak that doesn't like either." Across from me I looked at Dean, who was currently shoving pieces of hot dog in his mouth and getting ketchup all over his face, and noticed that beneath his open plaid shirt he was wearing a shirt with a Star Wars logo. Clearly, Trace had dressed him.

"Ketchup is gross," she countered, "and Star Wars is weird."

Trace gasped. "Take that back."

I laughed at their playful interaction. No matter how much they might banter back and forth, that was just their relationship, but you could always see the love shining through in everything they did.

Jude bumped my shoulder and I looked up at him with a smile. I giggled when I saw mayonnaise sitting in the corner of his mouth. I lifted my head to kiss it away.

"Are you happy?" Jude asked me.

"Very," I replied, and it was the truth. I couldn't remember a time when I'd been happier.

Jude grinned widely. "Do I make you happy?"

"The happiest," I responded.

Lowering his voice, he nuzzled his face against my ear. "I've wanted you for so long that I stopped believing we'd ever happen. Thank you."

"For what?" My brows furrowed together in puzzlement.

"For giving me your heart, your love, your future." He shrugged, squeezing my thigh. "Thank you for giving it all to me. You could've chosen any guy to love, but you picked me."

"I didn't pick you, Jude." I smiled, kissing his stubbled cheek. "We picked each other."

He chuckled. "That sounds about right."

Rowan bumped my shoulder, distracting me. I turned my head to look at her. "What?" I asked.

She giggled. "I was a bit afraid that the way you guys were staring at each other you might end up having sex on the table."

"Rowan!" I gasped in shock.

"Table sex?" Trace piped in. "Table sex is the best. I mean, all kinds of sex is the best—"

"Trace!" Olivia hissed. "Be quiet." She nodded her head at Dean.

Tristan and Ivy didn't seem bothered by the outburst—although, there was a bit of a blush staining Ivy's cheeks.

Olivia's warning came a bit too late though. "Sex! Sex! Sex!" Dean chanted, smacking his small fists against the table.

Olivia shook her head, her cheeks coloring with embarrassment. She slowly raised her hands to hide her face as other people gathered at the Memorial Day party turned to stare.

Trace put a hand over his son's mouth and waved at the staring people with a smirk on his face. "Nothing to see here folks. Look away."

Slowly, they turned away and back to their meals.

"Now, Dean," Trace said as he looked down at his son, still not moving his hand, "we can't say that word so loud, okay?"

The little boy looked up at his dad and nodded. Trace lowered his hand and then Dean started in again with a quieter chant of, "Sex, sex, sex."

"Oh, God," Olivia groaned. "Someone give him another word to say, *please*. Anything. I beg of you. He's like a parrot, repeating every thing you say."

Jude looked at Dean and said, "Tater Tot."

Dean quieted and tilted his head. "Tater Tot?"

Jude nodded. "This—" he pointed at me "—is Tater Tot."

Dean looked at me with a puzzled brow. "Tater, Tater, Tater," he began to chant.

Olivia shot Jude a smile. "Thanks."

"No problem."

"Why do you call Tatum that?" Tristan leaned around Trent and Row to peer at Jude.

"Because, her nickname's Tate and it sounds a lot like Tater, so I settled on Tater Tot. Plus, it used to make her ears turn red anytime I said it. Now she doesn't do it and I know it's 'cause she secretly likes it." He chuckled, rubbing my shoulders.

I didn't agree with him, but I didn't deny it either, because he was right. Now I loved that stupid nickname, because Jude was the only person that called me that. I'd missed hearing him call me that during our time apart more than I'd care to admit.

When we finished eating people came to clear off the tables and take them away so the whole lawn was free for roaming.

A DJ started up in the corner and Jude grabbed my hand, dragging me over to where others were gathering to dance.

"Dance with me," he pleaded, his bottom lip jutting out enough to be cute, but not look stupid.

I couldn't resist that face, so of course I said yes.

It was a fast-paced country song and Jude seemed to know all the words, singing them under his breath as he spun me around.

Somehow, I ended up with my back to his front. His hands fisted against the bottom of my dress, dragging it up dangerously high as I swayed my hips against his. He felt hard and lethal behind me, like a predator, but I wasn't scared. I craved his touch. I needed it more than I needed the air I breathed.

He brushed my hair over my one shoulder before his hands returned to my hips. He pressed his face against my neck, planting small kisses to the skin there. I giggled as his stubble tickled me.

"God, I love that sound," he groaned.

"What?" I asked, my voice light and carefree sounding.

"Your laugh." He bit my earlobe. "It's music to my ears."

"That's silly, Jude." I closed my eyes and reached up to wrap my arms around his neck. "It's just a laugh."

"Nah, with you it's not." His voice grew deep with seriousness. "You used to never laugh, and now you do it all the time. It always makes me smile hearing it—knowing that you're happy."

"Mmm." I leaned my body fully against him, playing with the hairs at the base of his neck. "I think you're trying to flatter me."

"Nope." He bit my neck lightly. "Just being honest, baby."

The song changed to something slower and he turned me around so we faced each other once more. I let out a small scream as I stumbled, but he was quick to catch me before I could fall.

He held me close, leaning down to brush his forehead against mine. He was dressed casually today in a pair of khaki shorts and a white t-shirt, but he also wore his favorite beanie.

"You know," I laughed, remembering a conversation we had so long ago, "you never told me what these rules were you made with yourself that you've broken with me. Care to tell me about it now?" I smiled up at him.

He chuckled, kissing the end of my nose. "I can't believe you remembered that."

"I did." I nodded. "So, come on, tell me. I'm curious."

"Well, it was only one rule to be honest."

I leaned my head back to stare into his warm brown eyes. "And what was it?" I asked, trying to keep the pleading tone from my voice.

He lowered his head to whisper in my ear. "Never fall in love."

I closed my eyes and let out a happy, contented sigh. I leaned up on my tiptoes, and with my fingers tangled in his hair I tilted his head down so I could reach his ear. "Funny, Brooks. I had the same rule."

He grinned down at me with a boyish smile. "It's amazing how these things work out, isn't it?"

I smiled in response and leaned my head against his chest. Listening to the steady *thump, thump, thump* of his heart. My laugh was music to his ears and *this* was my music. "Amazing," I agreed, letting my eyes drift closed.

"It's time for the fireworks!" someone yelled and the music cut off.

I jumped as one boomed in the sky and then my mouth fell open in awe at the display. These were *real* fireworks. Not the kind you got at the stand by 7-Eleven.

Someone handed Jude and me sparklers and then lit them for us.

Tristan ran by us with two in his hands, laughing as Dean chased him. Rowan cried after him, worrying about him getting burned, while Trent chuckled. "He's a boy, leave him alone."

I leaned my head on Jude's shoulder, a small smile on his lips.

I used to think I didn't have a family, but looking around at my friends and the man by my side that I loved more than anything, I knew that I did have a family. I wasn't alone. I was surrounded by people that loved me and I loved them just as much in return.

For so long I'd closed myself off from caring about anything and anyone. It was so much easier to build a fortress around my heart than risk getting hurt, but then this crazy cocky guy knocked it down and showed me what life was really about.

I smiled up at him and he turned his head to smile at me.

Fireworks lit up the night sky above us as we swayed our sparklers through the air.

A part of me wanted to stay frozen in this moment forever, but life didn't have a pause button and you had to keep moving forward. So, that's what I was doing.

CHAPTER THIRTY

As I drove to the farm my hands shook with nerves against the steering wheel. I wasn't even nervous for myself, oh no this shaking jittery mess I'd become was reserved solely for worrying about Jude.

I hoped and prayed that everything went okay when he met Julia and Archer. I was going to be there for support, but there wasn't much I could do to distract him if this turned out to be a really bad idea. On second thought, I could probably flash him my boob and he'd be a happy camper.

I'd stopped at Starbucks on my way to the farm and gotten myself an iced coffee. I hadn't gotten much sleep last night and needed the caffeine to keep me awake.

The lack of sleep was due entirely to the fact that while we were having lunch with Julia and Archer, my dad would be arriving home. Jude and I were supposed to have dinner with him and I was worrying myself sick over what might transpire between us.

Today was going to be full of family time, but I wasn't sure if that was a good thing or a bad thing.

When I pulled up in front of the farmhouse I spotted Jude sitting on the porch steps, his elbows resting on his knees with his head in his hands. He looked as tired as me. I got out of the car, coffee in hand, and sat down beside him.

"How are you feeling?" I asked, staring out at the horses grazing beyond us.

"Scared out of mind," he admitted. "I have a fucking brother, how weird is that, Tate?" He peered down at me with his dark eyes. "But what if he hates me? What if all this blows up in my face?"

I set my drink beside me on the step and wrapped my hands around his muscular arm, giving it a light squeeze. "You can't worry about that." I shrugged. "Think positive. He might be a really cool guy, or he could be a major douche nozzle, in which case I will gladly kick him in the balls for you." I smiled innocently, batting my eyelashes.

That got him to laugh, which had been my goal. "You'd do that for me, wouldn't you?"

"Uh, of course." I looked at him like I was crazy. "I already took on a guy three times my size for you. I think I've proven my worth. After all, look at this face." I pointed at myself. "No one expects me to be such a badass, so they never see me coming."

"God, I love you." He laughed, slinging his arm over my shoulders and pulling my body against his. He rubbed his face into my hair, humming under his breath.

I narrowed my eyes. "Are you trying to distract me with your declarations of love?" I slid away from him, quirking my lips so he'd know I was only joking. "Check out these muscles,

Brooks." I flexed my arms. "I'm like your own personal bodyguard."

"Gotta keep the chicks away from me, don't you?" He chuckled, reaching for me and lifting me onto his lap.

"Hell yes." I nodded with a grin. "You're a slut magnet. These bitches best learn to back up off my man." I wrapped my arms around his neck, staring into his eyes. "Don't worry." I leaned forward, my voice growing serious, "I trust you."

"You do?" he asked, surprise coloring his tone.

"I do," I stated firmly. My voice softening, I frowned. "I'm sorry I ever doubted you."

He smoothed his fingers through my blonde hair and then took my chin in his hand. "It's in the past now, baby. I'm over it. Sitting here with the woman of my dreams in my arms I've never been happier. *That's* what I choose to focus on. Every relationship has ups and downs, Tate." He smoothed his thumb over my jaw. "That's normal. I've learned to cherish every moment you choose to spend with me." His eyes dropped to my lips and his eyes darkened. "Because with you by my side, I'm the luckiest son-of-a-bitch on this whole damn Earth."

My lips quirked into a half smile. "That was quite the declaration."

"It's the truth," he stated flatly. His eyes darkened with heat. "You're worth it all, Tate."

I grinned at that and he chuckled.

"Ah, there's the dimple I love." He leaned forward, kissing my cheek. "I still don't get to see it often enough," he added with a slight frown. "We've got to work on that."

"Don't worry, Brooks," I began as I burrowed my body against his, tucking my head under his neck, "I think you're going to be seeing a lot more of it."

He didn't respond and I felt his body stiffen in my arms.

About that time, I heard the sounds of the car.

I eased off of Jude's lap to sit beside him. He reached over and grabbed my hand, squeezing it tight. His Adam's apple bobbed with nervousness.

"It'll be okay," I assured him.

He nodded, his eyes never leaving the car. It came to a stop and dust from the gravel clouded the air.

"What do I do?" Jude asked, sounding panicked.

I stood, giving his hand a light tug. "You go say hi and we go from there."

A tall guy got out of the SUV on the driver's side. He appeared as nervous as Jude. His dark hair hung in waves over his forehead and his eyes were a piercing gray. He stood against the side of the vehicle with his arms crossed.

A woman, Julia, I assumed, got out of the passenger side.

We all stood staring at each other for a moment and I decided it looked like I'd be the one to have to break the awkward silence.

I let go of Jude's hand and stepped up to Archer. "Hi." I squared my shoulders, determined not to show my nerves. "I'm Tatum, and this is Jude." I pointed my thumb over my shoulder in the general direction of where Jude hovered. "This is all very awkward," I whispered conspiratorially, like I was letting him in on a secret, "so why don't we all just introduce ourselves and head inside for lunch? Sound good?"

Archer chuckled, and his laugh sounded so much like Jude's I nearly reared back. Then, when he pushed his hair out of his eyes and I got a good look at his face I was even more surprised by the similarities. They had the same pouty lips and angular jaw. While their eyes were different colors they both had the same shape and piercing quality to them.

"I'm Archer, but I guess you knew that already." He winked.

Jude stepped forward and put a possessive hand on my shoulder. "Nice to meet you," he said, but there was a hardness to his voice.

Archer's eyes sparkled with mischief. "Don't worry, little brother, I'm not trying to hit on your girl." He held his left hand in the air, tapping his thumb against his ring finger. "Happily married for the last six months."

"Oh." Jude dropped his hand from my shoulder. Smiling sheepishly, he added, "Sorry."

Julia came around the vehicle and smiled pleasantly at the both of us. It seemed she'd needed a minute to gather herself. "I'm sorry, I … it's strange being back here after so long." She looked up at the house behind us. "I spent many years at this house when I was growing up." Julia turned and smiled at me, then at Jude. "Can I hug you?" she asked Jude.

He seemed startled by the question. He hadn't said it, but I knew he expected her to hate him. After all, she'd caught Jude's dad cheating on her with his mom. But looking at the kind woman in front of us, it was clear there was no bad blood—at least where Jude was concerned.

"Uh …," he paused, his brows furrowing together. "Sure."

Immediately, Julia enveloped him in her arms. It wasn't the hug of a stranger, either. No, she hugged him like a mom. I saw Jude relax in her arms and tears stung my eyes. Jude needed this more than anything else.

She released him and patted his cheek with a small smile curving her lips. "Where's Jerry?" She looked behind us, waiting for him to appear.

"He was taking a nap." Jude shrugged. "He should be up

soon. I ... uh ... I didn't tell you when we talked but he," Jude's face crumpled as he continued, "Pap has Alzheimer's."

Julia's mouth parted in surprise. "Oh."

Archer didn't have any obvious reaction, but I didn't expect him to. He didn't know Jerry.

"Yeah, he has good days and bad days. Today was a good day before his nap, so let's hope it stays that way. Come on, we don't need to stand out here all day. I already fixed lunch."

"You cook?" Julia asked with surprise, following Jude inside.

"Yeah," I heard him tell her as they stepped into the house. "I had to learn from a young age. Pap and—" They got far enough away that I couldn't hear their voices anymore since I still stood outside with Archer. Neither of us seemed ready to go into the house.

"So," he said, shoving his hands into his pockets, rocking back on his heels, "this is awkward."

I shrugged. "It only is if you make it." Growing serious, I narrowed my eyes at Archer. "Jude is a good person. His parents really fucked him up, so much so that there's a lot he won't talk about when it comes to them and I realize he'll probably never tell me everything because it's easier for him not to think about it, and all the family he has left is his grandpa. He needs you in his life. He needs someone he can depend on. Someone who's family. Don't hurt him," I stated flatly. "If you do, I won't hesitate to hunt you down and cut off your balls, and use them as ornaments to decorate my Christmas tree."

Archer busted out laughing.

I narrowed my eyes and widened my stance, with my hands on my hips. "I'm serious," I warned.

"You must love him a lot." Archer chuckled, trying to hide his smile behind his hand.

"More than I ever knew possible." I held my head high. Something about Archer made me feel intimidated, but I refused to show that I was affected by him.

He smiled slowly. "I guess we better get in there so I can get to know my baby brother."

As we headed slowly toward the house, I asked him, "Was it weird for you, finding out you had a brother?"

Archer halted his steps and looked down at me. Jude was tall, but Archer was taller. I swear he had to be at least six feet five. He was a giant. He loomed above me, an intimidating force. "Surprisingly, no." He shrugged. "I didn't know my dad at all, but I always assumed he moved on and married someone else, had a few kids ... a life without me," he said softly. "I know things will probably be awkward for a while, but I'm glad to know I have a brother and I want to have a relationship with him. My mom never remarried, so I was an only child growing up." His eyes flicked to the house and back to me. "At first, when my mom told me about Jude—before I talked to him on the phone—I was really mad, because he grew up with a mom and a dad. He quickly set me straight on that." Archer sighed heavily. "It seems like I got the better deal. My mom's awesome and she always made sure that I had everything I needed and provided me with a stable loving home. Jude didn't have that."

"At least he had his grandparents," I inserted. I nodded toward the front door. "Come meet Jerry. He's your grandpa too, and trust me you'll, never have met a more amazing person than him."

Voices were coming from the sunroom so that's where I led

Archer. Julia was sitting in a chair while Jerry and Jude sat on the couch. When Archer and I approached Jerry came to stand. His limbs were shaky and I knew it had everything to do with nerves and not old age.

His eyes lit on Archer and my mouth fell open in surprise as he began to cry.

He stepped forward and enveloped Archer in a hug.

Archer glanced at me in surprise, but slowly returned the gesture, patting Jerry on his back.

"I didn't know. I'm so sorry. I never knew," Jerry cried into Archer's shoulder.

"It's okay, Jerry," Archer said as they parted.

Jerry wiped the moisture from beneath his eyes. "Please, call me Pap." He clapped Archer on the shoulder and led him over to the couch so he could sit between Jude and him.

I went to sit in the other free chair, but Jude's hand snuck out, catching me around my waist and I was pulled onto his lap.

He kissed my neck, and whispered, "I need you."

I leaned my head on his shoulder in comfort. I understood completely what he meant. I'd do whatever it took to get him through this day, and if he needed me close to him then that's what I'd do. Tonight, I would need his support.

I rubbed the back of his neck soothingly, and kept quiet while he interacted with Archer and Julia. Things were a bit tense for a little while, but soon everyone got comfortable and we ate lunch in the kitchen.

Jude and Archer left so he could get a tour of the house and property.

Julia smiled at the guys as they walked off. She looked from Jerry to me. "I never thought this day would come."

"Did you know about Jude?" I asked with surprise.

She nodded with a sad smile. "I did, but the way things ended between Andrew and me, I didn't think it was the best thing for me to reach out." She shrugged, pushing her pretty auburn hair out of her eyes. For being in her forties I thought she was gorgeous. Her skin was flawless and her eyes were bright. Despite the bad hand life had dealt her, she'd come out better than most. It was obvious in the way she carried herself and the smile that was nearly permanent on her face that she was happy.

"I can understand where you were coming from," I assured her, not wanting her to think I judged her for keeping the brother's apart.

I sincerely hoped that Archer and Jude would grow close. Based on how things had gone so far today, I had nothing to worry about. There was definitely an awkwardness between them, but with each passing minute it lessened.

"You two seem very much in love," she commented.

Jerry chuckled, and his smile was pleased. I knew Jerry was looking forward to Jude and I progressing in our relationship—like marriage and babies, but he was going to have to wait a few years. At least for the baby part. I wanted Jude to myself for a while.

"Yes, we are." I smiled. I knew there was a happy flush to my cheeks. "I don't know what I'd do without him."

And that was the truth. I'd suffered nearly two weeks without him, and I'd been as depressed then as when I lost my brother.

"It's nice to see people young and in love. So carefree." She propped her head in her hand. "I miss that."

"You're still young—" Before I could continue, she snorted.

"No, really," I added. "You could still find someone and have your happily ever after."

She smiled sweetly, her eyes soft. "Honey, I did get my happily ever after, it just wasn't the one they write about in romance novels." She reached across the table and patted my hand in a motherly gesture.

Looking across the table at her I couldn't believe that we'd found Julia, and subsequently Jude's brother because of it. If Jerry had never called me Julia, I would've never started wondering about the mysterious girl. Life worked in funny ways.

I made a pot of coffee while we waited for the guys to return. When they did it was time for Archer and Julia to leave. Both promised that we'd meet up again next week for dinner—either at the house or a restaurant.

Jude's smile seemed permanently glued to his face. He hugged Archer and Julia goodbye, and I was surprised when both opened their arms to hug me.

I'd known Jude was worried that they might hate him, or just be horrible people, but everything had worked out perfectly. Jude had a brother who clearly wanted to get to know him, and given enough time I could see the two becoming close. Even Julia seemed genuinely interested in knowing Jude. I hoped she'd become a mother figure in his life since his was absent. I was beginning to wonder if I was ever going to meet his parents. He barely talked about them and seemed to have nothing to do with them. But I knew all about having shitty parents and let's face it if I completely blocked them out of my life it would be a whole lot easier than having to deal with them.

Unfortunately, or maybe fortunately, I never took the easy route.

My mom was still in a home for the foreseeable future—maybe even forever—but with my dad coming home today, I'd decided to try to have a relationship with him. I hoped our dinner went well and we could move past everything. After all, reading Graham's letter seemed to have a profound effect on him. I guess I only had to hope that it lasted and that his anger management had helped—even though he was out of the facility, he still had to attend meetings three times a week. I think more than anything, I just wanted to have a dad. I'd lost my brother, and my mom—because let's face it, she was off her rocker—so my dad was the only family I had left.

I shook my head free of my thoughts and followed Jude and Jerry to the porch, where we watched Archer and Julia get into the SUV and drive away.

"Well," Jerry smiled as he spoke, patting Jude's shoulder as he passed him on his way back into the house, "I don't think that could've gone better."

Jude nodded his head in agreement, watching until the SUV disappeared from sight.

While Jerry went inside, probably to watch TV, Jude and I stood outside for a while.

He seemed lost in his thoughts, so I let him think.

Eventually, he turned to me with a grin curving his lips. "Thank you."

I jerked back in surprise. "Thank you? Why are you thanking me?"

He chuckled, reaching for my hand. "Because, you're the one that said we should find Julia. Without you, I wouldn't have known about Archer ... That I had family."

"Jude," my throat constricted with emotion, "you never need to thank me for that."

"I know—" he pulled me in front of him and I leaned my head against his chest "—but I wanted to." He trailed his fingers over my stomach and up my t-shirt. Heat filled my body and I let out a small moan. It didn't matter how many times he touched me, I *always* wanted more.

Jude chuckled low against my ear. "Tate?"

"Yeah?" I panted as his hands skimmed higher, coming up to cup my breasts.

"It sounds like you want me." He bit my earlobe.

"I always want you," I replied truthfully. Anywhere, anytime. I was like a big ball of want when it came to Jude. What had he done to me?

"Really?" His teeth lightly bit into the skin where my neck met my shoulder.

"Mhmm," I hummed, my eyes closing.

"I like that, Tate," he growled low in his throat, "I love that what I do to you turns you on."

His thumb rubbed circles around my belly button.

My chest rose and fell with each heavy breath and I could barely keep my eyes open. "I need you. Now," I panted, and he hadn't even *really* touched me yet. Just teased.

"Your wish is my command," he growled, his voice low and husky. He turned me around and captured my lips with his own, before lifting me up and hauling me over his shoulder. The air got knocked out of my lungs and I was pretty sure his shoulder bruised my stomach. But I'd take the pain if it meant I got to have him.

Jude ran inside and started up the steps. "We'll be in my room, Pap ... cleaning."

I heard Jerry chuckle and call after us. "Cleaning? Sure, that's what they call it these days."

My cheeks flared with a blush, but I wanted Jude too bad to care.

He jogged down the hall into his room and slammed the door closed and locked it behind us.

He tossed me onto the bed and I bounced up and down a few times, letting out a small squeal as I tried to keep from falling off his bed.

While his bedroom at the townhouse was that of a man—gray walls, and black furniture—this was the bedroom of a boy. The walls were painted dark blue, the furniture was clearly hand-me-down and the comforter had blue and gray stripes on it. Clearly, he'd never bothered to replace it.

I didn't have long to look around, though.

He stalked toward me, reaching behind to hook his thumbs in the back of his shirt. He yanked it over his head and threw it across the room.

All that tan, muscled, and rippling flesh was a feast for my starved eyes. My tongue flicked out to wet my lips and then he crashed on top of me, pushing my body against the mattress. He pressed his whole body against me and took my face between his hands, staring into my eyes—staring right down to my very soul.

"I love you," he whispered, and before I could reply he kissed me.

My hands gripped his arms, my nails digging into his flesh.

I needed him closer.

I needed more.

This wasn't enough.

I pushed at him until he rolled over and I could straddle his hips. I leaned forward and my hair created a shield around us as I lowered my head to kiss him this time, taking control.

His fingers were bruising where he gripped my thighs and I knew he was struggling to hold himself back from taking things too fast.

He didn't understand yet that no matter what we did, fast, slow, easy, or hard, I loved it all, because it was with *him*.

I laid my lips against his, not really kissing him, just feeling him.

I then opened my mouth and pulled his bottom lip between my teeth—letting it go with a pop.

"Fuck," he groaned.

I ignored his comment and trailed my index finger over his nose. "I don't think I've ever told you how much I love these freckles."

You couldn't see them from far away, but when you were face to face like we were now there were small freckles sprinkled across his nose and more over the tops of his shoulders. I thought they were adorable and gave him a boyish quality. But honestly, I loved everything about Jude because I loved *him*. Inside and out.

"You like those, do you?" He smoothed his thumb over my cheek.

I nodded, biting my lip. "As much as you love my dimple."

"That's a lot then." He chuckled warmly. His voice lowered and he murmured, "Now, where were we?"

He closed the distance between us, kissing me sweetly.

My body turned to liquid as his hands rubbed my body.

"Jude," I gasped between our lips. "Please."

"Tell me what you want." He nibbled my lips with his teeth and massaged the nape of my neck. "Whatever you want, I'll give it to you."

"You," I breathed, my eyes closing, "only you."

He flipped me onto my back and eased my shirt off of my head. His movements weren't rushed. "You have me, baby." He growled low in his throat as he peppered kisses over my stomach.

My body squirmed against him and he pressed a hand against my chest to still my movements. He chuckled as his hot breath blew against the top of my shorts, making my hips buck. "Simmer down, Tate. I haven't even gotten to the best part yet."

Oh, God.

With his hand on mine he undid the button and zipper on my shorts and started to pull them down. I shimmied my hips a bit to help him.

"You're fucking gorgeous, you know that, right?" He stared up at me with hooded brown eyes.

"I know you make me feel beautiful." I gasped as his fingers parted my underwear and slipped inside me.

I fisted the comforter between my hands and hissed between my teeth.

"Don't ever forget that, baby," he murmured, and then his mouth was on me.

Sweet mother of all things holy!

My brain short-circuited from all the nerves tingling in my body.

"Jude," I moaned, squirming against him as his tongue laved at my center. My fingers delved into his hair and I wasn't sure if I was trying to pull him closer or push him away. "Jude," I tried to find my voice again, but it was barely above a pant. "I need you. Naked. Now."

He chuckled, his body vibrating against me and I almost came right then.

"My sweet Tate is so impatient today, but baby," his voice

lowered further and he looked up at me with darkened eyes, "you're going to have to find some patience, because this isn't going to be quick." His lips quirked up, promising delightful and devilish things.

"Can we do slow and then fast?" I begged, not even caring that my tone sounded whiney.

He bit my thigh and I yelped. With a smirk, he shrugged. "Whatever you want." And then his mouth was on me once more.

My breaths filled the air as I struggled to hold on, but the way he was working his tongue ... Well, I was a goner. A small scream escaped me as my body shook and then he was on top of me, his hand over my mouth.

"Shh," he soothed, "let's not scare the old man downstairs."

My cheeks colored with embarrassment. I'd totally forgotten where we were and that his grandpa was downstairs. In actuality, the house was large enough that there really was no concern of him hearing us, but that thought didn't stop me from feeling uncomfortable.

"Sorry, I didn't mean to kill the mood." His fingers ventured back down and my thoughts from before disappeared. I was pretty sure he could use sex to make me forget anything. "You have the sweetest pussy," he growled, pushing his fingers further into me. "You feel and taste so fucking good."

My cheeks colored at his words.

Jude raised his head and smirked when he saw the blush staining my cheeks. "Does my dirty talk embarrass you? 'Cause baby, that's not even as dirty as it gets."

My cheeks grew redder and I could feel the heat spreading to other parts of my body.

"It does," he chuckled, brushing his lips against my collarbone. "That's cute, Tate. Come on, say something naughty for me."

I wanted to bury my face in my hands, but my hands were currently grasping the comforter as his fingers worked me and I was pretty sure if I let go I'd float away.

"I don't know if I can," I panted, my hips grinding against him.

He kissed me deeply and released my lips. "Yes, you can. Please. For me?"

I was sure that my skin had to be an unattractive red color at this point. "Jude," I groaned, wanting to kick him.

His fingers left my body and he used them to trace my lips. My tongue flicked out automatically and I could taste myself on his fingers.

"You can do it, Tate," he murmured. "It doesn't have to be naughty. Just … push your limits a bit."

Fuck. He wasn't going to leave this alone.

He rolled off me and lay on his back, crossing his arms behind his head. He turned slightly to look at me. A playful smirk turned up his lips. "No sex for you until you say something dirty."

I eyed the bulge straining against his jeans and stared him down. "Really?"

"Really." Waving his hand over the top of his jeans he smirked. "I don't want to, but I can always take care of this myself." He then gestured with said hand to show exactly what he meant, as if I didn't already know.

I sat up, my hair falling forward to cover my breasts, which were still covered by my bra.

I bit my lip. Taking a deep, steady breath, I steeled myself to say something that made me horribly uncomfortable.

I leaned toward him and his eyes sparkled. I let my lips

brush against his ear and murmured, "I want your cock inside me."

Okay, so it *definitely* wasn't the dirtiest thing I could say, but for me ... it was pushing it. Jude smiled wickedly, seeming to like it, so maybe I'd have to get better at pushing my sexual boundaries.

In record time he unclasped my bra, took off my panties, and removed his jeans and boxers. He maneuvered me with ease so that my head was on the pillow and my hair fanned around me. He stared at me like I was the most beautiful woman he'd ever seen, but there was something else I saw in his eyes, and that look could only be summed up in one word.

Love.

L-O-V-E.

Four simple letters, but when you combined them together it created the greatest emotion we ever experienced as humans.

I'd never truly known what it meant to love another human being until I met Jude.

Yes, I loved my family, but that kind of love was different. It was the love of blood and bonds.

But the love I had with Jude it was a choice. *My* choice. He gave me happiness and he pushed me to be a better person. We had our ups and downs and more would come in the future, but I'd learned that it was worth working through, because this kind of love wasn't something you gave up on and you did have to work at it. It wasn't easy, but it was *right*.

He took my lips between his as he guided himself inside me. My body tightened at first and then relaxed to allow him inside.

He slid out all the way and murmured, "Say it again."

If this didn't feel so good, I'd probably kill him for torturing me.

Instead of whispering it, this time I clasped his face between my hands and stared into his eyes. "I want your cock inside—"

Before I could finish he pushed into me and I gasped.

He moved slowly, rolling his hips against mine in a way that had my back arching and my fingers clawing at his back. Sweat dampened our skin as we moved.

He lowered his head, swirling his tongue around my nipple, and then showing attention to the other.

I whimpered from the delicious pain as he lightly bit it. Fuck, he knew what he was doing. I was going to have to get over my embarrassment and read a book or something so I could show him the same kind of attention, because he deserved it.

He quieted my cries with a kiss when I came. When my body stopped shaking he pulled out, and I whimpered.

He climbed off the bed and grabbed my ankles. I yelped as he pulled me down the bed and turned me over. He smacked his palm lightly against my ass and I let out a squeal. "Jude!" I gasped with surprise.

His only reply was a chuckle. Figures.

He smoothed his hand over the spot he just smacked. "I couldn't resist."

He grasped my hips, positioning me the way he wanted. His fingers found my folds and then I felt his ... cock—maybe if I started thinking the dirty words more then they'd stop feeling so ... well, *dirty*—nudge my entrance.

He slid in all the way and my gasp was so loud that he gave my ass another light smack. "Quiet, Tate," he warned.

"Feels so good," I hummed, turning my head so I could see

him behind me. He stood so strong and powerful, but his hands touched me gently.

He leaned down so his chest covered my back. He grabbed my hair, pulling it away from my face. "You said slow, then fast, so get ready, Tate. I'm not holding back."

Oh, the look in his eyes. It was full of mischief and excitement. I felt my groin tighten around him. "Yes," I gasped. "Please. Hard. Fast. Now." Apparently, I could only speak in one-word sentences at the moment. Jude didn't seem to mind, though.

He lifted up and grasped my hips.

He slid out of me and back in roughly. The headboard banged against the wall and I would've thought it was funny if I wasn't too preoccupied focusing on the way his body felt joining mine.

Holy fuck, I really loved this position and wondered why we hadn't tried it before. He was so deep and hit something inside me every time he pushed into me.

"Fuck, Tate," he growled and his fingers dug into my hips harder. My legs began to shake. I turned my head further so I could watch him.

His head was bowed back, his eyes closed, and his mouth slightly parted. The muscles in his chest and stomach flexed and rippled with every movement. Watching him like he was now, I realized he'd been holding back on me. He hadn't wanted to push me too far, but this time he was letting go and taking what he wanted, and I fucking loved that I could give it to him.

He pulled out, stroking himself and then sticky warmth covered my back. He collapsed beside me with a grunt.

"Jesus," he groaned.

"My name's Tate," I retorted with a lazy smile.

He cracked his eyes open. "Such a wise ass," he chuckled. He reached over, running his index finger along my lips. "You're lucky I love this smart mouth of yours so much."

"Is that so?" I asked, stifling a yawn. After our lovemaking, I was exhausted. My lids lowered with the threat of sleep.

"Mhmm." He nodded, looking as tired as I felt. "Don't move," he warned, rising from the bed. He pulled on his boxers and headed into the hall.

He returned a moment later with a damp cloth and wiped off my back.

"There," he murmured, leaning further up my body to kiss the back of my neck.

I rolled over to face him as he tossed the cloth in a hamper.

He opened a drawer on his dresser and grabbed a shirt. He tossed it at me and I managed to catch it, despite the fact that my tired body didn't want to move. I slipped the long-sleeved shirt over my head, reveling in how it smelled like him. I nearly drowned in it, though. I knew when I stood the length would nearly hit my knees.

Jude climbed onto the bed beside me. He pushed the covers down and then pulled them over us. He spooned my body against his and yawned. "Nap time."

"What about dinner with my dad?" I rolled over to face him, suddenly alert.

He lifted his head so he could see the clock that rested on the nightstand. "We have plenty of time," he assured me. "Now roll back over, so I can hold you."

I did as he said, not because he was being bossy, but because I wanted to. I'd become used to Jude wrapping his body around mine as we drifted off to sleep.

In fact, it was getting more difficult to go to sleep without him.

Since we'd worked things out he'd brought up living together a few more times, but I always shot him down. It wouldn't take much more convincing on his part for me to give in.

The fact of the matter was, I wasn't scared anymore.

Jude told me he wanted it all with me—a future filled with marriage and babies.

I used to never imagine my future, but now I did, and it included Jude as my husband and a dark-haired baby boy.

One day.

One day soon.

I SAT STRAIGHT UP, staring around the dark room.

Wait ...

Dark. Room.

"Oh, shit."

My eyes darted to the clock and widened at the time.

"Jude," I groaned, pushing his shoulder.

"Hmmm?" He hummed in his sleep. He cracked one eye open. "What?"

"We were supposed to be having dinner with my dad an hour ago!" I slid from the bed, frantically searching for my clothes. "We slept too long!"

"Fuck," he growled hotly, rubbing the heels of his hands against his eyes. "I'm sorry, Tate."

"Don't say you're sorry!" I cried, grabbing my shorts off the floor. "Just get out of bed and get dressed. I have to call him and tell him we're coming."

"Oh, we came all right."

"Jude!" I picked his shirt up and threw it at his head, where he sat on the edge, deliciously rumpled.

He laughed as he put his shirt on. "It's true."

Once we were dressed we did our best to fix our rumpled appearance, but it was futile. It would take my dad two seconds to figure out what we'd been up to. I only hoped he didn't comment on it. I wasn't sure I could handle the embarrassment right now.

Since I'd driven here by myself we had to take separate cars to my house.

I used the time to try to calm down. I told myself repeatedly that everything would be okay, but so far, I didn't believe my own words.

It might've been better if Jude and I could've ridden together. I was sure he'd have done a far better job at making me feel better, because my self-imposed pep talk wasn't working.

When we got to my house I was shaking like a leaf.

"Everything's going to be fine, Tatum," I told myself one last time before pushing my stiff body out of the car.

Jude met me and took my hand, giving it a reassuring squeeze. "Everything is going to be fine." They were the same words I'd just told myself but they sounded more believable coming from his mouth.

Jude paused at the front door and gave me time to catch my breath.

When I knew I was okay—well, as okay I could be—I nodded and he opened the door.

The house was so eerily quiet that I almost believed he hadn't arrived home yet, but when we entered the kitchen it was lit up, and he sat at the same spot at the kitchen table where he'd been the last time. Only now, he looked very different. His eyes weren't angry and tired; instead they were full of trepidation and worry. He'd put on a little weight and his smile wasn't grim like it was before. He wasn't quite normal—or the smiling, loving dad I remembered from *most* of my childhood—but it was an improvement. So, I'd take it.

"Hi, Tatum." He nodded at me, clasping his hands, with a sad smile on his lips. "Jude." He nodded at him too. "Sit, please." He waved his hands at the free chairs. "I got your message that you were running late so I just ordered the pizzas. They should be here shortly."

"How are you?" I asked. I wasn't sure what the customary thing to say in a situation like this was, so I settled on that. It seemed harmless and safe enough.

"Better," he replied, his shoulders lifting slightly in a barely-there shrug. "I have a long way to go." He cleared his throat and looked between Jude and me. "I want to apologize about the horrible things I said to you both. I wasn't ... well." He flinched. "I hope you can both forgive me." I nodded and Jude did as well. Speaking solely to Jude, he said, "I'm so sorry for the hurtful things I said and that you witnessed. You are good enough for my daughter." Lowering his head, he mumbled, "You're a far better man than I am." He lifted his head gradually and when he looked at me tears shimmered in his eyes. "I was horrible to you, Tatum. I can't believe the things I did and said to you. To your brother. Your mom." He bit down on his fist and shook his head. Regaining his composure, he continued, "I will spend the rest of my life regretting everything I've done. I wasn't a good husband or father."

"You weren't always horrible, Dad," I interjected. "There were good times. Remember those too, they shouldn't be forgotten just because there's bad." I slid out of my seat and walked over to him. He startled when I reached out to hug him. "I love you, Dad." Pulling away, I looked into his eyes, "But you have to understand that I need to protect myself and if ..." I closed my eyes, taking a steadying breath so I could say what I needed to say. "If things go back to the way they were before, I will leave."

He nodded his head. "I understand. I'm trying my hardest to be better."

"I know." I kissed the top of his head. "I'm putting the past behind me and we're starting new." I stared into his eyes so he'd know I was serious. "It's up to you to decide where we go from here. Understand?"

His eyes closed and he let out a shaky breath. "I understand."

"Good." I stood up straight as the doorbell rang. Jude left to get the door and came back carrying the pizzas.

"Let's go to the family room and watch TV." I pointed and Jude immediately turned on his heel, heading out of the kitchen. I turned to look at my dad over my shoulder. "Come on, Dad. Let's put a movie on and eat. Like the good times."

"Like the good times," he mimed, pushing his hands against the table as he stood. He grabbed my arm, halting me in the doorway so I couldn't leave. My heart sped up and my throat closed with fear, but I forced myself to relax. My dad was better now, but that didn't stop me from fearing him. It would take time for me to completely be okay around him again, but I was going to do my best, because I wasn't lying when I told him I wanted us to move forward. He was my dad after all. "When did you get so grown up?" he asked me, his mouth tilted down sadly. "Where'd my little girl go?"

"My brother died." I shrugged. "My mom shut down and my dad ..." I eyed him, not in angry way, just bluntly. "Was an asshole. I didn't have any choice but to grow up at a young age." Shoving my hands in my pockets, I shrugged. "I'm twenty-two, I'm really not a kid anymore." Peering around the corner toward the family room where Jude waited, I added, "Love made me stronger. It gave me something to fight for when I didn't have anything else."

My dad didn't reply.

Forcing a bright smile, I brushed past him. "Let's eat."

CHAPTER THIRTY-ONE

The summer was going by insanely fast and before I knew it, it was the end of June and I was helping my best friend into her wedding dress.

Rowan Sinclair was thirty minutes away from becoming Rowan Wentworth.

I was nervous, so I had no doubt that she was.

"I'm scared," Rowan admitted, as she stared at her reflection. It was almost as if she'd picked up on my thoughts.

"Me too, and it's not even my wedding." I laughed. "But this is Trent and you love him more than anything. Everything will be okay."

"My heart's racing so fast," she breathed as I stepped away to make sure the dress was on properly. "I'm terrified, but at the same time I'm so ready to be his wife." She turned to look at me and tears shimmered in her eyes. I prayed she didn't start crying and mess up her makeup—the makeup artist would probably kill us. "I'm ready to take that next step with him."

I soaked in her words, words I'd been repeating in my head as of late.

While Jude and I had only been together for a few months, it felt like forever and I knew I would never want another man like I wanted him. I was still scared to take that leap, but I felt ready.

Rowan sat down and I fixed the diamond pin in her hair. Her hair had been curled in an elegant up-do. Olivia and mine had been done in a loose fishtail side braid—casual, but elegant.

Ivy was currently getting the finishing touches put on her hair. Even though she declared that she was too old she was going to be the flower girl.

Olivia sat in the corner rocking a fussy Grace.

"I swear," Olivia groaned, grabbing Grace's small fist before she could yank on her braid, "Grace only likes her daddy. She cries almost every time I hold her." She frowned, straightening Grace's peach-colored dress that matched the shade of ours.

"Aw," Rowan said with a frown, "you know that's not true."

Olivia's eyes widened and she laughed. "Oh, no, it's true. She's a very cranky baby, but Trace can work voodoo mind magic on her. I call him the baby whisperer." With a smile, Olivia asked Rowan, "So, when should we expect baby number two?"

Rowan's cheeks flared and her eyes flickered to her sister, me, and then back to Olivia. "That's what the honeymoon is for," she finally answered, lowering her gaze.

Olivia grinned and I tried to contain my laugh. I failed.

Rowan looked up at me and let out a soft sigh. "Trenton can be very convincing when he wants something, and the more we talked the more I could see where he was coming from."

"You don't need to justify it to me," I assured her. "As longs as this is what you want, I'll support you. Especially since it won't be my baby. I can spoil them and then when they cry I can give them back to you."

Rowan laughed. "Sounds like a plan."

Someone knocked on the door and then it swung open. It was Lily, Trace and Trent's mom, and she was dressed to perfection. Her gown was a lovely rose color that complemented her complexion and her dark-brown hair cascaded around her shoulders. She didn't look her age at all.

"Are you all ready?"

The lady finished with Ivy's hair and nodded her head.

"It's time for everyone to get lined up." Lily clapped her hands together. Her eyes softened when they landed on Rowan and she held back tears. "Oh, Rowan, you look stunning."

"Thank you." Rowan bowed her head slightly. Raising it, she bit her lip. "There's something I've wanted to ask you, but I've been too scared."

"Go ahead, sweetie," Lily encouraged, coming to stand by Rowan's side.

"Well ..." Rowan looked up at Lily. "I don't have any parents, so I was hoping, maybe ..." Rowan bit her lip, her eyes darting nervously from Lily to the floor. "That you'd walk me down the aisle."

Lily gasped and dove at Rowan for a hug. "Oh, sweetie, of course I will."

Rowan's eyes widened with shock as she lifted her arms to hug Lily back. Clearly, she wasn't expecting that kind of reaction.

The wedding planner showed up then, guiding us out of the room and to where we were to wait.

The wedding was being held on the back lawn of Wentworth mansion. I hadn't seen how it had been transformed yet, but I was sure it was magical. I knew not to expect anything less from the Wentworth's.

I caught sight of Tristan, who had Bartholomew—Trent's ferret—on a leash, and tied around the critter's neck were Trent and Row's wedding bands. I couldn't help laughing about it.

Rowan giggled as well. "Trent was adamant that Bartholomew be a part of the wedding in some way, so I let him have his fun."

We lined up in order and since Trace was Trent's best man he was to escort me, and Jude had Olivia.

Jude looked me up and down, licking his lips like I was a dessert he wanted to devour. When his eyes met mine, he chuckled at being caught and sent me a wink.

Trace held out his arm for me and I took it, adjusting my grip on my bouquet.

The music started up and that was our cue.

The aisle was made of white and pale pink flower petals—the ones Ivy dropped were painted silver—giving it a mythical appearance, like we were in a fairy garden or something. Trent stood beneath an arch of some kind of large white flower that I didn't recognize. His hands were clasped together and he looked dangerously handsome in his tuxedo—although, I had to admit I thought Jude looked even better in his. Poor Trent looked scared out of his mind, and he was probably afraid Rowan would change her mind and turn into the runaway bride. She'd run from him a lot, so his fears were justified, but I knew Rowan wasn't going anywhere.

Trace and I reached the end of the aisle and I released his arm. He went to stand by his brother—giving him a firm pat on his shoulder, before lowering his head to whisper something in his ear.

Jude smirked at me and went to stand by Trace.

The music changed and everyone rose to look at Rowan as she started up the aisle.

I heard Trent gasp and murmur, "Wow."

Rowan's eyes lowered and her cheeks flushed as her groom gazed upon her. She looked excited and scared all at the same time.

Lily kissed her on the cheek and gave her hand to her son.

"You're beautiful." Trent whispered to her as she handed me her bouquet to hold.

Their vows were exchanged quickly to the hoots and hollers of the friends and family gathered.

"You may now kiss your bride."

Trent grasped Rowan's waist and dipped her down, kissing her in a way that should be illegal in public.

I started to blush and turned away, feeling like I was invading on a private moment.

Trent lifted her back up and kept his arm wrapped around her. He swiped his thumb across her bottom lip as they were introduced as Mr. and Mrs. Wentworth.

They headed back down the aisle and everyone started to stand.

Jude came to stand by my side, his eyes excited. "Let's do that."

"What?"

"Get married. You said you'd marry me, so let's do it." He nodded his head excitedly.

"Today?" I gasped. "*Here*?"

"Why not here?" he countered.

"Uh ..." I blanched as people fluttered around us. "Because it's Trent and Row's wedding."

He waved his hand dismissively. "You know they won't care. Please, Tate." He reached for my wrist and I was sure his fingers felt my pulse jump. "Marry me today." Before I could reply he was dragging me through the crowd to where Rowan and Trent stood. "Would you guys mind if we got married today? I really can't wait another second to call this woman my wife."

Rowan's mouth fell open and she let out a squeal. "Do it!"

Fuck.

Jude turned to me. "See, they're cool. There's nothing but you stopping us now, Tater Tot."

"I-I—" I stuttered, looking from Jude to our friends. "But your grandpa isn't here. Or your brother. Or your friends."

"All it takes is a phone call to change that," he argued. Sobering, he let out a deep breath. "I know I said we'd wait till you were ready, but I don't want to wait, Tate. I know you're it for me and I want to be married to you."

I swallowed thickly, feeling panicky. Not because I wanted to say no, but because my answer was very much— "Yes." I grinned. "Yes, let's do it!"

"Ahh!" Rowan screamed, throwing her arms around me. "This is so exciting!"

I was surprised that she was so thrilled, because I really felt like we were hijacking their wedding. Trent seemed to find the whole thing very funny, standing there with a smirk on his lips and his hand on Tristan's shoulder.

"You two need to go get a marriage license," Rowan pushed Jude and I toward the French doors that led inside the house.

"I'm going to talk to Olivia and see if we can find a different dress for you. Something a little more ... bridal."

"Rowan, this is fine," I pointed to my peach-colored bridesmaid dress.

"No, no, no." She shook her head, her lips set into a firm line. "You need a proper wedding dress or something close to it. Now, go! Hurry!" She gave us another firm push toward the door.

Jude grasped my hand and we ran through the mansion. After a few wrong turns, we finally made it to the foyer and out the front door.

They'd hired a valet to park cars on the expansive property, so Jude handed one of the guys a slip of paper.

A few minutes later his truck pulled up and we left quickly.

He called Archer, telling him to pick up Pap and make sure they dressed nicely. He even extended an invite to his wife, who we hadn't met yet, and Julia. From what I could overhear of the conversation Archer was curious about what was going on but Jude wouldn't tell him that we were getting married.

He hung up from Archer and called Dylan, inviting the guys. He once again left off the part that we were getting married.

Jude seemed to know where we needed to go to get a marriage license. That made one of us. As the female I probably should've been the one to know this stuff, but I was clueless.

He parked the truck and we headed into the building.

It didn't take long for us to fill out the paperwork and sign our names.

Butterflies assaulted my stomach as I gazed at my signature. It was the last time I'd write my name as Tatum O'Connor. From this day forward I was Tatum Brooks.

I couldn't believe we were actually doing this.

Not after everything we'd been through and how much I'd fought the idea of marriage and living together.

But Jude won.

He was right; this was inevitable so why delay it? It was time for us to start the rest of our lives … together.

Before we went back to the mansion he stopped at a jewelry store.

"Gotta have rings." He grinned, turning off the truck.

We hurried inside the store and separated so we wouldn't know what each other picked.

I settled on a simple, but thick, platinum band for Jude. It wasn't flashy and I knew he'd love it. I shivered at the thought of seeing the ring on his finger, marking him as mine.

I gasped as I realized I hadn't even thought to call my own dad.

What the hell was wrong with me?

I guessed I'd spent so long with barely-there parents that I'd kind of forgotten about them. Horrible, I know, but it was the truth. I'd been on my own for years, so it was easy to forget to include them in my life.

Or in this case just my dad.

I didn't have my phone with me so I'd have to borrow Jude's when we got back in the truck.

Since it didn't take me long to pick and buy his ring I stood by the door waiting.

When he finally appeared, his grin was wide. "I can't wait for you to see this." He held the bag to his chest. Then, as if he couldn't help himself, he lowered his head to kiss me quickly. "Not long now," he murmured, his lips brushing mine as he spoke.

We climbed in the truck and I asked for his phone.

I gave my dad the same spiel that Jude had given Archer and Dylan. My dad sounded suspicious though and I really hoped he didn't figure out what we were up to. Regardless, I wouldn't apologize for doing this. I was finally allowing myself to do something that *I* wanted. I wasn't holding myself back and doing the responsible thing. I was letting my heart guide me.

Jude reached for my hand, entwining them together. "Are you second guessing this?"

"Not at all." I squeezed his hand. "I'm so ready for this." I grinned. True, I felt a little fear, but I figured most people felt that way on their wedding day. Mostly there was excitement.

Jude lifted our joined hands, kissing my knuckles as he drove.

"I don't want you to regret this."

"I couldn't regret you," I replied immediately. "Never."

He glanced at me and grinned. "God, I love you."

I laughed, my cheeks lifting as I smiled. "I love you too, Jude, and I always will." I laid my head on his shoulder.

He grew quiet and after a moment he said, "We need to make one more stop."

"Where?" I lifted my head as I asked him.

"You'll see." He grinned, his eyes sparkling with excitement.

I narrowed my eyes as I pondered what he could possibly be up to.

When he pulled up at the nursing home I was still confused. "Why are we here?" I unbuckled my seatbelt and followed him into the building.

Breezing past the sliding glass doors, he finally answered me. "Mr. Jenkins said he better be invited to our wedding, so

I'm breaking him out of this place and letting him come. The guy deserves a little fun in his life."

I smiled up at the man I loved so much. He had such a big heart and he never ceased to amaze me. I couldn't believe I used to hate him. I hadn't known him at all and once I did get to know the real Jude, I saw that there was no one else like him. He was special and he'd always be mine.

"Hi, Trudy," Jude greeted the lady at the front desk.

She looked up and smiled widely at us. "What are you doing here? Aren't you supposed to be at your friend's wedding?"

Jude nodded, and wrapped his arm around my waist, pulling me against his side. "Yeah, we were there, but now Tatum and I have decided to get married. Today," he added bluntly.

Trudy's eyes widened in surprise as she looked between the two of us. "Oh, wow. That's exciting."

"It is," Jude agreed. "But I was wondering," he lowered his voice and gave her his most charming smile, "if it would be possible for me to pick up Mr. Jenkins and take him with us. He was very adamant about being at my wedding and I want him there. Please, Trudy?" Jude batted his eyelashes.

I wanted to roll my eyes at his ridiculous display, but of course Trudy caved.

"I'll see what I can do."

Twenty minutes later we were on our way, Mr. Jenkins in tow, with strict orders to have him back by eight tonight.

"I knew you two would get married." Mr. Jenkins smiled proudly in the truck—I was stuck sitting in the middle, practically on Jude's lap. I didn't know how he drove.

"I knew it too," Jude agreed. "Even though Tate wanted to

fight me the whole way." Skimming his fingers along my neck, he murmured, "But no one can resist my charm."

He was definitely right about that.

We got back to the mansion and went in search of our friends. Rowan ended up intercepting me and shooing Jude and Mr. Jenkins away. I watched them leave, laughing at Mr. Jenkins' wide-eyed expression as he looked around the mansion in awe. It was pretty impressive so I couldn't blame him.

"Who's the old guy?" Rowan asked, watching them leave as well.

"Mr. Jenkins. He's a patient at the nursing home Jude works at." I shrugged.

"Oh, that's cool." She smiled. "It was sweet of Jude to want to bring him. Now come on." She grabbed ahold of my arm, dragging me up the main staircase. "We found a dress for you."

I was pulled into the bedroom we'd used to get ready in earlier. Olivia and Lily stood inside waiting for us.

I expected them to be angry about what Jude and I were doing—after all, Lily wasn't family to me, and I didn't really know Olivia all that well—but they were smiling happily and eager to help.

"Do you want to change your hair?" Rowan asked, already reaching to pull out the braid.

"I like it the way it is," I assured her.

She immediately dropped her hand and went over to the chair in the corner. She turned back around to face me with a white dress draped over her arm. She bit her lip nervously and held it up. "I hope you like it."

The dress was short and I knew when I put it on it would hit just above my knees. It was strapless with a sweetheart neckline and a silver sparkly band around the waist. The bottom of it flowed without being poufy. It definitely wasn't the traditional wedding dress, but it was perfect.

"I love it, Row." I reached out to touch the fabric. "This is perfect. How'd you find it?"

She shrugged. "It was mine. I got it for a homecoming dress in high school and never got a chance to wear it. Someone should."

"Please tell me you didn't leave your wedding to go get this," I frowned.

"No, of course not," she hastened to assure me, "I got someone else to go."

I reached for the dress and took it from her hands. "Thank you so much for this."

She waved her hand dismissively. "No thanks needed. I'm just happy to see my two best friends getting married." She clapped, doing a small happy dance. I still marveled in the differences in Rowan since she'd been with Trenton. Gone was the quiet girl only focused on school and creating a better life for her son and sister. She was so full of life now. "Now," she began as she held up a finger warningly, "don't try to hijack my honeymoon. I'm *not* sharing that with you."

"Deal," I agreed, laughing too.

Lily and Olivia left Rowan and I alone while she helped me into the dress.

Rowan grabbed some lip-gloss off a table and swiped it on my lips. "You look beautiful, Tate." She fixed a piece of hair back in place and put her hands on my shoulders. "It's time to get you married."

I soon found myself standing where we'd waited earlier before walking down the aisle.

I turned to Rowan, grabbing her arm. "Can you grab Jude's grandpa and my dad?"

"Of course." She smiled, and headed outside to get them.

When they stepped inside I pulled them away from the others so we could have the semblance of privacy.

"I'm sure by now you've probably figured out that Jude and I are getting married—" My dad opened up his mouth to speak, and I knew from the steep set of his brows he was going to try to talk me out of this. "No, Dad. This is what I want. Nothing you can say will change my mind." I squared my shoulders and took a breath. "I know it's customary for the father to walk the bride down the aisle, and while I want you to do that, Dad, I also want Jerry to be by my side." I turned to face Jude's grandpa and tears pricked my eyes. "You've become a huge part of my life and it doesn't seem right to celebrate this day without making you a bigger part of it. So, I'm hoping you'll walk me down the aisle as well."

"You know I'd do anything for you, Tatum." He reached out to hug me. Wetness stung my shoulders and I realized he was crying. I was relieved that he'd called me Tatum. A part of me was afraid today would be one of his unfortunate bad days, and he wouldn't remember Jude and I getting married.

Once everything was straightened out, Rowan stood as my bridesmaid and Trent was at her side.

"Oh." She shoved a bunch of Twizzlers tied together into my hand. "Jude told me to give you this as your bouquet. He said you'd understand." Lowering her voice, she said, "One day you really have to explain this whole Twizzler thing to me."

I laughed as I stared at the red candy in my hands. Only Jude. I was surprised he hadn't glued gummy bears onto the Twizzlers.

"You ready?" Rowan asked.

I nodded and she signaled to someone outside the doors.

Music started up and my heart lurched as my stomach dropped.

This was it.

The first day of the rest of my life.

Time seemed to speed up as Jerry and my dad walked me down the aisle and toward Jude who stood waiting for me.

He grinned proudly with his hands clasped together. His brown hair was gelled messily and stubble adorned his cheeks and chin. His brown eyes shimmered with happiness and I kept thinking *mine*.

When we reached him, he held out his hand for mine. I took it and my dad and Jerry drifted away to sit.

I'd been so focused on Jude that I hadn't realized that the crowd attending our wedding was much smaller than Trent and Row's. Everyone that had attended their ceremony must've been down on the grounds at the reception already.

I was glad for that.

This way it was only our friends and family, making it seem more like our own wedding—and not someone else's, which was exactly what it was.

Jude took both of my hands in his. He couldn't seem to stop grinning and neither could I.

The minister or preacher or whatever he was began his lengthy speech.

My heart thumped against my chest so hard I was surprised it didn't break free and fall to the ground.

Then, before I knew it, it came time for the vows.

Jude repeated after the man, "I, Jude Gabriel Brooks, take you, Tatum Elizabeth O'Connor, to be my wife, to have and to hold from this day forward, for better or for worse, for richer, for poorer, in sickness and in health, to love and to cherish until death do us part."

He slid two bands on my finger. The first was more of an engagement ring—a simple silver band with a modest sized diamond. "My Gram's," he explained. "Pap gave it to me to give to you ... when you were ready. I feel like I've been carrying it in my pocket forever, because when I asked you to marry me, I knew you weren't ready to wear this. But now you are." He grinned triumphantly. The second band he put on my finger was the ring he got today. I gasped at its beauty. It was an infinity band with many small diamonds. It was simple and stunning. Absolutely perfect. I couldn't have picked anything better for myself.

My body shook when it was my turn. I stared into his eyes as I spoke each word, so he'd know I meant them completely.

"I, Tatum Elizabeth O'Connor, take you, Jude Gabriel Brooks, to be my husband, to have and to hold from this day forward, for better or for worse, for richer, for poorer, in sickness and in health, to love and to cherish until death do us part."

Rowan handed me Jude's ring and my hands shook as I slipped it onto his finger. I smiled in satisfaction at seeing it on him and then turned my gaze to him.

We'd done it.

We were married.

It might not have been a traditional wedding—not by a long shot—but it was spontaneous, crazy, and fast just like the two of us and the journey of our relationship. I couldn't ask for more.

The man officiating the wedding smiled. "I now pronounce you husband and wife. You may kiss your bride."

"About fucking time," Jude groaned, taking my face between his hands and kissing my deeply. I felt his tongue press lightly against mine and I moaned into his mouth. With a hefty breath, he pulled back. "You're mine now, Tatum Brooks."

"I was always yours." I grinned back, staring into the loving eyes of my husband.

He looked over at Rowan, who stood behind me. He grinned proudly, and said, "I told you I was going to marry this girl."

This girl.

His girl.

Jude's girl.

Forever.

EPILOGUE

Two Years Later

ARMS WRAPPED AROUND ME FROM BEHIND AND I giggled as I was pulled against a hard chest. "Jude," I laughed. "I'm trying to cook."

He pressed kisses to the skin where my neck met my shoulder. "I've been working all day. I miss you. Let me kiss my wife."

I let go of the wooden spoon I'd been using to stir the sauce for the homemade spaghetti and turned around to wrap my arms around his neck. I stood on my tiptoes to give him a proper welcome home kiss. Jude put in many hours at the nursing home and I always missed him when he was away from home—and home happened to be his grandpa's farmhouse. Jerry still lived here, which worked out well since we could look after him, but he'd given us the deed to the house. A wedding present he said. Jude and I had spent the last two years working on fixing it up. We still had a few more things to fix, but it was almost complete. We'd had to halt renovations last month when our daughter was born.

So, she definitely wasn't Jude Jr., but Juliette was the light of our lives. I'd thought I'd loved Jude before, but having our daughter only made me fall in love with him more. He was so good with her, and the way he looked at her almost always brought tears to my eyes. What could I say; I was highly emotional these days. Having a baby will do that to you.

Seeing her daddy, Juliette began to stir in her bouncer.

Jude kissed my forehead and then went over to her. He lifted her out and cradled her in his arms. She was beautiful—not that I was biased or anything. She had light brown hair, her daddy's pouty lips, and my nose. She was perfect.

"Hi, my beautiful Juliette," Jude cooed to our daughter. "Did you miss Daddy? Because Daddy sure missed you." He kissed the top of her head and inhaled her sweet baby scent.

Once I found out I was pregnant I'd started looking for jobs I could do at home. The last thing I wanted was to miss out on any moment of Juliette's life, or any children we might have in our future. I'd been lucky enough to find a job writing for an online magazine. I got to do what I loved and be with my daughter all day. It was a win-win.

Jude rocked Juliette in his arms, singing to her. Her eyes grew large as she listened to him. Despite the fact that she was only a month old she was already Daddy's little princess. Jude spoiled her rotten. I knew as she got older he'd make sure she got everything she wanted. Except boys. I feared the day she started dating. Jude was going to go lose it.

Smiling at the loves of my life I couldn't help thinking how crazy it was that if Professor Taylor had never given me that assignment, and I hadn't needed Jude's help, we'd never be where we were now.

Things had worked out exactly as they were meant to and I couldn't be more thankful.

I had everything I'd never known to want.

"Thank you," the words tumbled out of my mouth before I could stop them as I gazed at Jude.

He stopped singing and stared at me. "For what?"

"Giving me this. You … our daughter. For never giving up on me."

"Oh, baby." His eyes softened as he stalked toward me. "You don't need to thank me for that." He kissed me slowly and Juliette stirred in his arms. I laid my head on his shoulder and closed my eyes, soaking in his warmth with a smile on my face.

Happiness came in many shapes and forms. This happened to be mine.

ACKNOWLEDGMENTS

Writing THE END on this book was an extremely bittersweet moment. I can't believe the Trace + Olivia series is over. It's been a crazy year thanks to these characters and I couldn't ask for more. I'm beyond shocked by the amount of love and support these characters have received. I hate saying goodbye to them as much as you guys do. But no matter what, their stories will always be there for you to go back to.

A tremendous thanks goes out to the fans of this series. Without you it would have never done as well it has. Thank you for embracing a crazy, ketchup-loving, plaid shirt wearing, mechanic in Finding Olivia. Thank you for loving these characters as much as I do and wanting more. Thank you all for your support, words of encouragement, and love. I know all authors say this, but I truly feel like I have the best fans in the world.

Thank you to my BAFF's Harper James and Regina Bartley for keeping me sane. (Okay, I'm probably not completely sane

... so let's go with mostly.) Thank you for staying up late and doing writing sprints with me, Regina. If it wasn't for you this book wouldn't be done yet.

Regina Wamba, you kicked cover design butt with this one. It's stunning and exactly what I wanted. Your talent never ceases to amaze me and one of these days I swear I'm going to watch you in action.

A big thank you goes out to Chloe and Max for bringing Tatum and Jude to life. You both did AMAZING and I couldn't ask for more.

Thank you to my beta readers, Haley, Becca, Kendall, Stefanie, and Heather. You're words of encouragement have meant the world to me. Thank you for shaping Saving Tatum into the book it is today. I know it's much better with all your help.

Becca deserves a special shout out for sending the gummy bear cake my way. As soon as you showed it to me I knew it would make the perfect apology cake. I also have to thank you for chatting with me late night during my many freak-outs and for your often hilarious beta reading comments. They always make me smile.

www.ingramcontent.com/pod-product-compliance
Lightning Source LLC
LaVergne TN
LVHW031608060526
838201LV00065B/4774